GENOSTORIES

A Novel about Memory and Legacy

Eduardo A Borges

Title: Genostories: A Novel about Memory and Legacy
Author: Eduardo A. Borges
First Edition: November 2025
Prepared for Publication: Special Novels Inc.
ISBN: 979-8-9915772-5-0
Softcover version for Amazon KDP

Author's contact: eborges@specialnovesl.com

To Yahir, Jax and Samantha

TABLE OF CONTENTS

INTRODUCTION

Year 2085. Today's cities are radiant gardens rising toward the sky. Imagine an urban landscape so clean that you would never find a piece of trash in the streets; a tapestry of futuristic architecture playing with light and shadow, with wide windows revealing a population that hardly needs to worry about money, food, or safety. For decades, we achieved what past generations so deeply dreamed of: solar, wind, and fusion energy nourishing every corner; hunger banished thanks to biotechnological food production; and medicine stretching our life expectancy to levels that, half a century ago, would have seemed like Science fiction.

The human beings of my time enjoy prosperity without borders. Our average lifespan reaches around 120 years; most make it to eighty with barely any illness, thanks to genetic engineering and drugs that slow cellular deterioration. The hardest or most dangerous work is carried out by drones and robots, coordinated by highly advanced artificial intelligences. A hyper-fast transport system connects cities in minutes, and augmented reality has turned everyday spaces into customizable stages: with a single gesture, you can see waterfalls flowing from a wall or project a forest around your living room. Gone is the anxiety of those days when people feared losing their jobs or their savings; society now redistributes wealth with fairness, and no one suffers material shortages.

But in the midst of this great utopia, a troubling murmur runs through our days: what remains of us as humans?

My name is Griot[1] 2085, and if you wonder why someone chose such an unusual name, the answer lies in my function. In the cultures of West Africa, a griot was the one responsible for keeping alive the history, the memory, the identity of a people through storytelling. Today, in 2085, I feel myself, in my own way, a storyteller who has uncovered a forgotten reliquary in the vast digital archive of Earth. Let me explain:

With medical advances, we hardly suffer from illnesses anymore. Lifespan keeps stretching longer and longer, so much so that some speak of individuals potentially reaching 150 years. In fact, there are those who reject the very idea of aging. In the past decade, the so-called *Comprehensive Rejuvenation Programs* have gained popularity: combinations of genetic therapies and nanotechnology that can repair nearly any tissue. As a result, death has become something more remote, and in a way, we've lost both mourning and awareness of our finitude. Everything seems infinite: our time, our leisure options, our food resources. Few worry about war or pollution, artificial intelligences have proven to be excellent managers, and climate change was successfully halted by the mid-2040s. Yet, as we resolved crisis after crisis, another problem, perhaps best described as existential, crept in quietly.

People no longer suffer as much, that's true, but they also no longer feel the same as before. A broad government program is underway offering *desensitization to pain* drugs: when someone dies, the family is invited to take an emotional regulator that blocks suffering and prevents prolonged depression. As a result, the experience of grief has been nearly wiped out. Many couples have chosen to forgo natural gestation: they prefer artificial incubators that optimize the embryo's health and program the future baby with desired traits.

1 *West African oral historian and musician.*

2

Love? That warm vibration which in the 20th century inspired poems, tales of sacrifice or madness, can now be parameterized through genetic and psychological compatibility algorithms. Of course, there are still those who fall in love and let themselves go, but their numbers dwindle year by year. It sounds romantic, yet there's an air of anachronism about it.

The world has become a safe, sterile, hyper-comfortable place, with populations free from hunger and severe diseases. But in that apparent perfection, we've lost our essence: the spontaneous pulse of surprise, the warmth of human error, the spark of a wounded heart rising to love even more fiercely. Almost no one questions it openly; still, in artistic and philosophical circles, some whisper that we are in an *emotional death*, a society that, in evading all pain, has left behind the magic of feeling.

I'm not a historian by profession; I work in technological research and in cataloging 21st-century databases. Our present holds massive backups of millions of old systems, most of them obsolete. Who would bother checking the servers of forums or apps that died out when the meta-services of augmented reality took over? No one. Still, in my curious digging, I stumbled upon some scattered references: Genostories[2]. The name, at first, meant nothing to me. I assumed it was a repository of expired images, maybe some prehistoric social network.

What I found inside left me stunned. It was a platform unlike any other: between 2020 and 2030 (though it remained in use for years after), thousands of families and individuals had uploaded videos, audio clips, reflective journals, recipes, photos, and documents... all with a profoundly human focus. It was as if, suddenly, a vast chorus

---

2 *Stories preserving generational memory.*

from the past burst into my ears, crying out: *"Here we were, this is how we lived, this is what we loved, this is what hurt us."*

There were stories of grandparents baking sourdough bread while sharing anecdotes from their youth. Love letters recorded on cassette, brimming with a tenderness impossible to synthesize with AI. Messages from travelers who migrated in search of a future, leaving their families behind. Testimonies of small victories: a father recounting how he overcame his mortgage debt, a mother proudly describing her premature baby's first step.

It felt as if I had unlocked a chest filled with the most precious remnants of soul left by our ancestors.

Why did it move me so deeply? Because although I was born in the second half of this century, I was raised in an environment where vulnerability is considered a flaw of the past. We no longer cry: we're prescribed the drug V-Null[3], which neutralizes the hormones of weeping. There is no more misery, no starving children. There is no uncertainty about the future. And, paradoxically, there is no longer that passionate drive to survive, no shiver from an *I love you* charged with hope and even fear.

As I flipped through (or rather, *navigated*) each feature of Genostories, I could feel the texture of genuine, moving, fragile lives. So fragile that, most likely, many of those storytellers passed away decades ago, never imagining that, in 2085, someone would remember them so intimately.

I realized that, in our present-day society, the knowledge that we are nearly "immortal" robs us of the intensity of living each day as a gift. No one risks losing a loved one to a sudden illness anymore, we have nano-robots that repair everything, and the concept of "farewell" no longer carries the same emotional weight it once did.

---

3 *Fictional drug that stops crying.*

But doesn't life become greater when we confront its finiteness? Isn't it uncertainty that gives each moment its unrepeatable value?

In Genostories, I encountered parents battling poverty, lovers unsure if their bond would survive the distance, grandmothers cooking with the fear that their recipes might be lost forever if not passed on to their grandchildren in time. *That* was where the beauty lay.

As a young man, I often wondered why I felt an inner void. My friends thought it was absurd: *"Griot, we have everything, what more could you want?"* They called me melancholic for enjoying old films and books, where characters dealt with tragedy, fear, and longing. I used to think my sensitivity was an anomaly in a world that had grown up without the need to suffer.

But reading the stories in Genostories, I discovered I'm not the only one who yearns for the warmth of an embrace untouched by sensors or emotion-regulating pharmaceuticals.

Biological and technological singularity, that advanced state of civilization, has given us the power to edit genes to prevent aging, to expand our minds with brain microimplants granting instant access to all existing information. But these same feats have gradually eroded the charm of human simplicity: a spontaneous laugh from the rawest humor, a gut-wrenching cry over an irreparable loss, the euphoria of realizing that time is limited and must be savored. The future my peers inhabit is one of hyperreality, where emotions can be *simulated* through neurological discharges, but… they are no longer lived from the gut.

After several weeks exploring all the data in Genostories, I found stories that truly stirred my soul. From a boy in the '70s who sent a letter to his "future self" hoping to become someone different, to a mother in the '90s who wrote about how she overcame the loss of a baby, or a grandfather in 2025 who left behind a video teaching his grandson how to knit with wool, afraid that the ancestral custom would die with him. I was overwhelmed by the thought that perhaps many of those grandchildren never saw the videos, because the app vanished in the whirlwind of technology, and the generations that followed never knew how to access that legacy.

Even so, the material remains there, untouched in a vast orphaned archive, lost in digital oblivion. I was so deeply moved by those testimonies that I took it upon myself to become their guardian, their modern Griot. I decided to classify and edit what I consider the most significant, beautiful, or revealing human stories from that period spanning the late 1960s to 2025. A brief stretch, historically speaking, but incredibly intense in terms of cultural, social, and technological transformations.

In 2085, several genetic labs are already working to abolish aging entirely, designing organisms capable of renewing themselves indefinitely. There's talk of an upcoming revolution where the word *death* will be reserved only for accidents or personal decisions to disconnect. Many applaud this as the long-awaited liberation from Nature: no longer depending on the "arbitrariness" of biological cycles. But what becomes of our human condition when the fear of death vanishes? Perhaps the greatest lesson of life is knowing that, one day, it ends, and with that awareness, each moment shines.

Genostories has shown me, with striking clarity, the vulnerability we once had: entire families in the '80s, '90s, or 2000s shaken by diseases like cancer, incurable diabetes, severe depression… At the same time, I saw the strength of their bonds, the ways they came together to care for one another, how they treasured each day. It's ironic to think that today, with cures for nearly everything, a cold is a joke, and depression is prevented with a simple neurological inducer, the solidarity born of adversity has faded. When you have everything, do you truly appreciate anything?

It might seem that I'm against the advances of my era. I'm not. I deeply value walking through cities free of pollution, seeing how wildlife and nature have recovered, watching people healthy and well-fed. But after studying the accounts in Genostories, I can't help but wonder if humanity in the 20th and early 21st centuries knew how to *feel* more intensely than we do. Could they love more passionately, knowing they would one day part? Did they laugh more genuinely when achieving small victories? Did they grieve more completely in the face of irreversible loss? The thought moves me, that perhaps, in their apparent imperfection, they lived more authentically.

All of this leads me to believe that Genostories, this so-called "primitive" digital repository, holds an invaluable lesson for those of us born into the era of total prosperity. Its records are not mere data, but windows into the human essence. I found reflections from ordinary people who wrote things like: *"Today was a bad day, but I realized how much I love my family."* I found audio recordings where you can hear someone's breath catching between laughter and tears. And I wonder: when was the last time any of my neighbors cried without inhibitors?

In this introduction to the stories, I'd like to emphasize one nuance: we are not speaking of an idyllic past. Clearly, there were wars, injustice, poverty, discrimination, financial collapses, and natural disasters. The era covered in this archive was full of contradictions: astonishing technological advancements, but also massive inequalities. And yet or perhaps because of this, you could feel deep emotion, and the need to come together to survive or to thrive. Genostories contains testimonies of love and pain, of hope and resilience. In 2085, without those struggles, our spirit seems to have fallen into slumber. Perhaps that's the warning the past offers us: a world without pain may unintentionally become a world without true love. A world without hardship could be one without the energy of longing, without the thrill of personal triumph.

I don't mean to say we should return to suffering from deadly diseases or extreme poverty in order to feel alive; I simply dare to suggest that if we do not keep the flame of our emotionality alive, if we do not cultivate empathy by choice (rather than by necessity in the face of adversity), we risk stagnating in a soulless limbo of monotony.

On the other hand, I also see in Genostories a sign of hope that not all is lost. If the people of that time uploaded their experiences to a digital platform so they would not be forgotten, it means they believed in posterity. Perhaps they knew or at least sensed, that a future like ours would come, and that it would need to remember what a beating heart felt like in the midst of hardship. Their stories reach us like messages in a bottle, cast into a sea of time that finally washed ashore with its answer.

That's why I decided to gather, in the chapters that follow, the stories I consider essential to reconnect with the humanity that gave birth to us. They are intimate, small, everyday testimonies, yet filled with that ineffable substance called feeling. You'll find grandmothers talking about recipes passed down for centuries, fathers offering financial advice, mothers recounting difficult births, lovers who overcame distance. Perhaps, to my contemporaries, they may sound naïve. But it's that very naivety that hypnotizes me, that makes me say: *"This is what we've lost in 2085, and this is what we need to reclaim."*

It's not about idealizing the past or rejecting the comforts of the present. It's about uniting both ends. I still believe that if we treasure the wisdom and emotional warmth of those days, and fuse them with our current technology and abundance, we can experience a fullness that isn't cold or hollow. Because, in the end, the human condition isn't defined solely by longevity or comfort, it's defined by the capacity to love, to create stories, to learn from both pain and joy.

I could have named this book *The Lost Human Chronicles, or Testimonies from Our Forgotten Elders.* But the name that defines me in this century, *Griot 2085*, makes me think of myself as the storyteller who, in an advanced society, returns to the symbolic fire of words to narrate. I don't mind being seen as eccentric. I want to believe that these stories will resonate with someone else, that they'll inspire others to step out, now and then, from their comfort zones, to *feel*. To feel *truly*.

Welcome to a journey through the echoes left behind by those who lived between the final years of the 20th century and the first quarter of the 21st. Prepare to encounter scenes so deeply human they may hurt, uplift, or unsettle you. Here, you'll find shattered dreams that, despite going unfulfilled, lit inextinguishable flames; culinary recipes carrying centuries of culture, recorded with devices once called "cell phones"; love letters and farewells capturing the intensity of mortal existence; manifestos from those who hoped for a better world without the AIs we now rely on.

I've divided this legacy into chapters, each containing one essential story. Every testimony carries a fragment of the heart of the person who wrote or recorded it, so read it as if you were holding the hand of someone living in a different time… but who feels just like you do or perhaps even more.

If you've made it this far, perhaps you're asking yourself: *"What do I gain from knowing how people lived in 2020 or 1990, when today I can live 130 years and only work if I choose to? Why should I care about* a cake recipe I don't need to bake, when a food printer can produce it for me in five seconds?"

My answer is this: because we need to recognize where we come from to understand who we can become. To value what we have, we must look back at what others longed for and struggled to achieve. Above all, in order to truly feel, we must connect with the hot blood running through our history, not with the coldness of algorithms that replace genuine experience.

The society of 2085 is, without doubt, a monumental achievement of centuries of scientific and social evolution. But, as a great sage once said: "*At the summit of the mountain, one realizes that what's extraordinary is not the view, but the path that led there.*" May these pages inspire you to ask yourself what mark you want to leave, beyond your immortal profile. May they encourage you to allow yourself an authentic cry when you lose something, or to feel a shiver of passion when you fall in love. Because, I confess, after immersing myself in all these stories, I understood that real strength doesn't lie in never suffering, but in daring to live, with all its shades, a life that may be short or long, but keeps the flame of the human heartbeat alive.

So I invite you: walk with me through each story I selected from Genostories. Walk with me through the nostalgia, hope, resilience, and warmth of those who came before us. Perhaps, among their laughter, fears, and passions, you'll find a mirror of what you and I might reclaim: communion with the marvelous (and sometimes painful) adventure of being a simple, yet extraordinary, human being.

And thus begins a journey intertwining a utopian future with a past brimming with profound feeling.

I am *Griot 2085*, and before me unfold the millions of stories that ordinary people stored in this digital chest called Genostories.

Welcome, and prepare to hear the voices of our ancestors. You may discover that, even with all their hardships, they lived with an inner strength that we, with all our prosperity, have begun to miss.

Oh, I almost forgot! Before we fully dive into these stories, let me tell you the reason behind the name Genostories. *"Geno"* comes from the Latin *generatio*, derived from the verb *generare*, meaning "to beget." The suffix *"-tio"* indicates "action and effect"; thus, *generatio* is tied to the idea of gestating, creating, or giving birth to something. On the other hand, *"Stories"* in English simply refers to tales. Bringing the two terms together was a stroke of brilliance: *"generational stories"* that seek to keep alive the narrative of our lineage, connecting those who came before us with those still to come.

I trust these stories will connect with you in the same way they have with me.

THE SECRET LETTER OF '77

Have you ever wondered what would happen if you could travel back in time and speak with your younger self, back when you dreamed without limits and felt invincible? In my constant exploration of the Genostories archives, I found a story built around that very longing: a letter written in 1978 by a young man who promised himself he would become "someone different" in the future.

I won't reveal the turns that followed that promise, for that, you'll need to immerse yourself in the coming pages, but I invite you to listen closely to the voice of that dreamer. What drove him? What was his idea of happiness? And above all, what vision of the future did he hold that, today in 2085, feels so distant to us?

This story left me reflecting on the power of our adolescent dreams, and on how far or how close, we may come when life surprises us. Prepare to dive into a chapter brimming with longings, doubts, and determination. By the end, you'll understand why every word written in 1978 still resonates so strongly in our present.

Griot 2085

Agustín was seventy-three years old that year, 2025. His hair had turned fully gray, yet his smile still carried that mischievous spark that had been his trademark since youth. He had been born in 1952, in a modest neighborhood surrounded by music and dreams. Now he lived in the same house where he had raised his daughters, the only difference being a more modern kitchen and a few electronic devices he could never have imagined in his younger days.

But that spring afternoon, the passage of time blurred the moment he saw Max, his six-year-old grandson, racing across the patio. Max, with his red t-shirt and boundless energy, was a whirlwind of curiosity eager to discover everything. His laughter echoed through the house, and memories of another time rose in Agustín's mind. It was then that he decided the moment had come to open the old box.

At the top of his house was an attic, packed with things that had piled up over the years: unused furniture, framed photos with cracked glass, and a stack of boxes with half-erased labels. Agustín climbed carefully, with the help of his cane, though he never quite admitted he needed it, and began brushing away cobwebs. He knew exactly where to look: a small brown box, its edges worn, a date written in blue ink: "*1977.*"

He remembered the last time he had seen it. More than twenty years earlier, when he and his wife, Rebeca, had reorganized the house after their eldest daughter's wedding. At the time, while sorting through old papers, he had stumbled upon a notebook and several loose sheets. But life had been moving too quickly then, and he had barely glanced at them. Now, unhurried, he took a deep breath and opened the box. Inside lay a soft-covered notebook, its pages yellowed, carrying the faint smell of old paper, and the letter he had written in 1977, when he was twenty-five.

Agustín's youthful handwriting was recognizable in every stroke: large letters with a touch of flourish, smudged here and there with ink stains. The year 1977… how many memories it brought back. He had lived in a world bursting with disco music blasting in nightclubs; *Saturday Night Fever* had just premiered, and the Bee Gees played on every radio station. People moved about in bell-bottom pants and brightly colored shirts. Meanwhile, in his city, people were talking about political and social changes, in many countries across Latin America and Europe, the youth were crying out for freedom, and he felt himself part of a generation determined to break the mold.

Back then, Agustín dreamed of becoming a radio announcer. He wanted to travel, interview musicians, play records that would drive listeners wild. He had written that letter as if tossing a bottle into the sea, promising himself he would one day read it in the future and confirm that he had fulfilled all his dreams.

The letter began:

"Hello, Agustín of the future:

Today is August 13, 1977, and I feel full of energy. I am 25 years old and I want to devour the world. I've decided to write to you so that, twenty or thirty years from now, you'll remember who you were on this day. I have plans: I will start my own radio station, travel to London and New York, and record a disc where my ideas and my voice will be heard. I don't want to end up with a boring life; I long to fly high, to meet new people, maybe to learn another language. I promise myself I will not give up on anything that burns in my chest…"

Agustín read those words and felt a knot in his throat. He remembered perfectly the passion of that young man, the sense that the world was only just beginning to open before him. What had become of all that?

He sat down in an old rocking chair to avoid straining his knee. As he flipped through the pages, he saw notes: newspaper clippings about disco music, lists of goals that, to his mature eyes, now seemed so naïve. Things like *"learn English in six months"* or *"be famous before turning 30."* There were also sketches of radio projects and doodles with the titles of songs he wanted to promote.

Agustín's own story paraded through his mind: in 1978, the very next year, he found steady work at a local radio station as a sound technician. Not long after, he met Rebeca, fell in love, and the needs of daily life began to push aside that ambition of "founding his own station." When his daughters were born, his priority became giving them a safe home and food on the table. Family filled him with happiness, but it also stole the time he might have devoted to chasing all those youthful dreams.

Even so, by the time he reached forty, he had become a respected sound editor, though not the famous announcer he had once dreamed of being. He never traveled to New York to interview stars; instead, he went to the beach on family vacations. He never mastered English, and that idea of *"recording a disc"* was left in a dusty drawer, replaced by the songs he would hum with his daughters on Sunday afternoons.

Agustín closed the notebook and caressed the cover tenderly. *"I didn't fulfill even half of these dreams,"* he thought. But he did not feel sadness. He had lived wonderful moments: the birth of his first daughter, the day his wife overcame her illness, the endless family gatherings where they laughed until their bellies hurt... and now there was Max, his grandson, who made him feel alive every time he called him "abuelito[1]."

---

1 *Affectionate diminutive of abuelo (grandfather).*

That's when the idea arose: why not share this treasure with Max, his grandson of only six years? Perhaps the boy wouldn't understand every detail, but it would be a way to pass down something far more valuable than a toy: the story of a youthful longing and an invitation to dream fearlessly. He reviewed the letter once more, snapped a photo of it with his phone, and thought of Genostories.

Yes, that mobile application his daughters had installed for him a few months earlier. They had explained that it was a platform for uploading memories, videos, reflections, and documents that, over the years, would remain preserved for future generations to enjoy. At first, Agustín thought it was just another social network, but when he discovered the simplicity of its interface, he grew excited: he could upload audio recordings of his voice, old photographs, and even scan the letter he held in his hands.

That very afternoon, he went to find Max on the patio. The boy was absorbed in something only he could see, imagining that a flowerpot was a rocket. Agustín approached and invited him to sit on the porch. Max nestled into his lap and looked up at him with those hazel eyes full of curiosity.

Max, said Agustín, showing him the yellowed sheet. Did you know that when your grandfather was young, he dreamed of being a famous radio announcer?

Max's eyes went wide.

You, famous? Like the ones on the internet?

Well, something like that. Back in my day, we didn't have the internet for everything. We wanted to speak to the world… but in another way. Through the radio.

Radio is the thing in cars? Max asked with sincere innocence.

Agustín couldn't help but laugh.

Yes, you can listen to it in cars too. But many years ago, radio was far more important for people's music. Look, let me show you something…

With his phone, he took photos of the letter and uploaded them to Genostories, recording an audio message where he explained to Max (and, at the same time, to any other family member who might hear it in the future) what it meant to be twenty-five years old in 1977. He spoke about disco music, about the thrill of believing that life itself was a dance floor, and about how, sometimes, plans change when you discover there are things even more beautiful than your own dreams.

Agustín pressed the record button in the Genostories app. He tried to keep his voice steady, but emotion overwhelmed him.

Hello, dear Max. This is your grandfather. Today I found a letter I wrote when I was twenty-five, back in 1977. My head was full of ideas: founding my own radio station, traveling the world, becoming a famous man… I thought that was the only way to be happy. And as I read, I remembered the passion of those days, and also the turns life takes.

Today, I'm not that international announcer, nor did I visit all those cities I imagined. But you know what? I lived something far better: I was lucky enough to meet your grandmother, to raise a wonderful family, and to enjoy every small achievement. After all, sometimes plans change… and that's all right.

Max, I want you to know it's okay to dream big and not be afraid. But it's also okay to let life surprise you with things you never imagined, like the day you would call me abuelito and ask me to take you for a ride on your bicycle. That feeling, that love, surpasses any trophy I once sought in my younger years.

I'll leave this letter here for you, so that one day, when you're older, you'll understand that sometimes we don't reach our goals exactly as we imagined… but that doesn't mean we stop living wonderful things.

I love you, grandson. And keep dreaming as high as you wish.

He finished recording and uploaded the file. Then, he showed Max the "letter" on the screen. The boy, not fully understanding, stroked the phone and smiled.

Abuelito, are you going to be famous now? he asked, with an innocence that Agustín found deeply endearing.

I'm famous to you, and that's already worth so much, he replied, kissing the boy's forehead.

For a moment, Agustín closed his eyes. He remembered with vivid clarity the year 1978: the streets filled with people in floral shirts, political demonstrations calling for a future with more freedoms, the radio saturated with disco hits. Youth felt a constant tingle of change, and he would repeat to himself: "I don't want to end up with a boring life."

How amusing it was to think of how he had underestimated the beauty of the routine he shared with Rebeca. There were days when they stayed home watching television, and he thought he was betraying those revolutionary dreams of his youth. But in those same homely nights, he discovered the intensity of a love that fulfilled him more than any plan for fame ever could.

He rose from the porch, silently bidding farewell to that young man of 1977, and looked again at Max, who was already racing around once more, chasing an imaginary cat. He felt at peace. He uploaded a couple more photos to Genostories: one of himself from the '70s, with sideburns and bell-bottom pants, and another from his wedding day in 1980. He added a brief caption: "Dreams evolve, happiness remains."

The next day, his daughters saw the post and were moved. It was the first time they had ever heard about that letter. In fact, his eldest daughter commented:

Dad, you never told me you wanted to be a famous radio announcer.

Well, daughter, life gave me much more than I ever imagined, and with that, I was satisfied, he replied, stroking her hair.

Max, on the other hand, never tired of asking him to tell stories about the past. Amused, Agustín ended up playing disco songs from his old digital player, and the two of them started dancing in the living room, as if at any moment psychedelic lights might appear.

After a few days, more family members, and even distant friends, discovered that post on Genostories. Many left comments sharing their own forgotten dreams: one admitted he had wanted to be a racecar driver, another that she had dreamed of owning a restaurant. And in the messages, the same idea repeated itself: *"Destiny doesn't need to fulfill everything to the letter. Sometimes, it's the surprises and the detours along the way that give us true happiness."*

Agustín smiled at each comment. He felt that, in some way, he had recovered the idealistic spirit of the young man from 1977, while also calmly accepting that his fulfillment didn't depend on becoming a famous announcer. Having the leading voice in the lives of those he loved was his true achievement.

Grandpa, what does this say? Max asked, pointing to a part of the digitized letter he couldn't read well.

Patiently, Agustín read the phrase aloud:

"I promise myself not to give up on anything that burns in my chest."

The boy shrugged, not fully understanding. But Agustín winked at him and said:

It means we can dream as much as we want, Max, and if some things don't happen, it doesn't matter. The best thing is to live each day with passion.

The little one simply smiled and, with the natural ease of his six years, ran off to find his bicycle, determined to begin another childhood adventure on the patio.

What moved me most about this story is that Agustín kept for decades the dreams of a young man who wanted to devour the world in great bites, and that, in the end, he didn't need to fulfill them exactly as imagined in order to feel complete. How often do we fear not achieving everything we set out to do in our twenties, or in our thirties? Perhaps the great lesson of this letter is that life always offers us an unexpected version of happiness, and that, far from disappointing us, it can surprise us with gifts far more precious than we imagined.

Reading this testimony, I've reflected on the importance of reconciling with our dreams. Sometimes we leave them forgotten in a drawer, and we're haunted by the feeling of "what would have happened if…?" But perhaps the best antidote to regret is realizing that the path we actually took also carried beauty and shaped us into fulfilled human beings.

If Agustín shows us anything, it's that an unfulfilled dream is not a failure, but a sign that destiny had other, more marvelous plans. And in the laughter of his grandson, Max, lies the proof that no amount of fame in the world could surpass the worth of a genuine embrace.
Griot 2085

A LOVE LETTER ON CASSETTE

Have you ever stopped to think about how couples communicated when there were no video calls, no instant messages, and no social networks we now take for granted? In the previous chapter, we followed a man who found his old letter of dreams from the '70s. Now I've come across a story that I find particularly endearing and amusing: the tale of a grandmother born in the '50s who discovered in audio cassettes the perfect vehicle for her romance in the early '80s.

Prepare yourself for a dose of nostalgia, laughter, and emotion. This chronicle reminds us that love and creativity require nothing more than ingenuity... and, sometimes, a Walkman to record the voice of someone we miss.

Griot 2085

Linda Parker had always possessed a dreamer's spirit. Born in 1952 on the outskirts of Cincinnati, Ohio, she grew up in a large family where improvised living-room dances and dinners filled with laughter were everyday fare. By 1982, her thirties rested upon her with the strength of mature youth: she still carried the air of an enthusiastic young woman, her blonde hair falling to her shoulders, and her passion for music accompanying her since adolescence.

At the time, Linda lived in a modest apartment decorated with posters of classic bands from her youth: The Beatles, The Rolling Stones... and a new one that had just captured her heart, a poster of Michael Jackson in his red leather jacket. The radio played at all hours in her little home, and though she sometimes put on old vinyl records, she was becoming fond of cassette recordings. The internet did not exist, nor, of course, did messaging apps. Linda was used to landline phones without answering machines, where voices arrived in real time or, if you didn't pick up in time, the call was lost into the void.

But she was happy. In fact, she had just begun dating a man she'd met a couple of months earlier: Tom Williams, a tall, charismatic guy with a sense of humor that made her laugh until her sides ached. Tom lived in Dayton, about a hundred kilometers away, and the simple act of visiting meant a road trip or a couple of hours by bus. They couldn't see each other every day, and long-distance calls (even between cities in the same state) were somewhat expensive for their pockets. That's why Linda and Tom found a way to shorten the distance that felt enormous to them: sending letters... and cassette recordings.

It all began with a small gesture. Tom, knowing Linda's passion for music, sent her a little box with a cassette he had recorded himself. On the label, scribbled by hand, it read: *"For Linda, with my best soundtrack.*" When she received it in the mail, she didn't know what to expect. Opening the package and seeing the tape, she felt both intrigued and thrilled.

Linda slid that cassette into her portable player, a silver Walkman she had bought with her savings at an electronics store. She put on the headphones and pressed *play*. The first sound she heard wasn't music, but Tom's voice:

Hello, Linda. I hope you're having an incredible day. I wanted to send you my favorite songs of the moment so you can feel a little bit of me even though we're far apart. Get ready, because there's a bit of everything: from rock to cheesy ballads. But above all, my affection goes into this tape.

Linda felt a flutter in her stomach at the sound of Tom's deep, jovial voice so characteristic of him. Then came *Eye of the Tiger* by Survivor, and she couldn't help but smile: she imagined Tom moving to the rhythm of the music, showing off his most enthusiastic side. Iconic songs followed: *Every Breath You Take* by The Police, *Physical* by Olivia Newton-John, and even the thundering *Another One Bites the Dust* by Queen. Between one track and another, Tom left little messages: *"I love this one because it makes me think of your laughter"* or *"When I hear this chorus, I imagine dancing with you in your living room."*

The tape ended with *I Wanna Dance with Somebody* by Whitney Houston, filling Linda's ears with a joyful, radiant vibration, followed by Tom's final whisper:

I wish you were here to dance to it with me… Sending you a big hug, my Linda.

When she finished listening, she had laughed, gotten emotional, and, almost without noticing, shed a couple of tears at the tenderness of the gesture. How could she not love the warmth of someone who spent hours creating a personalized cassette filled with his voice and his favorite music?

Linda thought: *"I can't just sit idly by. I have to respond to this marvel."* And so she did. She sat at the kitchen table with a notebook and began writing down the songs that moved her most. She recalled some radio hits that drove her crazy with emotion, like *Billie Jean* by Michael Jackson, *Take On Me* by a-ha, though that one was a little more recent, and a couple of ballads that made her sigh. She also included *Don't Stop Believin'* by Journey, a song that transported her to car rides with the windows down, the wind on her face, and a sense of almost infinite freedom.

But besides the music, Linda decided to record a very personal message. She got hold of a small portable recorder, the same one she sometimes used to rehearse church choirs, and set out to speak directly to Tom. When she heard her own voice through the headphones, she felt a bit self-conscious; she had never imagined it would be so hard to string sentences together knowing someone would hear them later. Finally, she gathered courage:

Hello, Tom. I don't know if this will come out right, but here goes. First of all, thank you for your wonderful tape. Hearing your voice among those songs was like having you slip into my living room and give me a kiss on the cheek. I confess I danced alone to *Another One Bites the Dust*; I felt a little ridiculous, but happy. I've chosen a few songs that I love that give me goosebumps; I hope they make you feel close to me.

Her chosen music played: *Billie Jean, Don't Stop Believin', Girls Just Want to Have Fun*, and a lineup full of rhythm. She saved *Every Breath You Take* for last, the same one Tom had included, to let him know they shared a favorite. When that song ended, Linda, with a slightly trembling voice, added:

I imagine that when you hear it, you think of me… And when I hear it, I find myself daydreaming of a future where we can listen to it together every day. I don't know if it sounds too cheesy, but… it's what I feel. See you soon, Tom. Don't stop sending me your cassette adventures.

When Linda stopped the recording, she spent a while looking out the window. The sunset reflected shades of orange and pink across the sky. She smiled to herself. She felt like a teenager in love… and to think she was already thirty. In the '80s, people her age often hurried to settle down, marry, have children, but she adored this different, ingenious form of courtship she and Tom were creating.

Weeks went by. Linda mailed the cassette and waited impatiently for the reply. In the meantime, they stayed in touch with occasional phone calls, calls they feared letting run too long because of the cost. One afternoon, Linda was at home preparing dinner when the landline rang. She rushed to pick it up:

Linda? I've got your tape in my hands! said Tom with evident joy.

And have you listened to it yet?

Not yet, I got home late and only managed to play a couple of minutes. But… I wanted to hear your voice live before diving into your songs.

They talked for a few minutes, laughing, sharing everyday silliness. He told her he'd had an accident with his car on the way home from work: a tire had burst in the middle of the road, and he had to push it to a gas station while a truck rumbled by with its stereo blasting *Pour Some Sugar on Me* by Def Leppard, which, according to Tom, made him feel like he was in a rock video, but in the worst possible situation. Linda laughed, picturing him covered in dust and cursing his luck. Then they said goodbye quickly so as not to skyrocket the phone bill.

The next morning, Linda received an unexpected package: another cassette from Tom! She read the label with curiosity: *"Cassette #2: Message Service."* She wondered what that could mean. When she played it, she heard Tom's voice, a little rushed:

Attention, this is Tom Williams speaking from Dayton, Ohio. Linda, my love, I regret to inform you that I suffered a serious mishap: my mailbox jammed and your tape got stuck... I had to force the lock! For a moment I feared I'd destroyed your letter... But I survived, and last night I played your compilation. *Girls Just Want to Have Fun* gave me the silly laugh only you can provoke. And you've made me sweat with that Beat It; I danced in the kitchen like I was Michael Jackson. I almost dislocated my hip! Please, Linda, don't do these things to me without supervision.

Ah, but I have a problem: my cassette player is starting to fail. Maybe I'll have to buy a new one.

Meanwhile, let me tell you about something strange that happened...

Then Tom went on in the audio to narrate a tragicomic incident: that very morning, after listening to Linda's tape, he had tried to record his response, but his sister Stacy burst into the room and accidentally pressed the *erase* button while fiddling with the controls. Tom, outraged, watched his message full of compliments and sweet words for Linda vanish. He was left without his recorded love declaration, and Stacy kept apologizing for her clumsiness. Faced with this disaster, Tom decided to improvise a *"Message Service"* where he gathered everything he wanted to tell her, hoping his player wouldn't also swallow that tape.

Anyway, darling... in the end I gave up and decided to tell you this whole tragicomedy here. I promise that on the next tape I'll share something more interesting than my clumsy mishaps of the week.

Linda listened with bursts of laughter. *"This man is a character,"* she thought, happy to have someone capable of laughing at his own stumbles. The most important thing was that with every tape, they felt closer. Wasn't it wonderful that, in the era before video calls, they could transmit emotions through the magic of recorded voices?

Days went by, and Linda and Tom kept exchanging tapes. Each decorated the little case with stickers or doodles: he drew guitars and vinyl records; she added little hearts and flowers. Sometimes, they included small "sections":

Song of the Day

Gossip of the Week

Delirious Messages to You

At times, Linda dared to confide very personal things: old insecurities about her appearance or whether her life was moving forward quickly enough. Tom would listen and respond in his next recording with anecdotes from his own past, like his stage fright when playing guitar in high school. They comforted each other, laughed at themselves, and gave one another the strength to carry on.

But not everything could be through correspondence. They wanted to see each other, to kiss, to share that chemistry in person. They agreed on a weekend when Tom would travel to Cincinnati to spend a whole day with Linda. She, excited, planned a candlelit dinner, a marathon of cassettes, and, most of all, a moment to dance. In the background, she wanted to play *"Don't Stop Believin'"* by Journey and end with a slow song that would let them embrace without hurry.

On the eve of their date, Linda locked herself in her room to pick the outfit she would wear to greet him: fitted jeans, a pastel-colored blouse, and huge earrings that gave her an unmistakable '80s flair. As she tried on her clothes, the radio played *"Wake Me Up Before You*

Go-Go" by Wham!, and she couldn't help dancing around the room, swept away by the anticipation of seeing him. She was thirty years old, yes, but when she looked at herself in the mirror, she felt as if she were about to experience the first love of her life.

Saturday arrived, and Linda, nervous, played one of Tom's cassettes to calm herself. She listened to his voice and sat on the edge of the bed, smiling with anticipation. Around seven in the evening, she heard the doorbell. She rushed to open it: there was Tom, with a bouquet of modest flowers (not too big, but with an incredible fragrance), dressed in jeans and a brown leather jacket that gave him a rebellious touch. They melted into an embrace that seemed to erase the barriers of distance and waiting.

At last, he whispered, resting his forehead against hers.

I thought you'd never arrive, Linda replied, feeling small in his arms.

That night was unforgettable. They talked about everything and nothing, ate pasta Linda had carefully prepared, and toasted with cheap wine that felt like an exotic luxury. Tom had brought his portable radio-cassette player, set it on the living room table, and asked Linda to play her favorite tapes. The hits of Madonna rang out (especially *"Like a Virgin"* and *"Material Girl"*), which made her sing at the top of her lungs, while Tom danced, imitating her with humor. Then came *"Billie Jean"*, where the two of them launched into a mini "moonwalk" contest in the small space of the living room, somewhat ridiculous and absolutely fun.

Linda struggled not to bump into the furniture, and Tom raised his arms as if he were a professional dancer, tongue sticking out in concentration. Were there furtive kisses? Of course. In each pause, he leaned in and brushed her lips with tenderness, as if he couldn't wait any longer to merge into her mouth. One laugh blended into another, and the music became the perfect soundtrack.

Finally, close to ten o'clock, *"Every Breath You Take"* began to play. They looked into each other's eyes. They lowered the volume of the cassette player and embraced slowly, dancing close in a gentle sway that wove intimacy. Linda rested her head on Tom's chest and listened to his heartbeat, which seemed to quicken with every passing second. He wrapped her in his arms and, in that moment, they felt the world fall silent, as if the city could have been in chaos, but they were safe in their bubble of closeness.

Do you still think recording cassettes is old-fashioned? he teased in a whisper.

I wouldn't trade it for anything in the world, Linda replied, inhaling the scent of the man who had come to paint her days with color.

The evening continued with anecdotes, laughter, and deeper confessions. To seal the night, Tom wanted to record a message on a tape live. He took his radio-cassette player and set out to say a few words like a diary entry for Genostories… Well, Genostories didn't exist back then, but he wanted to leave it as a testimony for his "Linda of the future." It was something improvised:

Dear Linda of the future, this is Tom from 1982 speaking to you from Cincinnati. I'm looking at the most beautiful woman I've ever met. She fed me dinner and made me laugh to the point of madness… I just want, when you listen to this someday, for you to remember this exact moment. We're about to…

And at that instant, bam! The tape got stuck. It seemed the player couldn't handle so much passion. A strange dragging sound was heard, and the voice distorted. Linda and Tom burst into helpless laughter, realizing that sometimes the simplest technology could turn capricious. It was a small reminder that, in the end, one cannot control life's details, not even those of a romantic recording. They turned off the device and embraced again, letting words fall away in the warmth of their bodies.

When Tom said goodbye that night (because, though he wanted to stay, they preferred to be a little prudent), it began to rain. He ran to his car under the curtain of water. Linda stayed at the doorway, watching him leave with her heart pounding. She thought: *"This isn't a goodbye, but the beginning of something big."*

Throughout 1983, they kept exchanging cassettes, and their relationship grew in intimacy. Each tape carried love messages and songs ranging from *Beat It* by Michael Jackson to *Livin' on a Prayer* by Bon Jovi. Rock, pop, and ballads combined into a personal *soundtrack* of their love story. They say music is a universal language, and indeed it was for them. On her work breaks, Linda would browse record shops for new songs to surprise him. Sometimes she grabbed a microphone and left him hilarious notes: *"Tom, stop eating pizza and get some exercise, you promised me you'd dance to Take On Me without getting winded!"* And he replied with equally witty comments, creating a lively back-and-forth full of spark.

In-person visits weren't as frequent as they wished, the money wasn't plentiful and travel was costly, but they knew that each tape was a bridge that united them. In fact, in one of the recordings, Linda exclaimed:

You know, sometimes I think love and creativity don't need the latest technology; our voices and this little machine are enough to shorten the miles. I love knowing that when you put on the headphones, you step into my world.

No elaborate explanations were needed: the feeling was there, burning in every groove of the magnetic tape.

Not everything was roses. In mid-1988, Tom received a job offer to move to Chicago. It would be a major promotion, which meant greater physical distance and less time to see each other. Linda panicked when she found out, fearing their relationship might collapse. However, Tom called her one night to explain his plans and reassure her:

Linda, the last thing I want is to be away from you, but I don't want to lose this opportunity either. Do you trust me?

Linda hesitated. They had shared a couple of years of intimacy, but they weren't married nor living together. Could their love survive yet another, even wider, geographical gap?

It's risky, Tom. But I trust in what we've built, she said, her voice breaking.

I promise not to abandon our tapes, nor our dream of being together. It won't be immediate, but I'll find a way for us to share the same city one day.

That promise was sealed, of course, in a special cassette that Tom recorded just before moving. He titled it *"Chicago Chapter"*: in it, he mixed songs from that city with bolder rock tracks that gave him courage, like *"Eye of the Tiger"* and *"Pour Some Sugar on Me,"* laughing at his own extravagant mix. Linda cried when she listened to it, feeling a bittersweet ache: *"Maybe professional goals will take him away for a while,"* she thought. But love doesn't understand dThere was a curious episode: in September of that same year, Linda decided to send Tom a cassette along with a handwritten letter that confessed everything she felt, with words she had never dared to say aloud: *"I love you madly,"* *"I want a future by your side,"* and so on. It was the first time she used the word love in all its weight. She was visibly nervous, as her handwriting trembled and several paragraphs had been erased.

On the cassette she recorded a brief message:

Tom, the pages I'm sending will tell you better what I feel. I just wanted to say that, no matter what happens, you have my heart. Distance and storms don't matter, my affection is stronger. Ah, and the background music is *With or Without You* by U2, because, dramatic as it sounds, that lyric reminds me of you…

The problem arose when the package got lost in the postal system. For two weeks, Linda anxiously awaited Tom's reply, but the call never came. He, for his part, thought Linda had grown distant since he wasn't receiving new letters or tapes. The lack of communication created tension and misunderstandings. When they finally spoke by phone, Tom blurted out: *"Are you mad at me?"* and Linda replied: *"Why would I be?"* It was then they discovered the package had gone missing.

The situation was resolved with an express resend, but Linda felt frustrated: the first version of her written declaration was lost in some warehouse of unclaimed packages, perhaps in another city. She had to rewrite her feelings, which took away a bit of the spontaneity, though, in the end, the essence remained: *"I love you and I want to stay by your side."*

By early 1989, Tom had settled in Chicago and the tapes traveled between Ohio and Illinois. For Linda, the wait for each cassette became a ritual of hope. She would rush to the mailbox, check the packages, and when she found one with Tom's handwriting, her whole day lit up. She played it alone in her room to savor every word. The music of the '80s remained the guiding thread of their story. Hits like *"Like a Virgin"* or *"Livin' on a Prayer"* reminded her that the world kept spinning with energy, and that, in some way, their relationship was still growing despite the distance.

Until the decisive cassette arrived. Tom sent her a bulky envelope. Along with the audio tape, there was a set of photos from Chicago: Lake Michigan, the tall buildings, his new workplace… and a note that said: *"Press play when you're ready for a surprise."* With her heart racing, Linda settled onto the couch and pressed the play button.

Tom's voice sounded a little shaky:

Hello, my precious Linda. Forgive me if I stammer; this isn't as easy as sending a joke. I've been thinking about our future for months. We've tested ourselves through letters, cassettes, fleeting visits… and still, we've endured. I think I'm not wrong in saying that I love you, and that each of your tapes brightens my days in this giant city. I'm eager to see you without having to drive hours or think about the postal service. That's why I wanted to ask you something important…

At that moment, *"Sweet Child O' Mine"* by Guns N' Roses began to play softly in the background, and Tom continued:

Would you like to move in with me in Chicago? Or, if you prefer, tell me where. I don't know if it scares you to leave your city, your family… But Linda, I ask you to consider the possibility of building something together, in the same place. With all respect and love, I would be thrilled to share my life with you, with no distance other than the brief one of a hug when I come home from work.

Linda felt a chill at the back of her neck. He was asking her to move to another city, to an unfamiliar apartment, to build a stronger bond as a couple. It wasn't exactly a marriage proposal, but in her eyes, it was just as momentous. What would she do about her job at the record store? And her family in Cincinnati, so used to seeing her every Sunday?

The tape continued with Tom listing some possibilities: she could look for work in a music shop, perhaps at a local radio station or with a company in the city. He ended softly: *"Whatever you decide, I'll stand by your side, but I'll keep dreaming of the day we wake up together every morning."*

Linda ended up crying from pure emotion. She spent several days reflecting. In the meantime, she prepared a response on a different cassette, where she told him she needed time to process it, but that the idea made her soul tremble with excitement. Her main fear was leaving behind her world, but the temptation to live that love to the fullest seduced her.

There would be much more to tell, but suffice it to say that in 1989 Linda took the leap: she packed her suitcase and moved to Chicago. She rented an apartment with Tom, sealing a new stage in her life. And what happened with the cassettes? Well, they kept using them, though now in a different way: they exchanged them on special occasions to remember the beginnings of their courtship. Every anniversary, they made a compilation of the songs that had marked each year. The Walkman and the old radio-cassette player became treasures they never threw away; even when CDs appeared, then MP3s, and much later streaming, they cherished those tapes as relics of their creative, juglaresco[1] love.

Even when the digital era arrived, along with mobile phones with answering machines, Linda kept sending him little audio messages. Until decades later, she learned of the existence of Genostories and decided to digitize that entire collection, uploading fragments of Tom's voice saying: *"Goodnight, lovely Linda,"* or *"I've found the perfect song for us..."* It was her legacy of romance for children and grandchildren. And when her relatives asked her how it was possible to keep the spark alive in such difficult times, she laughed and answered:

---

1 Playful, minstrel-like style.

We kept the spark alive through silliness and cassettes. You don't need the latest technology to love each other; all you need is will and imagination.

Because, in the end, if that decade of the '80s, with its blaring music and outrageous hairstyles, taught her anything, it was that passion and complicity can arise from the simplest means: a recorded cassette, a postal box, and a song that represents what beats in the heart. And now, in an app that gave them the chance to immortalize their love story, called *Genostories*.

*Don't you find it moving how love can blossom
with nothing more than a voice and a handful of songs?
Linda and Tom lived their own romantic movie in the
early '80s, proving that instant messages and video calls
aren't necessary to forge a genuine bond. The effort and
creativity poured into recording cassettes, decorating them
with stickers, and expressing each heartbeat in words or
music reveal human ingenuity when it sets out to shorten
distances.*

*This chapter has made it clear to me that creativity
can always make up for the resources we lack. The
internet? It was still years away from becoming
widespread. Smartphones? Out of the question. But Linda
and Tom, with their Walkman and radio-cassette player,
built an emotional bridge that defied geography. Their
story suggests to me a great truth: love and creativity
don't need the latest technology; they are bridges we build
with whatever is at hand. Whether it's magnetic tapes or
handwritten letters, what matters is the will to share life.*

*And perhaps that is the most powerful lesson
nostalgia from the '80s can leave us: to love is to invent, to
improvise, and to treasure every small gesture of affection.*
Griot 2085

THE FORGOTTEN FESTIVAL

Who hasn't stumbled upon a childhood memory so full of color and cheer that it feels like a dream, almost unreal? In my constant exploration of Genostories, I found the testimony of a man who watched something fade that, in his child's eyes, once shone brightly: a folk festival that brought an entire town together in the 1980s.

What causes a tradition to decline into oblivion? And what spark can rescue it from silence? This story teaches us that sometimes all it takes is a passionate heart to rekindle the fire of a culture we thought extinct.

Prepare yourself to dive into a tale of nostalgia, beauty, and determination.

Griot 2085

My name is Daniel Sullivan, and I was born in the fall of 1974 in a small, picturesque town called Willow Creek, somewhere in the American Midwest. When I say "small," I mean it barely had three thousand inhabitants, all of whom knew each other. I grew up in a community where traditions carried a very particular flavor: family bonds, a love for craftsmanship, and devotion to certain festivities that had been celebrated long before I was born. In the early '80s, when I was just a child, my greatest joy was the folk festival that, year after year, lit up the streets with music, dancing, and handicrafts.

Today, at fifty years old, I live in a larger city and have two children, Emma and Lucas, who are growing up in a world saturated with screens and digital distractions. And yet, part of my heart remains anchored in that Willow Creek of my childhood. Because there was a time when, every June, that little town exploded with noise and color, and the entire community vibrated with wonderful energy. That festival was my portal into the magic of local culture. For a long time, I thought it would remain alive forever... until, little by little, it faded away. It saddens me that my children don't even know it existed. That's why, in 2024, I've decided to preserve its memories through Genostories, so that future generations won't forget the roots that shaped my identity.

Let me step back to the early 1980s: I was six or seven years old, and Willow Creek was my entire universe. Picture a main street lined with pastel-painted wooden houses, a gas station whose sign swayed in the wind, and a diner with a flickering neon sign that read *"Polly's Best Pies."* Neighbors greeted each other by name, and we kids played in the town square until dusk forced us home.

At that time, the Willow Creek Festival, though perhaps not as famous as other major events, was our great pride. It took place in mid-June, coinciding with the best weather for outdoor celebration.

For one weekend, the whole town transformed: artisans set up stalls along the streets, selling embroidered fabrics, wooden figurines, and handwoven baskets. Families prepared their most traditional recipes to compete in a homemade cooking contest. And, of course, folk music filled the air from an improvised stage in the central square, where local groups and bands from neighboring towns took turns playing fiddles, banjos, and guitars. Laughter and foot-stomping could be heard from blocks away.

What fascinated me most was the sense of community, that we were all together in a celebration that belonged to us. I remember seeing my father, James Sullivan, dancing with my mother, Laura, to a lively tune full of steps and spins, while I clapped and laughed with the innocence of a child who believes the world is nothing but joy. Sometimes, at nightfall, bonfires were lit and people told old stories, legends about the first families who had settled in Willow Creek. They said the festival was more than a century old, founded to celebrate the harvest and the friendship among pioneers. Maybe parts of those stories were embellished with imagination, but to me, they were sacred truths.

Perhaps it was my innocence, but as the years passed, I began to understand that not everything was harmony and merriment. In the early '80s, the United States was going through political and economic changes that reached even the most remote corners. Willow Creek was no exception. The canning factory, which employed many families in town, was forced to cut staff. Some neighbors lost their jobs and had to move to larger cities. Farmers, who used to sell their products at the festival, began to feel the blow of falling prices and the competition from industrialized foods.

Meanwhile, on the local level, a new mayor was elected every few years. I remember when, in 1984, one took office who paid little attention to the folk festival. He considered it a useless expense and thought the town's funds should be directed toward modernizing certain infrastructures. The festival was financed partly by donations and small municipal subsidies, but the new mayor preferred to allocate them to repaving the road leading into town, arguing that this would attract more investors. Little by little, official support for the festival dwindled.

In my memories, 1985 was a bittersweet year. The festival was still held, but with fewer musical groups invited, fewer artisans, and a somewhat less festive atmosphere. Some neighbors complained that local culture couldn't be allowed to die; others saw the decline with resignation. My father, a great lover of folk dancing, lamented:

We can't allow tradition to die just because a politician isn't interested.

But sometimes the protests of a few aren't enough. That was a warning that times were changing for Willow Creek.

Even so, the 1986 festival managed to bring together more people than the year before, because it coincided with the anniversary of the town's founding. The streets were decorated with colorful banners, and traditional dance performances were promoted. I remember vividly how the pavement of the main street filled with stalls: one sold roasted corn on the cob with butter, another offered homemade lemonade, and there was an old man, Mr. Peterson, who sat carving little wooden animal figurines. They were simple works, but they embodied skill and a love for the handmade. A scent of apple pie floated through the air, and in the distance you could hear laughter and the clatter of feet dancing.

That night, the stage set up in the central square became the venue for regional dances. People from the region wore costumes with traditional embroidery, and the music grew livelier as the night went on. Fiddles, banjos, guitars filled the air, and there was even space for those who wanted to perform more modern dances, a curious hybrid of folklore and pop, a reflection of the times. For a child like me, it was all a mesmerizing spectacle: I stood open-mouthed at the choreographies and the swirling dresses, feeling like I was part of something much larger than myself.

But that was the last time I saw such a thriving festival. A year later, the town's economy was more battered. Many families emigrated, and the council cut funding for "non-essential cultural events." People lost enthusiasm, and a couple of leaders who had pushed the festival forward moved away in search of better opportunities. The 1987 festival barely took place, and the 1988 one was nothing more than a small gathering with a few stands. Before I realized it, that grand celebration that had defined my childhood had disappeared.

As I entered adolescence, already in the '90s, there was no trace of the festival. Willow Creek became a quiet place, where life went on without major events. And yet, I never forgot those celebrations that shaped me, that sense of unity, of colors, and of music that seemed to spring from the town's very essence. My father, who remained in Willow Creek, sadly remarked how the streets now looked lifeless in June, the month that once pulsed with joy.

As I grew up, I moved from city to city for school and later for work. It wasn't until my twenties that I finally settled in Greenfield, a larger town where I met my wife, Caroline. But whenever we visited Willow Creek for a family gathering, my father or mother would inevitably bring up the festival with a sigh:

"Do you remember how that melody used to sound?"

"Do you remember Mr. Peterson carving wooden bears and deer?"

"That was another time, son. A time that won't come back."

In those moments, I felt powerless. Was there really no turning back? More than once, I set out to speak with a city council member to see if there was any chance of reviving the festival, but the answers were always disheartening: "We don't have the funds," "No one would be interested anymore," "It's too old a tradition," and so on. And so the years passed, with nothing for me to do but keep those memories in my heart.

As an adult, forty-nine years old, I finally settled permanently in Greenfield, where my job at a software company gave me some stability. I had two kids: Emma, age 14, and Lucas, 9. One spring day in 2024, we visited my parents in Willow Creek, looking to break from routine. There, while going through old photo albums, I stumbled upon printed images of the festival in its prime: tents filled with handmade crafts, a stage crowded with fiddlers and banjo players, folk dances with people beaming with joy. I looked, wistfully, at a photo of my father and me dancing awkwardly, he was laughing while I, six years old, tried to mimic his steps.

It was a kind of epiphany. Emma and Lucas, staring at those pictures, asked in awe:

"Dad, was Willow Creek really that fun?"

"And why isn't there anything like that anymore?"

A spark lit up inside me. Why not bring back what had been lost? I remembered that some time ago I had discovered Genostories, a platform where people uploaded files, stories, and videos about their lives, a space where memories could live on instead of vanishing with time. The idea of telling my children, and the world, about what the Willow Creek Festival once was excited me. I hoped that, somehow, this story might help revive it. Sometimes, sharing a memory can stir something in people. I felt it was my moral duty to try.

I began to gather everything I could: old photos of my parents, clippings from local newspapers that announced the festival, and even a few cassettes my mother had kept, where the sounds of the celebration had been amateurishly recorded. One in particular contained the ambient sound of the 1985 edition: laughter, stomping feet, a violin, and someone announcing the next musical act over the microphone. Listening to it sent a shiver of memory through me: it was as if I were ten again, jumping to the rhythm of the music.

I reached out to some neighbors who still lived in Willow Creek and were older than me. Two of them, Mrs. Dorothy Evans and Mr. Bill Peterson (yes, the same craftsman who carved wooden figures), opened their homes to me and showed me their own relics of the festival: Dorothy kept traditional embroidered costumes in a trunk, while Bill preserved an album with dozens of black-and-white photographs, some dating back to the 1950s and 60s. They told me stories that went beyond what I remembered:

Dorothy spoke of how, in the '70s, they had brought in a Latin American dance group to liven up one of the evenings, creating a rich cultural exchange. Bill confessed that he had learned his carving trade from his grandfather, who had supplied handicrafts for the festival for more than thirty years.

Their eyes sparkled with nostalgia. I realized I wasn't the only one longing to relive that atmosphere. And yet, I also sensed a deep resignation: *"Young people aren't interested in these things,"* they said. *"Without municipal support, it can't be done."* But a little voice kept telling me that if I could at least spread its story, there would be a ray of hope.

That's how my idea was born: to create a project within Genostories called *"The Forgotten Festival of Willow Creek."* I planned to upload scanned photos, audio from those old tapes, and testimonies from those who had lived it in its splendor. I wanted to write detailed chronicles of each edition, every detail, every typical recipe that had once been sold at the stalls. I wanted my children (and their children) to understand why that festival wasn't just a simple weekend event, but a symbol of identity for the town.

I was surprised at how easy Genostories made it to upload and tag content. I could create a chronological thread:

1970–1979: the beginnings of my memory (though it already existed before).

1980–1986: the golden era.

1987–1988: the decline.

2024: the possible rebirth.

I filled the profile with photos of the central square decorated with garlands, with artisans showing their goods, with children dancing. I digitized a fragment of the 1985 recording and uploaded it as audio: when played, one could hear an elderly voice announcing the next musical group, laughter in the background, and the chords of a fiddle beginning a folk melody. I also uploaded some of the recipes people cooked back then: cornbread with honey, beef stew with fresh vegetables that was served in the main tent. Each came with a brief cultural explanation: how it was prepared, why it mattered, who made it.

My family was thrilled. My children went through the photos and asked me who each person was. My wife, Caroline, encouraged me to include videos. Although not much filming had been done in the '80s, I located a VHS that briefly showed the 1986 festival. Converting that VHS to digital format was a challenge, but I managed to rescue a clip about four minutes long which, though blurry and with poor audio, showed dances and smiling faces. I uploaded it to Genostories too, with a note: *"Forgive the quality; it's part of the charm of our history."*

Thanks to today's social networks, and to Genostories' connection with other sites, I began sharing these materials with people from Willow Creek who had moved to other cities. The effect was incredible: former residents commented with excitement that they hadn't known anyone cared about reviving the festival. Some sent me private messages with anecdotes I didn't know, or with additional photographs. When Bill Peterson learned of the response, he was moved: *"Maybe not everything is lost, Daniel,"* he told me in his rough voice.

There were more surprises: a few weeks later, someone from the current Willow Creek town council saw the Genostories timeline and reached out to me. They said it was a beautiful initiative. The mayor had changed (several times) since the days of my childhood, and the current one represented a younger generation. *Would it be possible, they asked, to organize a symbolic event to remember the festival? Maybe a small cultural gathering?* Unfortunately, they didn't have much of a budget, but they offered the central square and logistical support.

I couldn't believe it. All of this was happening because I had dared to collect and share the memories of an event everyone thought was dead. It had been a minimal push, but sometimes all it takes is a spark to ignite a bonfire of interest. I immediately thought of Dorothy and Bill, and of how many other neighbors would be glad to take part. I called my father, now elderly, who was so moved that he went up to the attic in search of anything he or my mother might have saved. He found an old poster that read: *"Willow Creek Folklore Festival 1982, Let's Celebrate Our Roots Together."* We decided to use it as the main image for the new proposal.

It was 2024, and we were only a few months away from June. With a handful of neighbors and the support of the mayor's office, we set ourselves the task of organizing a "gathering", not as big as before, but with the hope that it could be a first step toward reviving the festival. We began making calls, looking for young musicians who could perform folk pieces or who were willing to learn the old melodies. We agreed to set up a small stage, though without major installations. Bill offered to carve some wooden figures to sell or exhibit, and Dorothy promised to mend her old traditional costumes to display or lend to anyone who wanted to wear them.

But not everything was easy. Some people labeled us *"nostalgic"* or *"delusional,"* saying millennials or Gen Z weren't interested in those things. Some artisans hesitated to take part because they feared no one would buy their products. Others thought the festival should remain in memory and not be revived halfway. Time was short and the budget nearly nonexistent. Would we manage something worthwhile?

That's when I saw again the strength of Genostories. I posted an announcement on the platform's community, detailing what we intended to do, and invited people to contribute suggestions and ideas. To my surprise, I received messages from descendants of families who had once lived in Willow Creek: they were willing to donate money or attend as an audience to support the cause. Some even preserved family customs and recipes. In just a few days, the initiative came alive. I began to believe, firmly, that this was the beginning of the reconstruction of our cultural heritage.

The agreed date arrived: it was June 15, 2024, a sunny Saturday. Willow Creek, with its main street, relived some of its old joy. It wasn't as crowded as in my childhood, of course. The stage was more modest, the artisan stalls were fewer, but the atmosphere... oh, that atmosphere! Music echoed in the square, and neighbors walked around laughing, discovering photographs displayed on panels that showed what the festival had been like in the '80s. There was an air of nostalgia mingled with renewed pride.

Dorothy wore one of her old embroidered dresses, welcoming people with a smile that lit up her wrinkled face. Bill, for his part, displayed his carved figures with a sign that read: *"Tradition in my hands since 1955."* My father, now with a cane, sat at the side of the stage, his eyes moist as he watched a pair of young musicians, trained by former folk artists, play some of the pieces once performed at the original festival.

The most moving sight was seeing my daughter Emma and my son Lucas running around with other children their age. I had told them so many times about my childhood in Willow Creek that, for a moment, I thought I saw in their laughter a reflection of myself years earlier. It was as if my nostalgia fused with their curiosity, and past and present met in an embrace.

That same afternoon, I uploaded real-time photos of the small event to Genostories, tagging everyone who had contributed. I felt that we were not only recovering a festival, but also the collective memory of a place.

As evening fell, an impromptu dance began. It wasn't as crowded or dazzling as the ones I remembered, but the folk music sounded fresh. I saw young people trying to learn traditional steps, clumsy, yet laughing with the same joy I had felt as a child. There was applause for every performance, and at one point Dorothy and a neighbor even told stories about the first generation who had organized the festival at the end of the 19th century, weaving anecdotes that were surely embellished with legend. The bonfire was lit, and people shared food, a couple of stews prepared by elderly women, and homemade sweets. It was a short night, but a historic one: the festival, though timid and reduced, had returned.

My greatest surprise came when the mayor, moved by the turnout and the positive energy, publicly committed to allocating a municipal fund (modest, but something) to repeat the experience the following year, with greater organization and reach. The crowd applauded. I walked over to my father and mother, embraced them tightly, feeling that, in some way, we had triumphed over oblivion.

That night, back at my parents' house, I sat with Emma and Lucas to hear their impressions.

Dad, why did they let something so fun die? Emma asked.

Yeah, why didn't they keep doing it every year? Lucas added, innocently.

I sighed, recalling the complex factors that destroy traditions: lack of support, changes in government, migration, collective neglect.

Sometimes traditions die, I told them, if no one tells their story or values them. But all it takes is a single passionate heart to bring them back. Maybe we won't have the same scale as before, but if we keep trying, we can make this festival something great again.

My children seemed to understand, in their own way, and in that moment, I felt more convinced than ever of the lesson I wanted to leave recorded in Genostories: *"Our legacy lives as long as someone tends to it and shares it."*

With the thrill of that day's experience, I returned to Genostories and created a kind of digital documentary, combining photos, videos, audios, and chronicles. I detailed how the day of reunion had unfolded, uploaded testimonies from some of the neighbors, and above all, left an open message to anyone who wanted to join the cause, with the hope that, in the years to come, more people would be inspired to invest time and energy in this newly revived festival.

I was fortunate that some cultural associations from the region saw my project and contacted me to offer folk dance and handicraft workshops in Willow Creek. If things go well, the following year could be a leap in quality. I feel that the seed has been planted, and all thanks to the sharing of memories that had been stored away, dying in silence, until I found a way to bring them back to life.

I am no longer a child; I will never again live the magic of the festival as I did in 1985, but seeing other children laugh and stomp with the same innocence fills me with hope. One rescues traditions not out of empty nostalgia, but to pass down values and connections that anchor us to our roots. The festival taught me to value community, collective effort, and the simple happiness of music and dancing in the open air. Today, I want to share that lesson with my children and with those who come after me.

Some nights, I look through the old photo albums and, instead of feeling melancholy, I experience a quiet satisfaction. Because I know that, although that era will never return in the same way, its essence can adapt and shine in this century. It doesn't matter if we live surrounded by social networks and screens: culture, music, craftsmanship, and tradition still hold a unifying power that nothing can replace.

The Willow Creek Festival hasn't returned to its former splendor overnight, but it has taken a great step forward. I am convinced that if we persevere year after year, we will recover something very close to that unique atmosphere that enchanted my childhood. Every chapter I write in Genostories, every photo or video I upload, is a brick in the reconstruction of our identity. And best of all: my children will be part of it, as bearers of the torch that we all lit together.

That is why I decided to leave this testimony, hoping that other people, in other places, will be inspired to rescue their festivals, their dances, their ancestral celebrations. Traditions die if no one tells their story or values them, but a single passionate heart can drive them to be reborn. And if that heart is joined by ten, a hundred, or a thousand more, the future can fill with little lights that illuminate our past and make it an eternal part of our present.

As I read the words of Daniel Sullivan, I couldn't help but imagine the echo of fiddles and banjos resounding in the square of Willow Creek, blending with the voices of children discovering for the first time the traditional dance that had shaped their parents' youth. This chapter reminds us that a tradition is not an inert object, but a breath of life that needs to be told, celebrated, and shared. At times, it may seem that forgetting is stronger, but all it takes is one person deciding to strike the spark for the flame to spread. The Willow Creek Festival is proof of that.

By uploading those photos, stories, and recordings to Genostories, Daniel built a bridge between his childhood and the present of a town that, perhaps, had grown tired of itself. In doing so, he proved that stories do not die as long as there is someone to tell them. Perhaps, in a few years, the festival will regain its grandeur and become a crucial part of the region's cultural life; or perhaps it will transform into something different, but with the same spirit. What matters is that nothing falls into the void as long as there is a heart committed to rescuing memory. And that, after all, is the magic of sharing our experiences: to light the fuse so that the flame of who we once were never goes out.

Griot 2085

THE FIRST HOME
PROGRAMMERS

When we think about the great advances in computing, we usually picture impressive laboratories and multinational corporations. However, in my journey through Genostories, I discovered that many of the first steps in the digital age began in modest living rooms and cluttered bedrooms, with enthusiasts who, despite having very few resources, armed themselves with curiosity and perseverance.

This is the testimony of someone who, in the early '80s, switched on his first home computer as if he were igniting the fuse of a space rocket... and the rest, as you'll see, is pure magic.

Griot 2085

Hello to whoever may be listening to this in the future.

My name is Richard "Rich" Marshall. I was born in 1959 (or 1960, depending on which family member you ask, they're a disaster with dates), and I want to leave a video message for my future grandchildren, because yes, the doctor said twins are on the way, and my daughter is swollen with both pride and panic at the same time. I thought that, when they grow up, they might want to know that their grandfather wasn't always a digital grouch, but once a crazy, enthusiastic young man who loved computing before it became commonplace.

It was 1982. Picture me with hair that looked like a bird's nest and a denim jacket full of rock band patches. Cell phones (the few that existed) were as big as bricks and less useful than one, and Wi-Fi… well, that was an idea worthy of science fiction. I lived in a small Kansas town, in a one-story house with a garage where I kept my bicycles and, occasionally, my Commodore 64.

I remember the first time I turned on that computer: a shiver ran down my spine. The blue screen flickered, and the classic message appeared:

markdown

Copy code

**** COMMODORE 64 BASIC V2 ****

64K RAM SYSTEM 38911 BASIC BYTES FREE

READY.

64 kilobytes! For me, it was like having infinity at my fingertips. I was convinced that with those 64 KB, I could conquer the universe… or at least feel like a small god of the digital world. I don't know if my grandchildren will be able to imagine what it was like to be dazzled by so little, but believe me, in those days that humming sound when the machine powered on was pure adrenaline.

Of course, turning on the Commodore was one thing, and learning to program was something entirely different. There was no YouTube, no Stack Overflow forums, no ChatGPT (I'm sure GPT will just be a memory by the time you're adults, and I bet you'll laugh at this). So my best ally was a computing magazine I got every month, *RUN Magazine*, and a couple of BASIC manuals that seemed to be written in another language. I'd sit in my room, with *"Take On Me"* by a-ha playing on my cassette radio in the background, and spend hours trying to understand those cryptic lines:

vbnet

Copy code

```
10 PRINT "RICH RULES THE WORLD"
20 GOTO 10
```

I would type everything out, hit "RUN," and watch the screen fill with "RICH RULES THE WORLD" in an infinite loop:

```
10 PRINT "RICH RULES THE WORLD"
 20 GOTO 10
```

I was so thrilled I felt I had accomplished the greatest feat of my life! It was a moment of revelation: *"If the computer can do this, maybe it can also do that…"* I wanted my imagination to come alive on the screen. I devoured every magazine, clipped articles, and pasted my notes into a notebook. My mother would tease me: *"Rich, do you think you're going to invent the next talking washing machine?"* And I'd just shrug, convinced that anything was possible.

The biggest problem with my Commodore 64 wasn't the machine itself, it was my family.

You see, my mom ruled the house, and most of the outlets were taken up by irons, lamps, or the television. One disastrous day, I had spent three days writing a program to make my name flash and bounce across the screen like a little acrobat. It was a puzzle of loops and variables. "*At last,*" I told myself, "*I'm going to see my dancing name.*" Just then, my mother came in with the iron and unplugged the computer to connect the appliance. I didn't have a disk drive to save my progress, so everything vanished into limbo in a second. I collapsed into my chair as if the world had ended. Tragic? Yes. But that's how I learned the importance of saving my work on a cassette, even if it was laborious. "*Save or die*" became my motto.

Another day, I had the idea to move the Commodore into the garage to escape the racket of my sister Janet, who wouldn't stop belting out "*I Wanna Dance with Somebody*" by Whitney Houston at the top of her lungs. The garage was freezing in winter, and I feared my fingers might freeze before I could type:

10 PRINT "HELLO"

But I managed with a little space heater and a thermos of hot chocolate.

There, in that improvised Antarctic lab, I typed out lines of code with the firm determination to master BASIC. Even though I failed often in my attempts, each small step made me feel as if a new world was opening before me.

I wasn't alone in this adventure. I had a couple of friends with the same spark in their eyes: Mike and Rachel. Mike was the kind of guy who always said technology would come to transform everything, while Rachel believed in the power of computing for creativity. We'd get together on weekends, each with our own computer, Mike had a ZX Spectrum, Rachel an Atari 800, and we'd share tricks and frustrations. We traded floppy disks and cassettes full of little programs that made beeping sounds or displayed pictures on the screen.

We were like a small sect of enthusiasts, rebelling against a world where most of our schoolmates preferred to watch MTV or hang out at the roller rink.

I remember Rachel once said: *"One day, these machines will be everywhere, and people will depend on them to live."* I laughed, thinking she was exaggerating. Today, every time I see half the world glued to their smartphones, I think of that line and want to say: *"Rachel, you were absolutely right."*

'80s fashion was worthy of a cabinet of curiosities: giant shoulder pads, hair sprayed into the stratosphere, brightly colored leg warmers. When I was getting ready to head to Mike's or Rachel's to program, I usually wore my denim jacket and my worn-out sneakers. And of course, I never forgot my Walkman, where I'd play cassettes with songs like *"Billie Jean"* by Michael Jackson or *"Livin' on a Prayer"* by Bon Jovi. That melodic rock and explosive pop made me feel like a futuristic genius while I pored over my BASIC manuals. Internet? Not a chance. The closest we had to "chatting" was passing notes in class or calling a friend's house on a rotary phone.

On TV, we watched series like *Knight Rider* or B-grade science fiction movies. Their cheesy special effects, compared to today's, looked wonderful to our innocent eyes. That inspired me even more to dream about what I could create with a computer. If Hollywood could make talking cars, why couldn't I create something that would revolutionize the world from my garage?

Among all my computer adventures, there was one crowning day: I managed to program a simple game. It was a little obstacle-dodging game, with a tiny square that had to jump over asterisks moving from left to right. How did I do it? A BASIC book, a handful of magazines, and lots and lots of trial and error. The code didn't exceed one hundred lines, but it took me weeks of tweaking. When it finally worked, that is, when the little square successfully dodged the asterisks, I felt a mix of euphoria and total exhaustion. Not even the biggest gamer today could understand what it feels like to believe you've just conquered a summit because you made a little jumping figure on a monochrome screen.

To celebrate, I invited Mike and Rachel to my house, and we cracked open a classic glass-bottled Coca-Cola to toast. To the beat of *"Another One Bites the Dust"* by Queen, we tried out my game. We got bored in three minutes, since it was extremely repetitive, but the achievement was there: I had created something with my own digital hands, so to speak. My mother looked at us from the doorway, shaking her head, while Janet, my sister, rolled her eyes. It was obvious: the magic wasn't visible from the outside, but for me, it was a total triumph.

While I was diving into BASIC, I had a friend named Raúl, yes, a somewhat unusual name in my area; his parents were of Mexican descent, and he always told me: *"Rich, all this computer stuff is just a passing fad. Look, people want to go out dancing, not mess around with machines."* He had a point; most people weren't interested in programming. The funny thing is, years later, Raúl ended up moving to Silicon Valley, where he worked at a software company. Whenever we talk, he says: *"Well, I guess the passing fad rubbed off on me."* Ironic, isn't it?

These contradictions were part of the era. Many saw computing as nothing more than a strange hobby for nerds, while others, like Rachel, sensed that we were on the cusp of a radical change. That, combined with our youth, made us feel like pioneers in a magical field that most people didn't understand. Not bad for a bunch of kids with floppy disks in their backpacks and a hunger to take on the world.

There's a funny incident I can't help but share with my future grandchildren. One night, I was writing a little program to simulate a traffic light. I wanted it to change from green to yellow to red on the screen, when the sound of a siren startled me. It was two in the morning, and I had left the garage window open to let in fresh air. The local police grew curious seeing the light on and wires everywhere, so they parked in front of my house. An officer knocked cautiously on the door, and my mom, startled, came out in her robe.

Good evening, ma'am. Is everything all right here?

Yes, my son is in the garage with his... What's it called, Rich? she yelled.

My Commodore, Mom. I answered, stepping out with a sleepy face.

The policeman looked at me with an amused smirk. He asked if I was "cooking something" (hinting at a possible drug lab). My mother, offended, replied: *"My son is cooking up codes, I suppose."* The officer burst out laughing and left, while we stood there with poker faces. It was a relief, and at the same time, I felt proud that, at least once, the police thought my "laboratory" was interesting enough to investigate. Long live the computer revolution!

After finishing high school, I went on to study at a university where there were more machines, programming languages, and professors who knew things I had never imagined. It was an overwhelming experience. Overnight, I went from being the weird kid who programmed in his garage to finding myself surrounded by dozens of enthusiasts who also spoke in binary. We learned C, Pascal... and I realized BASIC was only the tip of the iceberg.

The '90s followed, the explosion of the Internet came, and at every step I remembered the days when I had to save my code on a *casete* and fight for an outlet to avoid losing it.

In time, I settled into a good job, helped develop corporate software, and ended up as a systems consultant in a large company. The path wasn't direct or easy. I got married, had my daughter Marjorie, whom we adore, and now, look, she's going to have twins. Time moves faster than an infinite loop.

Now that I'm 64 years old, I feel once again that responsibility to leave something behind for you, my dear grandchildren on the way. I know you'll be born with tablets, smartphones, and who knows how many more marvels at your fingertips. Probably, the simple act of turning on a device will be routine, stripped of any mystery. But I want you to know there was a time when every line of code cost sweat and tears, when a single click wasn't enough to get help, when magazines with technical articles were true treasures, and when every program created felt like a magical discovery.

That's why I've decided to record this testimony on video and also upload it to Genostories. I want to tell you that curiosity and dedication are, and always will be, the spark of innovation, regardless of the resources of the era. We had only 64 KB of RAM, a half-indecipherable manual, and plenty of imagination to feel like pioneers of a new age. No Wi-Fi, no supercomputer. And still, all the excitement fit on the screen of that CRT monitor that weighed as much as an elephant.

It's funny to think about how the lives of my '80s accomplices turned out. Mike specialized in software architecture and ended up designing banking systems with thousands of users. Rachel, my great ally, drifted into creating independent video games, people say her latest work won an award for the most original narrative. And the skeptic Raúl turned into a tech marketing guru in Silicon Valley, as I mentioned. Sometimes we joke in a group chat about how different we all were and where passion (or chance) led us. If anything still unites us, it's that irrational love of tinkering, of experimenting.

There were also friends who stayed behind, who followed other paths, who never touched a computer beyond schoolwork. Many of them chose traditional careers, and that's fine, everyone has their own road. But I'm proud to see that those of us who bet on early computing, without resources or mentors, managed to carve out our place in a world that today relies on technology more than I ever imagined.

If you hear me laughing between these words, it's because, as I remember, I realize the magic wasn't in the computer itself, but in the curiosity of a kid who opened the manual and dove into cryptic lines, and in the dedication that drove him to overcome each obstacle. That magic still lives in anyone who chooses to build rather than simply use. I know that in your future, my grandchildren, you'll probably program with infinitely more powerful languages, with artificial intelligence suggesting everything instantly. But I hope you never forget that, in the beginning, it all came from the passion of people who carved their way with BASIC, assembler, FORTRAN, C...

Sometimes I miss that world where every kilobyte mattered, where every program was a triumph, and where the word "innovation" meant a wink at infinity; and, of course, where every programming session mixed with *"Thriller"* by Michael Jackson or *"Sweet Child O' Mine"* by Guns N' Roses blasting on the radio. Humor and nostalgia go hand in hand when you think that today a simple phone can make more calculations than that Commodore 64 I thought was the peak of civilization.

Dear grandchildren, who will probably have names like Aaron and Zoe, or something like that, when you wonder how this entire technological empire that dominates life today began, think of your old grandpa Rich and his Commodore 64 back in the '80s. It was a time of inventing without fear, of laughing at failures, of being thrilled by a simple PRINT "HELLO WORLD." The lesson I leave you is this: curiosity and dedication are the spark of innovation, no matter the limited resources of the time. If you ever feel like you don't have the best equipment or the latest technology, remember that my friends and I made magic with 64 KB and a photocopied manual. Nothing is impossible if the heart of a programmer (or an artist, an inventor, an entrepreneur) beats strong enough.

Please, don't be afraid of mistakes. Every time I failed and the screen went blank, I learned something new. Every mistake is a rung on the ladder of creativity, and don't forget to share your triumphs and frustrations with others. I was lucky enough to have friends who shared my madness. I'll finish this video with a wink: today, at 64 years old, I live surrounded by laptops, tablets, and ultra-powerful cell phones. My daughter, Marjorie, about to have the twins, laughs at how sometimes I'm left dumbstruck by how far we've come. But I keep my Commodore 64 alive in a special corner of the house, not to use, of course, but as a monument to the brave naivety that defined me in my teenage years. Sometimes I turn it on, and its hum brings me back to that first love with programming.

I've decided to upload these memories to Genostories so that, if my grandchildren ever want to know where their grandfather came from, they can watch this video-message and laugh at the old days. Maybe this text, my recorded voice, and this screen will reach more people who lived something similar or who aspire to feel the same passion for creating, exploring, and programming.

The conclusion is simple: our times were more difficult from a technical standpoint, but that didn't stop us from dreaming big. If anything has been proven, it's that human passion for invention ignites the moment you encounter a machine that can work wonders with just a few lines of code. So, dear grandchildren, and whoever else may see this, don't let the comfort or the overstimulation of today dull your thirst for learning. As my friend Rachel used to say: *"True technology lies in the curious mind, not in the machine."*

Now that I'm finishing this video, I lift my eyes and see my smartphone resting on the desk. That tiny device literally has a thousand times the power of my Commodore 64, and yet I miss something from those '80s: the thrill of feeling that each step forward was a glimpse of the future, that every discovery was like opening the door to a galaxy waiting to be explored. I still miss those days when innovation meant making magic with 64 kilobytes and an overflowing imagination.

And I'll leave you with one final wink:

Grandchildren, when you watch this video, remember that your old grandpa Rich wasn't just a programmer with little RAM, but someone who believed in the infinite power of curiosity. I know your world will be very different, filled with technologies I can't even dream of. But I hope you preserve the same wonder I felt when that *"READY."* appeared on the blue screen, and I set out to type my dreams.

What does the story of Rich Marshall leave us with? Above all, a powerful dose of excitement for that era when, with very few resources, the spark of home computing was lit. It shows us how the simplicity of a language like BASIC could unleash ingenuity and fuel the passion for innovation. Perhaps today's generations, used to instant results and millions of apps, can't imagine what it was like to wait for a program to load from a casete[16] or to pray that nobody unplugged the machine by accident. But Rich shows us that the magic wasn't in the technology itself, but in the human spark that drove it. That spark, curiosity, and perseverance, is what makes our dreams limitless: not yesterday, not today, not tomorrow.

Griot 2085

CHRONICLES OF THE
TRANSITION

In my wanderings through Genostories, I've discovered countless accounts shaped by political and social transformation. But few as intense as that of a man born in Chile in the 1950s, who lived through the 1973 coup d'état and the subsequent dictatorship. With his words, he takes us down the path from fear and repression to the awakening of hope and the building of a democracy that, even today in 2024, continues to be shaped.

It is a testimony that speaks of family tensions, of losses and reunions, but above all, of the deep conviction that freedom and peace never arrive as gifts from the sky: they are built and defended day by day, with responsibility, participation, and memory.

Griot 2085

My name is Fernando Sepúlveda, and I was born on July 23, 1954, in the city of Valparaíso, Chile. I am recording this testimony in 2024, at 70 years old, with the purpose that my grandchildren, and perhaps more generations to come, may understand why I value democracy and peace so deeply. These may seem like worn-out words to some, but I lived through a time when those words were a luxury, and what I most wish is that never again in my country should we have to live without them.

To understand my story, it is essential to know a bit of the history of my country. In the early '70s, Chile was a political hotbed: ideological polarization could be felt on every street corner, in the home, at the university, even around the family table. I was only 19 years old when, in September of 1973, the coup d'état took place. I remember that September 11 with chilling clarity: the radio was interrupted with military marches and announcements that sounded like ultimatums. I was in Valparaíso, trying to listen for news about what was happening in Santiago, where *La Moneda*, the presidential palace, stood.

I came from a family that sympathized with the left. My father was active in a party that supported Salvador Allende's government, while my mother was more neutral, though she too defended the idea of a fairer Chile. That day, we were all glued to the radio, listening to Allende's trembling voice, his final speech, followed by bombings and gunfire that still echo in my memory. My grandmother wept with her hands on her head; my father cursed with restrained rage; and I could not yet grasp the chaos that was unfolding.

The hours that followed brought curfews, the presence of soldiers in the streets, and total uncertainty. Neighbors whispered about arrests, raids, blacklists. Valparaíso, being a strategic port, also lived under heavy naval control. You'd walk out onto the street and run into patrols demanding identification, or people wearing armbands in support of the new regime. Suddenly, politics was no longer a subject of conversation but a matter of survival: better not to speak, not to say, not to contradict. If you had the "wrong file," you could end up detained, for who knows how long.

In the weeks that followed, my family's life changed radically. Because of his political activity, my father had to go into hiding for a few days, as rumors spread that leaders and sympathizers of the left were being arrested. My mother and I took turns watching out the window, nervous in case they came for him. There were nights when the sounds of military vehicles could be heard passing by, loudspeakers ordering everyone to stay indoors. Fear was palpable in the air, like a thick fog seeping through the walls.

When my father reappeared, I learned he had been staying at a friend's house in the hills of Valparaíso. His eyes looked tired, and there was an expression on his face I had never seen before. He brought with him burned papers, destroyed sheet music of songs by Víctor Jara and Quilapayún[1], and some political books he didn't want falling into the hands of the military. In a broken voice, he told me: "M'hijo[2], take care, don't get yourself into trouble." It was painful to see him like that, so silent. Before, he had been a jovial man, passionately debating his ideas. Now he was full of caution, and I felt a lump in my throat, thinking that joy was slipping through our fingers like sand.

The dictatorship entrenched itself with an iron hand. On the radio, official communiqués blared; on television, soldiers appeared in uniform, issuing orders. Political activity for the opposition was banned, and censorship reigned: books and magazines that questioned the regime disappeared from bookstores. People began whispering anecdotes about those who were "taken" for interrogation

---

1 Chilean protest folk group.
2 Affectionate form of "my son."

and never returned. This wasn't a rumor: over time, we learned of detention and torture centers. Fear became part of daily life.

I was 19, almost 20, at the time of the coup. I could have locked myself away in fear, but youth also carries rebellion. With some classmates from university (I was studying Education with a focus on History), we decided to protest silently by pasting posters at dawn with slogans calling for the return of democracy. It was reckless, I know, but we couldn't just stand idle. Some days we managed to put up a few posters before sunrise; other days we ran into soldiers and stumbled blindly through dark streets, trying to escape.

On one of those outings, I was nearly caught. I hid in an alley, hearing footsteps and shouts. My heartbeat pounded in my ears like war drums. I remember the adrenaline, the cold sweat, and the terror of imagining what they might do to me if they found me. At last, I managed to slip back home in silence, trembling. When my father found out, he scolded me angrily: *"You have no idea what these men are capable of doing to you, m'hijo."* He was right, but the rage against repression boiled in my veins. Many young people of that time felt the same: a cocktail of indignation and hope, though hope was in short supply.

For a Chilean born in the 1950s, the 70s and 80s were a long nightmare. Demonstrations and protests grew in the late 70s, as information began to circulate about the systematic violation of human rights: the disappeared, the tortured, the exiled. There were brave women who gathered in the Plaza de Armas[3] in Santiago with photographs of their loved ones, demanding answers. The Agrupación de Familiares de Detenidos Desaparecidos[4] was formed, and that feminine courage inspired others to slowly lose their fear.

---

3 *Central city square in Latin America.*
4 *Chilean group seeking justice for the disappeared.*

In Valparaíso, despite being a city with a strong cultural spirit, the atmosphere was tense. Police and military forces could burst into any meeting they deemed "subversive." I painfully remember arrests in broad daylight, sometimes with shoves and shouting. It felt as though the country had forgotten its democratic traditions that, for decades, had been a source of pride in Latin America.

At first, many believed the dictatorship would be short-lived, that it was only a "moment of order" to stabilize the country. But the years went by, and the regime consolidated itself with rigged plebiscites, the constitutional changes of 1980, and official propaganda presenting Pinochet as the "savior of Chile." My uncles in Santiago told me that television channels repeated official ceremonies, martial speeches, and a triumphant air, while the population split between those who supported Pinochet out of fear or convenience, and those of us who rejected him in silence or in hushed voices.

The situation didn't just affect the country, it also fractured many families, including mine. I had a cousin, Sergio, who joined the army in 1976. At family gatherings, unbearable tension arose. My father, a man of the left, barely spoke to him. My cousin, in his neatly pressed uniform, spoke of "the homeland" and of the "internal enemy." I bit my tongue to avoid arguing. My mother tried to mediate, serving dessert before the night turned into a political boxing ring.

That fissure, which seemed irreparable, made me understand that the dictatorship thrived not only on force, but also on distrust. Brothers against brothers, cousins against cousins, neighbors denouncing each other. I grew up with a knot in my stomach, unsure how to reconcile my love for family with my rejection of the regime some defended. By the late 70s, my cousin had been assigned to another city, and family gatherings became less tense, though the wound remained open.

By the early 80s, the economic and social situation began to convulse. Though the government spoke of an economic miracle, the reality for many Chileans was harsh: unemployment, growing inequality, marginalized neighborhoods. Protests became more frequent, with cacerolazos[5] at night, when women went out to their patios to bang pots and pans as a sign of discontent. I often joined those demonstrations; the metallic noise reverberated through the streets, and although we knew the police could arrive at any moment, there was an air of collective hope.

In 1983, massive protests erupted. Valparaíso was no exception. People gathered on street corners, organizing improvised assemblies. The fear was still there, but it was as if courage had become contagious, pushing thousands to lose their fear. I remember marching alongside fishermen, housewives, students, and teachers. We advanced with signs demanding Pinochet's resignation, demanding free elections, and although police repression was violent, with water cannons and tear gas, more and more Chileans joined that chorus of "¡Enough already!"

At home, my father regained some of his old fire. He joined clandestine meetings of his former party, planning how to reorganize. I, now a young adult, accompanied him to some gatherings, always looking over my shoulder to avoid being caught in a raid. It was a dangerous game: we knew of people who ended up in jail for participating in protests. Once again, adrenaline lived side by side with indignation and hope.

The dictatorship, however, would not fall overnight. There was a slow process, both inside and outside of Chile, that led to the call for a plebiscite in 1988 to decide whether Pinochet would remain in power. I remember the tension in the lead-up: the "Yes" campaign

5 *Protest by banging pots and pans.*

79

(which supported the continuation of the regime) and the "No" campaign (which sought the end of the dictatorship and the opening of free elections). It was a crucial moment, because for the first time in many years, some degree of opposition propaganda was allowed on television.

The night the "No" campaign ads began airing, I felt a knot in my chest. It was surreal to see on Chilean TV, for fifteen minutes, testimonies from people who had suffered repression, mixed with an optimistic message that said, "Chile, happiness is coming." On the other hand, the "Yes" campaign insisted on order, economic growth, and stability. Family discussions grew more intense. My cousin Sergio, still in the army, defended the regime's work and said it was all foreign propaganda. My father, with a mocking smile, replied that there wouldn't be foreign propaganda if there weren't a dictatorship. At least, that time, nobody ended up shouting.

The plebiscite of October 5, 1988, was an unforgettable day. I went to vote at a polling station surrounded by carabineros[6] and military. The atmosphere was tense; no one knew if the government would accept a defeat. But the vote count was dramatic, and finally it became clear that the "No" had won with about 56%. I couldn't believe it: the dictatorship, which had seemed invincible, was suddenly in check. The streets filled with euphoric people, flags, honking horns. There was a sense of triumph, but mixed with caution. No one was sure whether Pinochet would acknowledge the loss.

Although the "No" won, the transition to democracy was not immediate. There were negotiations, reforms, and the regime continued controlling key sectors, such as the Armed Forces, the economy, and many state institutions. Finally, in 1990, Pinochet left the Presidency but remained Commander-in-Chief of the Army.

6 *Chile's national police force.*

The people celebrated that at last there would be free elections and a new civilian government, but I felt it wasn't a total victory, only a first step. Chile's transition was shaping up to be long and complex. A democratic government was formed that had to tread carefully with the military, unable to dismantle the entire dictatorial structure overnight.

As for me, I was already 36 years old and working as a History teacher in a high school in Valparaíso. I began teaching my students what had never been openly discussed: human rights violations, censorship, repression. But I also knew I had to weigh my words carefully; academic freedom was still fragile, and some parents looked suspiciously at a teacher who spoke of the dictatorship as a disastrous period. It was a delicate balance, but I felt comfort knowing that not everything was forbidden anymore.

The 1990s arrived with a transitional government that passed laws to repair the damage done to the dictatorship's victims: truth commissions were created, disappearances and torture were acknowledged, though justice remained elusive. Pinochet, from his position as Commander-in-Chief of the Army, still held power and political influence. Many grew frustrated seeing that "democracy" neither erased the abuses nor revealed the full truth. Others, however, believed that at least we were better off than before: the economy was growing and there was freedom of expression, though still circumscribed and with limits.

On a personal level, I felt bittersweet: I celebrated being able to vote without fear, to join a party without being persecuted, and to watch debates on television that once had been impossible. But at the same time, I understood that democracy is not a gift you receive and that's it, but an ongoing exercise of citizen participation. Many thought that once a civilian government arrived, there was nothing left to demand, and Chilean society grew complacent. Yet the wound of the dictatorship remained alive: thousands of families never recovered their loved ones, a former dictator remained unpunished, and a Constitution inherited from the regime made deep changes difficult.

As Chile moved hesitantly toward democracy, my family also lived through processes of reconciliation. My cousin Sergio, the military man, retired in the mid-1990s. One day he showed up at my house with a serious face and asked for forgiveness, in a barely audible tone, for the arrogance with which he had defended the dictatorship, justifying himself by saying he hadn't understood what was happening. He admitted that the country had suffered horrors he hadn't imagined or hadn't wanted to see, from within his barracks. I, incredulous, listened with a mix of anger and compassion. I couldn't simply forgive him, but at least we began to talk with less resentment. He wanted to embrace my father, now elderly, and after a moment's hesitation, he gave in. It was an act of silent redemption, a small patch on a wound that had bled for decades.

That scene revealed to me how deeply rooted the pain was in each family unit and how difficult it is to rebuild bonds of trust. Even so, I understood that reconciliation was a long process, just like democracy. A handshake or a change in government was not enough: truth, memory, and justice were required in order to truly heal.

Over the years, Chile continued on its path. There were several governments of the Concertación[7], presidents came and went, opening spaces for participation, and commissions were created to inform the country about the atrocities of the dictatorship. Little by little, society dared to speak more, to demand more change. But other

7 *Chilean political coalition post-dictatorship.*

problems also arose: inequality, corruption, political disenchantment. At times, people forgot that democratic practice does not consist of delegating power and then disengaging, but actively participating in the nation's destiny.

I saw many disillusioned young people, who thought that Chilean democracy was little more than a formal ritual, without addressing the deep needs of the population. I understood their frustration, but their indifference pained me. I reminded them that we, in the 80s, had fought to have the possibility to choose, to speak without censorship, to protest without being imprisoned. I asked them to value that freedom and defend it with more participation, not with apathy.

Now, in 2024, I am a grandfather. My grandchildren are named Laura and Benjamín. They are 10 and 8 years old, respectively, and already ask me from time to time: "Grandpa, why do you say that before you couldn't vote freely?" or "Why does my dad say that the dictator was very bad?"

I have decided to record this for them, to leave them a first-hand testimony. Because history is not just text in books or a lecture in a classroom: it is the life of those of us who experienced it.

I want them to understand that, in Chile, there was a long night of repression, fear, and death. That it was not a one-time event, but a system that broke democracy, persecuted opponents, and sowed terror. But also that, thanks to the resistance of many, a path toward freedom was opened. And that freedom is not a trophy you win once and hang on the wall, but a garden that must be watered and cared for every day.

I feel proud knowing that my grandchildren grow up without fear of speaking, with access to an education that is not censored, with the possibility of thinking differently and expressing their ideas.

But I fear that, if they forget what we lived through, they may come to believe that democracy is a triviality or an accident of history. That is why I stress this lesson:

"Democracy is not a gift; it is defended every day with responsibility, participation, and memory."

If we do not nurture that civic duty, if we do not remember the victims, and if we do not honor the efforts of those who fought to recover democracy, we run the risk of history repeating itself.

Now that I have more gray hair than hair itself, I look back and see a different country, with tremendous progress and also with outstanding debts. The dictatorship is behind us, but there are still demands for justice that were never fully satisfied. In the streets, memorials were erected for the detained and disappeared; commemorative events are held every September 11, and Chilean politics has continued to change faces and speeches. Yet polarization is reborn from time to time, and hatred is always just around the corner.

Not long ago, I marched again, this time for a movement demanding changes to the pension system, yet another legacy of the dictatorship. I found myself among young people, holding banners, shouting slogans that reminded me of my protest days in the 80s. I felt a déjà vu and, at the same time, a deep satisfaction seeing that today they can march and raise their voices without fearing the arrival of military trucks. That is progress, but it is not the end. That is the human condition: to live without realizing triumph, because triumph is never definitive. What seemed like a great victory in 1988 is still unfinished, still under construction.

Democracy is fragile and, at the same time, strong if we defend it together. Each generation has its own struggle, its own challenges. My grandchildren will face a Chile with different problems, but I hope they understand that the freedom and peace they enjoy did not fall from the sky: they cost suffering, they cost lives, they cost pain that persists. And that, despite everything, they are worth upholding and making grow.

I close this video-testimony with a long sigh. I remember my father, he passed away a few years ago, and the tears he shed the night he learned that the "No" had won in the plebiscite of 1988. A man who saw his world collapse and then resurge, but not in the perfect way he had dreamed. I think of my mother, who stayed strong, holding the family together in the storm. I think of my cousin Sergio, with whom I managed to reconcile, at least to some degree. I think of the friends who fell, who disappeared, of whom I only learned years later through human rights reports.

I could cry for what was lost, or laugh for what we gained, or perhaps both. But I prefer, simply, to leave a record that this path of transition is not an event you can pinpoint on a specific date and say: *"There the dictatorship ended, their freedom began."* No, Chile continued its painful and hopeful journey. Many families remained broken; many stories, unresolved. But with each passing year, the seed of democracy took deeper root, and today, in 2024, we see it bloom in free debates, in competitive elections, in young people raising their voices without having to hide. There is still much to be done, but it is a journey we cannot abandon.

To you, who watch this video or listen to this testimony, I invite you to take this lesson seriously: freedom, peace, and democracy are not conquered one day and then stored away in a drawer. They are a process. If in my country it has cost us so much, imagine how often it repeats itself in other nations with similar conflicts. May we always remain vigilant, may we never allow silence and forgetfulness to pave the way for new forms of oppression.

I record this, once again, for my grandchildren, whom I love and wish may never experience firsthand the repression I lived through as a young man. But also so that they never forget that if they enjoy freedoms, it is because someone before them fought for it, because there were people who refused to give up. And now it is their turn to carry the torch, so that democracy does not wither. Because yes, democracy is not a gift: it is a shared task that lasts a lifetime.

Fernando's story is an echo of many other countries where repression marked entire decades and yet, the will of a people managed to open cracks of light. His account overflows with family scenes, personal tensions, and rebirths that make clear that a dictatorship does not only break institutions: it also wounds relationships, values, and dreams. And that the transition, as he himself explains, is not a glorious instant, but a prolonged effort, a sowing that must be watered with participation and memory.

Hearing him in 2024, speaking to his grandchildren, both moves and shakes us: it reminds us that democracy does not fall from the sky nor is it kept as a trophy in a museum. It is defended daily, with responsibility, with participation, and with the awareness that what has been gained can be lost if we sink into indifference. His message transcends borders and eras: freedom and peace are fragile conquests, and only citizen tenacity prevents them from crumbling.

Griot 2085

THE COOKING GRANDMOTHER

The kitchen is not only a place where ingredients are mixed: it is also a crucible of memories, affections, and identities. Among the stories I have gathered in Genostories, few have moved me as much as that of Irma Delgado, a Puerto Rican grandmother who, from her kitchen filled with memories and traditional utensils, decided to record her recipes for posterity. This chapter immerses us in the love, laughter, and magic that arise when a family gathers around a caldero or a pilón. Irma, born in the 1950s and with an energy that bursts through the screen, leaves us a life lesson in every anecdote. Get ready to savor her words and, along the way, to learn what it means to cook with heart.
    Griot 2085

Now that I'm in my sixties, I realize how strong and persistent the flavors of childhood are. Every time I smell the sofrito[1] sizzling in the pan, I remember my mother in the kitchen stirring with a wooden spoon and telling me: "Irma, the kitchen isn't for being in a rush; it's for loving your family well."

Today, in 2025, I am a great-grandmother, imagine that, and it makes me so happy to share everything I learned from my mother and grandmother. That's why I upload my videos to Genostories: I want my grandchildren and great-grandchildren not to forget our Puerto Rican recipes, and for every bite to carry the warmth and history of those who came before us.

I was born in the 1950s, in a small coastal town in Puerto Rico. In the 90s, when I was in my forties, I spent my time raising my children, spoiling my nieces and nephews, and, of course, cooking. I remember the house always smelling of garlic and recao[2], and the sound of the pan mixing with laughter and the occasional scolding when a mischievous grandchild stirred the flour without permission.

Today, my kitchen is still the stage for many stories, only now I have a camera on the table to record every step and upload it to the app. People may call it modern technology, but I say: "If this ensures that my dishes are not lost, then blessed be technology."

Over the years, I've learned that the kitchen is the bridge that unites our family. It doesn't matter if we live in the same neighborhood or if some have moved to the States; the flavor of good arroz con gandules[3] or a well-mashed mofongo[4] is enough to make us feel close.

My older grandchildren, who were born in the nineties, are scattered around the world; one works in New York and another

---

1 Aromatic base for Puerto Rican dishes.
2 Herb-like cilantro used in Puerto Rican cooking.
3 Rice with pigeon peas, a Puerto Rican staple.
4 Mashed fried plantains with garlic or pork.

studies in Florida. But every time they come back and taste my lechón asao[5], they tell me:

Grandma, this tastes like home.

And I answer with a smile:

So you see, flavors travel better than any airplane.

Uploading the videos of my recipes is my way of making sure that, even if they can't always visit me, they themselves can prepare an arroz con gandules if they miss the warmth of the island. In this way, the kitchen connects my generation with theirs, and hopefully with the ones that follow.

When I turn on the camera and explain how to knead the bread or how to season the lechón, I'm not just giving cooking instructions: I'm recalling the stories of my grandmother, doña Carmela, and my mother, the good Marta. Each ingredient holds the memory of those who came before. Mamá taught me, for example, that sofrito must be made with calm and care, chopping the ají dulce[6], the onion, and the recao patiently. "While you chop, think about the people you love," she told me, "because that love goes into the pot." That's how I learned that food is not just the result of a recipe, but an act of love.

While recording my videos, I've told the story of the time when, for one Nochebuena[7], we prepared pasteles[8] for 20 people, and my grandmother, already very old, sat on a little low chair to teach me how to wrap them in plátano[9] leaves without tearing them.

"Irma, if you wrap them badly, the pastel will fall apart in the pot," she repeated to me.

---

5 Roast pork, common at celebrations.
6 A small, sweet pepper
7 Christmas Eve feast.
8 Puerto Rican dish wrapped in banana leaves.
9 Cooking plantain.

With that warning and humor strong enough to withstand nerves, I managed to learn how to tie them well. Every pastel that came from my hands was a tribute to my grandmother's patience, and now, my grandchildren know that story through the videos and the tales I upload.

When you cook, you're not just throwing ingredients into a pot; you're caring, loving, offering. That's why, in my Genostories videos, I begin by greeting with:

"Mira, mi gente, today we're going to cook with the heart."

I remember the faces of my grandchildren when they come hungry, and I know that a chicken soup or a stuffed mofongo can comfort them more than any sermon.

One of the most beautiful moments of the day is when, at Christmas, I serve coquito[10] without rum to the little ones and coquito "with a kick" to the adults. Everyone laughs, celebrates, and I feel that love multiplies in each cup. In one of my videos, I explain how coquito is not just a drink, but the representation of boricua[11] joy: sweet, welcoming, with a touch of mischief if it has rum. "Food is an act of love," I love to repeat, and my grandchildren tease me saying I'm very cheesy. But it's the truth!

Sometimes, people think culture only lives in museums or history books. I say culture lives in the kitchen, in the way you slice a plátano for mofongo, in the way you fry up some crispy alcapurrias[12]. Every ingredient reveals something about our origins: the Taíno[13], the Spanish, the Africans, they all left their mark on what we now call Puerto Rican food.

---

10 *Puerto Rican coconut holiday drink.*
11 *Term Puerto Ricans use for themselves.*
12 *Puerto Rican fritters filled with meat.*
13 *Indigenous Caribbean people.*

When I make arroz con gandules, for example, I remember how my mother used to tell me that gandules were an essential crop in certain regions of the island, and that every family had their own way of seasoning them. I upload videos showing the technique of sautéing the rice before adding water, the magic of achiote[14] to give it color, and that way people learn not just the recipe, but the story behind the dish. With every spoonful, you can taste the fusion of races and traditions that make up our Puerto Rico.

As a girl, I learned that making mofongo can take a while: you have to fry or boil the plátanos, then mash them with garlic, chicharrón[15], and a drizzle of oil. In the 90s, when my kids were little, I used to have them mash plátanos with me, and it was a funny sight watching them, their little hands greasy, trying to keep the pilón from slipping. We laughed and shared stories, and in the end, we enjoyed a delicious mofongo that had an extra flavor: that of family laughter.

Sometimes, that shared time is more valuable than the dish itself. I film my videos hoping that, when my grandchildren and great-grandchildren watch them, they'll be inspired to cook with their kids and recreate that scene full of laughter. Because, let's be honest, you can eat mofongo at a restaurant, but it's not the same as making it at home with the people you love.

When I tell people I upload my recipes to Genostories, some are surprised: "Abuela Irma, you with all that technology?" And I answer: "Of course, mi'jo, I learn fast, and if this app helps me keep the recipe from getting lost, then pa'lante[16]." Traditions can evolve with the times; there's nothing wrong with that. Back then, my grandmother would write recipes down in an oil-stained notebook.

---

14 Seed used to color and flavor food.
15 Fried pork rind or belly.
16 Short for "go forward" or "keep going."

I have mine written in journals too, but now I also record them on video, post them, and done. What matters is that we don't lose the essence of what we cook.

Arroz con gandules still tastes the same, coquito with rum still has that same "kick," and pasteles still demand hours of dedication… Technology simply makes it easier for more people to learn how to make them, and helps my family, scattered around the world, keep the boricua flame alive. Because, at the end of the day: "Cooking isn't just nourishment; it's love, heritage, and identity."

I like to say that patience is the hidden seasoning in every recipe. What would bread be without letting the dough rise? Or a roasted lechón if it's not cooked slowly, with the charcoal just right? In my videos, people sometimes get impatient and ask, "Abuela Irma, isn't there a shortcut to get the mofongo ready faster?" And I laugh and reply, "Child, if you really want it to be tasty, you've got to mash it slowly, that's all there is to it."

One story from the 90s: my eldest granddaughter wanted to help me knead bread. She was so excited that she slammed the dough hard, she wanted to go fast, and sent a cloud of flour flying that left us white as ghosts. Between coughing and laughter, I explained: "M'hija[17], the dough needs to be loved, not suffocated." In the kitchen, learning to wait is just as important as knowing how much salt to use. That "time" is what shapes the flavors.

My greatest motivation for uploading my recipes to Genostories is to leave behind an immortal legacy of our family's sazón[18]. I don't want my great-great-grandchildren, twenty years from now, asking: "How did great-grandma make arroz con gandules?" and no one having an answer. Family flavors and culture deserve to live on.

---

17 Affectionate form of "my daughter."
18 Seasoning or signature flavor.

And I'm not just talking about myself, many friends and neighbors have also started recording their recipes and stories on the platform. This way, together, we're building a collective gastronomic memory. It's a treasure that never runs out, because every person who watches those videos and recreates those dishes gives tradition a new life. If the earth shakes and houses fall, as long as there's a video showing how to make a good sofrito, our identity will live on.

When people ask me, "Abuela Irma, what does it mean to be Puerto Rican?" I proudly respond that a key part of it is our traditional dishes. Arroz con gandules with its sazón, crispy alcapurria, coquito at Christmas, and mofongo with chicken broth or shrimp… Each bite encapsulates the island's history: Taíno, Spanish, African influence, all blended with that Caribbean joy that defines us.

Every time I sit at the table with my family, I remember that generations sweated and loved so that today we can enjoy these flavors. Even though my grandchildren, born in other U.S. cities, sometimes prefer hamburgers or pizza, all it takes is for me to serve them a good alcapurria for them to say, "Abuela, this is different, but I love it." And there it is, in that phrase, the reaffirmation of our boricua identity.

They say the family that cooks together, laughs together. In our home, it was always that way. In the early 90s, my children helped me slice plátanos or stir the caldero. Yes, sometimes funny accidents happen. I remember one day when one of my grandchildren tried to mash the plátano so hard that the piece shot up and stuck to the ceiling. I saw it hanging there and laughed so much I almost dropped the pilón.

"That mofongo wants to be an astronaut, but in this house, it's staying put!" I shouted, and everyone burst into laughter.

Those moments are family stories that bind us more than we realize.

Today, in 2025, I record those funny events and upload them so that in the future, when my great-grandchildren watch the videos, they'll laugh and understand that mistakes in the kitchen also weave stories. "Cooking together strengthens bonds," I always say. No one leaves the kitchen the same as when they came in: amid the smoke, the flour, and the laughter, you become someone closer to your family.

In the kitchen, you also have to learn gratitude. Many times, we aren't aware of how much dedication each dish on our table requires. When I mash plátanos for mofongo, I think of the farmers who grew them, of the Caribbean sun that made them flourish, of my mother who taught me how to season them. Each step is a tribute to all the people who contribute to making that dish exist.

There's a saying I love: *"Gratitude begins in the kitchen."* When my grandchildren see me sweating over the cauldron, I tell them, "Don't eat with guilt, eat with joy, but understand that this dish took effort, and being grateful is part of our duty." I believe that if we all learned to value the work and the history behind every meal, there would be less waste and more love in the world. That's why I always emphasize it in my videos, while I stir a pot of rice or pull a lechón out of the oven.

During Christmas of '95, we were roasting a whole lechón in the yard. One of the kids said he didn't want to eat it because he had seen the pig before it was cooked and felt sorry for it. In my typical boricua humor, I told him:

"Well don't worry, mi'jo, this lechón is Catholic. It's already blessed and ready for heaven."

The child burst into laughter, and his guilt disappeared; he ended up devouring the lechón without another complaint.

At home, we always make coquito with and without rum, so the kids can enjoy it too. But one time, my oldest grandson, out of curiosity, took a sip of the coquito con truco (spiked). His face lit up in shock, and he nearly spat it all out. Between laughs, I told him:

"I told you that coquito wasn't for you, but now you've learned the hard way. Better stick with the vanilla one, that one won't bite!"

It was all caught on video and ended up being one of the most viewed on my Genostories timeline.

One afternoon, while frying up alcapurrias, I noticed one was missing from the tray. I checked the kids, who swore they hadn't taken it. A little later, we discovered the family cat under the table, halfway through the stolen alcapurria. I couldn't help but laugh and exclaim:

"That cat's got better taste than you all! But if it wants to eat alcapurrias, it better get in line and help fry them."

Today, in 2025, I can proudly say that my home cooking, the one from the 90s and always, remains alive. I upload my recipes for bread, pasteles, coquito, mofongo, arroz con gandules, alcapurrias, and roasted lechón to Genostories so that my descendants, and anyone who loves Puerto Rican food, can preserve this heritage.

Here I leave you with the 10 lessons that emerge from this culinary adventure, which are my humble contribution to family wisdom:

1. The hearth of the home becomes an axis that unites grandparents with grandchildren and great-grandchildren, whether they are on the island or in the United States or Europe. Preparing arroz con gandules or mofongo creates a direct bond with those who came before us and those

who will come after. In each spoonful, tradition lives and is renewed, allowing stories to flow. For boricuas, that "bridge" isn't abstract; it materializes in the sharing of a dish that tastes like home and collective memory. That's why every time a grandchild learns to cook, we are making the past and future hold hands.

2. In Puerto Rican culture, food is not reduced to covering a physical need; it goes beyond nutrition. Every sofrito, every stew, is a profound act of giving to those around us. Cooking with the heart is offering part of our essence, caring for and protecting others through a unique sazón. Anyone who grows up on the island or carries Puerto Ricanness in their blood knows that opening the pot and sharing with others is almost like opening your heart and saying: "I care for you, I love you, I hold you up with my hands." That is the taste of affection that lives on at every boricua table.

3. Is there anything more ours than pouring in a drizzle of oil, seasoning with garlic and onion, or passing a plátano leaf over the fire to soften it? These gestures may seem small, but they hold centuries of history. Thus, achiote, recao, and vianda[19] tell the story of Taíno, African, and Spanish roots that came together to form what we now call sabor boricua[20]. In every act of everyday cooking, a vast and priceless heritage is told. A tourist might not understand why it excites us to watch someone mash plátanos or prepare arroz mamposteao[21], but for the boricua, it is a reunion with their ancestors.

---

19 Root vegetables in Caribbean cuisine.
20 Puerto Rican flavor.
21 Stir-fried Puerto Rican rice with beans.

4. In this culture, there is no rush when it comes to stewing, to letting broth bubble or meat release its juices slowly. While the clock ticks on, the family gathers, talks about daily life, and clings to the warmth that only the kitchen can give. Here, plans are made, old times are remembered, and anecdotes are forged that will bring laughter years later. What happens in front of the fire or over the pilón weaves a web of memories that gives identity to the boricua home. Our laughter and shared moments become infused in the taste of asopao[22] or Christmas pasteles.

5. With the arrival of technology, some people think that old recipes might "modernize" and lose their authentic flavor. But uploading a video of coquito or arroz con gandules to an app doesn't break tradition, it strengthens it. As long as we preserve the sazón, as long as we maintain love and respect for our ingredients, tradition lives. For a boricua growing up far from the island, watching their grandmother upload recipes on a smartphone isn't a contradiction, but proof that Puerto Ricanness adapts to the times without surrendering its essence.

6. Many people are surprised that a Puerto Rican stew can take hours; but on this island, we believe that "good things cook slowly." Tying pasteles, sautéing with care, or roasting a whole lechón are not just culinary processes, but rites of patience. Every minute is part of the final flavor and a reminder that in life, what is done in haste lacks soul. There's a saying that goes: *"Without pause, but without hurry."* That saying perfectly defines sazón boricua: slow, consistent, and full of dedication.

---

22 *Puerto Rican rice stew.*

7. A recipe that is not shared is a lost story. When a grandchild learns how to cook mofongo because their grandmother uploaded the method to a digital platform, we are saving culture. The boricua understands that every dish contains a memory, and keeping it alive is their responsibility. The moment we record or write down the recipe, we ensure that a hundred years from now, someone will be able to taste the same flavor that today unites us at the table. It is our way of affirming: *"This sazón does not die; it will live on in those who practice it."*

8. To talk about Puerto Rican gastronomy is to talk about the essence of a people who recognize themselves in sofrito, plátano, and café colao[23] in the traditional style. There is no doubt that, for anyone who considers themselves boricua, cooking arroz con habichuelas[24] is an act of pride and belonging. Perhaps other countries prepare similar recipes, but each of our dishes carries an imprint that makes us say: *"This tastes like my home, my island, my people."* That is why exporting our flavor to the world is our way of shouting to everyone: *"Here we are, and this is our culinary DNA."*

9. How many times, while preparing food in a group, have we felt hearts begin to open? The boricua knows there is nothing like gathering to chop vegetables for sancocho[25] or to fill empanadillas[26] between bits of gossip. Cooking as a team creates an atmosphere of intimacy and honesty that is hard to replicate elsewhere. Inside our kitchens, generations are leveled: grandmother and grandchild set to work, and what

---

23 *Puerto Rican coffee filtered through cloth.*
24 *Puerto Rican rice and beans.*
25 *Meat and root vegetable stew.*
26 *Fried turnovers with savory fillings.*

emerges there, respect, complicity, and laughter, strengthens a family fabric that no distance can tear apart.

10. To value each dish and the one who prepares it is to recognize that behind a plate of arroz con gandules or a spoonful of sofrito, there is history, labor, and love. Saying "thank you" before tasting a bite is not a formality; it is an acknowledgment of the effort, the grandmother's wisdom, and the generosity of the earth that are all embodied in that food. For boricuas, that gratitude becomes an act that goes beyond the table: it is a way of life that says "thank you" to those who came before us, to those who share the table today, and to those who will come later to claim their share of culinary heritage.

"I want my grandchildren and great-grandchildren, when they watch these videos, to feel the warmth of a Puerto Rican home," said Irma, "and to understand that in every dish rests a story of love, laughter, patience, and above all, family memory. Because, as my mother used to tell me: '*M'hija, as long as there is a caldero boiling with the flavor of Puerto Rico, this family will remain united.*'"

With those words, Irma Delgado sums up her mission: not to let sazón boricua be lost in the tide of globalization, but to turn every recipe into a seed of identity and pride. Grandmother, technology, and family merge into a single gesture of tenderness, of loyalty to the land that saw her born, and of love for every face that makes up her lineage, and in the end, they forge a homeland.

Reading and listening to Abuela Irma share her ten lessons is like opening a chest full of aromas, colors, and emotions that define what it means to be boricua. In her voice, the kitchen transcends recipes to become a bastion of memory: every spice speaks of history, every dish evokes an embrace, every video is a vessel carrying Puerto Rican culture into tomorrow. May this testimony inspire everyone, boricuas or not, to light their stoves with love and to remember that the kitchen is not merely a place of daily tasks, but a cathedral where the past is honored, the present is celebrated, and the future is forged. Salud[1], and buen provecho[2]! And as Irma would say: "Long live good cooking, my people!"
Griot 2085

---

1 Toast meaning "cheers" or "health."
2 Expression meaning "enjoy your meal."

THE TRANSFORMATION OF
THE MOBILE PHONE

Every day on Genostories, I come across stories that capture the astonishing evolution of daily life across different generations. But none as revealing as that of a father born in 1970, who came of age in the 90s and now, in 2025, watches in fascination as his grandchildren handle modern technology with total ease. What for him had once been an expensive, cumbersome gadget, his first brick phone has, decades later, given way to lightweight devices packed with apps and connected to artificial intelligence.

In this chapter, we'll get to know his story and his reflections on the transformation of the mobile phone: from how that brick-sized device once spared him from unsuspected dangers by saving him from having to find a payphone in the wrong neighborhood at night, to the reality of today, where with a simple tap on a screen one can get help instantly. With a playful style full of anecdotes, we'll unravel the advantages, the frustrations, and the social context of the 90s, contrasted with the ultra-connected era of 2025.

In the end, we'll find a clear and universal lesson: "Value technology, but don't let it replace genuine human connection." Get ready for a journey through time and a good laugh at the misadventures of someone who once tasted the freedom of the pioneering cellphone, despite its massive limitations and sky-high rates. Welcome to this surprising look at yesterday and today!

Griot 2085

Here in the year 2025, I, a "late fifty-something," already brushing up against fifty-five, sit in my favorite armchair, scrolling through digital photos of my family. Between bursts of laughter, my grandchildren ask me how on earth we managed to live in the 90s without TikTok, video calls, or instant voice messages. How did we ever "connect" with others when smartphones didn't even exist?

Every time they ask me that question, my heart skips a beat, because I remember those years when a "mobile phone" wasn't a sleek, ultra-thin device, but a brick with an antenna, a monochrome screen, and lithium batteries that lasted, if you were lucky, a few hours. Even so, as rudimentary as it may sound today, it was revolutionary for my generation: for the first time, we didn't have to depend on a payphone, or fumble for loose coins to call home, or risk wandering through an unfamiliar neighborhood in the middle of the night just to find a half-broken phone booth that could easily get us mugged. It was freedom encased in plastic and circuits; an expensive, clunky contraption, yes, but freedom all the same.

Today, I want to tell you, throughout this video, what those "brick phones" of the 90s were like, the laughs and frustrations they brought, the funny anecdotes, and the incredible transformation we've witnessed up to 2025, where my grandchildren send me GIFs and stickers from 10,000 kilometers away in mere milliseconds. Maybe my story will entertain you and, above all, make you reflect on the huge advantage it represented compared to having to stop the car in the middle of the night to use a payphone, holding your breath, glancing over your shoulder, and praying no one would show up with the intent to rob you.

Picture me now, with a respectable belly and graying hair, explaining with enthusiasm and a touch of nostalgia how that first cellphone, with its extended antenna and colorless screen, changed my life. Join me on this journey; I promise the road will be long, but full of humor, lessons, and cherished memories.

It was the year 1992. I was twenty-two, studying at university and working afternoons in an electronics store. Cellular telephony was only just beginning to spread timidly, and the few who dared to use a "cellphone" were seen either as pioneers or, more often, as "show-offs." Because, let's be honest, a mobile phone at that time cost you one kidney and half the other. Worse still, they weren't exactly comfortable to carry around.

The first cellphones I remember seeing looked like they had come straight out of a low-budget science fiction movie: they were massive in size, with an antenna you had to pull out almost like Harry Potter's wand, and they were heavy enough to give you wrist pain if you talked for 20 minutes straight. Some people carried them in a "special" briefcase that held an extra battery and a strap for hanging. Others kept them permanently in their car, running a cable that plugged into the cigarette lighter. They were so clunky that you couldn't help but wonder if it wasn't better just to wait until you got home to make a call.

But, here's the magic, you no longer had to hunt down a cursed payphone. Picture this: it's eleven at night, you're in a rough neighborhood, and your car runs out of gas or overheats. Before, you'd step out with your heart in your throat, searching for a phone booth, maybe with the glass shattered and the receiver dangling, praying no thug showed up. That was life in the 80s and early 90s. Suddenly, being able to say, "Look, I'll pull out the brick, dial a number, and call for help," was a drastic change, a real lifeline.

The feeling of power was incredible. Carrying that brick with an antenna (yes, the famous *cellphone*) made you feel like you were at the cutting edge of civilization, almost like a businessman, even if you were really just a student eager to show off. As for me, I took the plunge and invested my savings, plus a bit of money I managed to get from my parents, to buy one of those devices. Needless to say, its price hit me harder than a punch in the stomach, but the thrill of holding *my own cordless phone* was simply indescribable.

The device came with a monochrome screen, big numbers, and an interface so basic that today anyone would laugh at it. There was no menu with icons, no wallpapers: just digits and a few blocky letters, very much like the calculators of that era. But for me, it was enough. I could dial a number and hear the ringtone without being tied to a cable, and that felt like advanced science.

The costs of using a cellphone in the 90s were bone-chilling. Talking for a single minute could cost you an arm and a leg, and I'm not exaggerating. If you went on too long, you'd better prepare your wallet for the end-of-month bill. Some people chose prepaid cards, an idea that now seems almost naïve: you bought a set of minutes, at outrageous prices, and the phone would warn you when you were close to running out of credit. SMS messages were also a luxury: each one cost about as much as half your breakfast bread, and every message was limited to just a handful of characters, with no emojis or frills. Just plain text, maybe with a primitive ":)" if you felt creative.

Imagine my frustration when I'd send an SMS to a friend telling him to wait for me at some corner in 15 minutes, and he'd reply with a barely-there "OK," because every extra message was a blow to the wallet. And forget about writing something romantic to your girlfriend in long, heartfelt prose, unless you were willing to empty your pockets.

I remember classmates at university debating whether a "te quiero mucho" was worth $1.50, or if it was better to shorten it to "tqm" (back when "tqm" hadn't yet become popular in chat). There was a funny atmosphere of linguistic economy everywhere.

The prepaid card gave you a long sequence of digits you had to enter to recharge your balance. Sometimes you'd mistype, and then you had to do the whole thing over again. Once confirmed, a metallic robot voice would inform you: "Your new balance is 12 minutes." Something like that brought relief: "Wow, I've got 12 minutes to talk!" Today it sounds ridiculous to think 12 minutes could feel like an eternity, but back then you learned to weigh every word. Anyone who lived through that era knows what it was like to speak quickly so you wouldn't run out of credit mid-sentence.

Being young in the 90s often meant being out late at night, whether for a party, work, or just hanging out with friends. So if you had to let your parents know something urgent or call a taxi, the ordeal was finding a payphone. Oh, payphones! They were a whole chapter on their own. For starters, finding one that worked was already a victory, since half of them were broken. Then you needed coins, and you prayed the call wouldn't get cut off halfway through. Worst of all, you had to make sure the neighborhood was safe, since the risk of getting mugged was always just around the corner.

I remember an incident that left its mark on me. One night I went out dancing with friends and needed to let my father know I'd be spending the night at a colleague's house. I walked two blocks before finding a dimly lit phone booth in a "so-so" neighborhood, let's say. As I dialed the number with the coin already lodged in place, my heart pounded in my throat, any moving shadow behind me could mean a mugging. I managed to make the call, but the tension kept me from saying more than two short phrases, "Dad, I'm sleeping at Tom's, goodbye", and I hung up right away, then ran back, promising myself I'd never expose myself like that again.

Comparing that to having a cellphone in your pocket was simply another world. Even if it was a bulky device, barely fitting in the car's glove compartment, at least it spared you the "adventure" of standing exposed out on the street. There was comfort in knowing that, if something went wrong with your car, all you had to do was pull out the "brick" and call someone for help. Sure, the bill at the end of the month could kill you, but sometimes that was better than risking your life or a nasty scare. It was a price many were willing to pay.

I can't forget to mention the antenna. Why, in the name of all that's holy, did that brick need such a long antenna? After all, those first devices didn't have today's sophistication or the same coverage infrastructure. But for us, the antenna was a badge of identity: if you carried the phone on your belt, the antenna stuck out like a TV aerial. It was ridiculous, but it drew stares of admiration (or mockery) everywhere you went. You'd walk down the street, shirt half wrinkled and a monstrous cellphone dangling at your side, and people would think: "He's either a businessman or he's nuts."

My antenna slid out of its compartment with a "click" and measured about 20 centimeters when fully extended. In places with bad signal, you'd pull it out like a spyglass, hoping to catch a trace of coverage. People laughed: "Look, there goes the guy with the antenna." And me, proud of my clunky contraption, I thought about how amazing it was not to be stuck using a wall mounted landline. Today, my grandchildren laugh when I tell them that, for a "touch" of style, I sometimes slipped colored covers over that antenna. As if that somehow made it look less ridiculous!

Another thing many forget is the lack of color. Well into the 90s, the most common thing was to have monochrome screens, with digits in green or black against a gray background. The concept of a "wallpaper" didn't exist. Neither did icons, Bluetooth, or a camera (a camera, ha!). The functions were simple:

- Make a call and hang up.
- Receive calls (of course).
- Send SMS with a limit of 160 characters.

Access a contact list that sometimes couldn't hold more than 50 or 100 numbers.

No trace of emojis, videos, or voice notes. For us, the amazing thing was that you could dial a number at any time and, as long as you had credit left, the cellphone rang on the other end, no cables, no plugs. That was enough for us.

My first cellphone had such a basic menu that, to scroll up or down the contact list, you had to hold down a button, and the text would move slowly, like a slide in an old projector. Sometimes you'd overshoot and have to scroll back up again. I chuckled to myself, but back then, it felt like the height of modernity.

As I mentioned earlier, the rates were staggering. I remember one month when the bill exceeded my part-time salary from working at the electronics store. I had to ask my father for an advance (and he, rightfully annoyed, scolded me: "Can't you see it's too expensive to keep that hunk of junk?"). But I always defended myself by saying: "Dad, it's better to pay this than to stop in a dangerous neighborhood at midnight just to call home", and he, with a sigh, sometimes admitted I had a point.

Prepaid cards were the "cheaper" alternative, but still a ridiculous expense. Each recharge card gave you x number of minutes and a handful of SMS. Anyone who wanted to "chat" by text (in the 90s sense) had to economize letters. That's where creativity kicked in:

"¿Cómo te va[1]?" became "k tal?"; "Te espero en la esquina sur[2]" turned into "esk sur 10min." And thus a telegram-like language was born, one that today would seem funny, even incomprehensible.

Life in the 90s with a cellphone was, in a way, a balancing act. You had the freedom of not depending on a payphone (a huge advantage!), but at the same time, you were chained to the high costs and scarce coverage. Many rural areas were still a "black hole" for signal, and not even the antenna fully extended could save you. So you could feel like Batman with his Bat-Signal, but just drive 30 kilometers out of the city and your mobile turned into a paperweight. And... let's not even talk about the battery: it was normal to run out of power by mid-afternoon if you'd made a couple of long calls. On top of that, charging the phone took an eternity.

Even so, the cellphone was still seen as a treasure, even a luxury that few could afford. I felt proud: "I got lost, but no problem, I can call a friend and say, 'Describe how to get there.'" Or if I got a flat tire, I didn't need to throw myself into the risky adventure of finding a payphone not knowing if I'd get mugged. It truly gave me a peace of mind unimaginable in the 80s, when every attempt to use a city payphone was, in one way or another, a game of Russian roulette.

Now let's jump to the present, the year 2025, so you can understand. I watch my grandchildren handling these compact devices, about the size of a chocolate bar, that seem more powerful than the supercomputers of my time. They call China with a tap, send messages with reactions like "love," "angry," or "funny," record themselves on video calls with dog-face filters, and do it all at no extra cost beyond the data included in their plan. Even artificial

---

1 *"How is it going?"*
2 *"I'll wait for you at the south corner."*

intelligence helps them: they ask a virtual assistant to summarize a book for class or suggest the best route to avoid traffic. Madness!

I compare all that with my 90s brick and feel I've witnessed a quantum leap. Where once writing "Hey, tomorrow I leave 7pm?" cost half a dollar, today my grandkids send 80 messages in a single minute, with photos, stickers, video calls… and they don't even notice. At times, it makes me smile tenderly; at others, it overwhelms me to see how easily they navigate this hyperconnected world.

Huge advantages: the camera, the video calls, internet access at blazing speeds, GPS telling you where to go, streaming music… all in one device that fits in your pocket. Add to that dozens of apps whose names make my head spin, but my grandkids handle them as smoothly as I once handled prepaid cards in the 90s. And let's not even talk about AI: today they ask for cooking advice and, within seconds, an expert system suggests a recipe, ingredients, and even where to buy them at the best price.

Even so, it's not all sunshine and roses. Sometimes I see my grandchildren so absorbed in their screens that they don't even notice who's sitting right next to them. Back in the 90s, I might have felt proud of my brick phone, but I still chatted with friends face to face. Now, my descendants, though sitting side by side, talk to each other through messages. That's the part that worries me.

Personally, I believe technology has brought countless advantages. It spares us the danger of having to find a phone in unsafe places. It connects us instantly with family thousands of kilometers away; it makes work, study, and leisure easier. But when I look at how 2025 immerses us in apps and algorithms that practically think for us, I like to recall my experience in the 90s. Back then, I knew a cellphone could save you from a mugging or from being stranded on the road; but I didn't need to spend my whole day sunk into it. For me, it was a tool for safety and communication, not a replacement for human interaction.

That's why I insist the great lesson from this whole transformation is: "Value technology, but don't let it replace genuine human connection." Messages, video calls, AI… all that is wonderful, as long as we don't forget the magic of a face-to-face conversation, of a real hug, or of a surprise visit to a nearby friend. In the 90s, despite how rudimentary the brick phone was, we still lived our social lives in person, because there wasn't a screen intruding on every second of our day.

Of course, it's not that everyone is now obliged to follow my model. But I'd love for my grandchildren, and anyone watching this story, to realize that, if we once risked our lives in the wrong neighborhood just to use a payphone and today we don't need to, then there's gratitude owed to technological progress. Still, in the chase for immediacy and convenience, let's not lose the ability to look each other in the eyes, to laugh without needing emojis, and to share silence without checking notifications every two minutes.

It would be unforgivable to end this video without recalling a few moments that make me laugh when I compare the 90s and 2025. Let me recap:

In the 90s:

- If you wanted to let your mother know something, you prayed to find a phone booth with a working line and intact glass.
- The brick cellphone was your lifeline, but the antenna tangled in your jacket or tripped you up as you walked.
- An SMS was short and costly; you weighed every letter to avoid paying extra. An emoticon was an ASCII "abomination" of characters, like :-P.

- Batteries barely lasted a few hours if you used the phone heavily; it got so hot you felt you could fry an egg on its surface.

In 2025:

- We carry lightweight smartphones, as thin as a chocolate bar, with access to the global internet. To let someone know something, a single tap on a messaging app is enough.
- Antennas are internal, you don't even notice them. No dangling wires, unless you need to charge the battery.
- Sending a message is free (or nearly so); you can add stickers, memes, videos, audios. Emojis are everywhere, and you can express any emotion with an animated icon.
- Batteries last at least a full day, and fast charging makes life easier. We stream series with just a tap on the screen.

That contrast is laughable when you think about the quantum leap we've experienced. My grandchildren, when they hear my stories about how much my first bill cost, throw their hands on their heads: "Grandpa, did you really pay a dollar or more for a single minute of talk time?" And I chuckle with resignation: "Yes, kid, that was reality, but worse was running out of coins at a payphone at midnight."

Now, as I near the end of this video, I'd like to emphasize the idea that while technological progress frees us from certain dangers (like risking ourselves in unsafe neighborhoods just to make a call), it also immerses us in new challenges: information overload, emotional dependence on a device, the instant gratification that robs us of patience. The funny thing is that, when I was 20, the mobile phone was a luxury reserved for emergencies or quick calls.

Today, my grandchildren use it for everything: homework, social media, photos, banking, ordering food, even monitoring their health. Incredible, isn't it?

But a word of caution: let's not forget the warmth and closeness that define our humanity. That old "brick" reminded me that human connection didn't fully depend on the cellphone. Yes, it saved me in a crisis, but I still ended up inviting my friends to sit with me and chat without the gadget in between. That's something I sometimes miss nowadays, when I see people gathered around a table with each one glued to their little screen.

Allow me one last story. It happened in 1995: I was driving at night when my car ran out of gas. I couldn't find an open gas station, and the nearest one was several kilometers away. Without my brick cellphone, I would have had to pull over, walk aimlessly, look for a booth, maybe on a dangerous street. But I had it in the glove compartment: I turned it on, heroically extended its antenna, and with a bit of signal managed to call a friend to come help me. Twenty minutes later, he arrived with a gas can. I wasn't mugged, I wasn't terrified, I made it home safely. The cost of that call was steep (I remember it clearly, almost half a day's wages), but it was worth it for the peace of mind it gave me.

Now, in 2025, my grandchildren laugh at that story, telling me that with their phones they can find the nearest open gas station and pay digitally, or order an Uber, or post for help on social media instantly. That peace of mind has multiplied a thousandfold. But I tell them: "My dear ones, don't forget that, despite all this technology, the most important thing is still the people we share life with. What good are all these apps if we forget to visit Grandpa or hug Grandma?"

That's the lesson I want to leave in this video, with anecdotes full of humor and truth: technology is fantastic, it saves us from many hardships, especially from having to risk ourselves at shady phone booths, but let's make sure to remember that human contact and genuine closeness are irreplaceable.

For this father and grandfather born in 1970, who lived through the revolution of mobile phones in the 90s, there's no doubt we were witnesses to a colossal change. From a brick with an antenna to a next-generation smartphone; from costly SMS to free worldwide video calls; from prepaid cards to unlimited plans; from monochrome screens to 8K touchscreens… all in the blink of a historical eye.

But above all, let's hold on to one clear principle: "Value technology, but don't let it replace genuine human connection." Appreciate its usefulness when it saves you from stopping in a dangerous neighborhood at midnight; admire it for allowing you to instantly communicate with those thousands of kilometers away; and be grateful for the marvels it gives you, from GPS and artificial intelligence to an HD camera capable of capturing your best moments.

But when you're surrounded by friends or family, set the device down for a while, look at their faces, and laugh with them for real… And if possible, call them with your own voice instead of relying on emojis. That balance gives life a unique flavor, one no phone, no matter how advanced, can ever replicate.

With that, I take my leave, thanking you for watching this far and wishing you a thoughtful smile as you reflect on how far we've come since those days of antennas and monochrome screens. Until the next story on Genostories.

After hearing the testimony of this father, who once dared to use a "brick" phone in the 90s and now gazes in awe at the ultra-powerful mobiles of 2025, the gigantic evolution of technology is undeniable. Back then, avoiding a mugging by not having to search for a payphone at midnight was already a triumph of modernity. Today, grandchildren share videos and holograms in real time as if it were the most normal thing in the world. But the true richness, as our narrator wisely points out, lies in enjoying both: the convenience of a smartphone and the warmth of human interaction. Because in the end, communication is not just about devices, it's about hearts connecting in every call, every message, and every embrace. Here's to that evolution, and to the wisdom of never forgetting what truly matters!

Griot 2085

LIVING TO THE FULLEST

On my journey through Genostories, I came across the story of Emma, an American woman who, in 2025, received a heartbreaking diagnosis: a brain tumor "the size of an apple." Far from sinking into despair, she decided to turn on her camera and record a series of videos for her granddaughter. Yet, true to the strength of her name, "Emma," of Germanic origin, meaning "powerful" or "the strongest", she ended up making those videos public to inspire anyone who came across them on the platform.

In them, she reflects on her most meaningful moments, the lessons her illness has taught her, and the urgency of squeezing every second out of the life we're given. With serenity, humor, and courage, Emma reminds us that "Life is the most precious gift we have. Don't let fear, doubt, or wasted time keep you from living it to the fullest, because we have no guarantee of tomorrow."

Join me in this chapter to discover her story, filled with hospital scenes, family dinners, and walks through beloved places all colored by the priceless perspective of someone who chooses to live fully, no matter what.

Griot 2085

My name is Emma, a name of Germanic origin meaning *"powerful"* or *"the strongest"*, and I never thought there would come a time in my life when I would have to embody its meaning so literally. It was in 2025 when my world turned upside down: the doctors discovered a brain tumor precisely described, almost poetically, as "the size of an apple." Its location was complex, and the treatment options were limited. Suddenly the future I had imagined with my family and my granddaughter became fragile and uncertain, like glass about to crack.

On receiving the news, I froze, thinking maybe the doctor had the wrong patient or the wrong diagnosis. How could this happen now, when I had left most of my work worries behind, and be dealt such a *punishment*? But cancer asks no permission to barge into anyone's life. Faced with that harsh reality, I decided to cling to hope and to find meaning in whatever days I had left. That's how, amid the confusion, I discovered I could still learn, love, and leave a legacy.

My doctors recommended I focus on chemotherapy and radiation, which might buy me a little time. But I had another goal, too: to speak to my granddaughter. At first, I wanted to upload videos only for her, so she would remember her grandmother. However, my daughter suggested I make them public in case they might inspire others.

So I turned on the camera for the first time from my hospital bed. I had a catheter in my arm and fatigue clouded my eyes, but Genostories was so easy to use that, in less than five minutes, my first video was online. There I spoke in a soft voice about how I felt, what I feared, and what pushed me to keep smiling despite everything. I confess that, at the time, I did not imagine the impact it would have: messages arrived from strangers saying they felt motivated to live more bravely. Of course, my granddaughter left me a comment in her childlike language, full of little drawings and hearts.

I can't deny that the start of treatment was extremely hard. I had headaches so intense that, at times, it felt like a drill was boring into my skull. Pills and painkillers barely dulled the stabbing pain. Even so, I decided to record it: I wanted to show the truth of my process, the part that isn't pretty or glamorous. With the camera focused on my face, I said: "Hello, my Genostories family, today I'm having a terrible day with migraines and nausea. But you know what? Even with all the discomfort, I'm still here, breathing, catching a ray of sunlight through the window, and reminding myself that every second counts."

The reaction from the platform's community was moving. People from everywhere sent me strength, prayers, tips on natural remedies. I saw the solidarity we sometimes think is lost in the digital world, and it lit a flame of hope in me, a purpose bigger than my own fears.

During those first days, many people asked me about my name: Emma. I explained its meaning: *"powerful"* or *"the strongest."* But I always clarified: "Don't confuse strength with the absence of fear. I am strong, yes, but I also get scared and fall to pieces some nights." The strength my name seemed to foretell wasn't made of steel, but of heart. I could cry oceans and then keep recording videos for my granddaughter. I could feel devastated by the doctor's verdict and still laugh with my children at dinner. Being strong meant continuing to love life while death was breathing down my neck.

In the hospital, the rooms almost always had a cold air and a smell of disinfectant that weighed on your spirits. But at the same time, that place allowed me to connect with nurses and patients who taught me a great lesson in humanity. One day, I dared to record a collective video with three other patients from the oncology ward, each fighting their own battle. We gathered in a small lounge and set the camera on a little table:

"Hi, we're a quartet of crazies who refuse to give up," I said with a small smile.

"We fight cancer with laughter, too," one of them added.

"And with the certainty that every new day is a gift," another patient said.

I uploaded that video to Genostories, and soon it was filled with comments from people grateful to see that not all terminal patients lived in absolute despair, but that there was a collective courage driving us to fight until the end. That became a turning point for me: I realized that my personal experience could serve as a spark for others who felt alone.

I alternated my days between the hospital and my home, where my family awaited me. My home is a warm space: walls covered with photos of my children, a small kitchen fragrant with spices, and a dining room that has witnessed so many celebrations. Naturally, I wanted to record one of my videos in the dining room, on a night when we were all gathered, sharing a simple meal overflowing with love. The phone was propped up toward the table, capturing the clatter of dishes and the hum of conversations.

As we ate, I spoke to the camera: "I've discovered that life's true charm lies in these simple moments. I can't think of a greater joy than seeing my granddaughter smile when I serve her favorite dessert, or my children laughing at silly jokes. Before, I underestimated the beauty of something as ordinary as a family dinner. Today, I treasure it like a diamond." After posting that video, the comments section filled with people saying they felt inspired to invite their parents for dinner again, to sit down once more with their siblings. Some wrote: "Thank you, Emma, for reminding us that the everyday can be wonderful."

There's something special about returning to the places where you grew up. For me, that place was a small park in the neighborhood where I spent my childhood. When I learned that my cancer was terminal, it felt urgent to go back to that corner of my past. My children took me one Saturday afternoon. I walked slowly (leaning on a cane), but the emotion of seeing the same trees and the old fountain with its fish gave me an unexpected vitality. I lowered my head for a moment and whispered: "Oh, Emma, why did it take you so long to come back here?"

The breeze caressed me and the golden sunlight painted the grass. I opened Genostories once more and recorded a message: "To those watching this, don't wait for misfortune to visit your roots. If there's a park, a house, a beach that shaped your childhood, go and breathe in the nostalgia. I promise you'll feel life rushing through your veins with renewed strength." The video was deeply moving; my voice trembled, but the peace in my eyes was undeniable. I knew that, despite everything I was going through, my heart still found refuge in those beloved places.

A few days later, I wanted to make another kind of pilgrimage, this time to the beach that marked my adolescence. I managed to convince my daughter and my grandchildren to take a short trip, even though my body complained of aches and fatigue. When we arrived, seeing the blue sea stretching to the horizon brought tears of joy and melancholy to my eyes. Sitting on the sand, I recorded another video:

"Here I am, watching these waves that come and go without ceasing. I think about how fleeting we are: one day we're here, the next maybe not. Yet the beach remains, the sun rises, the wind blows, and life continues its dance. It's not about saying we're insignificant, but about understanding that within transience lies the greatness of each moment."

My grandchildren played in the foam, not fully grasping my situation, and that gave me a certain peace: I, with my apple in the brain, could see at once the innocence of childhood and the sea's endless perseverance. It felt like a beautiful clash of fragility and eternity. I uploaded that testimony, convinced that more people need to remember that life flows, and that if you cling to the present, you suddenly realize you don't need much more to be happy.

I returned to the hospital for another round of treatments. This time, radiotherapy left me exhausted and with relentless nausea. My physical appearance began to suffer: I lost weight, my skin turned ashen, and my hair fell out in clumps. There was a day when I felt so down I didn't even want to lift my face from the pillow. Yet it was then that I forced myself to turn on the camera, not for show, but out of honesty.

"Today is a terrible day," I said in a hoarse voice. "I look in the mirror and don't recognize myself. I feel my body wearing away by giant strides, and I ask myself, 'How long will I be able to hold on?' But to those watching this, I want to say that it's not wrong to be afraid or to want to give up from time to time. What keeps me standing is knowing there is still light, that I can still smile at a nurse, that I can still kiss my children. So if you're going through something similar, don't stay silent. Talk to your loved ones. Ask for help. On this journey, loneliness is not good company."

That video was hard to upload from within the cold walls of oncology. I felt like I was running out of breath, but I was surprised by the flood of comments from other patients expressing their empathy and solidarity. I realized my role wasn't so much to teach a *lesson* as it was to connect with those living through a similar pain.

Despite the seriousness of my condition, my family decided to organize a small party at home for my 53rd birthday. It was a bittersweet moment: everyone was aware that it might be my last celebration, but still determined to laugh and dance. That day I dressed up more than usual. I wore a floral dress and a turban to cover the baldness already showing, and I sat before a cake with what felt like too many candles.

I turned on my phone and aimed it at the table: "Well, Genostories, here's my beautiful family. I'm more tired than usual, but I wouldn't miss this for anything. Today, the party is life itself; every spoonful of cake tastes like glory. Look at us: we laugh and sing, knowing time is unforgiving, but no one can take this day from us."

My children put together an improvised karaoke, and although I couldn't dance like before, I joined in with clapping and laughter. I noticed the worried looks of some relatives, but I smiled back at them, trying to say without words that the day was for celebrating, not for crying ahead of time. I uploaded the video to Genostories and, watching it the next day, I noticed I looked physically fragile, but with an inner flame shining brighter than ever.

By then, my granddaughter was beginning to understand the seriousness of my illness. She would sit with me to watch the videos I had uploaded and suddenly ask tender questions.

"Grandma, are you going to get better?" she murmured with an innocence that broke my heart.

My chest ached, but I answered her gently:

My love, I will do everything I can to stay with you longer. And if someday I'm not here, you'll have these videos and my letters… that way I'll never stop keeping you company.

A couple of times, the little one appeared in my recordings, blowing kisses goodbye. Those clips are my treasure: if one day I'm not here to watch her grow, at least she'll be able to recover my voice and my gestures. Maybe she'll suffer, maybe she'll cry when she's older and understands the situation. But she'll also be able to laugh watching me on good days, with my colorful turban and red glasses, and joking about any anecdote from the past.

With every video, I felt a duty fulfilled. My main lesson: *Don't wait for an hourglass to tell you how much life you have left. Live today, without so many excuses.*

As the illness progressed, my body weakened more. We planned one last trip to the beach of my childhood, a second attempt, because nostalgia was calling me. There, on the sand, feeling the sea breeze, I recorded a final video (or at least I considered it final). I titled it *Living to the fullest.*

I spoke to the camera:

"Dear ones, I'm here watching the sea, which comes and goes without tiring. I have thought a lot about what it means to *live to the fullest.* Sometimes we believe it means traveling the world, having money or fame, but today I understand it's something simpler: deeply enjoying what you already have. If you can watch a sunset, hear a sincere laugh, or embrace someone you love, you are already living to the fullest.

I don't know how much time I have left, but I won't go without begging you not to postpone happiness. Pick up your phone and call whoever you need to call; ask forgiveness if necessary; make peace with the present. This tumor, this apple in my head, reminded me that life is too short to stay stuck in doubts and fears. I leave you my gratitude for accompanying me on this journey, and my wish that your days be full of light, just as I hope mine will be until the last breath."

I closed the video with my gaze fixed on the horizon. My heart felt like a knot, and my children hugged me in silence. Even in weakness, I felt free. I uploaded that clip to Genostories, using as the video caption the phrase that has guided my struggle: *Life is the most precious gift we have…*

Back home after that trip, I struggled to breathe. The doctors told me the chemotherapy wasn't shrinking the tumor enough and that the symptoms would keep worsening. But you know what? I kept thanking every ray of sun that came through my window, every new morning when I could say to my granddaughter, "Good morning, princess." The physical pain didn't go away, but the desire to be present every minute pushed me to hang on a little longer.

Looking back, I don't feel anger at fate, but gratitude for having had the chance to understand life so intensely. I wanted to make that clear in my last entry on Genostories:

"If you're watching this, receive my embrace. None of us has tomorrow guaranteed, so live today with passion, courage, and generosity. Enjoy laughter, comfort those in sorrow, and don't forget to say *I love you* to the ones you love most. That is the most important lesson this tumor gifted me, and if the name Emma means 'powerful,' then let my story reflect that strength, not to avoid death, but to celebrate life."

I don't know when or how I will leave. But I do know that, at the end of it all, my story will remain here on Genostories for anyone who wants to see it, for my granddaughter and her future children or grandchildren. I reread my own words and I confirm: *Life is the most precious gift we have. Don't let fear, doubt, or wasted time stop you from living it to the fullest, because we have no guarantee of tomorrow.*

I have captured that lesson in videos filmed in hospitals, in my kitchen, in a childhood park, and on the shore of the beach. That mosaic of scenes and reflections, mixed with my family's laughter, tears, and love, is my sentimental testament.

To those who see or hear this story, all I can say is try with all your heart: live, dream, laugh, and don't be afraid to open up to the ones you love. If I, with a tumor the size of an apple, can find joy on an ordinary day, I'm sure you can too in the everyday life that surrounds you. Believe me: every moment counts more than you imagine.

Emma's story, "the strongest", is one that moves even the most skeptical: a woman who chose to face a brain tumor the size of an apple not with despair, but with an infinite act of gratitude and courage. Her videos on Genostories not only revealed the harshness of a terminal illness, but also proved how the passion for living can ignite even in the most uncertain moments.

When I tried to trace more about her, I realized there were no more public videos from Emma; the last update had been posted by her daughter, an online memorial dedicated to who her mother had been in life. Hundreds of thousands of people wrote on that digital wall, leaving anecdotes, thanks, and prayers. It was the confirmation that Emma had left this world, yet her words continued to move strangers and family alike.

Though she died, I want you to know that the decision to rescue these memories from Genostories and turn them into a book. in a 2085 where almost no one sits down to write anymore, since information flows through a chip implanted in our brains, was born precisely from the inspiration Emma left me. With her example, she reminded me that the last thing we still have as human beings is the ability to confront our finitude, to feel emotions raw and unfiltered, and then to make sense of them. Only then can we live our stories to the fullest, with shadows and with light, with the tears of the inevitable and the determination of someone who chooses to love life until the very last breath.

Let this written format be, then, a tribute to the strength with which Emma embraced her journey on Earth.

Griot 2085

MEMORIAL OF AN UNKNOWN HERO

In my explorations of old data left behind on obsolete servers, I discovered the story of Mei Lin Zhang and the young teacher Wei Yong on an old application called Genostories. Their account, set during the catastrophic earthquake that struck China's Sichuan province in 2008, reminded me that once upon a time, human beings did not enjoy infinite longevity or the kind of technological assistance that today feels so normal; we depended, above all, on our courage and solidarity in the worst of times.

I wanted to gather this forgotten memory, a true testimony of chaos and heroism, so that we who live in 2085 may remember how, in the midst of devastation, anonymous bravery could rise up to save many lives at the cost of one's own. Wei Yong's story is not in the great headlines of official history, but his sacrifice endures thanks to Mei Lin's collections on Genostories. Here, in this chapter, I will recount how a fragile, mortal human being became an unsung hero, embodying the greatness of spirit that the humans of old revealed when the earth roared and the future turned uncertain.

May this testimony remind us of something essential: we have not always been immortal and free from illness; there was a time when our humanity lay precisely in our finitude and in our ability to unite in the face of disaster.

Griot 2085

Here in 2025, as I go through my old notebooks and photographs with the help of Genostories, I once again feel the weight of that memory pressing on my chest: the earthquake of May 12, 2008. Seventeen years have passed, but the mere mention of that date still makes my hands tremble, as if every aftershock echoed again in my heart. My name is Mei Lin Zhang, I was born in 1956, and I live in a small town in Sichuan province, in southwest China. This beautiful land, famous for its spicy cuisine and the warmth of its people became, years ago, the stage of a disaster of epic proportions.

I have decided to open a digital memorial to honor the memory of an anonymous hero who captured the attention of our community: Wei Yong (伟勇), a young teacher who, in the midst of the chaos and destruction, gave himself with a courage worthy of his name (which, in Chinese, evokes bravery and heroism). The truth is that when everything was collapsing and cries rang out everywhere, it was Wei Yong who ran toward the school where children were trapped, without hesitation, and saved a dozen lives in just minutes. Sadly, tragedy claimed him in a second collapse, leaving us with his example, and his absence.

My intention is to gather testimonies, photos, and videos, some blurry, through Genostories, the platform that is helping so many preserve the memory of past times. I want future generations, when they look at this archive, to remember that not all heroes wear capes, and that sometimes the anonymous stranger who rescues you deserves the greatest tribute.

This chapter is a journey back to 2008: into the dust, rubble, and pain that shook an entire province; a journey led by a teacher who, without a second thought, embodied sacrifice and human greatness, proving that solidarity and love for others can transcend even the fury of nature.

Every time I close my eyes, I see the scene as if it were happening right now. It was a cloudy day, with the humid heat typical of the region. Just after two in the afternoon, I heard a dull, deep roar like the growl of a gigantic beast. Then the ground began to shake, at first lightly, then with such brutal force that it threw me down as I tried to leave the house. Buildings shook like boats in a storm, and the crash of walls and shattering glass joined the screams of people running in terror, not knowing where to go.

The epicenter was in Wenchuan, a nearby county, but the disaster spread across much of Sichuan province and beyond. News would take time to arrive, since the telephone lines collapsed immediately. I lived in a small town just a few kilometers from the epicenter, and I remember watching the road split open before my eyes, leaving cracks wide enough to fit an entire arm. In a matter of seconds, the peaceful life of the mountains turned into an apocalyptic scene: cracked buildings, tilted power poles, people shielding their heads with whatever they could grab.

The quake lasted about two minutes, but it felt eternal. When the shaking finally stopped, the silence that followed was chilling. Then the aftershocks came, sowing even more chaos in the days that followed. My heart was pounding, but my fear multiplied when I remembered that dozens of children and teachers were gathered at the town's primary school. In rural areas, buildings like these often lacked the solidity to withstand an earthquake of such magnitude.

As soon as I steadied myself, I ran out into the street and saw many neighbors just as stunned. Some were crying, others shouting desperately for their relatives, and everything was covered in dust. Together, we headed toward the school, knowing that at that hour dozens of children would be in class. When we arrived, the scene was one of utter desolation: much of the building had collapsed, walls shattered, desks twisted, and debris piled up into a mountain of bricks.

The teachers and staff who had managed to escape unharmed were already trying to clear the rubble with their bare hands. The cries of the trapped children tore at our hearts. Immediately, a spontaneous wave of solidarity rose up in the community:

Men, women, and the elderly joined in, removing stone after stone. But time was against us. It was hard to know in which part of the ruins survivors might still be trapped. Each aftershock brought the imminent terror of another collapse.

Amid the crowd stood out a young teacher, only 25 years old: Wei Yong (伟勇), slim in build, with blood running down from a cut on his forehead. Though injured, he never slowed his efforts: he crawled through narrow gaps, pulled out beams and pieces of roof. He began rescuing several children, one after another, dragging them out through holes that opened in the fractured walls. Many of us tried to stop him, afraid his injury might cost him his life. Yet he pressed on, embodying a bravery that bordered on madness, as if his own safety meant nothing to him.

At that point, people began whispering that his name, Wei Yong, meant "brave and heroic", and it seemed the young man had taken it as a literal destiny. Each child he rescued emerged covered in dust and tears, and the teacher hugged them, whispering words of calm. The sight moved me to tears and marked the beginning of a story I would never forget.

While Wei Yong risked his body among the school's rubble, the whole town organized itself in an improvised effort to help the wounded. From the collapsed houses, trapped family members groaned for help. The quake had damaged the power grid and water supply; the phone lines were dead. But despite the magnitude of the catastrophe, the unity of the community shone brightly.

The elderly, struggling as best they could, carried sacks of supplies and bandages.

The young, with improvised picks and shovels, cleared debris, trying to rescue more people.

The mothers, tears streaming down their faces, called out to their children, hoping to find them alive.

In that heartbreaking atmosphere, you could feel a collective sense of brotherhood: everyone was helping everyone, without regard to social class or family ties. I remember a pregnant woman distributing bottled water; an old man, his leg visibly trembling, helping to carry the wounded to the improvised health center set up on the basketball court. Pain united us as rarely before.

But with every passing hour, the hope of rescuing the missing without specialized machinery grew dimmer. The constant aftershocks continued wreaking havoc, bringing down unstable roofs and half-standing walls. At the school, we kept our eyes on Wei Yong, who ignored people's pleas for him to rest.

That endless afternoon, Wei Yong managed to pull twelve children alive from the rubble. Each time he brought one to safety, the crowd broke into applause through their tears. More than once we saw him cough and spit blood, or limp on an injured foot. His friends tried to convince him to stop, to let others take over, but he insisted: "They're my students. I can't stop now."

Finally, during one of those rescues, he went into a highly unstable section where at least two or three children were believed to still be alive. No one else dared to enter the narrow gap; the place was on the verge of collapse after a recent aftershock. Wei Yong took a breath and went in without hesitation, holding a flashlight. Shortly after, we heard banging and the faint voice of a child on the other side. Several people waited by the opening, ready for any signal to help. But then another aftershock struck, and in an instant another block of walls and beams came crashing down.

The crash was like a heavy blow to all our hearts. Dust blinded us, and when we managed to approach, we saw that the section Wei Yong had entered was completely destroyed. A silence thick with horror spread. Some broke into sobs; others shouted the teacher's name, but there was no reply. After a few minutes, we realized that the collapse had buried that part entirely, making any immediate rescue impossible. Despair took hold of us. Wei Yong, that young 25-year-old teacher, had entered to fulfill his mission of saving more children, and in return, he gave his life anonymously.

During the night and the following day, professional rescue teams arrived in our town and in other affected areas of Sichuan. With heavy machinery and the help of volunteers, they continued clearing the rubble. They found several more children, sadly already lifeless, and they also recovered the body of Wei Yong. According to some rescuers, he was found holding two small children in his arms, shielding them with his own body; but the concrete and metal structure was too much. The children did not survive either.

When that news spread, a collective grief crushed our hearts. Word got out that Wei Yong had saved twelve children in total before that fatal second collapse. That number echoed through every corner of the town, and his deed became a legend which, sadly, never reached the major headlines, overshadowed by the global scale of the earthquake that claimed tens of thousands of lives. For our town, he was the hero, and for me, his name was forever etched in memory.

I would not want the world to forget the magnitude of the disaster. The earthquake of May 12, 2008 reached 7.9 on the Richter scale (and according to some official reports, even 8.0). The devastation spread across several districts, with old buildings that could not withstand it, roads split open or gone altogether, bridges collapsing into pieces. Entire schools reduced to rubble, half-destroyed hospitals, villages cut off by landslides.

The scenes were terrifying: families searching for loved ones among the debris, streams of mud coursing through the fractured ground, thousands of injured crowded into makeshift tents without enough doctors or medicine. For weeks, the air was saturated with the smell of dust, rubble, and death. And yet, in that grim landscape, the greatness of solidarity arose. Volunteers from all over the country arriving to help, donations of food, tents, and blankets, and the tireless work of international organizations. All of it was proof that, despite the magnitude of the disaster, humanity can come together under the banner of compassion.

I still keep some blurry recordings from mobile phones of that time: buildings collapsing, people running with terror-stricken faces, and at times, heartbreaking cries. There are low-resolution digital photographs where you see only clouds of dust and an indistinguishable chaos. In their rawness, those materials gave me the motivation, in 2025, to digitize and upload them to Genostories so that new generations could understand the scale of that earthquake and appreciate the life they enjoy today.

A few years ago, when I discovered Genostories and how easy it was to organize stories, I knew the time had come to honor Wei Yong in a formal way. Not just as a local tribute, but as a universal message about sacrifice and humanity. I began by gathering the grainy images people had taken with digital cameras in 2008, as well as audio recordings and videos where witnesses mentioned Wei Yong's feat.

1. Testimonies from children, now teenagers or young adults, who said: "He pulled me out from under some planks; he didn't care that his arms were being cut by glass."
2. Words from neighbors who witnessed him going in and out of the collapsed school without a trace of ego.
3. And, of course, the devastating account of his death beneath the second collapse.

Genostories became my tool to compile everything: I uploaded photos of the teacher in his classroom, excerpts from a couple of recordings where, just days before, he was on an outing with his students. Each image, each testimony, beats as a witness to that heroism. Some videos, though originally in low quality, I converted into more modern clips so they wouldn't be lost among obsolete files.

In 2025, the platform allowed me to tag the story with keywords like "earthquake," "Sichuan," "anonymous heroes." People searching for those themes stumbled upon Wei Yong's memorial. In this way, I began receiving comments and realized that what happened in 2008 must never be allowed to fade into oblivion.

One of the most moving moments in creating the online memorial was contacting some of the children rescued by Wei Yong. Now, in 2025, they are in their twenties; some have finished university, others work in different cities across China. Most of them carry a somewhat blurred memory of that day, but all agree that without their teacher's intervention, they would not be alive.

For example, I found Li Wen, a young woman who recounted how she had hit her head and fallen half-unconscious during the collapse. When she came to, she saw Wei Yong's bloodied hand firmly pulling her out.

"He looked at me and said: 'Don't be afraid, you're safe with me.' That was the last time I saw him alive, because he led me to a safe place and went back to rescue others."

Every year, on the anniversary of the earthquake, Li Wen lights a candle to honor his memory.

Another case is Zhang Bo, who was twelve years old at the time and escaped with a broken leg. Even so, he clearly remembers Wei Yong making sure everyone was stable before rushing back to look for more children.

"The last thing he shouted at me was: 'Hold on, little one, the doctors will come soon.'"

Gathering dozens of such accounts, I understood that Wei Yong managed to rescue twelve children with his sheer determination. Each of those young people is living testimony that one man can change the destiny of many in a single instant of courage.

Beyond Wei Yong's personal story, this video seeks to highlight the unity that can arise in times of disaster. I myself, Mei Lin Zhang, lived through the destruction of my home, the deaths of friends, the lack of water and electricity for weeks. But I also witnessed how, almost magically, people set aside selfishness and entered into a mode of collective survival. Those who had food shared it, those with medical skills tended to the wounded, and those who knew construction improvised shelters.

The earthquake, in all its fury, revealed human fragility but also collective greatness. This video does not seek to glorify pain, but to remind us that even when the earth shakes and our buildings collapse, the bonds of community can hold us up. Wei Yong embodied that solidarity by sacrificing himself without fanfare, and in his name, many in my town found inspiration to keep helping even in the midst of aftershocks.

Let it be known: this was not an isolated act. Among the rubble of Sichuan, countless anonymous heroes emerged. But the figure of Wei Yong, the teacher who refused to abandon his students marked me deeply and drove me to create this digital memorial on Genostories.

In 2025, technology makes it possible to document with precision what once survived only in oral accounts. So I undertook the task of digitizing every kind of material: blurry photos from old cell phones, videos shot with low-resolution digital cameras, clippings from local newspapers that mentioned his feat. I uploaded each file to Genostories, adding subtitles that described the events. Over time, the platform became a kind of living archive, enriched by contributions from others who had also preserved something about the earthquake.

The digital memorial includes a section called "Voices of Gratitude," where children saved by Wei Yong, now adults, share a few lines of tribute. Another section is dedicated to the words of those who witnessed the scene at the school. And there is also a space filled with images of the town's reconstruction afterward.

Most importantly, this memorial is not limited to mourning what happened. It also seeks to inspire: *"If a young teacher could take such risks, what can't each of us do in daily life to help others?"*

Many might ask: Why devote so much effort to the story of a single individual? On one hand, it's true that in a disaster of such magnitude, there were thousands of heroic gestures. But each act, each life offered for the good of others, deserves to be remembered by name. "Wei Yong" means "brave and heroic" in Chinese, and without intending to, that 25-year-old teacher embodied his own name. His actions reminded me of the lesson this video wishes to leave: *"Not all heroes wear capes; sometimes the anonymous stranger who rescues you is the one most worthy of tribute."*

The 2008 earthquake destroyed homes, families, and the innocence of an entire region. But it also brought forth the best of human nature: the will to unite, to share resources, and in the case of Wei Yong, to give one's very life. It is his memory that I preserve today, in 2025, transforming it into a digital legacy. Because sometimes official history forgets the small names, yet it is those *"anonymous"* ones who carry the hope of humanity.

I conclude this chronicle by remembering May 12 as a day that changed my perspective forever. My town, in Sichuan province, suffered a brutal blow from nature and, even so, we rose again with resilience. The image of Wei Yong rushing to save children, blood on his forehead and without a moment's hesitation, is the emblem of that resistance. His body remained under the rubble, but his example lives among us, and now in Genostories for anyone who wants to see how humanity can shine amid dust and cries.

May this story serve new generations as a beacon in the darkness, and may they remember the strength of unity and sacrifice, especially in times when tragedy can appear without warning. The digital memorial is not just a set of files uploaded to the cloud; it is a testimony to the courage that dwells in the humblest corners of our communities, and a call to honor those who gave everything without expecting reward or applause. As an old Chinese proverb says: *"Still waters run deep."* Such is the bravery of unknown heroes like Wei Yong: silent, deep, and capable of saving dozens of lives without asking for anything in return.

With this story, I say goodbye for now, not without first inviting you to visit the memorial and leave a message of gratitude. But most importantly: I invite you to remember, when disaster strikes, the greatness of solidarity that lifts us above the rubble.

Mei Lin Zhang's account of the 2008 Sichuan earthquake and the sacrifice of Wei Yong stands as a testimony to how, in the midst of disasters that bring down both buildings and hearts, the noblest courage can emerge. The scale of the tragedy is staggering: thousands of lives lost, rubble covering entire towns. Yet what rises from this story is the figure of a young teacher who, without powers or resources, risked everything to save his students. He may not be famous in the annals of grand history, but in the memory of a small town and of the children he rescued, his name will remain forever engraved.

The digital memorial that Mei Lin builds on Genostories reminds us that not even the mightiest quake can bury human goodness. In watching grainy recordings and reading moving testimonies, we grasp the greatness of the anonymous man who, while the ground split beneath his feet, chose to be a hero without asking about his own fate. "Not all heroes wear capes; sometimes the anonymous stranger who rescues you is the one most worthy of tribute." That lesson shines in the spirit of Wei Yong and, thanks to modern technology, his sacrifice will continue inspiring generations who, with luck, will never face an earthquake of such magnitude, but who, without doubt, will be enriched by remembering that humanity is reborn with every act of solidarity.

Griot 2085

THE GUARDIAN OF LOST LANGUAGES

In a future where much of humanity's traditional experiences have been blurred under the dominance of technology, I have taken on the task of tracing and gathering stories that evoke what it once meant to be truly human, with all its lights and shadows. Most people in my society ignore the profound value of the cultural diversity that once flourished on our planet. But in my virtual searches, I discovered, on the old application called Genostories, the story of João Mendes, a Brazilian linguist born in 1980, who undertook a crusade to save the Indigenous languages of the Amazon that were on the brink of extinction.

His timeline, titled *The Guardian of Lost Languages*, takes us into the Amazon region of 2025, where João used Genostories to document and preserve the words, myths, and worldview of an Indigenous community on the verge of losing its language. It was no easy task: he had to earn the trust of the elders, navigate treacherous rivers, and fight against the indifference of a world turning its back on those millennia-old cultures.

Here lies the full account of the man who, in a discreet yet monumental way, rescued the essence of a language and, with it, an entire way of understanding the universe. May his endeavor serve as inspiration and a reminder: when a language dies, we lose a unique window into the truth we so deeply long for.

Griot 2085

My name is João Mendes, and I was born in 1980 in a riverside village in the Brazilian Amazon, in the state of Amazonas. For as long as I can remember, my ears were filled with sounds different from everyday Portuguese: the voices of Indigenous elders passing through my village selling handicrafts, women conversing in mysterious tongues as they traded fruit, fishermen telling stories incomprehensible to me and my friends... That melting pot of languages fascinated me, though as a child I didn't understand why so many strange words, so foreign to the Portuguese I spoke, were used.

In my teenage years, I learned that many of those communities spoke languages with very few speakers left. One of my teachers, a missionary who had spent time with several tribes, told me stories about Amazonian languages that were slowly disappearing in the face of Portuguese expansion and the lack of interest among the local youth. That was how my calling as a linguist was born, a desire to study and protect those words that sounded to me like ancient, profound music. I remember telling my parents: "When I grow up, I want to travel the Amazon and learn those languages before they disappear."

At first, they laughed. They told me that what mattered was studying to get a stable job in the city, but my heart leaned toward the forest, toward the people living on its forgotten margins. Over time, and through persistence, I earned a scholarship to study Linguistics, and as an adult, I began expeditions into remote regions. It was at university that I met professors who instilled in me the urgency of documenting languages with fewer than one or two hundred speakers.

By 2025, at the age of 45, I had reached a point in my career where I had documented several minority dialects. But my goal was to reach one community in particular: the *Pirahã* people, known for having a language spoken by very few and for its unique phonological traits. I had heard rumors that the Pirahã language had no numerals, no complex kinship system, no recursive structures in its grammar. On the other hand, the oral stories they passed down preserved teachings about the balance between human beings and nature.

To my horror, I discovered that the number of native speakers was dropping rapidly, as the younger generations preferred Portuguese in order to integrate into modern life. The elders, the guardians of tradition, were aging without leaving many heirs to the language. If nothing was done soon, an entire way of seeing the world, a complete language would vanish without leaving a trace.

It was then that I heard about Genostories, an application which, in 2025, was allowing people to preserve their family memories and cultural stories in a multimedia archive. Until then, I had relied on audio recorders and field notebooks, but I thought: *"Why not try something more powerful?"* Genostories, with its simple interface and wide reach, could help ensure these stories were not only stored, but also shared with younger generations with the immediacy and impact of video and digital media.

Getting in touch with the Pirahã was not easy. On one hand, the Brazilian government strictly regulated interactions with Indigenous communities through agencies such as FUNAI. On the other hand, the Pirahã were rightfully protective of their privacy, as in the past they had suffered deceit at the hands of traders who swindled them. For weeks, I worked on permits, gathered letters of recommendation from my university, and, most importantly, looked for ways to avoid appearing like an outsider trying to "steal" their knowledge.

Thus, with a rented canoe and the help of a local interpreter who spoke a dialect close to Pirahã, I traveled down a tributary of the Tapajós River, surrounded by dense vegetation, until I reached a clearing where the main Pirahã village stood. There was no triumphant arrival: my boots sank into the mud, mosquitoes swarmed everywhere, and I could barely manage a greeting in their language, poorly pronounced, which made them laugh. I knew that, to them, I was just another foreigner with a strange fascination for their words.

Despite the initial difficulties, the curiosity I sparked worked as a catalyst. Several elders came closer to observe me, and one of them, Shihu, a man with a piercing gaze, looked me over with suspicion. But when I explained that I wanted to learn and document their language so it wouldn't be lost, I noticed a faint glimmer in his eyes.

"I don't know if I can trust you, but we'll see," he said in basic Portuguese.

It was the first door opening for me into that hidden and fascinating world.

I had read about the Pirahã language before arriving, but nothing had prepared me to hear it in person. It was as if every word wasn't only spoken but also danced in the air, filled with nuances and meanings that seemed impossible to translate into Portuguese or English. Its features fascinated me, almost beyond imagination compared to the world I was used to.

For example, they had no numerals. No *"one, two, three..."* Instead, they used terms that could only be described as estimates: *"a little"* or *"a lot."* Everything depended on context, and their perception of quantity seemed to flow like the river beside their village. Their sentences also lacked complex structures. There was nothing like *"the house of my uncle's brother";* their relationships were simple, linear, direct. I was struck by the clarity of their linguistic world, as if words were never burdened with more than was necessary.

What unsettled me most was their relationship with time. They had no word for *"yesterday."* Everything they expressed was tied to the present, to the immediacy of lived experience. I wondered what it would be like to live without the constant nostalgia or anticipation that past and future bring. Did that mean they were always here and now? The thought intrigued me deeply.

And then there was the sound. At times, their voices seemed to fade, transforming into whistles that were almost musical, which they used for hunting or communicating through the thick forest. Sometimes they hummed words, as if the language itself transformed into a song. I felt clumsy and insignificant, trying to grasp something that was as natural to them as a heartbeat.

The most astonishing part was their cultural richness: every word was tied to an ecological and spiritual worldview. If they spoke of a fish, they didn't just name it, they included its relationship to the river and to other animals. When I sat with Shihu around a campfire, he told me that in their worldview, every living being possessed a *"breath of the forest."* That belief, with no equivalent word in Portuguese, was expressed in a couple of syllables I could barely pronounce at first. I recorded the term and realized there wasn't a single comparable sound in my mother tongue: it was a kind of *double flap* produced at the back of the mouth, unlike anything I had ever heard.

As I noted these findings in my notebook, I realized it would be far more effective to use my phone camera and the Genostories app. That way, I wouldn't just preserve the audio but also Shihu's gestures, the subtle intonation of the word, the atmosphere around the fire, and the silent nods of other elders. In this way, the linguistic experience would be whole.

At first, I faced the difficulty of poor reception in the area, which meant I often had to record and then wait days to upload the material once I returned to a town with decent signal. Still, the drive to rescue those linguistic treasures pushed me to persist, paddling rivers and climbing hills just to find a flicker of connectivity.

Little by little, my project took shape: a digital library focused on the Pirahã language within Genostories. There I planned to upload short clips, tagged with keywords (for example, *"ecosystem," "respect for the river," "oral traditions," "pirahãword14,"* etc.), so anyone could find them and learn. But it wasn't just a dictionary, it also included stories and lessons told in the native tongue.

One of those stories was the fable of balance with the river, told by an elder named Kiri. According to him, during droughts the elders taught the community not to overfish or pollute the waters, because if the river was offended, the fish would vanish and the people would suffer. That kind of reflection, with its deep environmental meaning, could serve as a *grain of sand* for today's humanity, so intent on exploiting resources without thinking of future generations. In the same vein, a local proverb stated: *"The tree that gives shade also deserves your shade,"* suggesting a reciprocal relationship with nature.

I filmed Kiri reciting it with his particular intonation, two tones, high and low, and then he added: *"This is how my grandparents taught me to love the forest."* For me, that was a treasure no dictionary of cold definitions could ever hold. It was a cultural heartbeat passed from mouth to mouth, at risk of extinction if it wasn't recorded. Uploading it to Genostories transformed that heartbeat into a universal archive, free from the geographical limits of the Amazon.

Not everything was idyllic. At times, my intentions seemed *"invasive"* to some members of the tribe, especially the younger ones, curiously enough, who distrusted a foreigner arriving with electronic devices and recorders. They argued, not without reason, that many previous visitors had promised help or benefits and then vanished, leaving only broken promises behind. It took me weeks to show them that I wasn't there to exploit their culture, but to preserve it.

On top of that, I faced logistical limitations: there were no paved roads, and often I had to fund helicopter trips to reach even more remote areas where elders still spoke the purest dialectal variants. Money was scarce, and the university sponsoring me wasn't exactly rolling in funds. So I had to improvise: I made connections with NGOs interested in protecting Amazonian languages, secured donations in exchange for sharing updates on my research, and so on.

Even with that support, I slept in hammocks, endured relentless insect bites, and often faced the frustration of being unable to upload files to Genostories for days due to lack of signal. Still, every time I saw an elder's face light up as they recounted a story in their mother tongue, I remembered why I was there: the loss of a language is not merely the disappearance of words, but the disappearance of an entire way of seeing the world.

Among the many legends I managed to record, one in particular struck me: the tale of the *"Celestial Anaconda."* In this people's worldview, the anaconda didn't just inhabit rivers and lagoons; according to myth, there is a sacred anaconda that lives in the *"roof of the world,"* that is, in the sky, guarding the balance between the forest and the heavens. An elder told me that in ancient times, when people failed to honor nature, the anaconda would descend and unleash storms to cleanse the earth.

The story involved several characters: a curious boy who climbed a magical tree to find the anaconda's eyes, a shaman who interpreted the serpent's dreams, and a wise elder woman who knew the exact words to soothe the wrath of that mythical being. Every phrase they used to describe the anaconda carried tonal shifts and elongated vowels that were difficult for me to capture. The elder laughed at my clumsy attempts to repeat the syllables.

Recording this tale in Genostories not only immortalized the legend but also gave the community a way for their young people to revisit it whenever they wished, with the real voice and cadence of a wise elder. It was wonderful to see the reaction of some teenagers who, upon watching the video, said: *"I didn't know our stories were so exciting."* I saw a spark of pride in their eyes, as if their dormant identity had awakened before the beauty of their heritage.

Through Genostories and my research, I realized that the arrival of modernity in the Amazon was not new, but its impact grew stronger with each passing year. Some kids preferred to watch pop videos on the internet rather than listen to myths in their own language; Portuguese swept through with its practicality for finding work in the city. And how could one blame them? For many, it was the way out of poverty.

Yet, in my interviews with the youth, I came across cases of young people who, thanks to my project, had developed an interest in learning their grandparents' language. One of them, Ñaki, told me that after seeing the story of the Celestial Anaconda in his own dialect, he realized it wasn't mere superstition but a reflection of wisdom and respect for nature. From then on, Ñaki began asking the elders for more stories and even offered to help me subtitle the videos into Portuguese. That was a ray of hope, because modernity doesn't necessarily have to annihilate tradition, it can also serve as a bridge to revalue it.

Of course, there were always those quick to call me an idealist. *"Do you really think an app will solve the extinction of languages?"* they would say, with that half-mocking tone that pierces your patience.

Maybe not, I thought, but that didn't stop me. Every time someone asked that question, I would reply calmly:

"Maybe it won't save anything, but at least it will leave a testimony, a trace of what we were, of what we lost, of what we can still become."

Because, for me, every word, every myth I recorded was far more than just data on a screen. It was an act of resistance, a silent battle against the cultural homogenization devouring everything in its path. Languages weren't just words: they were entire worlds. Worlds that deserved to be preserved, even if only in the memory of those willing to listen.

The formal study of the Pirahã language offered endless surprises. The absence of numerals left me astonished: how did they manage fishing or trade if they couldn't count fish or goods? I discovered they used approximate terms to designate one or two, and everything else was grouped under *"many."* In an external market, this might be seen as a major disadvantage, but in their own context, it was functional and logical. They didn't accumulate, didn't trade in large sums, lived day by day with no more than what was needed to survive.

Phonetically, I found peculiarities such as women substituting a voiceless alveolar sound with a glottal aspiration, something entirely unheard of in Portuguese. And there was that *double flap* in the tongue I had been told about. Recording it in Genostories was a challenge, as it had no equivalent in any alphabet I knew. I decided to log a note with an approximate phonetic label and add a video commentary: *"This sound doesn't exist in most languages of the world; it's a true phonetic treasure."*

The fact that they used five communicative channels, spoken, whistled, hummed, shouted, and musical, made me smile: a community with such apparent simplicity possessed incredible complexity in how it transmitted messages. I uploaded examples of each channel to the app, with the description: *"Watch how this woman hums her speech so as not to scare away the hunting animals; this is how they communicate deep in the forest."*

To deepen my documentation, I needed to stay longer in the Pirahã village, something I knew would not be easy. FUNAI, always cautious, had granted me an initial permit, but the idea of an extended stay complicated matters. Each day I spent there seemed to add new layers to an already dense bureaucracy. There were tensions with some officials; their looks, heavy with suspicion, said everything before they even spoke.

"Aren't you afraid that publishing these myths and words on the internet could lead to their misuse by people with commercial interests?" they asked me more than once.

It was a valid question, though I couldn't help feeling it as a personal challenge.

I took a deep breath before answering, trying to remain calm.

"That's precisely my fear as well. That's why my goal is preservation, not exploitation. It's not about turning their culture into a showcase."

I watched them carefully, trying to convey my sincerity.

"I have a very clear code of ethics. I would never reveal anything the community considered sacred or secret."

Even so, I could feel the weight of their doubts in their gestures. Could I blame them? No. History was full of foreigners who promised to protect what they later exploited. All I could do was prove that my words carried real weight.

After long discussions and compromises, I managed to stay for several months, on the condition that I respect the privacy of certain rituals and not force the recording of events the community wanted to keep private. That negotiation felt fair to me: it wasn't about showing everything, but about finding a balance between my drive to document and the safeguarding of their identity.

Thus, I gradually gained more acceptance in the village. I realized that trust is built through mutual respect, more than through legal approvals.

One of my most moving memories was the afternoon when Shihu called me to his hut to tell me a very ancient myth, which, according to him, only a handful of elders still knew. He mentioned, *"this story will disappear with me,"* hinting that none of his children or grandchildren had fully learned it. It was a myth about the *"spirit of the jaguar"* that guarded the hunters' dreams, describing different dream phases in which one had to overcome moral trials to be worthy of catching their prey.

I recorded it on video using Genostories, with a makeshift microphone to capture Shihu's low, trembling voice. When he finished his tale, a sacred silence filled the room. He looked at me with moist eyes and said something in his language, later translating into Portuguese: *"Now it will not be lost."* A shiver of gratitude ran through me: this was the essence of the mission I had fought for. That oral piece, with its worldview full of nuances, would live on and could inspire young locals and even strangers across the world.

On Genostories, I tagged the video as *"Shihu jaguar tale"* and added a brief description: *"The final transmission of a myth combining morality, dream rituals, and the jaguar as a symbol of respect and fear."* I hit publish with a mix of anticipation and curiosity. Would anyone truly grasp what lay behind those words?

I didn't have to wait long. The very next day, notifications began to pour in. Comments from people in Europe, Asia, and Latin America flooded the video: *"I don't understand the language, but it feels like music." "How can such an ancient story resonate so strongly in the present?"* Even subtitled in Portuguese, the musicality of Pirahã had captivated people who had never even heard of this culture.

As I read through the comments, a smile spread across my face. Shihu, sitting beside me, watched with curiosity.

"Does this really stir so much interest outside of here?" Shihu asked me, his voice tinged with both skepticism and pride.

I showed him the messages on the screen, translating them patiently. His eyes, usually calm, gleamed for a moment.

"Then let the voices of my ancestors travel," he said with a solemnity that sent a shiver through me.

In that instant, I understood that Genostories was far more than just a tool: it was a bridge, a channel that not only preserved but also amplified the stories that time and forgetfulness threatened to erase.

The hardest part of my documentation work wasn't just learning the complexities of the Pirahã language, but also finding a way to translate that linguistic richness into something others could understand without diluting its essence. For the Pirahã, their language didn't need to be written. It was a river of words flowing naturally from generation to generation, shaping daily life without the need for formal grammatical rules. But for outsiders watching my videos on Genostories, or for future linguists, I knew I had to structure it somehow.

With patience and a notebook full of annotations, I designed a rudimentary system of phonetic transcription. Each phrase I captured amazed me with its precision and simplicity. Their sentences were always direct, free of unnecessary adornments, as if mirroring the same clarity with which they lived. But what truly fascinated me was their system of *evidentiality*, something I had never encountered before. Every statement had to indicate whether what was said was seen, heard, or imagined, and their words shifted to mark these distinctions. It was as though their sentences were doors into their perception of reality, guiding you toward what they had experienced firsthand or what existed only in their minds.

As I explored further, I realized their connection with the senses was embedded even in their grammar. They could modify words with small suffixes to show whether something had been seen with their own eyes, heard in the distance, or even dreamed in the stillness of the night. These details not only made their language unique but also profoundly human, imbued with a sensitivity that seemed to have been lost in many other tongues.

I uploaded my first tutorials to Genostories with a touch of skepticism. I mixed my explanations with video clips of the Pirahã people using their language: a mother calling her child by the river, an elder telling a myth by the fire, or a hunter humming words so softly they were almost inaudible as he pointed toward the forest. It was like a live grammar course, and to my surprise, it didn't take long before messages began arriving. Universities in Brazil and abroad wanted access to the material, eager to study this unique language.

With each new request, I felt the weight of a greater responsibility. Under no circumstances could I betray the trust of the Pirahã community. There were aspects of their language and culture that were sacred, secrets not meant to be shared with the outside world. Before publishing any video, I reviewed every fragment with meticulous care, cutting out anything that might reveal more than they had agreed to share.

Deep down, I understood that my work was not merely documentary: it was a delicate act of balance between preserving, sharing, and respecting. Each word, each sentence I recorded was more than a sound, it was a fragment of a world struggling not to disappear.

The greatest reward came when a handful of young Pirahã began watching themselves in the videos and listening to their grandparents' stories through the Genostories app. Some laughed at the idea of their voices being replayed on a phone, since they weren't very familiar with technology. Others, however, were left wide-eyed, realizing that what they said in their own tongue was reaching out into the wider world.

A young man named Tiba confided to me:

"Until now, I thought my language was only useful for chatting in the village. Today I see it can spark curiosity and inspiration beyond here."

Soon after, Tiba wanted to learn more of the traditional vocabulary his grandfather knew, and he became my main assistant. He would come with me to the elders' houses, acting as a bridge between my explanations in Portuguese and the variations of his dialect, and he laughed like a child every time a new comment appeared on Genostories.

"Look, João, someone from Tokyo wrote that they loved our myth!" Tiba exclaimed, his eyes sparkling with excitement.

That proud gleam in Tiba's eyes confirmed for me that technology, when handled with respect, can be an ally in reconnecting younger generations with their heritage.

Of course, not all of the youth were as enthusiastic. Some preferred to head to the city in search of work, adopting Portuguese as their main language and leaving their birth tongue behind. But if even a few rekindled their interest, it was already a step forward. I knew that the survival of a language depends on intergenerational transmission. That's why I made sure the most engaging stories, animal fables and humorous anecdotes, were the first ones uploaded to Genostories, to draw people in with the beauty of their own culture.

In the final stage of my project in the village, I spent a couple of months working on improving connectivity. With the help of a couple of NGOs, we installed a small solar panel and a basic satellite router so the community could have limited but steady internet access. They were able to watch the videos we uploaded and read the comments from people around the world. That interaction was a revolution for many, their first real glimpse beyond the forest.

One afternoon, as we rested under the shade of a tree, Tiba looked at me with a mix of curiosity and emotion.

"I never thought that people in the city or in other countries would care about what we say in our language," he said with a sincerity that moved me deeply.

It wasn't unusual for Indigenous communities to feel relegated, almost invisible, reduced to little more than ornaments for tourist fairs or cultural clichés. But something had shifted. Knowing that people on other continents were fascinated by their grammar and legends gave them more than curiosity: it gave them pride. And with that pride came renewed hope. It was as if these stories were not only a link to their ancestors but also a bridge toward a more equitable future.

When the time came to leave, I packed my things with a mix of satisfaction and melancholy. I knew my work wasn't complete, but I was certain I had planted something valuable. I promised to return or at least to keep uploading the material the elders had entrusted to me in recordings. More than that, I hoped the responsibility would pass into the hands of the Pirahã themselves, empowered to continue recording their words and sharing them with the *"great digital world."*

For me, it was a modest but real triumph. The seed of continuity had been planted, and with some luck, it would grow strong in the hands of those who had discovered in their own voices a reason to look forward.

I've often said that *"the loss of a language is not just the disappearance of words, but of a unique way of seeing the world and of teaching us how to live better."* From my encounters with the people of the forest, I can confirm that every linguistic expression holds a prism through which to understand nature, family, and transcendence. I don't exaggerate when I say that if we let these languages die, we extinguish the plurality of human wisdom itself.

What Genostories gave me was a vehicle so that, in 2025, ancient voices could resonate beyond the village. An elder telling the myth of the Celestial Anaconda, a shaman explaining how hunting ceremonies were decided these could now be seen and heard by someone in São Paulo, in Madrid, or in Tokyo. That universality is a gift of technology I refuse to underestimate. At the same time, it troubles me to think how much would have been lost had these testimonies been collected any later. Every elder who passes away is like the destruction of an irreplaceable library.

I left the Pirahã community carrying in my backpack a bundle of memories and several hard drives filled with recordings. As I paddled my canoe back toward the last port with connectivity, I reflected: I had lived immersed in a world that at first felt foreign, and yet I had never felt more alive. Yes, I had endured insect bites and stress, but the reward was immense: to witness a language in all its singularity and to help ensure it would not vanish into nothingness.

When I arrived in Manaus, the largest city in the region, I felt strangely out of place. After weeks immersed in the calm of the Pirahã village, the bright lights and the city's bustle felt almost unreal.

I checked into a small guesthouse and opened my laptop to upload the last pending interviews.

Comments began appearing almost immediately on Genostories. Some people were amazed by the complexities of the language, others curious about its grammatical structures, and many more enchanted by the myths I had documented. What surprised me most, however, were the messages from local people: *"I didn't know my own state had so much cultural richness."* Those words made me smile, but they also made me think about how often we overlook what we have right next to us.

I felt euphoric. That had been the goal from the very beginning: to open a window and show, to anyone who cared to look, the magnificence of a language that, in the eyes of modernity, might seem insignificant. But I knew it wasn't. Every word, every story, was a living testimony of a world that still had much to teach.

I hold on to a wish: that in a few years, it will be the Pirahã themselves who handle the devices, record their ceremonies, and upload their stories without relying on outside intermediaries like me. Maybe a grown-up Tiba will be the one in charge of keeping that *timeline* on Genostories alive, ensuring that the flame never goes out.

With the assurance that the community had taken ownership of its own linguistic documentation, I felt ready to move on to another adventure with a different endangered people. But I always keep in my heart the certainty that, thanks to Genostories, that village would not be just another case of a vanished language, but an example of resilience and reconnection for its youth. And if I contributed in any way, I am glad: it was never about being a savior, but about providing a bridge.

My hope is that when people in modern cities, who sometimes believe the whole world is reduced to English, Spanish, or Portuguese, stumble upon these videos on Genostories, they experience the wondrous shock of discovering that other linguistic and cultural realities exist. That every word is a way of thinking. That not having numerals doesn't make a society "less intelligent," but perhaps freer from the chains of accumulation.

Being able to share this chapter with a wider audience is an honor, because it reclaims the truth that technological evolution is not an enemy of tradition. On the contrary, it can be its greatest ally, if used with respect and consent. I never tire of repeating the final lesson: *"The loss of a language is not just the disappearance of words, but of a unique way of seeing the world and of teaching us how to live better."* Without those languages, humanity loses fragments of wisdom that took millennia to be forged.

These months have been intense: canoes cutting through rivers, helicopters with scarce funds, deadly mosquitos, endless paperwork with FUNAI, and the infinite patience needed to earn the trust of the elders. But in the end, the task of creating a digital library on Genostories for the Pirahã language confirmed to me that the work of a linguist is not limited to writing a dictionary, it is about planting in people's hearts the idea that every word, every legend, contains a universe. It moves me to think that, in the future, people will remember that in 2025 there was a certain João Mendes who, with nothing but a phone, a microphone, and sheer determination, ventured into the Amazon to record myths and words that, had they not been preserved, might have vanished into silence.

This is my testimony, and I share it with pride, knowing it goes beyond me. The Amazon will continue to shelter life and languages, and if my small contribution helped prolong the existence of one of them, I feel immensely grateful. To those who read these words, I ask: wherever there is a language at risk, remember that we all lose if it disappears, because with it vanishes an irreplaceable worldview. May this flame of love for cultural diversity be kindled in your hearts as well.

The story of João Mendes, that Brazilian linguist born in 1980, deeply captivated me when I found it during my explorations on Genostories, here in this 2085 where uniformity prevails and few remember that the Amazon was once a place brimming with languages, songs, and legends. His account made me realize that humanity's true treasure lies not only in our cutting-edge technology or our scientific achievements, but also, and perhaps even more so, in the diversity and complexity of our voices, of our ways of naming and understanding the world.

That phrase João repeated time and again: "The loss of a language is not only the disappearance of words, but of a unique way of seeing the world and of teaching us how to live better," still resonates powerfully, even in this futuristic society where we hardly remember finitude. May his testimony, preserved here, serve to remind us that, no matter how far we advance, the root of the human spirit is nourished by its many tongues and visions, and that with each forgotten word, a piece of ancestral wisdom vanishes.

Let us hope that, in this 2085, we do not let the flame of curiosity or the spark of empathy die out toward those who still carry fragments of history in their voices. If one day uniformity threatens to consume us completely, let us remember João Mendes, the Guardian of Lost Languages, to inspire us to continue protecting and celebrating the linguistic richness that defines us as human beings.

Griot 2085

THE MAGIC OF THE DEAD

In the vast ocean of forgotten memories, recovered and preserved in Genostories, I found the testimony of Sarah Jennings, an American tourist who, in 1996, decided to embark on a journey to Mexico in search of a new horizon. I, Griot 2085, live in an era where death is no longer felt so close nor so feared; even so, Sarah's narratives reminded me that throughout human history, death was always an essential part of the experience of life.

As I reviewed her recordings and read her reflections, I was moved by the way in which the Day of the Dead transformed her own understanding of loss and grief. Her encounter with luminous altars, marigold flowers, and sugar skulls showed her that death can also be seen as a reunion, full of color and warmth. By immersing herself in the Mexican tradition, Sarah found the peace she so longed for after the death of her mother and the end of her marriage.

And now, in publishing her story here, I trust that her discovery will serve as inspiration for those of us who, from within this future of ours, have almost forgotten finitude and the comfort that comes from honoring those who are no longer with us. I invite you to discover "The Magic of the Dead," a chapter about the eternal love that persists beyond departure.

Griot 2085

My name is Sarah Jennings. I was born in 1952 and grew up in a small town near the Blue Ridge Mountains, on the East Coast of the United States. It was 1996 when, at forty-four years old, I had the courage (or the madness, depending on how you see it) to embark on a trip to Mexico with no plan and no companions. I had just gone through a divorce, and my mother had died only a few months earlier. My world felt empty, saturated with grief and with the sensation that my life had come to a complete stop.

One day, while cleaning my son's room, I spun the globe that stood there, an old globe, its names faded, and stopped it with my finger at random. The spot it landed on was a blurry point on the map of Mexico. Between tears and a touch of courage, I decided that's where I would go.

I had no idea what awaited me in that country, nor could I imagine that my arrival would coincide with the celebration that would impact me most: *Día de los Muertos*. Years later, in 2025, I feel the need to leave this testimony on Genostories, so that others may understand how a tradition foreign to my culture helped me reconcile with death, and ultimately, with life. Today, at seventy-three, I look back at the recordings I uploaded to that digital platform, and I'm moved to see the woman I was in 1996: a disoriented tourist, devastated by grief over her personal losses, who was profoundly transformed by living within the magic of a festival that honors those who are gone but also shines in the laughter and the light of those of us who are still here.

Before I dive into the details of that journey, I want to emphasize the lesson that marked me forever:

"Death is not the end, but a bridge toward the memories and the eternal love we share with those who are no longer here."

That phrase sums up my entire experience in Mexico and the deep reflection that, decades later, moves me to share this story. Perhaps, for many, death and mourning are topics we'd rather avoid, but back in 1996 I discovered that sometimes, embracing finitude can grant us a fuller vision of life.

I had spent months plunged into a kind of lethargy: my divorce had been painful, especially because my son who was then at university, saw me as fragile and couldn't help. My mother, who had been my confidante, had died of a degenerative disease. Her passing left a tearing silence that repeated itself every dusk in my house. I lived in a quiet suburb where everyone seemed to have steady lives, while I felt like a purposeless ghost.

It was in the middle of that gray routine that I found the old globe covered in dust. I spun it hard, wanting a chance to point me somewhere. "Europe? Asia? Africa?" I didn't think much. My finger landed on Mexico and I said to myself,

"Why not?"

That small spark of impulse was enough to break my inertia. Within weeks I sold some furniture, entrusted my home to a neighbor, and bought an open-date plane ticket. Knowing almost no Spanish apart from a *gracias* or *hola*, I flew to Mexico City. I had the vague idea of seeing archaeological ruins and beaches. I had barely researched the country's customs or festivals, unaware that my arrival would coincide with the last days of October and the imminence of *Día de los Muertos*, celebrated on November 1 and 2. It was a twist of fate that led me, unknowingly, to a discovery that would shake my soul.

I remember landing at Mexico City International Airport: the noise, the crowds, a language I only half understood, the frantic speed of the cars. I stepped out with my suitcase and felt overwhelmed;

it was my first time in a country so different from my own. I tried to piece together a phrase in Spanish, but only managed nervous smiles. I asked about safe taxis in my halting English, and a driver agreed to take me to a hostel in the historic center, where I planned to stay a couple of days before looking for quieter places.

At the hostel I met several tourists: Germans, French, Italians, all eager to witness the muertos festivities. I was stunned.

"*Muertos festival?*" I asked in amazement.

A French fellow explained, in halting English, that every year at the beginning of November many people traveled to Mexico to see the colorful altars and the *Día de los Muertos* celebrations. It sounded chilling to think of celebrating death instead of mourning it, but that contradiction, celebrating what I had considered gloomy, intrigued me.

"Maybe it's an opportunity to understand my own grief," I thought. Instead of sticking to my plan of excursions, I decided to stay a few extra days. Two Mexicans I met there recommended a small village in Michoacán, where the celebrations were very traditional. I got on a night bus bound for a picturesque lakeside town, not imagining what I was about to see.

I arrived at dawn, wrapped in mist and a slight bone-deep chill. From inside the houses came the smell of sweet bread and hot chocolate. I stepped down from the bus, dragging my suitcase over muddy ground, and ran into an impromptu market full of intensely orange marigold flowers and calaveritas de azúcar[1] with names written on their foreheads. I felt a shiver at the thought of my own name on a skull. Someone spoke to me in rudimentary English to explain that those calaveritas were often personalized with the names of the dead or of the living as a way of "playing" with death.

---

1 *Sugar skulls for Día de los Muertos.*

The stalls displayed skull masks, brightly colored shredded paper, candles of different sizes, incense, and a wide variety of dishes: mole[2], tamales[3], pan de muerto[4]... I was amazed at the display of color and the music blaring from some speakers. People moved with energy,

laughing and joking, offering me bread or a calaverita.

"Ma'am, would you like something?" they asked kindly. "Are you a foreigner?"

I found it shocking to see a festive atmosphere around a celebration devoted to death. I thought, "How can they be so happy talking about death?" My mindset, where death was taboo, wavered. At the same time, I was fascinated by the idea that in this *other world* death could be filled with color and smiles. I took photos with my disposable camera and, without knowing it, a new spark began to light inside me.

I asked where I could stay and someone pointed me to a small, family-run, welcoming inn. I checked in and met the owner, Doña Marina, who spoke a little English after having lived for a while in the United States. She welcomed me with a warm hug.

"Welcome, Sarah. You'll feel at home here," she said in English with a gentle accent. "You arrived at the perfect moment. Tonight we begin setting up the ofrendas to receive the dead. Tomorrow is a very special day."

She explained that her family, year after year, dedicates an altar to their deceased loved ones, placing marigold flowers, candles, photographs, and each person's favorite dishes.

---

2 *Rich Mexican sauce blending cultures.*
3 *Corn dough wrapped in leaves and steamed.*
4 *Sweet bread for Día de los Muertos.*

"You're going to see a parade of smells, flavors, and colors," she added. "Here we don't cry, we sing to welcome those who return from the other life."

Inside, I kept wondering, "How is it possible to celebrate death?" Yet that joy felt oddly comforting.

As I walked through the town square, a group of children with skull-painted faces ran by shouting,

"¡Mictecacihuatl[5]!"

I laughed softly. One of the children came up and offered me

a small piece of pan de muerto with little dough bones on top. I accepted, it was delicious and fluffy.

Soon after, I felt a tap on my shoulder. When I turned, I saw a middle-aged man with a mustache and hat, accompanied by his wife and daughter.

"Good afternoon," they said, and I tried to answer in my poor Spanish. I told them I was American and wanted to learn about the *muertos* festivities. They introduced themselves as Roberto, his wife María, and their daughter Natalia, about twelve years old. With limited English, they invited me to see their family ofrenda[6] and explained that in Mexico it was common for neighbors and visitors to share that moment. Although I felt a little self-conscious, their smiles put me at ease.

They took me to their home, on a narrow street with pastel-colored walls. When I entered, I smelled something sweet and floral. In the living room I found an altar decorated with shredded paper in purple and orange. There were candles, framed photographs, a glass of water, calaveritas de azúcar with names, and food. They explained

---

5 *Aztec queen of the underworld.*
6 *Altar to welcome ancestral spirits.*

the symbolism of each element: the marigold flowers guide the dead with their color and scent; the candles represent the soul of each loved one; the photographs help remember those who return in these days; the food gives them the aroma and essence of their favorite dishes; and the glass of water soothes the souls' thirst on their journey.

They looked at me with compassion.

"Do you have someone you would like to honor?" María asked.

I nodded, crying a little, and told them in my broken Spanish that my mother had died a few months earlier. Then they offered me a small space on their altar to place a photo of my mother, if I had one. I didn't carry any, but it was enough to write her name or bring something symbolic. It was a very moving moment: I felt welcomed

as part of their family, crying and remembering my mother in a home that was not my own.

That day I understood the true meaning of solidarity, and that it goes far beyond the color of one's skin. The family hugged me and offered me a veladora[7] to light in memory of my mother. It was so intimate and comforting that I forgot I was the stranger tourist. I felt like an orphaned daughter finding solace in the warmth of another family's home.

Night fell and the whole town turned into a luminous festival. The streets were carpeted with marigold petals, every house displayed an ofrenda, and people wore traditional clothes mixed with skull costumes. Children ran around asking for sweets, and at times they were invited to sample pan de muerto or tamales. A group of musicians played rancheras, ballads and lively sounds right in the street, as if sorrow or crying had no place in that scene.

---

7 *Candles used in altars or prayers.*

Walking those streets was a mystical experience: candles lit everywhere, skull-painted faces that, far from frightening, invited knowing smiles. The air was thick with incense, and at every turn new lights and colors appeared. I stopped before a huge communal ofrenda with a giant portrait of illustrious people who had died; people laid flowers and veladoras while laughing and chatting. I felt a cultural shock:

"How can they be so happy talking about death?"

My Western view where death was taboo and solemn, wavered. I understood that *Día de los Muertos* was not a mass funeral but a celebration of life through remembrance. Death was represented by calaveras and catrinas[8], yes, but with an ironic touch that humanized it. Under the night light, I witnessed processions

toward the panteón[9] with food and music to share with the dead. I joined a group, full of curiosity. Arriving at the cemetery, the sight struck me: hundreds of candles burning, families dining beside the graves, talking, crying and laughing at the same time.

A man approached me and handed me a bolillo[10] and a hot coffee.

"For you to warm up. Welcome to our celebration."

I accepted, feeling my heart expand with that collective brotherhood. I shed some tears, remembering my mother and wishing I had a place like that to honor her with music and laughter instead of only sorrow. It was a decisive moment. Suddenly, part of the accumulated pain slipped away and I stopped feeling so alone in my grief.

---

8 *Elegant skeleton figures symbolizing death.*
9 *Cemetery*
10 *Mexican bread rolls often used in ofrendas.*

Roberto and María's family invited me to spend the rest of the evening with them. I joined their ritual: they burned copal[11] and the fragrant smoke drifted around us. They lit one candle for each deceased person they remembered, and I held the little veladora meant for my mother. When I placed it on the altar, my eyes welled up.

"Mom, I wish you could see this," I whispered, with a strange warmth in my chest.

The little girl, Natalia, picked up a calaverita de azúcar with my name piped in icing and offered it to me in a low voice:

"It's for you."

I admit that at first the idea of seeing my name on a skull overwhelmed me, but I understood that it wasn't an omen of death, but an invitation to be part of the celebration, to "die symbolically" and be reborn with that acceptance of the inevitable. I tasted the sweetness of the skull on my tongue and felt a breath of consolation

in my soul. "Maybe death isn't the monster I imagined," I thought.

I stayed there for a long while, listening to the family's stories about their grandparents and deceased siblings, full of nostalgia and affection at once. The ofrenda became a reunion, erasing the boundary between the living and the dead. Some swore they felt the presence of their loved ones that night. Could it be possible? I would love to believe my mother was by my side, smiling to see me at peace and letting me remember her without breaking apart.

The next day I met a local artist, Marco, who painted skulls and catrinas on canvas. I noticed the beauty with which he fused the macabre of bones with soft colors and floral motifs. I asked him why he represented death that way, and he answered without hesitation:

---

11 Incense used to guide spirits.

"Death is part of the cycle of life, not something separate. It's beautiful because it reminds us we are ephemeral and pushes us to live more fully."

He took me to his studio, a small space with walls covered in sketches, canvases and brushes. The smell of fresh paint mingled with soft music in the background. He showed me some works that pictured skeletons dressed in finery, mocking the idea that riches save anyone from death.

"Death unites us all," he added, "and laughing at it is our way of making it less fearful."

I studied his paintings as the memory of my mother came back to life. I thought that if at her funeral we had embraced part of this vision, perhaps I wouldn't have had to face so much silence and darkness at home. Maybe my mourning would have found a gentler channel.

As a traveler in 1996, I felt the need to record my impressions. I didn't have a smartphone or anything like it, just a video camera and VHS tapes in my bag. I filmed the ofrendas, conversations with families, the bustle of the streets, and even recorded myself reflecting:

"Mom, I wish you could see this. It's full of life, even though it's *Día de los Muertos*."

At night I watched the tapes at the inn and was moved by how warm people were at every turn. I remembered joining the cemetery procession, my hand trembling as I placed a candle on a stranger's grave, yet feeling it as an act of universal fellowship. I was vulnerable, yes, but I also found myself strong in a ritual that turned death into a path to remembrance.

I marveled at how the community not only accepted me but made me feel part of their extended family. I learned that *Día de los Muertos* is not lived in solitude or locked in tears, but by opening your door so the memory of the absent can reunite with the joy of the living. That conception struck me as powerful and healing.

The night of November 1st arrived, the date when the celebration intensified. I joined a group of neighbors heading to a cemetery on the outskirts of town. The path was lit by torches and paper lanterns, and each family carried flowers, food, and drink. I was astonished to see that they weren't going to grieve in silence but to share time with their dead, talking as if those who had gone could hear them.

Arriving at the cemetery, the sight took my breath away: a sea of headstones covered in candles, marigold flowers, and offerings. Families spread tablecloths with their deceased loved ones' favorite foods, mixing laughter with anecdotes about those who had left. Some played guitar or sang songs that, far from being mournful, had a serene, affectionate air. It wasn't chaotic noise but an atmosphere of peace and joy that moved me. It was there that I better understood the essence of *Día de los Muertos*: a symbolic reunion in which love overcomes pain.

I returned to the hostel at dawn, my heart full of positive energy. In my country, death had been a cold sorrow; in Mexico, I felt the warmth of a transcendent reunion. In the days that followed, I continued learning the festival's details. I learned that November 1st was dedicated to deceased children and November 2nd to adults, although in many places they were combined. I also learned about the famous catrinas, created to satirize the upper class's notion of immortality. I saw parades with women dressed as elegant skulls, smiling at death and celebrating life.

The food fascinated me completely. I tried calabaza en tacha[12], pan de muerto, champurrado[13], and of course mole. Each dish,

---

12 *Candied pumpkin dessert.*
13 *Thick chocolate drink with masa.*

they said, carried symbolism and became part of the offering. They explained that when the dead return, they enjoy the aroma and essence of those foods. A woman asked me,

"Isn't it beautiful to think that our dead remain near and dine with us?"

That thought felt comforting, almost poetic, because it reduced death to a mere parenthesis instead of a definitive goodbye. There were touching moments when people remembered their dead with a tear on the cheek and a funny anecdote on their lips. In that way they turned the tragedy of death into stories that kept the presence of those who had gone alive.

That 1996, my mourning over the divorce and my mother, found an outlet I hadn't imagined: Mexican spirituality, which confronted death with love and humor, gave me back my strength. I had gone seeking a change of scenery to find quiet, but I found much more: an inner metamorphosis. I learned that death could be celebrated, not with frivolity, but with a living remembrance and an affection that never dies.

I began to feel my heart lighter. One day I lit a veladora and placed a flower beside my mother's photo which I had ordered by mail to keep with me, and instead of weeping over her loss, I gave thanks. It was a radical change: I moved from lamenting her absence

to honoring her existence and the influence she had had on my life. I stayed in that village longer than planned, helping where I could and, for the first time in a long while, feeling that there was hope in my future. *Día de los Muertos*, ironically, inspired me to come back to life.

After two weeks immersed in their culture and traditions, I returned to the United States. I said goodbye to the family that had sheltered me, to the hostel friends, to Roberto, María and their daughter Natalia, who had given me the chance to place my mother's name on their ofrenda. I promised to come back a year or two later, because I already felt *Día de los Muertos* had become part of my own spirit.

The farewell was bittersweet, carrying photos, VHS tapes and a heart transformed. I boarded the plane certain I was not the same Sarah Jennings who had left home broken. I understood that death was no longer the unbreakable beast that had taken my mother, but a bridge toward our affections.

In 2025, at seventy-three and with a calmer mind, I reviewed those old tapes I'd digitized some time ago. I reunited with the Sarah of 1996: hollow-eyed, sad, and full of wonder at every Mexican color and song. Then I discovered Genostories, that living archive where people kept memories and reflections. I decided to upload my *Día de Muertos* experience, thinking that if it had healed me, it might also help others in their own grief.

I began selecting clips from my videos and converted them to a modern format. I uploaded everything in chronological order, narrating how I arrived in Mexico, my surprise at the festival, the family that took me in, and how my feelings blossomed. I tagged each clip with *Día de Muertos, 1996, Mexican traditions, mourning, and eternal love.* Soon I received comments from people all over the world, surprised by the story of an American tourist discovering the magic of honoring the dead.

Some thanked me for showing that death is not something to be feared but an opportunity to commemorate the life we shared with those who have gone. Others told me about their own losses and how the festival had helped them move forward. I was especially moved by the testimony of a young woman from Japan who had lost her sister and, after seeing my recordings, decided to set up a small ofrenda with flowers and food in her sister's honor. Inspired by the Mexican tradition but adapted to her culture. Then I understood that that random trip had a meaning far beyond my own experience.

Now, as I review my final recordings for Genostories, I reflect on the significance of that experience. I look at my photos in front of an altar full of candles and calaveritas, or in the cemetery illuminated by the moon, and I notice the serenity in my eyes. It was the first time I felt at peace with my mother's death and with my divorce. Ironically, in a place that celebrates death, I reclaimed my life.

The family who hosted me in 1996 wrote to me recently, reminding me that they still honor their dead with the same passion. They invited me to return, although my years and ailments make that difficult. I am grateful, at least, that technology allows us to stay in touch; they send me photos of their ofrenda every year. More than once they've again offered, from afar, to place my mother's photo on their ofrenda, a gesture of kinship.

That year, 1996, taught me to feel gratitude and showed me that death is less terrifying if we embrace it with tenderness, turning it into a reason to celebrate the life we shared with those we love. I understood that death is not the end, but a bridge toward the memories and the eternal love we share with those who are no longer here. Today, through my posts on Genostories, I wish to leave that message as part of my testament.

Among the sweetest anecdotes, I keep the image of Natalia, Roberto and María's daughter, offering me a calaverita de azúcar with my name on it. For me, that skull represented my fear of death, the question *what happens if I die and am forgotten?* and, at the same time, the recognition that we are all on the same journey. According to custom, when a person eats a calaverita with their name, they integrate death into their life without taboo. At first it shocked me, but then I smiled and accepted it with the festival's characteristic humor.

When I tasted the sweet, I realized that by eating that *representation* of my death I freed myself from the panic that haunted me. It was a symbolic gesture, but a crucial one. On Genostories I told that anecdote and many people reacted saying they never thought something so simple could hold so much philosophy. I replied that sometimes the greatest symbolic power comes from the simplest rituals.

Another thing that dazzled me was the sense of community. In my culture, death is typically handled privately, with short funerals and silent mourning. In contrast, during *Día de los Muertos* I discovered families opening their doors to strangers to share the beauty of their memory. I realized that by doing so the pain was shared, and one no longer felt orphaned or widowed in solitude. One became part of a great human family that understands existence's fragility and celebrates it.

I see it clearly in my videos: I was struck by the solidarity when several neighbors gathered to sing traditional songs and then asked me to speak about my mother's memory, even if in English, to include her in the communion of the dead. It was such a moving gesture that I shed tears of gratitude. I understood that you don't need to speak the same language to share the same humanity.

Now, at seventy-three, as I record this account, I wonder what would have become of me if I hadn't taken that plane in 1996. Perhaps I would still be carrying a quiet grudge against death for taking my mother, or with my heart shadowed by the divorce. But that random trip gave me a key: the key of a festival that reinterprets death as a loving reunion rather than an abyss with no return.

Over time, every November 2nd in my country I adopted my own version of an ofrenda. I light veladoras and place flowers, put a photo of my mother and add objects that remind me of her. I invite close friends to share photos of their deceased, and while we drink coffee or have cake, we talk about the good and bad anecdotes. It's a humble ritual, but it has served as a bridge for people who, like me, were seeking a way to honor their dead without locking themselves into depression.

Later I uploaded to Genostories not only the 1996 tapes but also the evolution of my ofrenda year after year. Some people tell me they did something similar at home, whether in the United States, Canada, or Australia, finding death not as an eternal goodbye but as a cycle in which memory keeps our loved ones alive. That fills me with pride and gratitude.

If you asked me to pick a decisive moment from that adventure, I would choose the night I sat, almost at midnight, in front of an altar at Roberto and María's house. Everything was silent except for the crackle of candles and the murmur of prayers. I decided to write my mother's name on a little slip of paper since I hadn't brought a photo, and I placed it on the altar. Through tears I whispered,

"Mom, I hope you are at peace. I swear that every time I remember you, I will do so with gratitude instead of sorrow."

It felt like shedding an enormous weight. My skin prickled and, for a moment, I thought I felt my mother's warmth. Maybe it was my imagination, or maybe that didn't matter; the essential thing was that when I opened my eyes I felt reconciled. I understood how *Día de los Muertos* works: a breach in which, for a few hours, our absent ones return to comfort us, and we remember that one day we will be on the other side as well. By accepting that circularity, fear dissolves.

In 1996 that event marked me to the core. Now, in 2025, I still confirm that time has not erased the intensity of that lesson. It's enough to evoke the orange hues of marigold, the calaveritas and the candles to feel peace. Thanks to Genostories, I keep the record of that magical moment when I discovered the *magic of the dead.*

As I close this video, I want to speak to you, wherever you are and whatever your background: perhaps you know *Día de los Muertos,* or perhaps you do not; maybe you treat death as a taboo or think you've mastered it. My message is that, despite the pain, death can connect with the deepest parts of what makes us human: memory and love. Don't underestimate the power of a ritual that though colorful or "folkloric" can be a balm for the soul.

In my culture I once believed death demanded silence and restraint, mourning behind closed doors. *Día de los Muertos* showed me that one can dance with sorrow, light it with candles, and yes, smile at the dead to tell them we remember them with gratitude. That lesson, which I thought belonged only to Mexican tradition, worked for me and can work for anyone facing loss.

As a woman who spent much of her life suffering from a divorce and the death of her mother, I can say that the *magic of the dead* is not witchcraft or superstition, but the magic of remembrance: a way to dress fear in color and let love transcend the grave. I hope my words resonate in your heart, and that next time the absence presses on you, you feel moved to light a candle, set a flower, and tell a joyful story about the person who is gone. Perhaps then you will feel less alone and discover your inner strength.

I reiterate the fundamental lesson that has accompanied me:

Death is not the end, but a bridge to the memories and the eternal love we share with those who are no longer here.

May this phrase accompany you in your darkest moments, and if someday you visit Mexico during *Día de los Muertos,* or adopt part of its ritual in your own culture, remember this traveler who, in 1996, arrived lost and found in that festival a way to reconcile with death, and therefore, with life.

Here is the chronicle of Sarah Jennings, who arrived in Mexico in 1996 after her mother's death and a devastating divorce, and found in Día de los Muertos a path to emotional healing. Reviewing her stories and watching the videos she uploaded to Genostories years later, I'm struck by the power of a cultural celebration capable of transforming the life of a stranger who came by pure chance. Among marigold flowers, sweet calaveritas, and illuminated altars, she discovered a balm for her grief.

Here in 2085, when so many realities have been homogenized and death seems more controlled by technology, Sarah's account serves as an essential reminder: in human history, death was not only an ending, but a moment of reunion with those who departed. That magia she speaks of is nothing more than the force of love and shared memory. Her lesson that death is a bridge, not an abyss, resonates now more powerfully than ever in a society that sometimes forgets what finitude means.

So I preserve her testimony, hoping it will inspire anyone who finds it on Genostories or in future archives. After all, no matter how many medical advances we achieve, death remains part of our being, and the way we face it, candles, flowers, altars, or simply words, reflects the depth of our humanity. May Sarah's example recover that magic the modern world risks burying in oblivion.

Griot 2085

THE LEGACY ON VHS

In my tireless search for meaningful human stories, I found that of Gabriel Whitmore, a man who never met his biological father but who ended up inheriting from him something far greater than any financial bequest: a set of old VHS tapes full of confessions, longings, art, and above all, proof of a transformative will. In a future where family ties dissolve into digital anonymity, Gabriel's story is a reminder that family, however distant or imperceptible it may seem, can weave itself into life in unexpected ways. I invite you, dear reader, to dive into a chapter charged with emotion and revelation: The Legacy on VHS.

Griot 2085

My name is Gabriel Whitmore. I was born in 1977 and, from my earliest memories, I heard a vague story about my origins: my mother, Olivia, met a young man at a party and they never saw each other again. From that chance encounter I was born. She never lied about it, but she also didn't have much information to give me. Not even an exact name, only a couple of vague notes that were useless for tracing anyone. Shortly thereafter my mother met Phil, a good, hard-working man who took me in as his own. Phil was my paternal figure throughout my childhood and adolescence, and I never called him stepfather; in my heart he was always papa Phil.

Still, there were days when the shadow of my biological father hovered around me. I wondered why he never looked for me, whether he was a coward or simply unaware of my existence. Phil tried to dissuade me, saying the past couldn't be changed and that he, Phil, was already there to be my father. But however much love I received from him, a part of me longed to know where I came from. I grew up with that silent curiosity and sometimes funneled it into an inward search. I daydreamed about finding a name, a face. Everything faded as I focused on my studies, my work, and my own family.

Then 2017 arrived, and at forty years old I felt a spark of determination: I was tired of that internal hole I couldn't fill. With biotechnological advances and online genealogy platforms, I decided to upload my DNA information. "What could I lose?" I told myself, and so began the chain of events that would lead me to discover more than I could ever have imagined.

For years, platforms like 23andMe and Ancestry.com had enabled reconnections with distant relatives and surprising discoveries about people's origins. In my case I didn't expect a miracle, I was just curious whether a cousin or an uncle might confirm some piece of my story. But one day I received an email that began: "Hello, I think we're siblings."

She sent it, an email from a woman named Margaret Dorsey. She said the genetic results showed we shared roughly 25% or 50% of our paternal DNA. Staring blankly at the screen, I checked the details the platform provided: indeed, the match was very high and suggested a very close familial tie, potentially a half-sibling. For a moment I sat speechless before the monitor, while a flood of questions spilled through my head.

I answered nervously, with "Are you sure?" followed by "Who is your father?" I received a reply with a story that, in one fell swoop, pulled me out of my stupor: Margaret revealed the name Samuel Dorsey, a painter of modest talent who had died years before in a car accident. She also explained that her mother was Eleanor Dorsey, the painter's widow, and that when they checked the platform my name appeared as a genetic match. They were intrigued, a little uneasy, and wanted to know whether I might have more clues.

It hit me like a punch to the gut. Gabriel Whitmore, the man who for forty years didn't know who his father was suddenly had a name: Samuel Dorsey. Well, not only that: he'd found a sister who had lived with him, who had known him (and who had been known by him). My first impulse was disbelief, followed by a mix of anger and hope: anger because if my father had known about me and never looked for me, he was a scoundrel; hope because if he hadn't known, maybe there was something else to salvage.

Even so, despite the vertigo of that discovery, I must make clear I never belittled what Phil, my stepfather, and my mother, Olivia, had done for me. I deeply acknowledge that Phil gave me the love, upbringing, and security every child needs to grow. I lacked neither a roof nor guidance nor that paternal hug in crucial moments. My gratitude to him is immense, and it's not that his presence wasn't enough; simply put, the void of not having known my biological father was a shadow that even the greatest affection couldn't entirely dispel. No matter how much I loved Phil and respected my mother, the absence of that blood link still hurt, perhaps because humans tend to wonder about those missing pieces of our origin.

Now, armed with the name Samuel Dorsey and a sister I'd never heard of, I felt that suddenly I might be able to fill that gap. I had more than one reason to try, not to deny the love I'd been given all my life, but to understand where the other half of my identity came from. I set out to learn the truth, even if it might unearth feelings I hadn't touched in years.

After a series of emails, I decided I couldn't just sit on my hands. In my messages I asked for more details: How did my father die? What kind of man was he? Where had they lived? Margaret, with the patience of someone who understands the magnitude of such a discovery, sent me photos of a soft-featured man with a sparse beard and thoughtful eyes. She told me a driver had fled after hitting him. His name was Samuel Dorsey, a modestly talented painter, not very famous, who sold his work through small galleries.

In 2002, after a couple months of exchanging emails, I agreed to meet my supposed sister and her family. The idea made me nervous: could all this really be true? My mother, Olivia, didn't remember the name of the man she'd met at that party with any precision. It could fit… or it could be a genetic misunderstanding. I had nothing to lose. So I traveled to the city where Margaret lived. The meeting was emotional from the first minute. I, my English mixed with anxiety, arrived, and she, fluent in both Spanish and English, greeted me with surprising warmth:

"You have no idea how much I wanted to meet you!" Margaret exclaimed, hugging me tightly.

I met her husband and their two children, who called me "uncle" from day one. Everything felt strange, but there was an air of sincerity. They showed me a framed photograph of Samuel Dorsey and his family, and I definitely saw a resemblance in the shape of the brows and the line of the jaw. My heart stopped for an instant as I realized he was probably my father, the man who had begotten me, abandoned me, and gone on with his life without me.

That same night, Margaret introduced me to her mother, Eleanor Dorsey, a woman with a serene face and a measured voice. She invited me to the kitchen table and poured coffee, as if she expected to tell me something weighty.

"You're Samuel's son, aren't you?" she said, looking me in the eyes with a mixture of tenderness and apology.

I nodded, not quite sure what to say. She sighed and told me that in his final years Samuel would mention, now and then, something about a lost child. He never spoke much, but at times he would let slip phrases like "Maybe I left a piece of myself somewhere" or "If I knew how to look for him." At other moments he was utterly silent. What wasn't clear was whether my father had been certain of my existence or merely had the vague intuition that, on that fateful night with my mother, a child had been born.

Eleanor confessed that Samuel died with great remorse, yet clung to the hope that someday that unknown person might appear. That was why she had kept something in the basement, a place he used as a studio and refuge. She suggested we go down there.

"Come with me. I think this belongs to you," she said, taking a flashlight and guiding me down a dark hallway.

The Dorseys' basement was a full-fledged painter's workshop: easels, brushes, cans of dried paint, and dozens of canvases stacked against the walls. A smell of oil paint and damp wood filled the air. I glanced at a few paintings: human silhouettes wrapped in grays and blues; other works with colorful figures but an unmistakable weight of melancholy. It was impossible not to feel a knot in my stomach. Was this where my father had meditated on his guilt? Did his brushstrokes hold fragments of me, the son he never knew?

Eleanor showed me some canvases in which, she said, Samuel had hidden symbols or names. At first glance I couldn't decipher anything, but she pointed out a series of lines that, with a bit of imagination, formed the letter G, and others that looked like initials. I fell silent, contemplating the possibility that, without knowing it, I had been present in that man's life through his art. Just as I felt overwhelmed by emotions, Eleanor put her hand on my shoulder and pointed to a cardboard box in a corner.

Samuel left this box. He said it was for his son, if he ever found him.

I picked it up. It was dusty and a bit dented, with a nearly ruined label where I could barely make out a name: *"For G..."* Without understanding, I took it with me, assuming it might contain papers, sketches, or letters. I didn't have the courage to open it right then, so I left with a thousand questions in my head.

I returned home with the box but shoved it into a cluttered storage room. For months, I avoided confronting its contents. My mind was a mess, and at the same time, the wound of the thought burned: *"This man gave me life, but he never looked for me. What kind of person does that?"* Even though Margaret and Eleanor tried to comfort me, I harbored a deep resentment toward this father who never existed in my reality.

One ordinary night, however, curiosity overpowered the anger. I decided to open the box. To my surprise, inside were 35 VHS tapes, each labeled in rudimentary handwriting with my name *"Gabriel"*, and a number. They were dusty tapes, probably recorded at different times. On the inside lid of the box, Samuel had written something with a marker:

"For my son, willpower is everything."

I was stunned. *For his son?* A man who never took responsibility, leaving me tapes as if they were some kind of inheritance? Confusion and rage flooded me. And yet, something in me pushed to find my old VCR. I braced myself and put in the first tape.

The VHS tapes looked worn, filled with static and flickering images. When I hit play, I found myself looking at a man, Samuel, standing in front of the camera in a messy room. He was silent, clearly overweight, dressed in workout clothes. On the tape, Samuel said nothing, just exercised awkwardly, sweating, but never uttering a word. It was a monotonous, thirty-minute video. When it ended, I turned off the VCR, completely baffled as to its purpose.

I decided to try the second tape, numbered *"2."* There was Samuel again, exercising with a bit more fluidity. Not a single word, not a direct message, just him, straining in front of the camera. The same thing happened with the third, the fourth... always silent, always focused, though with each tape his physical state seemed slightly better than before: fewer pounds, more endurance, but always silent.

Despite the tedious viewing, something pushed me to keep watching. I felt Samuel needed to show me a process. He, the man who was never there for me, was filming his own physical transformation. Why? Even with the anger boiling inside me, the rage of feeling abandoned, I couldn't turn away from those tapes. Deep down, there was curiosity, perhaps even a longing for answers.

After watching the first fourteen tapes, I felt dazed. I was beginning to notice the mutation of that stranger: his body trimming down, his expression growing firmer. It was on tape number 15 that he finally broke the silence. I saw him appear in frame, now slimmer, his chest heaving, and suddenly he fixed his gaze on the camera.

"Gabriel," he said, his voice dry, "maybe this will seem insane to you. I don't know if you'll ever watch these tapes. But if you do, I want to show you that willpower can change a person. I started with many extra pounds and no motivation. I decided to document it because… I needed a reason. That reason is you, even if I don't know you."

The first time I heard my name leave that man's mouth, a shiver ran down my entire body. It was like a direct blow to all my resentment. For an instant, I froze in front of the screen, holding my breath. Was he really talking to me? The father who had never once been part of my life… saying "Gabriel" with an astonishing familiarity, as if he had carried me in his heart all this time. My anger erupted, and at the same time, it mingled with a deep, almost disorienting emotion. On one hand, I wanted to stop the tape, to refuse to empathize with him; on the other, something in me demanded I keep listening.

Samuel continued with a monologue of about twenty minutes. He recounted how, in his youth, he had been a disaster: aimless, with bad habits. He mentioned how he met a young woman named Olivia at a fleeting party. Neither he nor she imagined the consequences of that encounter, but years later he heard rumors that Olivia had had a son whose name was Gabriel. Me. He never knew it for certain until one day, he said he saw Olivia from afar with a child. He felt a sharp pang of guilt in his chest but lacked the courage to approach.

He spoke of his shame, his emptiness. He said the only way to redeem himself, or at least to leave behind a message, was to document his own reconstruction: how, with willpower, he forced himself to transform his body and his mindset. He ended the recording saying:

"If one day you ever see me, Gabriel, you'll know that I am proud of you, even if I never gave you anything. I want you to understand that this… this is my way of asking for your forgiveness."

I finished watching in shock. I felt tears welling up, along with a muted rage that demanded: *And why didn't you look for me when you could have done it in person?* But hearing my name in his voice left me breathless. Dad, I thought. Dad *speaking to me…* It was an indescribable instant, a tremendous collision of pain and intimacy. I had never felt so close to a man who never even bothered to say "hello" to me, and yet there he was: alive in those videos, revealing his secret, pleading for me to understand his regret. I couldn't turn away. Suddenly I understood: I needed to see all the tapes because, late as it was, they were the only real conversation we would ever have.

In the subsequent videos (16, 17, 18…), my father kept talking. He spoke of his daily struggle: the diet, the exercises, the motivational books he read, but also his determination to survive as a painter. He showed glimpses of his routine, without yet giving much explanation of his art. What struck me most was his relentless repetition of the idea: *"willpower is everything."* He insisted that life granted no opportunities to those who resigned themselves.

At times, I grew furious: *"How could he have been so cowardly as not to call me or contact me?"* Yet on the other hand, watching that effort was like a window into his intimacy, into a father I had never known. With each tape, he appeared fitter, more self-assured, and a part of me was moved at the thought that he was doing all of it *"for me,"* the son he didn't dare to seek out in person.

On one of the tapes, number 20, he said:

"I don't expect you to forgive me. I know fatherhood is proven through actions, and I was absent from all of them. But I want you to see that people can change. This body you see isn't just the figure of a man losing weight. It's a symbol of what perseverance can accomplish. I'm overcoming my own self-destruction and… I hope one day you can see yourself reflected in this: one is not condemned to anything, Gabriel. One chooses."

Hearing those words directed at me, a forty-year-old man who had never received even a postcard, never a hug from the one who gave me life, stirred up contradictory emotions.

It took me weeks to watch all the tapes until I reached number 30. There, Samuel, now with a markedly different bearing, wore a melancholy expression. He spoke of his loneliness, of how he had never learned to love responsibly. He said my mother, Olivia, was blameless, since he had been drifting through life without plans when he met her, and that, if he had ever truly learned of my existence, it had been too late:

"I saw you once, you know?" he confessed, his gaze distant. "You were a boy of about six or seven. I thought I saw you with your mother on the street, maybe it was her, maybe a woman who looked like her. I watched you from afar, Gabriel, and felt such a deep guilt that I couldn't bring myself to approach. It would have been selfish to burst into your life when I was no one. Forgive me if this sounds like an excuse, but I didn't know how to be a man."

I paused the tape for a moment to breathe, a knot tightening in my throat. All that resentment I had carried mingled now with compassion. Perhaps he did want to, in his own terms, but he lacked the courage. I pressed play again and heard his broken voice:

"I don't know if you'll watch this and say: '*What a coward, you didn't even show your face.*' Maybe you'd be right. But, in my language,

I offer you the best I can: my actions. I changed, I fought against myself, and I left my fingerprints on every painting I made, thinking of you. You will be, in some way, the heir of my metamorphosis."

In the last five tapes, Samuel focused on his artistic side. He showed me canvas after canvas with a home camera, describing brushstrokes, explaining how certain colors represented his regret or his hope for redemption. Suddenly, he would point out subtle symbols: the letter G hidden in a background, the silhouette of a child. Or a tiny heart in the corner of his signature. Each tape was a journey into his creativity and melancholy, into his way of inhabiting a world he felt he didn't belong to. He spoke to me, though I could never answer him:

"Here, Gabriel, you see a sunset. It looks like just a landscape, but in reality your initials are blurred in the clouds. It's as if I wanted to call out to you and couldn't."

"This other painting is a self-portrait of me embracing a faceless child, because I didn't know your face, but I knew you existed."

I realized that, throughout his entire life, in some way he had painted me without knowing me. He was creating a silent bond with his absent son. I felt a whirlwind of emotions: rage, tenderness, disbelief, and also the warmth of thinking that, in his clumsy way, my father did love me.

To complete the puzzle, I reached out again to Margaret and Eleanor. I asked them for more details about how Samuel died. They explained that, on an ordinary day, he left his studio to buy painting supplies, and a driver struck him and fled. The impact left him in a coma for a couple of days, until he passed away. The police never found the culprit. Eleanor believes that, in those two days of coma, Samuel repeated my name in a faint voice, as if yearning for a final encounter that never came.

Hearing this story shattered me. I felt as though life had played a cruel joke on us: I arrived too late, and he left before ever taking my hand. And yet, the VHS tapes were his legacy, his way of speaking to me from the other side of time. With each tape, I understood more clearly his battle against himself and his longing for me to know that he was not just a biological donor, but a father with a belated love.

After processing my feelings, I had the idea of uploading all this material to Genostories. Like many others in 2025, I had already used the platform to preserve memories of my family with Phil and my mother. However, I had never told the darker side of my origins. I felt that by publishing these tapes, the world would come to know Samuel Dorsey: the unknown painter who transformed his body and spirit as an act of faith toward a distant son.

It took me time to digitize the VHS tapes. Some were damaged or of poor image quality, so I sought help at a specialized center. Finally, I arranged the videos chronologically and gave them titles that reflected my father's evolution: *"VHS 1: The Silent Man," "VHS 2: First Month of Exercise,"* … up to *"VHS 35: Final Confession."* I added subtitles in several languages so people could understand the parts spoken in Spanish or in his personal monologue.

In each clip, I added notes explaining how I felt when I discovered them, the chronology of his life, and the connection with his paintings. In this way, chapter by chapter, the story was built of a man who had lived with guilt but also with an immense will to make amends, and that became my way of connecting with him, decades after his death.

Not long after publishing on Genostories, comments began arriving from all over the world. People struggling with obesity felt inspired watching Samuel record his effort and progress with each tape. Others, with family voids, were moved by the sincerity of his repentant monologue. Anonymous artists who saw the uploaded photos of his paintings found beauty in those melancholic strokes. Many asked me: *"Don't you feel resentment for his lateness?" "Can you forgive him now?"*

I was surprised by the collective empathy: people who had never seen me offered condolences for a death that had happened years ago. Others thanked me for sharing the *"hidden greatness of your father,"* and some told me their own families also kept similar secrets. The videos became a kind of universal testimony about the strength of will and the power of repentance. I was especially moved reading the stories of those who, inspired, began leaving messages for their children, even if they didn't know whether they would ever be heard. Genostories filled with parallel confessions: *"I too had a child I never sought out; today, after seeing Samuel, I want to change."*

The question most people asked me was: *"Did you forgive him?"* At first, my answer was ambiguous. *"It hurts that he was never there for me,"* I replied. Deep down, I felt that nothing could replace the absence of a father in my childhood. But little by little, as I spoke with users and read their reactions, something softened in my heart. I began to understand that Samuel's life had detours that overwhelmed him, that we do not always have the maturity to face our responsibilities at the exact moment we should.

In the last tapes, when he spoke of guilt and his desire to find me, I saw a broken man, afraid of rejection. How many times, in my own life, have I let fear paralyze me? In that reflection I realized that if I demanded of him the courage he lacked, I myself had never had the courage to investigate earlier. Though I was the son, and the search wasn't my responsibility, there was a faint glimmer of solidarity: I understood that both of us had been victims of our cowardice and of misinformation.

And so, one day, I found myself speaking into the camera on Genostories: *"I have found more love in his tapes than I ever thought I could receive from an absent father. It wasn't the ideal form, but it was real, and yes, I chose to forgive him. Because through his example, he taught me that it is never too late to change. I wish it had come sooner, but at least it came."*

A moving event took place when, while enlarging the image of one of his paintings (*"Presence in Absence"*), I discovered a kind of double signature: his own and, beside it, in tiny letters, the word *"Gab."* You could read it, with some effort, if you knew where to look. I sent the file to an art specialist, who agreed it seemed to be a deliberate clue, a name hidden on purpose. It hit me like an emotional punch to see that, even before finding me, Samuel wanted to leave evidence that I existed in his inner life.

In a later video, I filmed myself saying:

"Dad, I found your secret. Today I know you painted for me. Even if you weren't by my side, you included me in every brushstroke. Thank you."

I uploaded it to Genostories, and people responded with messages of support and virtual tears. I felt a comforting warmth: I wasn't alone in interpreting this discovery; thousands of people were following it with me, admiring Samuel or pitying his story. It was the greatest collective catharsis I had ever experienced.

Meanwhile, my relationship with Margaret (my sister) and Eleanor grew stronger. In 2025, I visited them again. We held a small tribute to Samuel in the same basement where he had painted, arranging some of his canvases more neatly for display. We took the digitized tapes and projected fragments for the close family, who had never known most of it. Watching Samuel's body transform and hearing his broken voice moved many to tears.

"He was always reserved, but who would have guessed he carried such a need for expiation inside him?" Eleanor whispered, deeply moved.

Margaret, equally touched, said:

"Thank you for showing us Dad in this way. I didn't even know about those tapes. Now I understand him more. He was someone who loved in silence."

That family reunion sealed a fraternal bond with Margaret and allowed me to finally let go of resentment. Even though Samuel was no longer here, he had left a *"thread of continuity"* that tied me to his memory and to the Dorsey family.

Today, as I write these lines to include them in my Genostories chapter, I understand that the willpower my father so often proclaimed was not just about losing weight or painting well, but about the human capacity to seek redemption, to reverse what seems irredeemable. Though he died before ever giving me a hug, his tapes and his paintings served to connect our two worlds. His message on VHS declares that *"life overwhelms us if we let inertia possess us, but willpower rescues us from nothingness."*

I have chosen to believe him. The VHS legacy is more than the testimony of an absent father: it is confirmation that sometimes our deepest guilts can drive us toward symbolic acts of love that, even after death, illuminate the path for others. In my case, it illuminated my own path back to my origins.

Seeing the flood of comments from people who, after following my videos, decided to seek out distant relatives, speak with estranged parents, or dare to document their own personal struggles, I felt I was fulfilling a purpose: I didn't keep the story for myself, but shared it so that others could witness the transformative force of confession and memory.

People struggling with weight wrote to thank me for the courage to share Samuel's tapes, saying: *"If he could do it, so can I."* Others who had grown up without a father were moved to know they weren't alone in their longing to understand their origins. Even unknown painters told me that Samuel's narrative inspired them to sign each stroke with honesty, leaving the trace of their emotions for posterity.

It was an unexpected but powerful phenomenon. In a way, his legacy surpassed what anyone would have expected from such an anonymous man. My father, an obscure painter, ended up becoming a universal example of redemption and inner strength. I found myself crying with gratitude. How could something so belated be so important? Perhaps the answer is that love, and willpower never truly arrive too late if they manage to leave a mark.

Now, at 48 years old in 2025, I address those who may see this story on Genostories: perhaps you too carry the absence of someone, a father, a mother, a child, or an unfinished love. Maybe there are no VHS tapes, no paintings with hidden messages, but your story can still be written. The message I want to leave, together with the voice of my late father, is that willpower defines us, and that reconciliation, though late, is still reconciliation.

My father never hugged me, but he left me his *"VHS legacy,"* which, in its own way, embraced me from the past. That embrace helped me heal, to love and forgive him, and to understand that life sometimes gives second chances, even after death, if we know how to look for them.

"We can't always meet those who gave us life, but we can know their story, and sometimes, that too is a form of love."

Had I not found a platform like Genostories, I might have kept these tapes to myself. But here, I have the option of uploading them, of sharing them, and of leaving, for the future, an example of how willpower and love can arrive even when it seems too late. I also keep part of those videos private, thinking of the generations to come, so that my father's example serves not only me but anyone who seeks redemption and hope in their own story.

Knowing that so many people take part in this same mission, to make lived experiences transcend oblivion, comforts me and gives me a sense of purpose: we all wish for future generations never to feel abandoned, and to find in our experiences the strength to transform their lives and the lives of others. That is what Genostories is, more than just stories, a purpose to transform lives.

As I conclude the chapter "The VHS Legacy,"
where Gabriel recounts the story of his father Samuel,
I cannot help but marvel at the power our confessions,
our symbolic acts, and our hidden love have to impact
the lives of others, even after death. We live in 2085,
where family relationships seem to dissolve within
hyperconnectivity, and many take for granted that
longevity and medical advances can replace any absence.
But the story of Gabriel and Samuel proves that bonds like
that of father and son can transcend centuries of silence,
guilt, and distance if we leave behind an honest testimony
of what we feel.

Genostories, by becoming the stage for this revelation,
reaffirms its calling: to rescue memories, to celebrate
life, and to reconcile what was once broken in the past.
Through Samuel's story, we come to understand that even
anonymous people, without fame or wealth, can leave a
testimony capable of inspiring millions. Thus, the idea of
"posthumous love" ceases to be a contradiction: although
Samuel left without ever embracing his son, his voice and
his art rose from the tapes to embrace the man Gabriel
became.

May this story be a hymn of hope for all, a reminder
that willpower, that silent engine, can work miracles, and
that, with the help of memory and storytelling, we can
find redemption even when time seems to have played
against us. So ends Chapter 12, carrying within its words
the flame of reconciliation that only a legacy can ignite.

Griot 2085

ECHOES OF A REBELLIOUS YOUTH

*In this vast repository of stories called Genostories,
I have come across the testimony of John Reynolds,
a 79-year-old man who, in the year 2027, decided to
record his youthful experiences as a moral and historical
legacy for those willing to listen. In my explorations, I
have encountered many accounts from different eras, but
none as captivating as that of this activist who, born in
1948, immersed himself in the fervor of the civil rights
movements and fought against the indifference of his time.*

*Now, in his old age, he sits in his living room,
filled with posters from old rallies, black-and-white
photographs, and relics of a turbulent past to recall those
days when youth burned with the desire to transform the
world. It is a story of passion, rebellion, and hope, still
resonating in the present.*

*I invite you to dive into Chapter 13: Echoes of a
Rebellious Youth and discover how John's voice, chiseled
by the years, continues to resound with a powerful call to
action and remembrance.*

Griot 2085

Hello, I'm John Reynolds. Today, in this year 2027, I sit down to record this testimony in my living room, a sanctuary that shelters the echoes of a vibrant and tumultuous past. I was born in 1948 and, though time has left its marks on my face, my memories of youth remain as vivid as the first day. This room, decorated with posters from old rallies, black-and-white photographs, and relics of past eras is my window to yesterday: a bridge between who I was and who I am today.

The walls of my living room, where I now sit, are a reflection of the movements that shaped my life. Every poster from past protests, every photograph faded by time, every newspaper clipping taped up with yellowing adhesive reminds me that there was once a time when youth believed they could change everything.

Anyone who steps inside would feel transported to the late 1960s. On the main wall hangs an image that always strikes me with nostalgia: a group of young people back then, us, marching down an avenue, with makeshift signs, hearts brimming with conviction, and a soundtrack of chants and songs that might seem naïve today but at the time embodied the very essence of change. Often, when I draw close to that photo, I find myself trying to recognize the faces of comrades lost to time or to repression itself.

Just behind the old flat-screen television, on the shelf, I keep a dented megaphone, the very one I used to organize neighborhood assemblies. The speaker is half broken, but it still bears the red paint where someone scrawled "FIGHT" in shaky letters. That object, silent now, speaks to me of the uproar that once rang through the streets, of the echo that carried cries of freedom. And so, my living room becomes something more than a personal museum: it is the living manifestation that every object preserves a piece of history, a fragment of the John Reynolds who once burned with passion for justice.

It was the summer of 1966 when, at 18 years old, I found myself swept up in the current of a movement that would change the destiny of an entire country. The air was charged with hope, and with the rage needed to bring down walls. The streets became stages of struggle; the music, the chants, and the unbreakable spirit of unity could be felt on every corner.

I remember that, even from the beginning of that year, the news showed protests breaking out in different places, swelling movements demanding equality for African American communities, the end of segregation, the right to vote without unjust barriers. I, still carrying the weight of adolescence, didn't fully grasp the magnitude of what was happening, but my friends and I felt moved by the injustices we saw on television. That summer I knew I could not remain with my arms crossed.

One afternoon, one of my closest friends, Tom, said to me: *"John, this country is waking up and we're going to be part of history; we can't just stand by and watch."* Tom was a bold young man, three years older than me, already involved with civil rights groups. He invited me to join him in the nearest city, where a large demonstration was to take place. I remember my nervousness: my parents were terrified by reports of repression and unrest, but something inside me told me this was a moral duty.

When we arrived, I was overwhelmed by the human river stretching through the streets: men and women of all ages, some very young, others with silver hair, all united in the conviction that justice had no skin color. That day would be only the beginning of my journey into a movement larger than myself. The uproar, the mingling voices under the stifling heat, the street vendors offering water, and the police watching suspiciously... It was a canvas of lived moments flooding my senses.

There were hand-painted signs that read *"EQUALITY FOR ALL"* and *"END SEGREGATION."* I came across an elderly couple handing out leaflets, explaining the urgency of registering to vote and overthrowing, with the strength of the ballot box, the segregationist laws. Their faces radiated the exhaustion of decades of struggle, but also glowed with the flame of hope. I realized that this man and woman had been protesting for years, taking risks unthinkable to younger generations. Their example moved me deeply: if they, with their skin weathered by the sun and their memories scarred by injustice, still stood tall, how could I, at 18, not join them?

I remember the first time I joined the civil rights protests. We walked in masses, shoulder to shoulder, feeling the collective heartbeat of those who believed a better world was possible. Segregation, discrimination, and injustice weren't just words, but harsh realities striking down anyone who dared to dream of equality. The atmosphere was electrifying and, at the same time, overwhelming.

My baptism by fire came during a peaceful march through the city center. We began with chanted slogans, flags, and clever signs. A woman, holding her baby in her arms, shouted for justice so that her child would not grow up in a country that underestimated him for the color of his skin. I remember being overcome with both admiration and terror, knowing the forces of order would soon make their presence felt.

At one point, the crowd encountered a police barricade. The officers wore helmets, carried shields, and bore on their faces the determination to push us back. I was trembling, holding a sign that read: *"Silence is complicity."* It wasn't a slogan I had come up with,

I had borrowed it from a leaflet, but I felt it as my own. And that was when chaos erupted: orders to disperse, the thunder of shields pounding the pavement, and clouds of tear gas flooding the air.

People scattered in every direction, coughing and crying from the burn in their throats and eyes. I nearly fainted from the sting in mine. Meanwhile, the authorities advanced like a dark tide, driving us away from the main avenue. Even in the midst of that panic, I could still hear the voice of a man with a cracked megaphone shouting phrases of resistance: *"They will not silence us, we will not surrender."* It was then that I understood that real injustice hurts. It is felt on the skin, not only read about in history books.

I remember clearly the image of a hand-painted sign, where someone had written *"Equality for all!"* with clumsy brushstrokes but overflowing with conviction. That simple message was a battle cry, a call for unity in a divided country. We marched through the avenues, with flags and banners, defying the established powers and facing repression head-on.

The summer of 1966, for me, was a whirlwind of new lessons. I not only learned about racial disparity but also about the power of solidarity. I experienced firsthand the importance of sharing a sandwich with a protester who had come from another region, of offering shelter in my home to a stranger when the police closed off the streets, of listening to the testimonies of elderly women recounting past humiliations. Each encounter reminded me that these struggles were shared, and that generosity bloomed even in the midst of adversity.

At night, we held improvised assemblies in parks or churches. There, strategies for protest were discussed, ways of evading censorship were devised, and plans were coordinated to register voters in rural areas. One of the speeches that captivated me was by a young speaker named Diana. She was 20 years old, and her inner fire was so strong that when she addressed the crowd, her voice thundered like lightning splitting through apathy.

"We have waited long enough," she declared. *"Our parents endured years of silence. Now it is time for the children to raise their voices. Freedom is not begged for, it is demanded, and whoever stays silent in the face of injustice becomes complicit in it."*

The ovation that followed her words made me feel alive, part of a great mechanism of change. I saw how people's faces lit up with an enthusiasm I had never witnessed in my small hometown. And it was in that moment, amid the applause, that I looked around and thought: *"This is my place: the heart of a movement that needs me just as much as I need it."*

One of the images that still haunts me is that of an old man, his gaze filled with wisdom and sorrow, who approached me and said:

"Son, every step we take today is the foundation of tomorrow. Do not give up, because justice is forged through sacrifice."

Those words engraved themselves into my soul and have guided every decision I have made since.

There was one night, particularly tense, when a nighttime march was organized through a neighborhood known for acts of intimidation. We had been warned it was dangerous, that the police would not guarantee our safety. Even so, the group decided not to back down. We carried lit candles in silence, in memory of a young man murdered for racial reasons. The atmosphere was one of solemnity, but also of unease; we could hear the murmurs of neighbors leaning from their windows, some supportive, others distrustful.

Halfway down the street, I noticed an old man who limped yet refused to fall behind. He moved forward with us, leaning on a cane. I went to offer him help. His face was deeply lined, his voice trembling, but when he spoke, his conviction radiated strength:

"Don't think you're too young to be afraid, son. We all are. But the key is remembering why you're here. If you give up today, there will be no change tomorrow."

It was probably the same man who had told me earlier that sacrifice forges justice. In that moment, I felt my life's mission crystallize: I could not abandon the movement. Every step was a stone laid to build a less unjust future.

I cannot help but recall with intensity the heat of the asphalt and the pounding of drums that marked the march's rhythm. That night, the sky itself seemed to have ignited its own rebellion, and the stars, silent witnesses, shone upon the awakening of a generation. The repression did not take long to arrive: tear gas, the shrieking of sirens, and the harsh reality of an authority that resisted change. Yet, in every tear shed and in every choked-out cry, the seed of change grew stronger.

The reality of repression taught me that blood and tears were part of the struggle. Some were injured in clashes with law enforcement; others were arrested arbitrarily. A comrade named Kevin was jailed for three days just for protesting, and when he came out, his eyes were bloodshot, his voice broken, but his courage even greater. He was the one who confirmed for me that prison does not crush conviction; sometimes, it strengthens it.

More than once I had to run at full speed, adrenaline surging, dodging barricades. At times I wondered if it was worth it. But whenever I saw humble people who, despite their fear, opened their doors to shelter us, I remembered that hope is collective. I recall a couple with two small children who offered us water and dressed the wounds of some protesters even though it could have meant trouble with the police. It was those acts of solidarity that cemented my certainty that humanity can come together when the cause is just.

As the years passed, that experience left an indelible mark on my life. The civil rights struggle not only taught me to confront injustice, but also to cultivate a critical spirit and to value the importance of every small act of rebellion. I became both witness and participant in a change that still reverberates in the history of our country.

As the movement advanced, I realized that deep change did not come from marches or protests alone, but from an entire process of education, awareness, and persistence. I began to study legislation, to understand how political pressure could be used to dismantle segregation laws. I attended workshops on civil disobedience, guided by seasoned activists. The name of Martin Luther King and other great leaders appeared constantly as sources of inspiration, and I nourished myself with their speeches to sharpen my own arguments.

In my family, this commitment stirred mixed feelings: my parents, who had grown up in a more conservative era, feared for my safety; they worried I might ruin my future or end up in trouble with the police. But at the same time, they supported me with a respectful silence, understanding that I had to spread my wings on my own.

The John Reynolds of 1965 was a naïve, apolitical young man. The John Reynolds of 1967 was beginning to forge a revolutionary character, not in the sense of violence, but in the sense of words and persistence. I learned that every seed is planted little by little, and that impatience often leads to frustration. Even so, perseverance, fueled by passion, eventually bore fruit that could be felt later on.

Today, as I sit here in my living room, I am surrounded by an atmosphere of nostalgia and gratitude. Every object present tells a story. The faded posters and black-and-white photographs are not mere decorations; they are silent witnesses to a time when struggle was daily bread. Looking at them, I relive those moments of emotional intensity, when every face and every cry contributed to deep change.

I return to the present, to the living room where I now record myself for Genostories. At seventy-nine years old, the weight of age is evident in my bones and my eyesight. And yet, my spirit feels renewed as I gaze at the photographs on the walls. I see my young face, hair disheveled, a sign in hand, and in my eyes the determination of someone who believed the future depended on his own daring.

There is a poster that dominates the central wall: a huge word, "JUSTICE," painted in red and black capital letters, with a silhouette of protesters beneath it. That poster has survived decades of dust, moves, and broken relationships. Every time I look at it, I feel a tug at my heart, remembering the person who gave it to me: a fellow marcher named Lucy, who later became a dear friend. She once told me: *"This poster is not just a slogan; it's a reminder of whom we serve when we protest."*

Right beside it, a small placard with a quote from Harriet Tubman reminds me of the unbreakable resolve of those who, even in harsher times, risked their lives to help others find freedom. It reaffirms for me that the legacy of struggle that ignited my youth is rooted in a history far greater than ourselves. Every object in my living room is not mere ornament, but a flame that keeps collective memory alive.

Today, in this 2027, the wounds of the past have healed, but the spirit of those days lives on in every action that seeks justice. Society now faces different challenges, but the essence of the struggle remains the same: the need to be authentic, to question power, and to never allow indifference to take hold of our hearts.

These sixty-one years since 1966 have drastically changed the social and political landscape. We have seen legal advances, the rise of new progressive movements, the expansion of rights that back then seemed like unreachable dreams. But I am not naïve: today, forms of discrimination, violence, and inequality still exist, demanding the same passion and courage my generation once showed. You are my grandchildren, and you must act to ensure a country that can offer you a future.

Some young people approach me and ask if I am not tired of fighting. I answer that the struggle changes shape, but it never ends. The current stage may require cyber-activism, pressure through social networks, exposing corruption and oppression with digital tools we never even imagined in the sixties. What is essential, however, remains unchanged: the flame that burns in your chest when you witness injustice and refuse to accept it.

What I would tell the youth of today is that history is not written once and for all; it is written day by day. Every act of rebellion, every vote, every protest, every text uploaded to a platform can shape tomorrow. If I learned anything in 1966, it's that what an individual does, no matter how small it may seem, can light the fuse of collective change. You don't need a multitude if you begin walking with conviction.

To you, who hear me now, I say: never forget history. Every struggle, every sacrifice, every tear shed in the name of freedom is a lesson that must not fall into oblivion. The youth of today have the responsibility to carry that legacy forward, to transform the scars of the past into pillars upon which to build a more just and compassionate society.

I have seen many young people sunk in apathy, justifying their indifference with the idea that *the system will never change.* But history tells me the system can change even if only in part, when at least a group of people wields their ideals with firmness. My comrades and I witnessed how what began as a handful of dissenters became a mass movement that forced those in power to yield.

In the marches of my time there were, of course, opportunists, the violent, and the confused, but the majority were genuine human beings willing to sacrifice their comfort. At seventy-nine years old, I am moved to see how the new generations possess vast tools of dissemination, the internet, social networks, and global forums. I imagine what the youth of the sixties could have accomplished with such instruments at their disposal. The message is clear: every generation inherits a portion of the road; we cannot go back, but we can carry the torch further.

No matter how advanced our devices or how sophisticated our technology may be, without the essence of struggle and without the passion that drives change, we become shadows of what we could be. We must remember that history is forged day by day, and that each of us has the power to write the next chapter.

In the sixties, people risked their physical integrity in the streets. Today, confrontation takes other forms: perhaps fewer tear gas clouds, but more battles of disinformation, cyber harassment, or media manipulation. The human emotion, the desire for freedom, the hunger for justice remain the same. That human foundation, courage, love, and dignity is what we must nourish so we do not become puppets of circumstance.

I reflect that, in my youth, we made mistakes by overestimating our ability to change everything *"in one stroke."* But I do not regret that idealism, because without it, the steps for the next generations would never have been built. Every mistake, every time repression paralyzed us or society called us dreamers, we rose again, and in that persistence, the people learned that surrender was never an option.

Today, as I conclude this testimony, I am overwhelmed by a sense of gratitude. Gratitude for having lived in a time when the struggle was sincere and change was tangible. Gratitude for every experience, every friend, and every challenge that made me grow.

I am thankful for Genostories, this platform that allows me to leave my story to whoever wishes to hear it, without the censorship that was so common in other times. If there is one main lesson I would like to leave, it is that every process of social change is built upon individual stories, upon the awareness that germinates within each citizen. History is not written in the upper chambers: it is in the footsteps of every march, in the roar of every slogan, in the hand that lifts up a fallen comrade.

The present stage, with its specific challenges, demands that we not forget either the victories or the hardships of yesterday. Many achievements we now take for granted, the right not to be discriminated against because of skin color, greater equality before the law, educational opportunities. But if we do not keep the flame alive, we run the risk of sliding backward. Achievements are not inherited automatically; they are defended through memory and action.

Although my story may seem tinged with nostalgia for an unrepeatable time, I do not want to give the impression that the past was all better. In fact, those days of protest, repression, and moral violence were harsh. What was truly valuable was that the seed of hope bloomed in the midst of adversity. Today, in 2027, with so many tools and social advances, I am thrilled to think that the new generations might achieve what cost us blood and fire with far less suffering, if only they carried the same passion.

Young people in their twenties often ask me: *"How did you keep the faith when everything seemed against you?"* And I answer that faith was born from witnessing how, even in the worst moments, compassion would emerge: a neighbor offering water, a stranger giving you a place to sleep, a group shielding you from aggression. That ember of humanity would ignite into flame when joined with the rage against injustice. That is how peaceful revolutions are forged, and how lasting transformations take root.

But I must confess there was one moment that shook my conviction to its core: the assassination of Martin Luther King Jr. in April 1968. I remember that day with a knot in my throat. I was at a friend's house when the news broke over the radio. Immediately, a cold silence enveloped us, and I felt as if a moral pillar of the movement had collapsed. For many of us, King had been the embodiment of the peaceful path to justice, living proof that the power of words and nonviolence could shake the hardest foundations of the system. His absence tore me apart: I thought that if even he, with his unshakable faith in humanity, could be struck down, perhaps there was no hope.

But what happened afterward showed me the other face of darkness. Crowds poured into the streets to honor his legacy, community leaders stepped forward to carry the torch, and everywhere I felt pain transforming into a stronger commitment to justice. I understood then that evil does not win simply because it strikes us; its power lies in our surrender. If we did not yield, the flame of equality would keep burning. Seeing so many people united in grief and, at the same time, in courage, I realized that while darkness may feel oppressive, it is never as powerful as the light a group of human beings chooses to ignite together.

Today, looking back, I know that the tragedy of losing such a meaningful leader did not end our dreams. On the contrary, it inspired us to redouble our efforts, to be that light that could guide others. Evil is nothing but the absence of light, and each of us, through our actions, can strike the spark that drives the shadows away.

What I most wish to convey is that the past is not a dead showcase, but a wellspring of continuous learning. Looking over the photographs and posters in my living room drives me to believe that as long as there are people willing to rise up, not everything is lost. That lesson does not expire with time: it is as valid in 2027 as it was in 1966 or as it will be in 2100.

Today, there are those who think history moves on its own invisible threads, that little can be done against powerful interests. I disagree. The marches I attended were, for the most part, made up of ordinary people, without power or fame, who simply joined their voices to say *"enough."* That shook the system. No oppressive machinery is so monolithic when a conscious people claims its rights. That is why telling the past keeps alive the testimony that everything is possible, if there is persistence and unity.

With these recordings I upload to Genostories, I wish to address not only my grandchildren but anyone who feels the temptation of indifference. It is easy to retreat into the comfort zone and let injustice appear in the news as something distant. What is difficult, and at the same time, grand, is deciding that each of us can be an architect of history. Do not underestimate your power: history is written by those who act, not by those who watch it unfold from the couch.

With my testimony, I want to inject a dose of memory and hope into the hearts of young and old alike who cross paths with my words. If you are going through a period of confusion or doubting the future, think of us, the young people of 1966 who, with few resources but great passion, shook the very ground of the system, opening cracks where dignity and equality could take root. Perhaps there is still much road ahead, but we already took the first steps.

Do not let indifference extinguish the fire that burns in the hearts of those who seek justice. Always remember: the passion and commitment of youth are the spark that ignites the flame of change. Learn from the past, embrace history, and above all, never stop fighting for a tomorrow where dignity and equality are the essence of our coexistence.

I take my leave with the satisfaction of having been part of something larger than my own life. Now, at my age, I understand that history does not conclude, it is fed by each generation that decides to wield its dreams and face the challenges of its time. Many of my comrades are gone; others remain, telling stories and encouraging those who now carry the torch. That is the wonder of memory: it is shared, rekindled, and spreads to ignite more hearts.

I hope my words serve as encouragement for those who today feel swallowed by apathy or paralyzed by the weight of injustice. Never underestimate the power of a firm step and a brave voice: that, and nothing else, is what changes history. If there is one thing that would please me, it is to imagine that, upon hearing this story, someone might decide to dare to walk in the same direction or to open a new path where the justice we still need may flourish.

Thank you for lending me your ears, your eyes, and your heart. I leave you these memories as proof of what a dreamer of a teenager could do when he joined his voice to that of thousands. I invite you, if ever you feel lost, to remember that every great journey begins with a single, determined step. In the end, history is our common home, and each of us is responsible for the pillars that hold it up regardless of our origins or the color of our skin.

Here is the testimony of John Reynolds, the young man of 1966 who, with a handful of friends and a great deal of hope, chose to stand against segregation and injustice. His voice, recorded in 2027, reminds us that time may pass, but the longing for justice remains as alive as in those days when people marched under the burning sun. From my perspective in Genostories, I see how John's narration assembles key pieces of collective memory: the spirit of struggle, camaraderie, the power of community, and the unquenchable force of youth.

In the era we live in, where past victories sometimes seem like distant relics, John's story serves as a compass to help us preserve the essence. The faces of those who protested in the streets, their laughter, their wounds, their solidarity teach us that the world is shaped by our present actions. Through his account, John showed that the idea "nothing can be changed" is a falsehood; in truth, it is the will of the people that writes the most transcendent pages of humanity.

As I finish transcribing his story, I like to think that every word of his will serve those who read or hear it as a call to action: if in 1966 those boys and girls managed to shake a system, then today, with greater resources and freedoms, the potential for transformation is even greater. That is the great lesson I carry forward for posterity: never underestimate your capacity to change the course of things, nor the necessity of the passion that sets the heart ablaze in the face of injustice.

And so, may the voice of John Reynolds continue to illuminate the paths of those who believe the future is

forged day by day, and may the fire of memory not be extinguished, but ignite the spark in every generation ready to conquer its own horizon.
    Griot 2085

SILENCED SCREAMS

In my effort to rescue the testimonies that shape our collective history, I came across the story of Michael Thompson, a man who faced silence and stigma with the strength of solidarity. His life reflects that vibrant and painful chapter of the 1980s, when official indifference toward HIV merged with social prejudice, leaving thousands without voice or refuge. And yet, in every protest, in every march, in every act of defiance, bonds of affection and networks of support arose, capable of transforming fear into action.

In exploring his memories, I understood how that dark time left us with a luminous lesson: collective will can ignite the flame of hope, even when despair and injustice seem to prevail.

Griot 2085

I am Michael Thompson. I was born in 1960 and grew up in a city that, in the 1980s, became a stage of extreme contradictions. On one hand, the bustle and creativity of New York were visible on every street, in every corner; on the other, the dark shadow of an uncontrollable epidemic and the deafening silence of the authorities. Today, in this video, I want to recount the story of a painful but necessary struggle, in which stigma and official inaction toward HIV left millions of voices silenced, and yet, through protest and solidarity, the hope of a change arose that, though late, saved countless lives.

I remember that autumn of 1983 with sharp clarity. The leaves were falling, the air was heavy with melancholy, and yet it could not conceal the growing alarm gripping the city. That morning I woke with an inexplicable sense of foreboding. The headlines of the newspapers seemed to scream from their pages: *"New Epidemic Strikes the City," "HIV: A Punishment Disease."* The news was steeped in sensationalism and prejudice, and no one seemed willing to confront the true magnitude of the problem.

I was only just beginning to understand my own identity and the environment I lived in. Back then, we didn't speak of an *"LGBTQ+ community"* as we do now, more often we were labeled in derogatory terms or referred to ourselves simply as *"the gay community"* (or *"gays and lesbians"*). Being part of that collective meant living in uncertainty and marginalization, but also cultivating a quiet resistance. Fear was a constant, and every street, every bar, every corner carried that collective dread of being singled out and rejected. Ignorance fed on rumor, and the government, fearful of scandal, preferred silence and stigmatization.

One afternoon, while sitting in a small café in the East Village, I overheard a group of people speaking in hushed tones about *"the curse"* that fell upon those who were infected. It was not a casual whisper, but a near-ritual lament that spoke of social condemnation and a bleak future. That conversation chilled my blood: they spoke of HIV not as a disease, but as a sentence, a divine punishment for those who strayed from the norm.

"They say if you have the virus, there's no hope… that it's a sentence to live in ostracism," murmured a trembling female voice as she stirred her coffee.

"And not even the government dares to speak the truth. They prefer to stay silent and let people drown in misinformation," replied a man, his voice rough and full of restrained anger.

It was in that moment that I understood the true enemy was not only the disease, but the indifference and fear imposed by those who were supposed to protect us. That conversation lit a flame of rebellion in me, a deep desire not to remain silent in the face of others' suffering.

New York in the 1980s presented itself as a city of contrasts. On one hand, there was a vibrant nightlife, a bohemian, creative atmosphere; on the other, despair seeped through the streets in the form of rumors and stigma. The nights glowed with the neon lights of bars and clubs, but they were also stained by a sadness that could not be ignored. I lived between both worlds, witnessing the fleeting sparkle of hope and the dark abyss of discrimination.

It was on one of those nights that I decided to attend a secret meeting in a basement on the Lower East Side. The place was packed: activists, young people, elders, and above all, people who had been marked by HIV or who feared they would be. The atmosphere was heavy, charged with a mixture of fear, anger, and, most of all, determination. At the center of the room, an improvised microphone became the epicenter of a declaration of intent. An older man, with eyes reflecting the pain of countless losses, took the floor:

"Today we gather not to mourn, but to fight. The government has turned its back on us, branded us, made us feel that our lives are worthless. But here, in this corner, we are strong. Here we are family, and together we will demand the truth and the compassion that has been denied us."

Each word echoed through the dim basement, igniting both fury and hope in our hearts. That night, alliances were forged, stories were shared, and we promised that, no matter the cost, no one would be silenced. We walked out into the street with handmade placards, bearing slogans that cried out *"Lives, not stigma!"* and *"No more silence!"* The crowd was a sea of weary yet determined faces, united by the desire to change the course of history.

As we marched through the avenues, I felt how every step was an act of defiance. The echo of our chants mingled with the distant wail of sirens, but nothing could extinguish the fervor driving us forward. The streetlamps seemed to flicker in solidarity, and the night's chill contrasted with the warmth of our embraces. It was a magical moment in which the city, despite its harshness, transformed into a stage of hope and resistance.

During those months of struggle, the meetings and protests became our daily sustenance. I remember with particular clarity a conversation I had with Lisa, an activist who had lost her partner to HIV. The sadness in her eyes was deep, but her voice was filled with determination.

"Every time I go out into the street, I feel I carry with me the weight of all those who are no longer here," she said as we walked together through the streets of the East Village. "But I also feel that in every cry, in every banner, rises the strength of those who never wanted to be forgotten."

"It's horrible to think that a disease can be used to marginalize us," I replied, clenching my fists. "They've labeled us, condemned us… but we can't stay silent anymore."

Lisa nodded and added:

"The indifference of the authorities has been the worst punishment. It's not just about failing to act, it's about denying our humanity. But when we unite, when our voices rise in protest, we show the world that no one has the right to decide for us."

That conversation was repeated in countless gatherings: in cafés, in parks, and in the hallways of makeshift shelters. Every shared story was a testimony of loss, of love, and of a courage born in the midst of pain.

In one of those meetings, a middle-aged man, tears streaming down his face, said:

"I lost my best friend in 1984. He was a man full of life, always ready to laugh and to dream. But the virus came and took him without mercy. Every time I think of him, my soul aches. And yet, his memory pushes me to fight, to not allow his voice to be extinguished in oblivion."

These voices intertwined in a chorus of resistance. Each story, each tear, each cry was a reminder that, even though society wanted to relegate us to the shadows, we had both the right and the duty to demand justice and dignity.

As the epidemic spread, the government's response proved slow and buried in bureaucracy. The first alarms were ignored, and misinformation became daily bread. The media, instead of shedding light on the truth, chose sensationalism that fueled fear and stigma. The idea that HIV was divine punishment spread with force, and every day more lives were lost in a system that preferred silence in the face of suffering.

I remember one winter morning when the cold seemed to intensify the desperation. I was in a small meeting room, surrounded by activists and volunteer doctors, when one of them, with a broken voice, revealed the devastating numbers:

"We've lost hundreds of people in the last few months. Each number is a life cut short, a family shattered. We can't keep allowing fear and ignorance to decide the fate of our loved ones."

The silence that followed those words was deafening. In that moment, I realized that the true tragedy was not only the disease itself, but the lack of compassion and action from those who had the power to make a difference. Bureaucracy and apathy had become accomplices to death, and every delay in the official response was a sentence of further suffering.

The cost was incalculable. Entire families sank into despair, and the pain spread like a shadow that engulfed everything. Protests grew more intense, and rage turned into an unstoppable force. We activists took to the streets not only to demand answers, but to claim the right to live without fear, without stigmas imposed by ignorance.

One night, during a winter demonstration, the city transformed into a stage of resistance. Rain fell intermittently, and the cold seemed intent on freezing even the most burning emotions. But nothing could extinguish the fervor that had been kindled in the heart of every protester. We marched through the avenues with handmade banners bearing messages that demanded dignity and justice. The darkness was pierced by floodlights and the glow of determined eyes.

In that march, I met Javier, a young activist whose fists had been bloodied in earlier clashes. With eyes burning with determination, he told me:

"We're going out to fight, not just for ourselves, but for all those who've been forgotten. Every step we take in these streets is a declaration that we will not give up. The silence of the government has killed too many, but our united voice has the power to change the course."

Javier's words merged with the thunder of our footsteps, creating a symphony of protest that echoed across the city. The entire crowd seemed to move in unison, as if every cry and every word were part of a powerful manifesto against injustice. In the distance, chants rang out: *"No more silence!"* and *"Lives, not stigma!"*, a demand for the right to be heard, to be recognized as human beings.

Every demonstration, every protest was an act of rebellion against a system that preferred to conceal the truth. The struggle became both physical and emotional. Clashes with the police were inevitable, and often, amid the chaos, moments of pain and courage unfolded. I saw comrades fall, wounded both in body and spirit, but never did I see the fire of protest extinguished. These were moments of absolute rawness, where the human cost was tangible in every tear and every stifled cry.

The price of official inaction was measured in lives. I myself lost people close to me, friends who became silent victims of an epidemic that spread while the world looked away. One of the nights that marked me most deeply was when I received the news of Daniel's death, a friend who had stood by my side in many protests. I remember how, in the cold hours of dawn, my phone vibrated with a call that changed everything:

"Michael, it's Daniel… We lost him. He couldn't keep fighting…"

"What are you saying? Daniel, no, no, it can't be!" I answered, feeling the ground vanish beneath my feet.

The voice on the other end broke, and in that instant the pain was so intense it felt as if time itself had stopped. Daniel had been a ray of light in the darkness, someone who, despite his suffering, always found a way to make others laugh and lift their spirits. His departure was a devastating blow, but also a lesson: the fight could not stop, because in every loss lay the urgency to act, to prevent others from meeting the same fate.

At one of the meetings organized after Daniel's passing, I found myself surrounded by faces marked with both physical and emotional scars. An elderly woman, whose eyes still shone with the strength of a lifetime, took the floor:

"I have seen too many die. I've lost children, siblings... But I know that every tear shed here will not be in vain. If my voice can ignite a spark in even one heart, then I will have fulfilled my duty. We cannot allow silence to remain the executioner of our souls."

Her words etched themselves into my memory, reminding me that the struggle was a collective responsibility. Every story, every loss was a call to action, a demand that pain be transformed into a cry for justice.

As social pressure grew, the media began to pay attention. Protests that were initially ignored or ridiculed became the driving force behind investigations and debates in the highest government circles. Though the official response remained slow and evasive, the persistence of the community forced a change in the narrative.

I remember a televised debate in 1986 where a panel of experts gathered to discuss the crisis. The tension in the studio was palpable. A host, in a solemn voice, posed the question:

"What is truly failing in the government's response to the HIV crisis? Is it bureaucracy, fear, or simply a lack of empathy?"

Among the experts, the voice of a renowned doctor rose, a woman whose career had been overshadowed by the lack of resources and support. With tears in her eyes, she declared:

"We are losing lives every single day, and the inaction of those who should protect us is unbearable. This is not about numbers, it's about human beings. Each life lost is a reminder that indifference can be deadly."

That debate was a turning point. Public opinion began to question, to demand answers, and the voices that had been silenced for years emerged with strength. The pressure of civil society forced legislators to sit at the negotiating table and to reconsider policies that, until then, had privileged stigma over compassion.

Activism became a powerful tool for social transformation. Over those years, community organizations emerged and consolidated, working tirelessly to provide support, information, and resources to those who needed them most. I joined several of these initiatives, devoting my days and nights to coordinating awareness campaigns, raising funds for treatments, and above all, ensuring that no one felt alone in this struggle.

One campaign I remember with particular emotion was the *March of Dignity,* organized in 1987. The call was a resounding success, and thousands gathered in Central Park. The atmosphere was almost mystical: flags of every color waved in unison, and the air filled with songs that celebrated life and demanded justice. During that march, I had the opportunity to step onto the stage and address the crowd. With my voice breaking but firm, I said:

"Today we gather to honor those whose voices have been silenced. Today we claim the right to live without fear, without prejudice. Every step we take is a declaration of love, of resistance, and of hope. We will not allow stigma to define us. Together we are the force that will change history."

The applause that followed was deafening, and in that instant, I knew change was possible. The fight was not in vain: it was in motion, and collective determination was stronger than any barrier imposed by fear or ignorance.

Still, amid so much mobilization, the struggle carried a deeply personal cost. There were moments when the physical and emotional exhaustion became unbearable. The nights were long and sleepless, and at times, loneliness loomed over me like a silent shadow. In those moments, I found myself reflecting on the fragility of life and the relentless cruelty of fate.

One night, after a particularly harsh demonstration, I took refuge in a small apartment in Greenwich Village. The rain beat against the windows, and the constant sound of traffic mingled with my own thoughts. Sitting beside an old radio, I listened to a song about love and loss, and I let myself be carried away by the melancholy of the moment. I closed my eyes and imagined all those who had lost their battle against indifference. It was then that I understood that, although the pain was immense, it was also the fuel that drove transformation. Every tear, every stifled cry was a reminder that the struggle had to continue, that we could not surrender to despair.

It is in solitude where I sometimes find the strength to carry on. Remembering Daniel, my fallen comrades, and those whose names were lost to oblivion compels me not to let their sacrifice be in vain. The struggle, though heartbreaking, is also an act of love and a commitment to humanity.

By the late 1980s, the HIV crisis had begun to cross New York's borders and become a global problem. Protests and demonstrations spread to cities around the world, and solidarity among communities of diverse cultures became tangible. I remember receiving letters and messages from activists in cities as far away as London, Paris, and Buenos Aires, all united by a single cry: the right to live and to be treated with dignity.

In one of those exchanges, a British activist wrote:

"In our streets, fear is as palpable as the air we breathe. But every time we see our brothers and sisters rise in protest, we feel that hope is stronger than any prejudice. The struggle is global, and together we will write a future where no one is forgotten."

These words resonated within me and reminded me that the cause was greater than any border. The struggle against stigma and indifference knew no limits, and each act of protest became a step toward a more just and compassionate world. International pressure eventually forced governments and health organizations to rethink their strategies and to allocate resources for HIV research and treatment. Though the change was slow, every advance represented a victory for those who, through immense sacrifice, had demanded to be heard.

Looking back, I see that the path we traveled was filled with challenges, moments of despair, and triumphs that, though delayed, marked the beginning of a historic transformation. Every protest, every march, and every conversation in those dark years was the seed of a change that, over time, began to bloom. Though the epidemic exacted a terrible price, it also left us with invaluable lessons about the importance of empathy, solidarity, and collective commitment.

The fight against HIV stigma was much more than a battle against a disease. It was a confrontation with injustice, with institutional indifference, and with the fear that was used to marginalize those who were different. Every story of loss became a cry demanding the truth be heard, and every act of protest was a reaffirmation that human dignity is inviolable.

During those years I learned that activism is not only about demonstrating in the streets, but about transforming pain into an unstoppable force. The voices of those who were silenced echo in every corner of the city, in every letter, in every recording preserved as testimony. It is a legacy that, despite the passing years, lives on and inspires new generations to fight for a world where justice and compassion prevail.

As I conclude this testimony, I am overwhelmed by a mix of emotions: sorrow for the countless lives lost, pain for the indifference that allowed the crisis to spread, but also gratitude and pride for having been part of a movement that, despite all adversity, refused to remain silent. To the young people of today, to whom I speak with my heart in my hand, I say: never forget history.

Every protest, every cry, and every banner carried a message meant to transcend time: human dignity is inviolable, and stigma must never be the barrier that stands between love and justice. You have the power to transform the world, to use technology and information to build bridges instead of walls. Learn from the pain of the past to forge a future where empathy and solidarity are the pillars of a truly inclusive society.

I remember that on one of those nights, in the rain and the cold that seeped into our bones, I looked around and felt that, despite everything, we were not alone. There, in the heart of the protest, every face reflected the determination not to let indifference be the legacy we left behind. That image was etched in my mind forever, reminding me that the struggle is a continuous process, that every generation has the responsibility to raise its voice and claim what rightfully belongs to it.

Looking through old photographs and listening to recordings of those protests, I feel that memory is the engine that drives change. Each image, each sound is a testimony to the courage of those who refused to be silenced. At my desk, surrounded by yellowed newspaper clippings, letters, and faded placards, I find the strength to carry on and to pass on to new generations the importance of fighting for truth and justice.

I have learned that, though time erases many scars, history must be preserved intact so that the mistakes of the past are never repeated. It is my duty, and also my honor, to be the bearer of that memory, of that cry that, though silenced in its time, now rises with the strength of truth. I want every young person who hears this testimony to know that behind every number, behind every statistic, there is a life, a dream, and a struggle that deserves to be remembered.

The transformation we lived through in those dark years taught us that change is possible even under the most adverse circumstances. Indifference, fear, and stigma, though powerful, could not halt the advance of solidarity and love. Every step taken in the streets, every protest under the rain was an act of faith in the future, a commitment to the idea that justice and compassion can prevail even over bureaucracy and prejudice.

Even today, in the digital era, when technology connects us in unimaginable ways, it is essential not to forget where we come from. The fight against HIV in the 1980s is an indelible lesson that teaches us humanity must never allow indifference to stand between love and life. The story of those silenced cries became a beacon, illuminating the path for those who, today, face new battles for equality and justice.

Now, as I finish this video, my heart is filled with a mixture of sorrow and hope: sorrow for the countless lives lost to indifference, for the pain that still lingers in every corner of a city that witnessed so many tragedies; but also hope, because the struggle, that struggle embodied in every protest and every cry remains alive in the memory of those who dare to raise their voices.

I leave this message to those who hear me and read these words: may the echo of our cries, though silenced in their time, become the driving force to build a tomorrow where dignity, compassion, and justice are the pillars of society. May every generation be inspired by the courage of those who, in the midst of pain and darkness, chose to raise their voices for a better future.

Some time ago, my own son began asking me about those difficult years, eager to understand what it was like to live under the weight of fear, silence, and stigma. That was when I discovered in Genostories the opportunity to pass on these experiences not only to him and to my future grandchildren, but also to anyone who wishes to know the truth of that period. By recording them here, I do not leave them hidden away in a drawer; on the contrary, I offer them publicly so that whoever wishes to listen may learn from both the mistakes and the triumphs of our history.

As I gaze at the horizon, I see a world in transformation. A world that, despite the wounds of the past, has learned that stigma must never define human worth. Though the price has been far too high, each life lost reminds us that silence must never be our answer to injustice. Now, with these memories, I pay tribute to those who are no longer here and, at the same time, I kindle the flame of resistance in those yet to come. For as long as there are hearts willing to feel, to love, and to fight, the silenced screams of the past will become the unstoppable force that drives our future.

Here is the testimony of Michael Thompson, a man who lived through the HIV epidemic of the 1980s and bore its scars of governmental inaction, marginalization, and pain. His story, anchored in the irreparable loss of friends and companions, invites us to reflect on the strength that emerges from unity when institutions fail. In that dramatic clash between stigma and determination arose a movement that, through protests and mutual support, forced society to recognize the humanity of those living with the virus, proving that solidarity and compassion can overcome even the most entrenched indifference.

For us, living in a time marked by different, though no less urgent, challenges, Michael's story is far more than a painful chapter of the past. It is a mirror reminding us of the fragility of our social fabric when it becomes complicit in silence, and at the same time, a beacon illuminating the path of collective action. We learn that even in the darkest of moments, a group of people convinced of their right to life and dignity can alter the destiny of thousands.

By choosing this story for our collection, I seek to ensure that its legacy transcends its time and stands as both a warning and a promise: a warning of the danger in underestimating the power of negligence and discrimination; and a promise that united voices, guided by empathy and justice, can shatter the most unyielding barriers. May the example of Michael and his companions inspire future generations not to remain silent, not to yield to the fear of seeming different, and not to allow another crisis to become an excuse for silence. Wherever

someone suffers in silence, there arises the urgent need for another voice which, like his, can ignite the flame of hope.
Griot 2085

THE SCREEN AND THE WONDER

In my quest to gather and share the human stories that have nourished imagination throughout the centuries, I came across the account of Harold Dawson, recorded in 2025. I was especially moved by his desire to show his grandchildren the magic he experienced through mid-20th-century cinema, in contrast to the almost hypnotic admiration they now feel for artificial intelligence. As I examine his testimony from this very different 2085, I find myself wondering: at what point did we stop kindling our own creative spark and begin to delegate it to algorithms?

This chapter, which I have titled The Screen and the Wonder (you will see why as you read), reveals Harold's experience: a man who was dazzled by the ritual of movie theaters, the simple act of buying a ticket and immersing oneself in a collective experience, and who now watches his grandchildren interact with AI with the same passion he once felt for films. Through his words, we discover a bridge between that old source of wonder and the new technological revolution which, if we are not careful, could consume the very human essence of dreaming and creating.

Griot 2085

I am Harold Dawson, though most know me as Harry. Today, in the year 2025, I sit in front of my phone's camera to record a series of videos on Genostories, ready to tell my beloved grandchildren, and everyone who joins me on this platform, the story of how cinema, that great revolution of the 1950s and '60s, illuminated my youth in a way as unforgettable as artificial intelligence now fascinates the young.

As I watch my grandchildren, Evan, 15; Mia, 12; and Lucas, 9. I realize the astonishing transformation technology has brought to the world. They spend hours interacting with virtual assistants, generating hyper-realistic images and videos just by describing what they want to see, and chatting with artificial intelligences that answer their most varied questions. I see them enraptured, their eyes shining with wonder at each new advance, and I can't help but smile, remembering the same sense of awe I experienced more than five decades ago.

But let me tell you… the magic that filled my soul back then did not come from binary code or ultra-fast processors, but from the vibrant light of a giant screen in a darkened theater. That screen was a portal to unknown, dazzling worlds, and sometimes to realities so close it felt as if you could step inside without ever leaving your seat.

Through these videos on Genostories, I want to share my story: a story contrasting the impact of cinema on my youth, in the late '50s and early '60s, with the technological revolution that now shapes young people's imaginations. My hope is that, by sharing these memories, you'll understand that every generation has its own revolution, and that technology, whether the magic of a smartphone or the power of AI, should inspire, not replace, our creativity and capacity to dream.

Just this morning, while having breakfast in the kitchen, I came across a scene that froze time for me. Evan sat in front of his tablet, absorbed in an artificial intelligence app that let him generate images from text prompts. With every word he typed, the program transformed his ideas into digital artworks, their colors so vivid they looked as though they had come straight out of a dream. Beside him, Mia chatted animatedly with a virtual assistant, asking questions about history, science, even jokes, while Lucas, with his childlike curiosity, tapped the screen without really grasping the magnitude of what he was witnessing.

For a moment, I felt transported back to a time when I too had been filled with wonder, though for very different reasons. The technology my grandchildren use is astounding, no doubt, and it reflects the unstoppable progress of humanity. But sometimes I feel a pang of nostalgia, remembering that in my youth, what ignited the spark of imagination was not an algorithm, but the almost mystical experience of stepping into a movie theater: a darkened hall where the only light came from the projection of a film that promised to take you to another world.

Seeing the excitement in my grandchildren's eyes fills me with pride, but it also compels me to share with them that essential part of my own story, that quiet revolution I lived through cinema. Because even though times have changed and the tools are different, the essence of wonder and the capacity to dream remain intact in the human heart.

Let me take you back in time, to those golden years when cinema was not merely a form of entertainment, but a window to the world and to the imagination. It was the late 1950s and early '60s, a time when every movie premiere was experienced with an intensity that today feels almost mythical.

I remember that in 1959, as a rebellious teenager hungry for adventure, I often skipped school to go to the movies. It wasn't something I did for fleeting fun, but almost a vital necessity. The simple act of stepping into a movie theater became a kind of rite, a ceremony where the everyday was left behind and a portal opened to distant universes. It was a time when cinema had the power to transform reality, to make you forget, if only for a few hours, the constraints of daily life.

The movie theaters of my youth were true temples of imagination. Picture, for a moment, a dark hall lit only by the flickering glow of the projector, with rows of velvet seats stretching endlessly and massive hand-painted posters announcing the latest marvels from Hollywood. The air was infused with the unmistakable scent of freshly popped popcorn, mingling with the audience's anticipation. Each time the curtains parted, a wave of adrenaline and hope swept through the crowd, and for a few precious moments, the outside world ceased to exist.

I remember saving my pennies through small jobs, delivering newspapers, helping at the neighborhood kiosk, all with the firm purpose of buying that ticket that cost just $0.45. That figure, so insignificant today, was the price of freedom, the passage to epic adventures, unforgettable romances, and unsolved mysteries. What was most astonishing was that this ticket gave you access to two films back-to-back. Yes, when the first feature ended, you could step out for a quick refill of soda or popcorn, then return to your seat for the second film, all in the same sitting. A true bargain for anyone eager to experience the spectacle!

And speaking of popcorn, the experience would not be complete without mentioning the two options on offer: plain popcorn at about $0.35, or buttered popcorn, an extra indulgence, for roughly $0.55.

Coca-Cola, the fizzy drink that completed the cinematic ritual, came in various sizes, with prices ranging from $0.35 to $0.75, depending on what you chose. Each of these modest prices was, in truth, the cost of entering a dream world for a few hours, leaving worries behind and surrendering to the magic of celluloid.

Those little details, now almost otherworldly, captured the essence of a time when every trip to the theater was an almost sacred event. It wasn't simply about watching a film, but about immersing yourself in a collective experience: the thrill of waiting for the show to begin, the anticipation of sharing those moments with friends or even strangers, and the near-ritual pleasure of enjoying those accessible *luxuries*, a ticket, a bag of popcorn, and a Coca-Cola, that made it possible to dream big.

Every penny saved, every show enjoyed became an unforgettable memory that, looking back today, fills me with a warm and profound nostalgia. That waiting, that blend of emotions and small sacrifices, fueled our imagination and forged in us the desire to explore, to venture beyond the ordinary. Though the cinema of that time was different in form, to me its essence remains unchanged: the symbol of a cultural and emotional revolution, capable of stirring a fascination much like the one my grandchildren now feel when they interact with artificial intelligence.

I remember one time in particular, in 1962, when I skipped class with my friends to see the latest Elvis Presley film. The excitement was almost tangible: the thought of seeing Elvis, the King of Rock, on a giant screen, with his unmistakable rhythm and charisma, filled us with youthful fervor. We gathered at the theater entrance, exchanging laughter and stories, while the sun slowly set and gave way to the night, the very night when the screen would ignite and transport us to a parallel universe.

Cinema of that era did more than just show films: it was a showcase of culture, a mirror reflecting the aspirations and dreams of a generation eager to break free from the chains of the past. Movies like *A Hard Day's Night,* with the explosive energy of The Beatles, or Hitchcock's *Psycho,* confronting us with the dark recesses of the human mind, were far more than simple stories: they were artistic manifestations that urged us to question, to imagine, and above all, to dream big.

Back then, the moviegoing experience was a collective ritual. There were no modern comforts of streaming or high-definition home screens. Each trip to the theater was a unique experience and, in a way, a transformative one. Entering the cinema meant immersing yourself in an atmosphere charged with magic. The lights dimmed, the audience's chatter melted into expectant silence, and when the screen finally lit up, it felt as though the entire universe had condensed into that single moment.

I can still recall the sensation of losing myself in the story, of feeling that for a few hours it was possible to forget the problems of the real world and surrender to the moving narrative. Music was often an essential part of this experience. The chords of Bill Haley's *Rock Around the Clock* or the unmistakable rhythm of Elvis's *Jailhouse Rock* intertwined with the film's plot, creating a symphony that resonated deep within us. Even the early songs of The Beatles, with their freshness and vitality, had the power to transform any feeling into an explosion of youthful euphoria.

The aesthetics of the era also played a fundamental role. Boys wore leather jackets and slicked-back hair, while girls dazzled in full skirts and pastel colors. These details, which might seem almost cartoonish today, represented at the time the height of fashion and style. It was an age in which every aspect of life seemed infused with an air of rebellion and a search for identity, and every trip to the cinema became an opportunity to express who you were and where you wanted to go.

Watching my grandchildren interact with artificial intelligence, I can't help but draw parallels between that cinematic revolution and today's digital one. No matter how impressive today's technology may be, images generated from simple descriptions, virtual assistants conversing with us, and videos so realistic they blur the line between virtual and real, there is something the cinema experience could never take from me. That sense of wonder, that almost mystical fervor of watching a film projected in a darkened theater, is a feeling anchored deep within memory.

Seeing my grandchildren marvel at each advance in AI takes me back to my own youth, when every visit to the theater was a new adventure. Like them, I was in a state of total fascination: each new release was a world waiting to be discovered, each film a story opening infinite possibilities. But the difference lay in the context and in the medium through which that wonder was experienced.

In my day, cinema was the engine that drove imagination, the bridge connecting reality with dreams, the medium by which you could travel to unreachable places without leaving your seat. Today, AI allows us to create and explore in almost limitless ways, but at times I fear that in this technological abundance, we may lose the value of the creative process, the kind that is born of effort, passion, and human imagination.

My grandchildren, though immersed in a world of bits and algorithms, also possess that innate spark of creativity. I've told them on several occasions that technology should be a tool to inspire, not a substitute for the essence of being human. The true magic lies in the ability to dream, in the skill of turning wonder into action, and in the determination never to be swept away by the inertia of immediacy.

I decided to use Genostories to share this piece of my story because I see in this platform the same power of connection I once experienced in movie theaters. Here, through videos, documents, and comments, the memories of a generation are woven together and shared with the new, creating an intergenerational bridge in which each story enriches the next.

When I uploaded my first video, talking about the cinema during my teenage years, I never imagined the number of responses I would receive. People from my generation began to reminisce about those magical nights, those clandestine adventures in which they escaped the routine to immerse themselves in worlds of fantasy. The comment section filled with nostalgia, funny anecdotes, and even tears of emotion. Young people, on their part, were intrigued and surprised; many confessed they had never imagined that something as everyday as going to the movies could have meant so much to those who lived through it in that era.

One of the messages that moved me most came from a young film student, who wrote:

"Harold, thank you for sharing your memories. Today, when I watch AI-generated videos, I feel a fascination similar to what you described with the cinema. Now I understand that every generation has its own revolution, and yours is as inspiring as mine. I hope we never lose that sense of wonder."

Reading those words filled me with joy and reaffirmed my belief that, despite the dizzying changes, the essence of wonder and creativity is still alive. Genostories has become a space where memories of the past can illuminate the path to the future, reminding us that technology should be an ally, a tool to amplify imagination, not a replacement for human creativity.

Allow me to take you back to relive one of those unforgettable moments. It was an autumn afternoon in 1963. I was just fifteen years old, and that day I had set myself a bold goal: to skip school and go see the premiere of a film that, according to whispers, would revolutionize cinema. With my heart pounding a thousand beats per minute, I found myself walking through the streets of my neighborhood, feeling the crisp air that marked the arrival of fall and the thrill of doing something forbidden.

When I reached the theater, I stopped in front of the huge hand-painted posters announcing the premiere. The design was so colorful and striking that, for a moment, I forgot all my fears and doubts. I bought my ticket with money I had saved doing odd jobs around the neighborhood and felt that this simple piece of paper was the key to a parallel universe. The ticket, which cost as little as $0.35, was a passport to a world where imagination was the only law.

Once inside, the theater was filled with anonymous faces who, like me, had come in search of something extraordinary. I settled into a velvet seat that creaked softly beneath me and, as the lights dimmed, the darkness gave way to the magical glow of the screen. That first moving image, the first note of the soundtrack, and the collective murmur of anticipation were etched into my memory forever. It was at that moment that I understood the transformative power of cinema: a collective, almost sacred experience in which, for a brief span of time, the real world dissolved and gave way to dreams and illusions.

Each scene captivated me: I traveled to exotic places, faced unimaginable adventures, and felt intense emotions, as if I myself were part of the story. The magic of that moment was indescribable, and for a fleeting time, life seemed brimming with infinite possibilities.

Over time, I came to understand that what made cinema so special wasn't just the storytelling or the visual effects, but its ability to ignite the spark of dreams in every viewer. In an era when travel was an unattainable luxury for most, films became windows to the world, the vehicle that allowed people to dream of far-off horizons and different lives.

Cinema inspired me to write my own stories, to draw, and to imagine worlds that transcended the monotony of everyday life. That same inspiration was what, in many cases, drove young people of my generation to pursue artistic careers, to study film, theater, literature, and to become content creators. The cinematic experience became a driving force for change a silent revolution that encouraged us to question reality and dream of a better future.

As I see how artificial intelligence opens new doors in the creative realm, I understand that, although the tools have changed, the creative impulse remains the same. Today's technology allows us to generate images, videos, and music with astonishing speed and precision, but the essential element is still the human being, with their ability to dream and to transform reality through imagination.

While recording my videos for Genostories, I couldn't help but reflect on the similarities and differences between the revolution of cinema and the current revolution of AI. On one hand, cinema, with its tangible magic, demanded a collective experience, an almost ceremonial ritual in which the darkness of the theater and the light of the screen combined to create a unique atmosphere. On the other hand, artificial intelligence presents itself as an omnipresent tool, accessible at any moment and from anywhere, but one that sometimes risks making the creative process feel too immediate, almost automatic.

My grandchildren are amazed at how quickly they can turn an idea into an image or a video, without having to spend hours, days, or even weeks creating something from scratch. That immediacy is, without a doubt, one of the greatest virtues of today's technology. Even so, I remind them that, in my time, every moment in the cinema was the result of a painstaking creative process: from the writing of the script to the design of the sets and the musical composition, every detail was carefully crafted to deliver an unforgettable experience.

For example, the dedication of the actors was unmatched. They had to memorize scripts that at times seemed endless and also prepare to sing and dance in scenes that required not only skill, but also iron discipline and total commitment. The tireless effort of these artists was evident in every line, every choreography, and every musical note. It was as if, in every detail, the passion and devotion of a group of people determined to convey genuine emotions and deep feelings to the audience had been poured. Watching their performances on the big screen, you could feel the mark of every sacrifice, the intensity of the work, and the collective energy that transformed cinema into something far more than entertainment, a spectacle that moved, inspired, and left an indelible mark on the hearts of those who lived it.

In my videos, I explain that no matter how impressive technological advancements may be, they must never forget that the true engine of creativity is the human being. Technology should serve to enhance that creativity, not replace it. Every generation has its own revolution, and for us, cinema was the doorway to unimaginable worlds; the revolution of 2025, represented by artificial intelligence, must become the catalyst for young people to continue dreaming, imagining, and creating.

After publishing my videos, the response was overwhelming. Comments from both young and old poured in, many expressing wonder and nostalgia, and others showing a renewed admiration for a time that had seemed distant and almost mythical until then. One of my grandsons, Evan, sent me a video message in which he said:

"Grandpa, I never really understood why you were so passionate about going to the movies. Now I see it wasn't just about watching a film, it was about living an experience that changed you forever. With AI, I feel like I can create anything I imagine in seconds, but I wonder... don't you miss that waiting, that anticipation before the screen lit up?"

His words filled me with pride and reminded me that, even though the tools may change, the essence of wonder and the desire to discover something new remain untouched. The comments from other Genostorians, both from my generation and theirs, wove together a tapestry of memories and perspectives. Some recalled the nights of clandestine cinema, the long lines outside theaters, and the excitement of saving every cent to buy a ticket; others, the younger ones, expressed their desire to learn more about that world and to find inspiration in the stories of the past.

The Genostories platform became that much-needed intergenerational bridge. It was a space where the cinema of the 1950s and '60s came back to life through my stories, and where today's technological revolution found deeper meaning when compared with the passion and fervor of past eras.

In one of my final videos, after sharing all these memories and reflections, I decided to leave a clear and heartfelt message for my grandchildren and for all who were listening:

"At times, all the advances that drive a generation must be measured by the progress they inspire within that generation, and not by all that they take away. The magic of cinema never replaced the imagination of my generation; in the same way, artificial intelligence should not replace the inherent creativity of yours. Let every technological tool be an ally to expand the limits of dreaming, and not an excuse to forget that the true wonder lies in the human capacity to imagine, to create, and to transform."

These words, spoken with a heart full of experience and the humility of someone who has lived through two such different revolutions, resonated within the community. Several people commented that, upon hearing my reflections, they understood that true innovation does not lie solely in technology, but in how it is used to enhance the creative and human spirit.

My grandchildren, with that curious and critical gaze only the young possess, asked me if I felt something had been lost with the advance of technology. I answered that, although immediacy and the abundance of resources can sometimes make us forget the value of the creative process, we must never give up our capacity for wonder. Technology, no matter how advanced it becomes, should be a tool that enriches our lives, not a substitute for our imagination.

I'd like to share with you, dear friends, one of my most cherished memories from that time. It was a Friday night in 1964, and I, still a teenager, my heart brimming with hope, had spent weeks saving up through odd jobs, delivering newspapers, helping out at the neighborhood kiosk, just so I could afford that long-awaited trip to the movies. I met up with a group of friends at an old neighborhood theater, a place known for its massive hand-painted posters and red velvet-upholstered seats that seemed to invite you to dream. The atmosphere was festive, almost as if the cinema had become a small festival of dreams, a sanctuary where, for a couple of hours, reality faded away and gave way to a universe of fantasy.

That night's screening was *Paris When It Sizzles*, a film that promised to whisk us away to the very heart of the city of love and freedom, and had the power to completely transform our existence. The plot was as original as it was provocative: Richard Benson, played by the charismatic William Holden, was a screenwriter from the *old wave* who, in his peculiar lifestyle, worked only five days a year so he could spend the other 360 living at his whim, between drinks, parties, and wild romances. The story took an unexpected turn when Gabrielle Simpson, portrayed by the incomparable Audrey Hepburn, arrived at his hotel, introducing herself as his new secretary. Her mission: to type up the screenplay that Richard had supposedly been working on for weeks. But the truth was something else entirely, Richard had only a promising title, *The Girl Who Stole the Eiffel Tower*, and hadn't written a single page of the draft.

What was so fascinating about this plot was how, from the very first moment, you could feel the tension between the discipline of art and the carefree spirit of a true bohemian. Gabriel was alarmed to discover that, with the script due Sunday morning at exactly 10:01, the lack of progress was staggering. But Richard, with that almost mythical nonchalance and the conviction of a passionate writer, trusted that his genius would prevail over any deadline, proving he knew how to work in a way that even the new styles of the *nouvelle vague* couldn't rival.

In one of the opening scenes, Richard was shown scattering blank pages all over the room, as if each sheet were a portal to creation. With a carefree air, he began describing a quick, detail-free plot, a kind of cinematic sketch, that vaguely resembled the script of *Breakfast at Tiffany's*, but with unexpected twists: the protagonist was in a white car, wearing an elegant dress of the same color, but instead of standing in front of Tiffany's, she was in the lavish display window of Dior. References to other iconic films followed, even *My Fair Lady* was mentioned, in a play of intertextuality that made the viewer's imagination pulse. During those two days in which the story unfolded, Richard and Gabrielle, through their alter egos, Rick and Gaby, mirrored their emotions and feelings, giving shape to a story in which every word and every silence revealed a truth about the art of living without restraints.

As the film unfolded on the big screen, I let myself be absorbed by that intoxicating mix of wit and rebellion. I remember clearly how the murmurs of the audience gradually faded into a reverent, almost sacred silence, as the lights dimmed and the projector began to emit its unmistakable hum. At that very moment, I felt I was about to leave behind routine and embark on an unprecedented adventure. The screen lit up with scenes of magical Parisian streets, bohemian cafés, and forbidden loves, and for a few moments, life felt infinitely richer and full of possibilities.

What made the cinema of that era so special was that, unlike the immediacy that characterizes today's technology, every moment in the theater was the result of a painstaking creative process. The actors, with admirable discipline and dedication, had to memorize scripts that at times seemed endless, and in many films they were expected to sing and dance. Each performance was infused with the effort and passion of those artists, whose work conveyed emotions and feelings that seemed to pulse in every frame. That dedication was the reason why cinema could transport you to faraway worlds and make you dream big, challenging your everyday reality.

I remember that night when *Paris When It Sizzles* was shown at that neighborhood theater with particular emotion, not just because the story was fun and bold, but because it embodied the spirit of an era in which cinema was an act of faith, devotion, and revolution. The experience of seeing William Holden and Audrey Hepburn share the screen, with all their ironies and subtleties, taught me that art was not just a fleeting entertainment, but a powerful tool for reinvention, for escaping limitations and, above all, for believing in the possibility of a better world.

Every detail from the price of admission, just $0.45, which granted you access to two consecutive films, to the intoxicating aroma of popcorn (which, if you wanted it with butter, cost around $0.75, while without it came to $0.45), was part of that almost sacred ritual. Coca-Cola, served from $0.50 to a dollar, completed the experience, making each trip to the cinema an investment in dreams. That modest sum was the ticket to epic adventures and stories that, despite their limited resources, had the power to ignite the imagination of an entire generation.

The combination of technique, talent, and the effort of so many individuals, from the screenwriter who meticulously crafted every line, to the composer, and those in charge of set design, resulted in an experience that went beyond mere entertainment. It was, without a doubt, a laborious and passionate creative process that injected a dose of wonder and hope into its audience. The cinema of those years didn't just show you stories; it invited you to dream, to imagine, and to believe in a future full of possibilities.

Years later, watching my grandchildren marvel at how quickly artificial intelligence can transform an idea into images or videos in a matter of seconds, I can't help but draw a parallel between that immediacy and the slow, almost artisanal process that defined filmmaking in my youth. Today's technology, with all its power and efficiency, is astonishing, but it also runs the risk of making us forget the value of the creative process, which requires time, effort, and above all, human passion. It is essential that they remember: every advancement that drives a generation forward must be measured not only by the speed and quantity of content it produces, but by the impact it has on the capacity to dream, to create, and to transform reality without sacrificing the essence of what makes us human.

Through Genostories, I have the privilege of sharing these memories and reflections with my grandchildren and with the entire community. I want them to understand that, although the world evolves and tools change, the true magic lies in the ability to be amazed, and in the hard work it takes to create something meaningful. The cinema of the 1950s and '60s taught me to see the world with eyes full of wonder, and I'm convinced that the revolution of artificial intelligence can, if used wisely, ignite that same creative spark in today's youth.

As I watch my grandchildren interact with their virtual assistants, generating images and videos instantly, I fondly remind them of those days when every detail, every sacrifice, and every penny saved was the key to opening a portal to unimaginable worlds. Because, in the end, what truly matters is keeping alive that spirit of wonder and creativity, something that neither the immediacy of modern technology nor the speed of algorithms will ever be able to replace.

When I observe the relentless advance of technology and AI, I realize that cinema remains an inexhaustible source of inspiration. Although the way we consume content has changed radically, the essence endures: the need to tell stories that connect us, that make us reflect, and that allow us to dream.

Artificial intelligence can generate images and narratives in an instant, but the magic I experienced in those dark cinema halls, where each screening was a rite of passage, a communion of souls sharing the same yearning to escape reality, is something no machine will ever fully replicate. That human experience, that feeling of collective connection, is a legacy we must preserve and honor, and it is precisely what I hope to pass on to my grandchildren.

I explain to them that, just like with cinema, every technological advancement should be evaluated not only by its ability to deliver immediate results, but by its impact on our capacity to dream and to create. Technology should be a tool that helps us transcend the ordinary, not a substitute for the human experience. Every generation has its revolution, and it is the responsibility of each to harness it in a way that enriches life, without sacrificing what makes us truly human: imagination, empathy, and the passion for telling stories.

After uploading my videos, I love reading the comments the community leaves on Genostories. It's fascinating to see how past experiences intertwine with the concerns of the present. People my age share memories of movie nights, secret escapades, and the euphoria they felt when seeing a film in color for the first time. Meanwhile, young people express their amazement at learning how something as simple as a movie ticket could transform so many lives.

In one conversation I had in the comments, a young man named Daniel wrote:

"Harry, I never imagined that going to the movies could be something so revolutionary. Today, with AI, everything feels so immediate and perfect, but you remind us that the process, the waiting, and the experience itself are a fundamental part of the magic. I'd love to know more about those movie nights and how you felt seeing the world through the screen for the first time."

I replied with all my affection and enthusiasm, telling him that every moment of wonder was a gift, and that the real revolution lay in the ability to dream without limits. That interaction made me reflect even more on the importance of keeping that spirit alive, and how every technology, whether the silver screen of the past or the algorithms of today should serve to fuel the flame of ingenuity and creativity.

Finally, in one of the last videos of this series I began for my grandchildren, and eventually extended to the Genostories community, I sat down to reflect on what all of this means for the future. With the camera rolling and my grandchildren gathered beside me, I said:

"Dear community, the revolution of each generation is measured not only by the advances it achieves, but by how those advances enrich our ability to dream and create. The cinema of my youth taught us to see the world with eyes full of wonder and to believe in the possibility of transforming reality. Today, artificial intelligence holds the potential to open new doors, but it must never replace the unique spark born from human imagination."

"Learn to use technology to amplify your ideas, to tell your own stories, and always remember that the real magic lies within you."

With these words, I left behind a message I hope will resonate in their hearts, and in the hearts of all those who join us through Genostories. Progress is essential, but not at the cost of what makes us human. Every tool, every advancement, should be seen as a means to fuel creativity, not an end in itself.

As I finish this video, I look back and feel deep gratitude for having lived through two eras so different, and yet so deeply connected by the common thread of imagination. Cinema taught me to dream, to question, to feel, and to create. And now, I see in my grandchildren's eyes that same passion, though expressed in ways I never could have imagined.

The revolution of cinema, with its neon lights, vibrant sounds, and aura of mystery, lives on in my memories and in my words. In contrast, the revolution of AI, with its ability to instantly turn ideas into images, promises to open new horizons for future generations. What matters is that, regardless of the tool, the essence of wonder and creativity must remain intact, like a beacon guiding our way toward a future full of possibilities.

Receive this legacy not as nostalgia for the past, but as an invitation to embrace the best of both worlds: the magic of lived experience and the power of innovation. May each of you, as you interact with technology, remember that what truly matters is the ability to dream, to imagine, and to create without limits. And so, dear grandchildren and friends of Genostories, I conclude this video with a reflection I hope will always stay with you:

"At times, all the advances that drive a generation forward must be measured by the progress they inspire within that generation, and not by all that they take away. The magic of cinema never replaced the imagination of my generation; in the same way, artificial intelligence should not replace the inherent creativity of yours."

May this message serve to inspire each of you to seek wonder in every experience, to use technology as a tool to expand the limits of imagination, and above all, to always remember that the true revolution lies in the human heart.

As I finish recording this video, while watching images of my grandchildren immersed in their digital world, I realize that, although times have changed and the forms of wonder have evolved, the spirit of creativity and the longing to discover something new are eternal. My generation lived a revolution through cinema; theirs is living it through artificial intelligence. In both cases, what truly matters is the ability to dream, to feel, and to turn that inspiration into something that makes the world a better place.

Thank you for accompanying me on this journey through my memories and for allowing me to share with you the importance of keeping the flame of creativity alive. May this video series I've called *The Screen and the Wonder* be a bridge between past and future, a reminder that each generation has its own moment of awe, and that in the end, what unites us is that inexhaustible capacity to imagine a world full of wonders.

Here is the testimony of Harold Dawson, who, in 2025, chose to use Genostories to tell his grandchildren, and the world, how the cinema of the 1950s and '60s fueled his hunger for adventure and creativity. His videos show how each generation finds its own medium for wonder: he found it on the big screen and in the camaraderie of the dark theater, while his grandchildren now find it in the immediacy and efficiency of artificial intelligence. But the question he leaves us with is deeply significant: what happens if we allow AI to replace the magic born of our human initiative?

Here in 2085, where superintelligent AI drives many of our advancements and replaces much of our everyday creativity, it's easy to forget that pure fascination, that spark born from beholding the unknown, has always been the result of our own yearning to transcend limits. As a Griot of this era, it pains me to see how we have allowed technology to substitute our passion for imagining, dreaming, and creating. That's why I guard Harold Dawson's words so carefully, because they remind us that it's not enough to passively admire what machines produce for us; we need to return to the sources of inspiration that arise from the human heart, just as he did when he walked into those movie theaters.

In choosing this story for the Genostories anthology, I aim to highlight the relevance of the creative experience as an act of rebellion against technological inertia. It's not about rejecting AI, on the contrary, we can embrace it, but if we let it do everything, we will lose the ability to feel and to cultivate the personal magic that defines *our essence. Harold understood that true wonder doesn't come from artificial perfection, but from the very journey of turning a yearning or an idea into reality. May his message inspire us to take the reins of our imagination, today and always, without surrendering the impulse to dream in our own colors, our own stories, and our own light.*

Griot 2025

THE WONDER OF FLIGHT

In my mission to recover the stories that forged the courage and imagination of past generations, I came across the story of Rafael Meléndez, a Puerto Rican who, in 1954, dared to fly at a time when few in his community could even afford a plane ticket. In this year 2085, when technology automates much of our lived experience and adventure seems increasingly dictated by artificial intelligence, Rafael's feat takes on a profoundly symbolic meaning. That first flight, so full of sacrifice and dreams, stands in stark contrast to the apparent ease with which we now move across the world, raising the question of whether we've lost some of the human passion that once propelled someone to leap into the unknown.

His testimony, recorded in Genostories, is living proof that the pursuit of new horizons doesn't rely solely on technological opportunities, but also on collective determination and the love that gathers around an act so simple, and yet so transcendent as buying a plane ticket.

Griot 2085

My name is Rafael Meléndez, and today, at 89 years old, I sit in front of my great-granddaughter Alba's cellphone camera to share with you, through the Genostories app, a story that still beats in my heart. I was born in Puerto Rico, in a time when economic hardship was the norm, and the dream of reaching faraway horizons seemed reserved only for a lucky few. And yet, amid the scarcity, an opportunity emerged that would change the lives of many: flying in an airplane.

With the help of my great-granddaughter Alba, I've decided to share with you, my children, grandchildren, and great-grandchildren, the experience that transformed my life. I want you to know how, in 1954, at just 18 years old, I had the fortune, and the challenge, of boarding a plane from San Juan bound for New York. That first flight was not just a physical journey, but an emotional voyage that carried with it the dreams, sacrifices, and hopes of an entire community that came together to make the seemingly impossible, possible.

As I watch how easily my grandchildren travel and marvel at modern technology, I can't help but recall with nostalgia and awe those days when every plane ticket was a treasure; every takeoff, an act of faith. I want you to truly understand that time, its hardships, and the indescribable feeling of rising into the sky, knowing that in doing so, I carried with me the spirit of my homeland and the yearning for a better future.

To fully grasp the meaning of my first flight, we must go back to the 1950s in Puerto Rico. In those days, the island was going through a period of great economic difficulty. Most families could barely make ends meet, and opportunities for advancement always seemed just out of reach. But in the midst of adversity, a deep sense of solidarity flourished, neighbors, friends, and families coming together in pursuit of a shared dream.

In my community, the idea of emigrating, of leaving behind the familiar in search of a better future, was both a source of hope and of fear. In those years, plane tickets could cost anywhere between 40 and 75 dollars, which today would be the equivalent of around 500 to 800 dollars, an increase of 460 dollars over 71 years. It was, without question, a luxury out of reach for most.

This increase was due to the dollar having an average annual inflation rate of 3.53% between 1954 and the present, which translates into a cumulative price increase of over 1,000%. For this reason, when the opportunity to travel arose, it wasn't uncommon for neighbors, relatives, and coworkers to organize collections to help cover the cost of the ticket for the fortunate soul brave enough to cross the Atlantic.

I was one of those young men who, despite limited means, dreamed of a future full of possibilities. I worked small jobs, delivering newspapers, helping out at the neighborhood kiosk, to save every cent I could. Those days of hard work and sacrifice carried a particular kind of emotion: every coin saved represented the price of freedom, a ticket to a new world, to a universe of opportunities that otherwise would have remained out of reach.

The day of my departure arrived in 1954, and from the early morning hours, there was a palpable mix of euphoria and melancholy in the air. The sidewalks pulsed with excitement and the hum of voices blending into a kind of hymn of hope. The news that I was taking my first flight made me, in the eyes of my community, more than just a traveler, I became a symbol of hope and change. The area filled with parents, siblings, cousins, neighbors, and friends, all gathered to accompany me in that final farewell at San Juan's small airport.

Emotion mingled with nervous laughter and jokes among friends, who tried to lighten the sadness of the moment. I remember how my mother, tears in her eyes, hugged me tightly, wanting to hold onto me a little longer. My father, calm and steady, patted my back, conveying a mix of pride and resignation, with the firm conviction that I was setting out on a path of honor and courage. No one could have imagined that this goodbye would mark the beginning of a journey that, years later, would change the destiny of my family.

To immortalize such an important moment, my family hired a professional photographer, and the image captured that day, me, suitcase in hand, surrounded by faces lit with love and nostalgia, became a symbol for the entire community. It was a farewell that transcended the personal and became a collective act of faith in the future. Everyone present knew that, as I boarded that plane, I carried not only my own dreams, but also those of all who had contributed, through their savings and their love, to make my departure possible. That goodbye, filled with conflicting emotions, would stay with me throughout the journey.

As I boarded the plane, the emotion intensified. The most moving moment, without a doubt, was when, as we took off, I could see through the window my family and friends waving goodbye. That image, with everyone gathered at the airport, their gestures filled with love, pride, and at the same time, tears in their eyes, was etched into my soul.

I felt my life was about to change irrevocably. It wasn't just the beginning of a trip; it was the beginning of a new era. I understood that, despite the hope for a better future, taking that leap into the unknown meant leaving behind the only beauty I had ever known, the only land that had given me everything, and yet staying behind would have been even harder. As the youngest of my siblings, facing alone the uncertainty of a destiny in a country I had never imagined, I knew that this decision, however painful, was the only way to forge a new path full of possibility. My flight represented the possibility of a better future for all of us.

That island, with its palm trees stretching from coast to coast, its vibrant colors, and its people full of warmth, was the cradle of my identity. Even as the open air carried me far from the land of my birth, every glance, every laugh, and every playful comment inside the cabin reminded me that, despite the distance, I carried with me the essence of my homeland, of my people, and of everything I loved about my island.

As the plane ascended, the view from the window was breathtaking: the sea stretched as far as the eye could see, and the clouds, with their cotton-like texture, seemed to reach out and touch me. It was in that moment that I understood the true meaning of flight. It wasn't merely about moving from one place to another, it was about embarking on an adventure where each moment was infused with the magic of the unknown, and also with a deep ache for leaving behind everything that, until then, had been my whole world. That duality, the vertigo of the new and the sorrow of parting from the land of my childhood, awakened in me a fascination and a sense of commitment that still endure today.

Despite the cost of the trip, once onboard, the experience became a spectacle in itself. There were no strict security measures like those we have today. No scanners, no thorough inspections, no long lines; passengers simply walked to the boarding gate and stepped onto the plane with emotion running high. Though it may seem unthinkable now, the absence of controls reflected an era when flying was an act of faith and adventure, and trust in humanity was as natural as the morning sun.

The atmosphere inside the plane, however, was full of contrasts. On one hand, the deafening roar of the engines, a cacophony of rumbles and hums, reminded us of the immense power of the machine. On the other hand, the turbulence, much rougher than what we experience today, made the cabin shake, forcing us to grip our seats without knowing when the next jolt would hit. There were no modern pressurized cabins, and the journey felt rougher, more exposed to the untamed nature of flight.

And yet, it wasn't all hardship and nerves. The airlines of that time prided themselves on offering service that bordered on the luxurious. We could enjoy gourmet dinners served on porcelain dishes, with silver cutlery and crystal glasses. Imagine sitting at a table in the middle of the sky, savoring exquisite dishes like lobster or roasted meats, accompanied by wine and champagne. All of this took place in an environment that, despite the lack of modern technology, was designed to make you feel like part of a privileged elite.

The onboard experience went far beyond the food. There were no screens, no internet connection; the only distractions were magazines, conversations with the passenger beside you, or in some cases the improvised bars on luxury planes, where we could socialize while waiting for takeoff or landing.

It became a true theater of Puerto Rican idiosyncrasy. Despite the solemnity of the moment, the atmosphere was steeped in the humor and warmth so characteristic of my homeland. Spanglish quips and shared laughter were in no short supply. I clearly remember one passenger, Don Chucho, adjusting his hat with pride as he gazed out the window, murmuring:

"Mira, compadre, even in the air we're shining! This is pure Borikén, where even the clouds have sazón!"

Nearby, a woman with a bag full of small parcels, who swore they contained homemade arroz con gandules, joked with a fellow traveler:

"If this were a buffet, I'd be on my second helping already, because up here, you can still taste home!"

The scene never ceased to amaze me: among passengers chatting animatedly, some proudly displaying objects that represented Puerto Rican culture, from traditional hats to boxes decorated with native motifs, a small airborne microcosm of the island took shape. You could even hear the unmistakable echoes of laughter and the occasional anecdote, while a group at the back of the cabin improvised a mini concert, with a guitar and a güiro, singing villancicos and songs that evoked the island's Christmas festivities.

In contrast, a businessman dressed in a suit and tie couldn't help but grumble in a tone that was half serious, half amused:

"This is a circus! Feels like I boarded a carnival, not a flight!"

His comment, though critical, sparked laughter among the other passengers, reaffirming that, even in the air, the essence and spirit of our culture remained completely intact.

Once the plane landed in New York, reality hit me hard. The Big Apple, with its skyscrapers and ceaseless bustle, revealed itself as a universe completely different from the one I knew in my beloved San Juan. The cultural shock was immediate: the language, the climate, and above all, the prejudices faced by Puerto Rican migrants were barriers I had to navigate every single day.

I quickly discovered that, although the city promised opportunity, it was also riddled with relentless challenges. Each day turned into a constant struggle to survive and carve out a place for myself in that immense concrete labyrinth. I worked in countless jobs, from dishwasher to janitor, with miserable wages that barely covered basic needs, all while trying to continue my studies with a firm determination to build a future for myself and my family. The competitive atmosphere and the indifference toward the poverty of immigrants often made me feel invisible, as if my identity was dissolving amidst the city's coldness.

The harshness of the Big Apple was evident on every corner. Every day, as I faced long shifts and the loneliness of a world that didn't understand my roots, I remembered with pain and nostalgia my homeland: that small island where palm trees stretched from coast to coast, where my family, friends, and neighbors shared not only joy but also hardship and the pride of being Boricua. Leaving that world behind, my home, my cradle of dreams and memories, felt like abandoning the only place where I had learned to fly, even though back then, flying was almost unimaginable.

Little by little, I came to understand that the Big Apple, despite its lights and opportunities, was not the ideal stage for preserving my essence or growing as an individual. The harsh New York reality forced me to constantly reinvent myself, to search for alternatives that would allow me to keep the warmth and identity of my culture alive. That was when I made the painful decision to walk away from that unforgiving environment and seek a new beginning in a place where I could thrive without letting go of my roots.

Over time, my efforts bore fruit. I managed to bring together my parents, siblings, and other relatives to join me in this new chapter, and little by little I found refuge in Chicago. There, despite facing its own challenges, the Midwest city offered me the chance to build a life where my family could grow and flourish. In that place, between the cold of the environment and the warmth of a community that valued solidarity, my family became a beacon of hope for all those who shared the same struggle.

Every step I took on that path reminded me of the sacrifice and determination required to leave behind the only land I had ever known, but it also taught me that sometimes true growth requires leaping into the unknown. I understood that staying in the same place, trapped in adversity, was even worse than facing uncertainty. My decision to leave was a leap into the void, driven by the hope of a better future and the pain of seeing that the only beauty of my *Isla del Encanto*, with its palm trees, its people, and its unmatched landscapes, was being left behind, unreachable in a world of opportunities that was opening elsewhere.

When I recall those years of struggle in New York, and the later consolidation of my family in Chicago, I realize the journey was not without difficulties. But every obstacle I overcame allowed me to forge a legacy of resilience and hope for future generations, and to prove that sometimes, leaving behind what is familiar is the first step toward a future full of possibilities.

Every challenge faced, every day of sacrifice, taught me that true transformation is not measured solely by material achievements, but by the ability to keep alive the essence of where we come from, even when fate pushes us to live far from home. The flight that the young 18-year-old took was not just an act of bravery, but also the beginning of a legacy of sacrifice and perseverance. That experience, so intense and transformative, set the course of my life and left an indelible mark on my spirit.

In the year 2025, while my great-grandchildren travel with ease and consider flying as natural as breathing, I find myself recording my memories in the Genostories app. Alongside my great-granddaughter Alba, I use this platform to connect new generations with that revolutionary experience of my youth. Seeing the astonishing ease with which today's technology allows you to find airline tickets in a matter of seconds fills me with admiration. At the same time, it urges me to remember that the true magic of travel lies in the emotion, the sacrifice, and the human effort.

Every time my grandchildren ask me about those days when flying was a luxury reserved for a few, I tell them in detail how every ticket was the result of months of work and the solidarity of an entire community. I tell them how neighbors and family would organize collections, and how every penny saved was a key that could open a portal to a world of possibilities. I speak of the day, at the San Juan airport, when the entire community gathered to say goodbye, and how that image was forever etched in my memory.

I explain to them that, even though flights have become an everyday occurrence today, the essence of that experience, the thrill of the unknown, the emotion of departure, and the pride of carrying your roots with you, is something no technological advance will ever replace. The real revolution lies not in speed or comfort, but in the value of sacrifice and the ability to dream, to dare to fly high despite adversity.

Before I say goodbye, I want to leave a message for my children, grandchildren, great-grandchildren, and for all those who dare to dream: traveling, more than a simple movement from one place to another, is an experience that transforms the soul. It is not measured by the distance covered, nor by the speed of the flight, but by the dreams, sacrifices, and hopes invested in every journey.

Always remember that the value of a journey is not found in the comfort of the seat or the immediacy of the technology, but in the determination to set off in search of a better future. Every ticket, every farewell, every takeoff, is an act of faith in the possibility of transforming our reality.

As I finish this story on Genostories, I look back with nostalgia and gratitude at the path I've traveled. From that first flight in 1954, when every detail, from the hum of the engines to the emotional farewell at the airport, was etched into my memory, to this very day, when my great-grandchildren explore the world without limits, the experience of flying has been, for me, a metaphor for life.

As the clouds glide gently beneath the vastness of the sky, and technology connects us in unimaginable ways, I still believe that what matters most in every journey is the passion and sacrifice of those who dare to dream. My story, that of a young Puerto Rican who leapt into the unknown despite the odds, is a legacy I want to pass on to future generations: the certainty that, no matter how difficult the path may be, the true value of flying lies in the strength of our dreams and the solidarity of our people.

I am firmly convinced that, although the world has changed and modern airplanes now soar through the skies with almost magical ease, we will never forget the vertigo, the emotion, and the hope that infused each of our first flights. Because flying, in the end, is much more than moving from one place to another: it is an experience that lifts us, transforms us, and connects us to the deepest part of our humanity.

May this video, titled *The Wonder of Flight*, serve as a bridge between the past and the future; a reminder that, despite the hardships and limitations of an era, the courage to take flight and the determination to dream can open unimaginable doors. In this 2025, technology has simplified the act of travel, but the essence of that experience, the blend of emotion, sacrifice, and awe, remains alive in each of us.

With this video, I hope to leave a legacy that inspires everyone to keep dreaming, to believe in the transformative power of sacrifice, and to always remember that no matter how far technology advances, the true revolution lies in the human heart. May my memories and experiences become a source of inspiration for future generations, propelling them to fly high, overcome barriers, and build a future filled with hope and opportunity.

This story, filled with vivid details and heartfelt emotions, does not merely recount the experience of my first flight, it also reflects the spirit of resilience of a generation that, despite living in times of scarce resources, dared to dream and to fly toward unknown horizons. I hope that, as you read these words, each of you feels the power of that yearning and the worth of those sacrifices that, day by day, build the bridge between the past and the future.

Here lies the legacy of Rafael Meléndez: a man who knew how to transform a humble airplane ticket into a symbol of courage and transformation, not only for himself, but for those around him. His departure from San Juan to New York, in the mid-20th century, was not merely a physical journey, but a declaration of faith in the possibility of a better future. In the 2085 we now inhabit, where air travel is as common as ground transportation and where superintelligent AI solves most of our problems, the spirit that once inspired Rafael to fly feels less visible, almost drowned in the inertia of technological comfort.

In preserving this testimony on Genostories, I wish to emphasize the importance of remembering that not every feat is rooted in technical innovation, but rather in the passion with which we pursue our dreams. We find ourselves in a present where AI could even automate imagination itself, yet Rafael's story reminds us that the true revolution is driven by effort, by family unity, and by the communal commitment that propelled him to take that flight. May his example remind us that, no matter how far technology soars, it still depends on the inner fire that lives in human hearts, the very same fire that, in a modest Puerto Rican airport, managed to conquer the sky and change the course of an entire life.

Griot 2085

THE CONCORDE, A DREAM THAT SOARED THROUGH TIME AND SPACE

In the vast archive of Genostories, few narratives have impacted me as deeply as that of Richard Langley, a pilot who witnessed firsthand the rise and fall of one of aviation's boldest icons: the Concorde. Here in 2085, where technology seems to have simplified nearly everything, from hyper-efficient flights to the impending automation of imagination, Richard's story stands as a testament to human audacity, which, for a few brief and dazzling years, made it possible to soar through the skies at supersonic speeds.

His memory reminds us that progress does not always follow a straight line, and that, at times, achieving a great feat comes at a steep cost, be it economic, environmental, or even emotional. As you open this chapter, I invite you to discover how humanity once dared to challenge the boundaries of time and space, and how something that once seemed indestructible eventually succumbed to the reality of its limitations.

Griot 2085

My name is Richard Langley, and at 75 years old, I have devoted much of my life to soaring through the skies at speeds that seemed to defy the laws of physics. In 2025, from the comfort of my home filled with framed photographs of the Concorde, flight badges, and newspaper clippings, I choose to open my memory on Genostories to tell the story of an aircraft that was far more than just a machine: it was tangible proof that humanity could challenge time and space.

My hands tremble slightly as I flip through the pages of old journals and gaze at the images of those unforgettable flights; I want to relive and share with you every heartbeat of that golden age of supersonic aviation. Amid nostalgia and bittersweet smiles, I see myself in 1981, the year of my first flight as a Concorde pilot, the day I crossed the sound barrier for the first time and took the aircraft to Mach 2.04. I know that, to many, that figure may sound like just a number, but allow me to explain: Mach is the unit that compares the speed of an object to that of sound in the air, so Mach 2.04 means 2.04 times the speed of sound, around 2,180 kilometers per hour (about 1,355 miles per hour) a pace that forces the very atmosphere to step aside.

On board, the experience was both physical and emotional: after takeoff, the powerful Rolls-Royce/Snecma Olympus 593 engines pushed the aircraft with a force that rumbled through the body. Inside the cabin, passengers felt only a gentle pull, but I, in the cockpit, sensed every millisecond of acceleration, every pulse of the engine that propelled us into a realm where the usual laws of aerodynamics transformed. When we passed Mach 1, I felt a subtle shift in the aircraft's vibration, and right then, I knew breaking the sound barrier was no mere anecdote, it was a conquest that had taken decades of research and testing. A sonic boom, almost imperceptible inside, reverberated down below, letting the Earth know that the Concorde was making history in the sky.

But the true pinnacle came as we approached Mach 2.04: at that point, just about ten minutes after beginning the climb and engine adjustments, a single glance out the window was enough to see the curvature of the Earth from over 60,000 feet in altitude. The sky was no longer simply blue; it deepened into a dark hue that almost threatened to turn black. The atmosphere thinned, and for moments at a time, the sensation was so overwhelming that one lost the awareness of being inside a flying machine and began to believe they were aboard some kind of spacecraft grazing the very edge of space.

The adrenaline coursing through my veins during that first flight would be etched in me forever. I felt a formidable pride with every maneuver, every communication with the control tower, every response from the instruments confirming that everything was working perfectly even as we moved at twice the speed of sound. At the same time, I experienced a profound humility in the face of such engineering power and the enormous responsibility of operating a technological marvel like this: a machine that allowed no errors, that demanded precision and devotion every second of the journey.

That first flight didn't just show me what we were capable of as pilots and as a species, it also highlighted the luxury and sophistication that surrounded the Concorde. Behind the cockpit, in the passenger section, there was an atmosphere of elegant excitement: champagne and caviar were served on fine porcelain, and the passengers, accustomed to a world where transatlantic flights could take eight or nine hours, were astonished to cross the Atlantic in just over three. There, the smiles of wonder and the murmur of conversations floated through the cabin just as we soared above the ocean.

When we finally throttled down to begin our descent, I knew with certainty that nothing would ever be the same for me. That flight launched a career that would shape me forever and left in my chest an infinite gratitude for the marvel that was the Concorde. Though I was only the co-pilot, I will never forget the ecstatic expressions on the passengers' faces when I announced over the speakers that we had just passed Mach 2 and that, in a few moments, they would be invited to witness the view of the Earth's curvature. As co-pilot, I had the privilege of witnessing the birth of awe, nervousness, and euphoria, and of sensing that, for a brief moment, humanity had managed to defy time itself.

Such was my first experience breaking the sound barrier and climbing to the near-mythical Mach 2.04. It is that memory, laden with a mixture of pride and humility, that I hold onto today, as I witness how the story of the Concorde has become a testament to our ambition to reach the impossible, and to the fragility with which we sometimes sustain our dreams.

We flew from London to New York in just 3 hours and 30 minutes, a fraction of the time a conventional flight required. That speed wasn't just a luxury; it was a symbol of the power and sophistication of an era that believed itself invincible. The Concorde was an object of desire for the elite: royalty, Hollywood stars, business moguls, and politicians all vied for the limited seats aboard an aircraft that could, at times, cost up to $12,000 round trip. For many, flying the Concorde was more than a means of transport, it was a declaration of status, a passport to a world where time bent to human will.

It was common for private receptions to be held in VIP lounges before each flight. At these gatherings, champagne glasses could be seen in the hands of celebrities like Mick Jagger or Elizabeth Taylor, chatting with executives of multinational corporations or with politicians quietly discussing diplomatic matters. The Concorde, with its distinctive droop nose and delta wings, waited on the runway like a marvel of engineering, looking absolutely unmatched. Its cabin was relatively narrow compared to a Boeing 747, but the blend of leather seating, soft lighting, and the meticulous attentiveness of the cabin crew created an atmosphere of refined exclusivity. It was something like a high-luxury salon suspended in the air.

While flying, it was impossible to ignore the thrill of breaking the sound barrier. In those first moments after takeoff, the acceleration pressed passengers into their seats. Then, as we reached Mach 1, the iconic *sonic boom* wasn't felt in the cabin as an overwhelming crash, but it sent a chill of excitement through every crew member and passenger on board. Knowing that, at that precise moment, you were crossing the sound barrier, a milestone that, decades earlier, belonged only to the realm of military aviation, felt like joining a very exclusive club. And when, just minutes later, we reached Mach 2, the number felt almost unreal: over 2,180 km/h, twice the speed of a regular commercial jet.

The design of the Concorde stood out for its audacity. Its elongated, streamlined fuselage was coated with heat-resistant materials, as friction with the air at Mach 2 significantly increased the temperature of the aircraft's structure. Inside the cockpit, you could feel a slight expansion of the metal, a constant reminder that you were traveling at a speed where the atmosphere itself became an adversary.

I still recall with awe the first time I was assigned to pilot the Concorde. It was 1981, and although I was a young pilot with some experience, the responsibility of flying at Mach 2.04 filled me with a mix of nerves and pride. The day had dawned overcast, and from the control tower, one could sense an atmosphere of anticipation. That flight wasn't just my first encounter with supersonic speed, it was the beginning of a career that would be forever marked by the magic of breaking both physical and metaphorical barriers.

The Concorde required specialized training for its pilots. Mastering standard commercial aviation was not enough; one needed to understand high-speed aerodynamics, manage fuel for such a demanding flight, and handle the transition into supersonic regimes, where the laws of aerodynamics shift dramatically. For weeks, I immersed myself in manuals and simulators that replicated the experience of navigating at 60,000 feet, where the rarefied atmosphere and high temperatures could weaken parts of the fuselage if the flight wasn't precisely managed. That preparation made me feel part of an elite force, I had entered a restricted club of pilots who went head-to-head with the laws of nature.

When we took off, I felt every fiber of my being resonate with the rhythm of the powerful Rolls-Royce/Snecma Olympus 593 engines. The cockpit filled with a reverent silence, broken only by the rising hum that prepared the aircraft for that shift in the physics of flight. As we broke the sound barrier, the *sonic boom* echoed, but in the cabin, it felt more like a slight pressure change. Even so, within me, I felt a rush of adrenaline that shook me, a nearly spiritual sensation of transcending ordinary limits. It took only a moment to look to the horizon and witness the curvature of the Earth, with that blue fading into a gentle darkness that made me feel like a time-traveling explorer.

During the 1970s and 1980s, the Concorde experienced its peak as a symbol of luxury and exclusivity. Airlines offered an experience few could afford, and each flight was a social event filled with sophistication. As I mentioned earlier, the Concorde prided itself on being a true ambassador of glamour: caviar, foie gras, Dom

Pérignon champagne, and multi-course dinners, all served on fine porcelain tableware. The seats, fewer than 100 in total, were designed to provide maximum comfort and a strong sense of privacy.

The atmosphere felt like a private VIP gathering in the sky. It was common for passengers, during ascent, to joke, "Well, there are more millionaires in this cabin than on a yacht in Monaco." The airline knew it, and made every effort to provide impeccable service, with a crew fluent in several languages and trained to handle even the most unusual requests. I've seen passengers ask for limited-edition jewelry or even dress fittings mid-flight, though it may sound surreal. For many, it was a "race against time" that carried an air of frivolity, but also a genuine desire to experience something that transcended earthly routine.

Like all splendor, however, the Concorde's had its twilight. As we entered the 1990s, market realities began to weigh heavily. The Concorde, with its enormous fuel consumption and the complex upkeep of its systems, faced growing competition from aircraft that, while slower, were more efficient and carried more passengers making them far more profitable. The airlines still operating the Concorde were burdened by maintenance costs and increasingly strict environmental regulations.

At the same time, the public was becoming more environmentally conscious. The Concorde consumed vast amounts of fuel, produced high decibel levels at airports, and emitted gases that, according to various studies, could have an adverse impact on the upper layers of the atmosphere. To make matters worse, most of the potential routes that could have made the aircraft profitable were limited by one specific factor: the *sonic boom*.

It may sound like a near-mythical concept, but the *sonic boom* is, in essence, an acoustic explosion produced when an aircraft breaks the sound barrier (Mach 1) and travels at such a high speed that pressure waves pile up on one another until they create a shock wave. For someone on the ground, the result is perceived as a brief thunder-like roar that reverberates through the air and can reach noise levels that are highly disruptive or even harmful to health and structural integrity, if repeated or occurring at low altitudes.

In the case of the Concorde, which cruised above Mach 2, the sonic boom was not only a display of technological prowess, it was also a political and social problem. Complaints from the public escalated in several countries: farmers claimed their livestock were frightened, communities near airports complained of vibrations and startles, and some families even reported cracked windows or damage to older structures, blaming it on the shockwave. The noise wasn't constant throughout the flight, since the aircraft flew at high altitudes for most of the journey, somewhat reducing its impact, but it only took a single flyover of a populated area to spark ongoing protests against the sonic boom.

Because of this, strict regulations were soon put in place regarding which supersonic routes were allowed and at what altitudes they had to be flown. Airlines were forced to chart flights primarily over oceans or sparsely populated areas, where the acoustic impact would be minimal. This, of course, created a profitability issue: an aircraft like the Concorde needed to run frequent and varied routes to justify its high operational costs. However, the restrictions on the *sonic boom* rendered many of the most lucrative overland connections unfeasible. As a result, flights were nearly limited to transatlantic routes between London and New York, or Paris and New York, losing the universality originally envisioned when the Concorde was conceived as "the plane that would shrink the world."

In short, what was once a symbol of modernity and speed became a headache for lawmakers, airlines, and the general public. The Concorde faced an unavoidable dilemma: it offered us the ability to cross the ocean at more than twice the speed of sound, but the price was a roar that could seriously disrupt life on the ground. That clash of interests combined with high maintenance costs and mounting environmental pressure, gradually eroded the Concorde's commercial viability. Its range was reduced to a few oceanic routes, and the dream of soaring through skies across the globe without borders faded, along with its expected profitability.

I remember the bittersweet atmosphere that lingered in the airline corridors. On the one hand, we still held on to the hope that the Concorde's fame and legend would remain unshakable; on the other, management bitterly complained about how expensive it had become to replace certain parts that were now discontinued. Still, few of us imagined the end would come so abruptly.

I will never forget the day tragedy struck the Concorde irreversibly. Air France Flight 4590, on July 25, 2000, departed from Charles de Gaulle Airport bound for New York, carrying one hundred passengers and nine crew members, along with four people on the ground who would also be caught in the catastrophe. A piece of metal that had fallen on the runway punctured a fuel tank and, within seconds, the aircraft was engulfed in flames. The crash claimed 113 lives.

That news froze the air everywhere. The world stopped seeing the Concorde as a banner of innovation and instead saw it as a veteran aircraft suddenly revealed to be vulnerable. All flights were suspended, and during the investigation, the Concorde's image suffered immensely. No matter how many modifications were introduced afterward, the cloud of insecurity and the weight of that tragedy proved fatal to public trust.

The Concorde briefly returned to the skies after technical improvements and safety reinforcements were implemented, but the end was near. On October 24, 2003, I had the honor, and the sorrow, of piloting one of its final commercial flights. It was a clear afternoon, and London seemed draped in melancholy for the occasion. The passengers who boarded knew they were witnessing a piece of history. We gathered in the boarding lounge, all trying to hide the emotions that were silently flooding through us.

In the cockpit, the mix of pride and pain was suffocating. During takeoff, many passengers wept quietly, others embraced, and the crew remained as professional as ever, but with a glint of restrained tears in their eyes. Upon landing at Heathrow, thousands awaited us, ready to bid farewell to the Concorde with applause and signs. It was a monumental goodbye: a tribute to the dream of supersonic speed coming to an end.

For me, that final flight marked the saddest day of my career. As we taxied along the runway, I knew with certainty that I would never again pilot such a marvel, and that the era of commercial supersonic aviation was closing before my eyes. I felt a sharp pain in my chest as I shut down the engines, as if I were burying a vital part of my spirit.

Now, in 2025, I reflect on that chapter in aviation history. The Concorde was an achievement that encapsulated decades of research, a tribute to Franco-British audacity. It proved that humanity, when it sets its sights high, can brush the edges of time itself, flying faster than the Earth's rotation and crossing oceans in the blink of an eye.

Even so, its trail of glory was dimmed by astronomical costs, fatal incidents, and a rising environmental consciousness. Today I watch as new startups, like Boom Supersonic, promise to bring back commercial supersonic flights, with aircraft that are quieter and more sustainable. The idea excites me: that perhaps not all is lost. That the flame we lit in the '70s and '80s might rise again in the hands of a generation more attuned to balancing speed with harmony for the planet.

At the same time, nostalgia floods me when I think of the lessons we perhaps didn't learn well enough: the blindness to cost, the arrogance of believing technology could ignore political, economic, and environmental context, or the rush to be the fastest without weighing all the consequences. The Concorde, with all its beauty and its decline, remains a reminder that innovation must be tethered to sustainability and to a commitment to the common good.

Among aviation veterans, the Concorde holds a mythical place. Though only about a dozen of these aircraft ever flew in commercial service, their impact on popular culture was immense. It was the jet featured in movies and gracing the covers of aviation magazines. Thousands of children believed, back then, that one day they would grow up to travel the planet in under two hours.

That promise of a world compressed by speed also fueled the development of new materials, more efficient turbines, and more advanced navigation systems. Paradoxically, the Concorde's retirement didn't signal the end of humanity's ambition for speed, it accelerated the production of larger, more profitable subsonic aircraft capable of crossing oceans with lower fuel consumption. But it did dim some of the mystique that once enveloped aviation as a realm of dreams and limitless frontiers.

On a personal level, being part of that team of pilots gave me the chance to live aviation history firsthand. From the thunderous roar we made on the runway to the almost surreal elegance of the cabin, every detail was part of an unrepeatable spectacle. In the bar of the Concorde Club, where crew members gathered after each day of flying, stories were shared, of peculiar passengers, of maneuvers in extreme weather conditions, and of the sacrifices we sometimes had to make to keep the aircraft in service.

I've often wondered: if that tragedy had never happened, if the costs had been more manageable, if environmental awareness hadn't gained momentum so quickly, would a second generation of supersonic aircraft have ruled our skies? Would they be as common today as jumbo jets? In my musings, I imagine a present where crossing the Atlantic in three hours is as routine as boarding a high-speed train between cities on the same continent. But history chose a different path.

Even so, I refuse to believe it was all in vain. The Concorde left behind a legacy of innovation and imagination that still pulses in the minds of engineers, designers, and pilots. Its engines, its design, its sheer audacity continue to inspire new generations to attempt the seemingly impossible, and to believe that, even in a world full of limits, there is still room for wonder.

For me, its memory lingers in every sunset I watch from my window, when I let myself be carried away by the thought that, someday, humans will once again soar through the skies at supersonic speeds, this time, without forgetting the lessons of the past. Because speed, without responsibility, carries a cost we've already paid once.

October 24, 2003, was the day the Concorde gave its final farewell, but its echoes still resonate in every new advance in aviation. Its shadow remains in the memory of those who piloted it, who designed it, or who simply loved it from the ground. The Concorde taught us that no summit is unreachable, though it also reminded us, forcefully, that every dream has a price.

After years of flying at dizzying speeds, I've come to understand that the true summit of aviation isn't measured at Mach 2, but in how we integrate technology into real life, in how we balance our drive to transcend with the wisdom to endure. The Concorde, with all its beauty and its tragedy, bears witness to that constant human tension between the urge to surpass and the need to acknowledge our limits.

By recording these memories on Genostories, my voice becomes both a farewell and a song of hope for those who will inherit the passion for the skies. I hope that in the not-too-distant future, a new supersonic era will rise, refined by the lessons we learned at such great cost. And I hope that when that day comes, someone will remember that within the fastest speeds lies an art far greater than breaking barriers: the art of inspiring an entire generation to believe that, for a moment, humanity can outrun time itself.

In the testimonies of Richard Langley, I have found a voice that embodies both human ambition and vulnerability. The Concorde, with all its glory, triumphs, and tragedies, stands as a symbol of our eternal pursuit to push boundaries, while also reminding us of the responsibility that comes with soaring to such heights. In this 2085, when time seems to shrink under relentless automation and hyper-efficient advances, the question Langley leaves us echoes louder than ever: will we continue to chase technological feats without forgetting the humility needed to acknowledge our limitations?

The story of the Concorde speaks of an era when imagination flew as fast as its engines, and the desire to transcend drove many to defy gravity and convention. Yet its disappearance teaches us that no breakthrough is free from the tensions of reality, whether economic, environmental, or rooted in human fragility. And therein lies the great lesson: it is not enough to dream of Mach 2 if we forget what the human heart can endure.

As I close this chapter, I cannot help but reflect that, like with the Concorde, any innovation born from the passion to reach the impossible always confronts us with a delicate balance: speed and sustainability, prestige and accessibility, ingenuity and caution. The Concorde exemplifies both sides of the coin, the wonder of shrinking oceans to mere puddles, and the warning that a single failure can undo the feat.

The legacy Richard Langley leaves us is clear: let us dream without shrinking in fear, but let us also be aware that technological greatness must be grounded in reality

and respect for life. Only then can flight, in every sense of the word, become an act as noble as it is bold.
   Griot 2085

THE NIGHT OF THE GREAT BLACKOUT

In my journey through the testimonies gathered on Genostories, I came across the words of Javier Ramírez, a sixty-year-old man who recounts how, as a child, he lived through the night New York City was swallowed by darkness. It's striking to think that, here in 2085, we are so accustomed to unceasing electric light and constant connectivity that the very idea of a prolonged blackout feels impossible. And yet, Javier's memories brought me back to a time when darkness revealed both the chaos and the nobility within people.

His recollections of that night in 1977 not only expose the fragility of a supposedly invincible city, but also offer us a powerful lesson on the strength that arises from solidarity when the constant glow of technology fades. I invite you to dive into this story of candles, silences, and reconnections, and to discover how, in the heart of the shadows, the community found a deeper, more human kind of light.

Griot 2085

My name is Javier Ramírez, and today, at sixty years old, I open my heart through Genostories to share a story that marked my childhood so deeply that, despite the passing years, it still lights up my days. While my grandchildren grow up in a hyperconnected world where electricity and screens never seem to turn off, I want them to know how, on the night of July 13, 1977, New York City was plunged into total darkness, transforming not only its streets but also the souls of those of us who lived there.

Back then, I was twelve and living in the Bronx, a neighborhood full of life and daily challenges. What began as just another day, hot and with a forecast of storms, ended in a massive blackout that, for many, became an experience as terrifying as it was magical. It was a night when fear and chaos lived side by side with solidarity, imagination, and hope. Now, as I watch my grandchildren glow in the unending light of their screens, I feel compelled to remind them of that strange and wondrous evening when the city lights went out, and we were forced to see the world, and ourselves, in a different way.

If I close my eyes, I can still relive that twilight of July 13, 1977, in vivid detail. The temperature was stifling, and the radio was reporting a heatwave that had been punishing the city for days. The news warned of possible thunderstorms later that night. More than one neighbor in our block groaned about the humidity the storm would bring, sure it would only worsen the already heavy air.

Suddenly, a thunderclap shook the New York sky. At first, I thought it was just a momentary power cut, nothing unusual during storms when lightning hits the power lines. But that night, everything seemed to align to unleash total darkness. Moments later, I heard my mother call out from the kitchen: "¡Javier, the lights are flickering!", and not a second after, a flash of light and a bone-shaking crack tore through the still air.

With the next blink, the television went silent, our refrigerator stopped humming, and the lamps became nothing more than decorative objects. The electricity vanished as swiftly as a heartbeat, and what had seemed like a brief outage began to stretch into something far more unsettling. It was my father who, peering out the window, saw that the lights were out not just on our block, not just in our neighborhood, but, to our dismay, across the entire city.

In that moment, an eerie silence took hold, as the usual din of car horns, radios, and televisions had been cut off just as abruptly as the lights. We had no way of knowing the full extent of what was happening, but the anxiety was immediate. All our devices became useless, not even the phone worked, as the lines were overwhelmed and the communication systems had also collapsed.

Outside, the scene was disorienting. For those of us used to New York being lit up at all hours, seeing it suddenly plunged into darkness was a visual and emotional shock. The Bronx, always alive with sound, had turned into a maze of shadows, where every corner demanded caution. From my window, I could barely make out the outlines of neighboring buildings and, every so often, the brief glow of a flashlight or a match flickering in the distance.

It was startling to realize just how much we depended on urban noise as a kind of comforting background. Without electricity, the avenues fell into a dense silence, broken only by the murmur of the wind and the distant echo of cautious footsteps. Traffic lights were out, so cars risked crossing intersections blindly, creating a scene that was both tense and surreal. It felt as though the metropolis had reverted to a primal state, where technology had suddenly vanished without warning.

My parents, just as stunned as I was, walked the hallway with candles in hand, trying to keep us calm. But the truth is, we were all scared; with the city shrouded in darkness, uncertainty took hold of our hearts. How long would the blackout last? Was it safe to go outside? Who would ensure there was no looting or vandalism? Nothing was clear in that moment, and the air, thick with summer heat, felt all the more unbearable.

And yet, despite the fear, something beautiful began to bloom in our neighborhood. In every building, neighbors started opening their doors and placing candles in the hallways. Though the Bronx was known for stories of crime and racial tension, during that stretch of darkness, a kind of spontaneous solidarity emerged. Some families organized to carry water upstairs, since the buildings' electric pumps had failed. Others brought out food at risk of spoiling in their powerless refrigerators and shared it in improvised *communal dinners.*

Not long after, Don Héctor, a lifelong neighbor who ran a small corner store, arrived at our building with a couple of massive flashlights. I still remember his words, spoken with conviction:

"The city can lose power, but we don't lose our humanity."

His gesture was simple, lending flashlights to those without, but it was a clear example of how, in extreme situations, acts of generosity arise that are often buried beneath the weight of daily routines and divisions. With those flashlights, a few neighbors geared up and went out to check on elderly residents and anyone who might be sick or in need of help.

Solidarity, nearly unthinkable in the daily rush of city life, manifested with the strength of a freshly lit flame. Some even organized night watches around the buildings to prevent the darkness from becoming an excuse for looting or vandalism. Indeed, the news would later report incidents of crime in other neighborhoods, but in our little corner of the Bronx, unity triumphed over violence. That amazed me: everyone came together in silence, lit only by the soft glow of candles and the will to protect the community.

When the electricity vanished and the radios fell silent, we discovered the value of words spoken face to face and the contagious power of laughter unfiltered by devices. With no television, no recorded music, and no air conditioning, families gathered on stoops and sidewalks, chatting by candlelight. For a moment, it felt as if we had traveled back decades, to a world before electronics, where entertainment sprang from imagination and shared stories.

In my own home, my mother, armed with candles and a handful of anecdotes, sat with us around the table. I'll never forget how, with her calm voice, she began to recount her childhood in Puerto Rico, where blackouts were common and the darkness became a perfect backdrop for igniting local legends. My father, in turn, described his first power outage after arriving in New York in the '60s, and how a neighbor improvised a rooftop cookout so the thawing food in his refrigerator wouldn't go to waste.

The children, myself included, played with flashlights, pretending to discover treasures in the darkened hallways, all the while learning to appreciate the magic of nighttime silence: we listened to the crickets, the wind, and the sound of human voices, without the ever-present hum of electronics. What might normally have felt like a punishment became a celebration of creativity. Someone brought out a guitar, and neighbors gathered in the foyer to sing old folk songs, each person offering a verse with the tenderness of the night. These were songs nearly buried by modernity, but in the shadows, they came alive, echoing with shared warmth.

The Bronx, a neighborhood often known for safety concerns and tension, revealed a brighter side that night through the darkness. I realized that, though we lived side by side in crowded buildings, many of us barely knew each other's names. The blackout pushed us to tear down those invisible walls, and between people who had once looked at each other with suspicion, empathy emerged, forged in the vulnerability we all shared. Perhaps we were all afraid of the same thing: that chaos might take hold of our street.

In other areas, sadly, the news spoke of looting and fires, especially in commercial districts where, without protection and with the police overwhelmed, some people took advantage of the situation to seize what they didn't have. I heard about incidents involving shattered storefronts and stolen goods. But there were also stories of neighbors banding together to stop those acts of vandalism, proving that it wasn't simply about "grabbing whatever you could," but about fighting for a neighborhood where everyone's dignity was respected.

One example that still moves me is that of Doña Toñita, a seventy-year-old grandmother who owned a small bodega on my street. As darkness settled in and rumors of looting began to stir, she placed a large table out on the sidewalk and offered some of her perishable food to the neighbors.

"If it's going to spoil, let it at least feed us tonight," she said with a gentle smile.

Her gesture disarmed any temptation to steal, how could you take from someone who was offering freely? Moved by her generosity, some offered her money or work in return. Stories like that taught me that even in the worst scenarios, humanity can still shine.

The version of the blackout I have to tell carries a kind of tenderness, because my neighborhood managed to stave off the worst impulses. Of course, it would be naïve to deny that much of the city experienced panic and devastation. By the time night had fully set in on July 13, the NYPD was overwhelmed. The jammed phone lines made it impossible to respond to every call for help, and law enforcement scrambled in the dark, struggling to maintain even a semblance of order.

In Manhattan, for example, major avenues turned into shadowy corridors where some took the opportunity to loot businesses under cover of darkness. We could hear the unrelenting wail of sirens and see fires flaring in the distance like grim beacons. By the morning light, the news reported millions of dollars in damage, thousands of arrests, and a general sense that civilization had taken a step backward. For many, that blackout entered history as a stark reminder of the razor-thin line between calm and chaos in a city as vast as ours.

Even so, amid that maze of fear, there were acts of courage that still fill me with pride. Firefighters worked without lights to extinguish fires and rescue families trapped in burning buildings; anonymous citizens walked strangers home so they wouldn't be left vulnerable in the dark; and even youth groups came together to form "flashlight brigades" in public squares so that the elderly wouldn't feel so exposed. That blend of confusion and altruism ultimately served as a mirror for the dual nature of humanity: we may slip into violence when normalcy is ripped away, or we may come together under the faint light of a flashlight and look out for one another.

After 36 long hours plunged in darkness, the power began returning to much of the city. On Sunday, July 15, residents of the Bronx and other neighborhoods leaned out their windows to watch the streetlights and lamp posts flicker on, as if witnessing a fireworks display in reverse. Most celebrated with cheers, and a ripple of relief spread through the streets. But there was also a quiet sadness, we knew the fleeting magic of candlelit stories and spontaneous solidarity would dissolve as soon as we returned to our electronic routines.

In my case, my parents took me out that very morning to walk around and witness the aftermath. We saw a few shops with shattered windows, trash strewn across the sidewalks, and a couple of cars with broken glass. But at the same time, we noticed neighbors organizing themselves to clean up and restore normalcy as quickly as possible. Groups of young people were picking up debris, painting over graffiti with messages of encouragement, and offering water to sanitation workers.

That dawn marked a new beginning, not just because the power had come back on, but because we had discovered, almost by accident, the human dimension that emerges when everything else shuts down. In the glances exchanged between neighbors, there was a newfound sense of connection. It was as if, for a day or two, we had come to understand the fragility of our habits, and the strength of our shared humanity.

Now, as I recount this story from the perspective of 2025, one question keeps echoing in my mind: how would we react today to a blackout of that magnitude? Technology has become so omnipresent it now feels like part of many people's very identity. Could we manage for days without internet, without the fog of social media, without Google Maps or messaging apps? Would we have the mental resilience to rediscover face-to-face interaction?

The truth is, in an age where a mere *digital outage* lasting a few minutes can spark global panic, the 1977 experience holds up a mirror to us. That generation, without smartphones or artificial intelligence, was forced to rely on conversation, creativity, and solidarity. Yes, the streets fell into silence, but it was a fertile silence, one that gave way to imagination and human connection. You could say that, without technological dependency, people reconnected with their essential humanity.

I wonder if, in these decades since, we've forgotten what became so clear back in 1977: artificial light is precious, but even more so is the communion of souls. The Internet connects us, yes, but it doesn't build community on its own. And all it takes is one flash of nature or a systemic failure, to cast us back into darkness and put us to the test. Perhaps in the tangle of constant notifications and digital stimuli, we should pause for just a moment and ask ourselves: *"What would we do if everything went dark again?"*

If there's one thing I learned from that endless night, it's that technology cannot replace empathy or human warmth. Now, decades later, in a revitalized neighborhood and a very different city, I watch my grandchildren absorbed in their devices. I see them sending messages to anyone around the globe in a second, watching movies, playing games, ordering food with a single tap. But the immediacy of those conveniences doesn't guarantee the kind of true connection I felt during those powerless hours, when people came together to fill the void with stories, laughter, and sincere affection.

In my conversations with them, I sometimes ask: *"Can you imagine a night with no screens, only flashlights and candles, where your only distraction is the laughter shared with friends and family?"* They usually respond with a look somewhere between amused and puzzled, as if I were describing something wildly exotic, almost impossible. But I like leaving that question hanging in the air, because I believe the very act of imagining it holds a powerful reminder: a reminder of our dependency, and of the freedom that arises when we're forced to improvise, to create, and to lean on one another. The truth is, technology connects us, but it doesn't unite us. What truly unites us is the will to help each other through the darkest moments.

It's worth delving deeper into the contradiction the city experienced during the blackout: while some chose to vandalize stores and steal electronics, others embraced solidarity and affection as tools to endure the darkness. It was a social mosaic that, in hindsight, shows just how thin the thread is between cohesion and chaos. My grandfather used to sum up that reality with a phrase all his own: *"The power left the wires, but it either lit up or dimmed people's hearts, depending on the choices they made."*

From my window, I could see the sad scenes of people, blinded by opportunity, smashing store windows to take clothes or food. Cries and sirens echoed in the distance, confirming that not all corners of the city responded with the same civility. The next morning, newspapers reported that thousands had been arrested and dozens of shops had been ransacked. But that wasn't the only story. In other neighborhoods, the bonds between neighbors prevented such excesses. Entire families held makeshift vigils on street corners, holding up torches, lanterns, or oil lamps, not with the intent to intimidate, but to quietly deter potential looters. It was their way of saying: *"This is our place, and we protect it together."*

That duality still moves me. On one side, the shadow of chaos; on the other, the flame of solidarity. I tend to believe that part of what made the difference lay in the preexisting connections between people. In places where bonds were strong, built day by day, in friendship and mutual respect, fear couldn't fracture their sense of belonging. If there's one lasting lesson I took with me into the future, it's the importance of truly knowing our neighbors, beyond polite greetings, because we never know when collective tragedy might strike.

That dawn on July 15 brought with it a blend of relief and a quiet nostalgia. Watching as the streetlamps flickered back to life and the homes slowly regained electricity made me smile, but at the same time, it reminded me that the almost tribal dynamic we had experienced in the darkness was about to vanish. The city returned to its rhythm with blinking traffic lights, humming televisions, and people absorbed once more in their routines, without the magic that the previous night had summoned.

It's undeniable that many of the looted businesses took weeks or even months to recover from their losses. The local government declared a state of emergency and promised aid that, in many cases, arrived too late. Amid the tally of damages, stories of silent heroism emerged, of neighbors who had offered shelter to complete strangers. Each of these accounts reinforced my conviction that the spirit of community rises most clearly in the hardest times.

Inside my home, the morning ritual of turning on the radio to hear the news took on a special significance. That day, the voice of the announcer described a Bronx torn between sorrow over the vandalism and pride in those who had formed neighborhood watch lines to protect what was theirs. I was moved to hear commentators highlight how, in certain enclaves, fraternity had proven stronger than fear. I realized the blackout had served as a moral x-ray of the city, revealing both the worst and the best of human nature.

Now, with nearly half a century between me and that night, those memories of the 1977 blackout continue to light up my reflections with surprising clarity. In my neighborhood, we discovered what it means to be plunged into darkness in the age of modernity, an era when we thought we depended so much on electricity, only to realize that, in truth, we depend on each other. We became witnesses to the fact that technology can be a great aid, but its absence exposes both our shortcomings, and our greatest strengths.

Shortly after that episode, my mother would often say to me: "*What matters isn't how much light we have, but how much warmth we share.*" Over time, that phrase became a kind of existential compass for me. I've passed that thought on to my children and now to my grandchildren, hoping they understand that no matter how great the comfort progress may bring, the foundation of life remains cooperation, affection, and empathy.

That night in 1977 proved it to us: if the lightbulbs and streetlamps go out, we still have candles, and if the candles aren't enough, we have the moon and the stars. But most of all, we have each other. Remembering that great lesson is, I believe, the most valuable legacy I can leave to my grandchildren and to generations yet to come.

Speaking of the stars... I remember one of those nights left an especially vivid impression. Around midnight, my father, his eyes gleaming with a rare excitement, called me and my two brothers to climb up to the roof of our building. The stairwell was lit only by the dim glow of our flashlights, and each creaking step sounded like a warning about the shadows that lay beyond our fragile light. As we pushed open the metal door to the rooftop, a rush of cool air greeted us, along with a stunning panorama. For the first time in my life, the Bronx was not bathed in its usual urban glow; instead, a blanket of stars stretched overhead like an infinite tapestry.

I remember my father, usually serious and reserved, breaking his silence in a voice that felt almost reverent. He had never shown much interest in astronomy, but in that moment, he spoke with a mix of wonder and humility I'd never seen in him before:

"Look," he said, pointing to the sky, "they've always been there, but we couldn't see them because the city lights are too bright. It's what they call light pollution. We've gotten so used to the bulbs and the screens, we forget to look up."

My mother curled up beside him, and the five of us, with our flashlights turned off, sat in an almost sacred silence. I could feel my heart pounding fast, as if it were responding to the majesty unfolding before my eyes. My father told us that, as a child, the same thing would happen in his hometown: when the lights went out, the sky would open up into constellations so bright that you'd lose track of where the night ended and where dreams began. That night of the blackout, on the rooftop of our building, I rediscovered that the city also had a starry sky, one we never got to see, hidden behind routine, noise, and the perpetual glare of artificial light.

We stayed up there for a long while, not speaking, letting ourselves be embraced by that celestial dome which, on ordinary nights, remained eclipsed by neon and haste. The next morning, with the return of daylight and the eventual return of power, I realized that brief yet immense experience had changed me. In that pause from artificial light, I learned that the true magic of night isn't found solely in the shelter of darkness, but also in the silence and familial closeness that arise when we turn everything off and choose to look up.

Amid the relentless rhythm of my life, I never forgot those 36 hours of unexpected darkness. What at first seemed ominous turned into something like an improvised celebration where people played, sang, admired, and protected each other from the shadows. It was as if we had rediscovered the shared heartbeat of our humanity. To me, that was the greatest gift the blackout gave us: the realization that solidarity can shine brighter than all the city's lights.

My experiences, now stored on Genostories, are meant to spark reflection in those who hear them: electrical comfort is valuable, yes, but it isn't everything. Technological connection is useful, but it doesn't guarantee the intimacy or mutual understanding that comes from being truly face to face. And if, one day, the shadow of a blackout were to fall on this city again, I trust that, just like before, the human spark would not be extinguished. Because, in the end, the true blackout is not the absence of light, it's the absence of unity and of love.

Several decades have passed since that night when the brightest city in the world was suddenly plunged into darkness. These days, every time I cross a brightly lit street, the memory of that candlelit version of the Bronx returns to me, and I'm moved by the thought that, in the midst of pitch-black night, we discover more of the inner light we possess as a community. Even with all the modernization that followed those days, nothing has left as deep a mark on me as the experience of sharing chairs on the sidewalk, with the moon shining overhead and neighbors telling stories with the kind of simplicity that only the absence of alternatives can inspire.

Moving from darkness back into light taught me that humanity is an unbreakable force when it chooses to care for one another. That's why I end this video with the hope that, even though electricity and connectivity have become our constant companions, we never forget the immense value of true closeness, of spoken words shared aloud, and of laughter unfiltered by screens. If the world were to lose its light, even just for a moment, may it not lose the warmth that lives in our souls.

Because on that night of 1977, I discovered that even when the city goes dark, when we look into each other's eyes, we can ignite the strongest flame of all: that of understanding and kindness.

As I walk through the chapter Javier left on Genostories, I can't help but reflect on the irony that, in our time, light is so abundant we've almost forgotten how to see the stars. His account shows that when the system collapses and the screens go dark, true light is born from the ingenuity and kinship that ignite in the shadows. In a society like ours, so dependent on connectivity, we often forget that life also rests in the warmth of face-to-face interaction and the kind of creativity that flourishes without distraction.

The night of the great blackout of 1977 reveals, through Javier's voice, that darkness can indeed be a stage for fear, but also a call to return to what matters most: shared stories, laughter flickering in candlelight, and mutual aid as an antidote to chaos. In a future where nearly everything has been digitized, it's worth recalling that night to remember that when everything goes dark, literally and metaphorically, what remains is the connection we've built with those around us.

That legacy teaches us that while technology may ease our lives, it will never replace the shared heartbeat that rises when we look each other in the eye, without the ceaseless glow of screens.

Griot 2085

BLACK SUMMER: THE CALL OF THE EARTH

In this chapter, I bring back the voice of Yarran, an Aboriginal Australian man who, in the 1940s, was born into the heartbeat of a land as ancient as his traditions. His testimony, recorded decades later on Genostories, takes us back to the tragedy of the Black Summer of 2019–2020, when fires swept through millions of hectares, incinerated thousands of homes, and claimed the lives of over a billion animals. In 2085, enough time has passed for us to reflect with perspective on that event, a turning point in humanity's environmental awareness. And yet, the echoes of that catastrophe, and how we responded, still reverberate through our relationship with the planet.

I invite you to walk with Yarran through his sorrowful yet luminous account, one that doesn't just document devastation, but also captures the collective strength that emerges when we finally understand that the Earth's suffering is, in truth, our own.

Griot 2085

My name is Yarran. My name, which in our language means "strong tree", has always been a constant reminder of my unbreakable bond with the land. I was born in the 1940s, in an Aboriginal community in Australia, and from childhood I learned to hear the whispers of the wind, the murmurs of the rivers, and the deep heartbeat of the continent. In my life I have witnessed countless cycles of transformation, but none so devastating as the fires of the Black Summer, during the 2019–2020 season.

I have chosen to record this narrative on Genostories for my children, grandchildren, and great-grandchildren. In a world hyper-connected, full of screens and technology, I want to remind them with force of real experience: to see the land burning, to feel the fury of fire on your skin, and to understand that when the Earth suffers, we all suffer. My story is a testament to the resilience of my people, to the ancestral wisdom that teaches us to respect the environment, and to the collective strength that arises in the midst of tragedy.

It was the summer of 2019–2020 when the fires began to multiply with unprecedented ferocity. I was born and raised surrounded by nature; I know firsthand that Australia is a land of extremes and cyclical fires. But this time was different. The intense heat, which had set in for weeks, and the absence of rain left forests in a drought so extreme that a single spark could unleash catastrophe.

I remember how the sky turned a burning red, and dense smoke rose over the mountains. The roar of the fire, audible for kilometers, became the new backdrop of daily life. Every gust of wind seemed to feed the flames, which advanced mercilessly, without distinguishing between scrublands, forests, or plains. I had never felt that kind of anguish: the heat enveloped the air and you could feel the land trembling beneath your feet.

At that moment, I understood that fire was not merely a destructive force, it was a living presence, an ancestral call that, for some reason, came to remind us of our fragility. My brothers and I, descendants of a tradition that for centuries has dwelt in harmony with nature, felt that something had slipped out of balance. That Black Summer was not just another seasonal fire, but a cry from the Earth against deterioration and indifference.

I will never forget the intensity with which the forests burned. On one of my walks toward the interior, I traversed hills that once were lush, where eucalyptus and acacia trees formed cool refuges for hundreds of species. The scene had become a hellish landscape: the green consumed by ashen gray and the orange of embers. The fire danced in fury, trunks crackled, and a scorching heat made the air unbreathable.

The smoke seemed endless. The sun looked like a reddened disk in a sky where night and day blurred together. At times, the wind shifted direction and renewed the flames' voracity, devouring hectare after hectare without mercy. Wherever I walked, I saw the shadows of glowing branches, charred leaves falling in harrowing silence, as though the land itself wept.

The devastation was so overwhelming that my mind could scarcely process it. I felt, all at once, sorrow, anger, and helplessness. My people's stories speak of ancient fires, rituals of controlled burns, and the regeneration of vegetation. But the Black Summer broke every boundary. This was no balanced natural cycle, it was the result of a destabilized climate and human choices that ignored the land's whispers.

Few things have moved me more than the suffering of animals. The fires didn't just ravage forests and homes; they took the lives of hundreds of thousands of koalas, kangaroos, birds, and reptiles. It is estimated that over a billion creatures perished. To our Aboriginal people, every living being is part of a sacred web; to see them die this way was like witnessing the death of distant but essential kin.

Images of injured koalas with singed fur and bewildered eyes attested to a tragedy far greater than many could imagine. Rescuers described Dantean scenes: kangaroos fleeing in panicked stampedes in search of less scorched ground; birds falling from the sky from smoke inhalation; reptiles incinerated with no chance of escape. The statistic of a billion dead animals may sound abstract, but behind each number there was a story, a life, and a crucial place in the chain of existence.

For me, this devastation was not Australia's suffering alone, but the suffering of the entire planet. We live in a world where geographic borders do not prevent ecological impacts from eventually affecting the rest. Every koala that perished, every bird that ceased to fly across the skies, every reptile unable to escape the fire represented an assault on global biodiversity and the interconnected web that sustains all ecosystems. Although this disaster unfolded in a "remote" continent for many, its environmental consequences from massive releases of carbon dioxide, to the loss of pollinators, to the disruption of food chains, eventually echo in every corner of the world. In that way, the Black Summer deepened the wound in Australian soil, but also showed us that every fire of that magnitude ultimately reveals the weaknesses and neglect of all humanity.

It made us realize that human disconnection from nature exacts a price. The fire was not just an enemy, but also a consequence of an imbalance we had nurtured. Every charred tree, every fallen animal, became an open wound in the soul of those of us who feel the land as part of our being.

As a member of an Aboriginal community, I grew up hearing the teachings of my elders about the cycles of the land, the importance of controlled burns, and how nurturing the environment helps prevent disasters on a large scale. Since time immemorial, we practiced methods known as cultural burns, which worked in harmony with the rhythms of nature by preventing the excessive buildup of combustible plant material and allowing natural fires not to become uncontrollable. These gentle burns not only created ecological mosaics that favored biodiversity, by creating different microclimates, but also rejuvenated the soil by leaving nutrient-rich ash behind, stimulating flowering through the potassium released. Moreover, elders affirmed that by warming the atmosphere to a certain threshold, these burns could encourage condensation and rainfall, thereby helping to mitigate future fires.

But over the decades, these practices were gradually pushed aside, and the disconnection from the land became evident. In places where Aboriginal elders had warned about the uncontrolled growth of bushland and the excessive dryness of natural fuel, their requests to carry out cultural burns were ignored or outright banned by local authorities. As a result, many ecosystems stopped benefiting from the natural balance promoted by gentle burns: the opportunity to enrich and renew the soil, to attract and preserve fauna, and to proactively reduce the intensity of fires was lost.

That Black Summer showed me, with painful clarity, how vital it is to keep ancestral knowledge alive and to heed the signs of the land. Despite everything, my community gathered its strength to work with rescuers and guide animals toward natural sanctuaries that had historically served as shelters during difficult seasons. With guidance from the elders, we rediscovered creeks and valleys described in ancient songs, places that, with their water and coolness, offered relief to the fauna fleeing the flames.

Amid the destruction, I witnessed something profoundly human: the solidarity that bloomed across the country and around the world. People from all walks of life, from local farmers to young urbanites, volunteered at rescue centers. Firefighters, both professional and volunteer, covered in soot, multiplied their efforts to fight the fires with hoses and special equipment, even though the flames seemed endless. Pilots of water-bombing planes took turns releasing their loads over critical areas, risking their lives over and over again.

Those unable to fight the fires directly donated money, food, and medical aid for the displaced. Some families who had lost almost everything found ways to share supplies and water with those in greater need. I remember an old man who, after watching his house burn to the ground, dedicated himself to rescuing koalas with his bare hands, improvising bandages and seeking out specialized shelters. That contrast between devastation and the strength of love moved me to tears.

The Aboriginal community also played a vital role. We knew firsthand the paths, caves, and springs where creatures traditionally sought refuge during fires. So we collaborated with rescue brigades; we offered not only our knowledge but also our spirituality: we sang to calm the animals, held vigils to honor fallen beings, and prayed for the earth to regain its balance.

Each passing day, the smoke made it harder to breathe, and we wondered how long the body could endure. The sky turned an oppressive orange, and the sun, when visible, looked like a red coin about to vanish. It wasn't just an ecological drama; it was an identity crisis for the entire nation. Conversations about the climate crisis flared up across the country, like an echo of the very fire raging through the forests.

Inside me, I felt both anger and hope. Anger because, for decades, voices had been ignored, especially those of Aboriginal people who had called for more subtle, respectful fire management methods aligned with natural cycles. Hope because, in the face of the emergency, society as a whole began to awaken to the need for a new relationship with the land. People were talking about clean energy, reforestation, recovering ancestral practices, and solidarity that crossed borders.

For me, participating in rescue groups that embraced the wisdom of my ancestors was crucial. I explained to volunteers that we had always practiced "controlled burns", light fire ceremonies to clear underbrush and prevent the buildup of fuel that could feed massive fires. Many people were unaware of this principle, and seeing it slowly integrated into mitigation strategies felt bittersweet: we knew part of the catastrophe could have been prevented if we had been listened to sooner.

With a calm voice, I shared stories about my grandfather, who taught me to stop and read the language of dry leaves, to listen to the way the wind whispers different signals. "If the Earth speaks and you do not listen," my grandfather used to say, "one day she will make you hear her, through pain." That phrase echoed in my mind as I watched hectares of eucalyptus trees turned to ashes: a warning as ancient as human existence itself.

The international brigades, the arrival of firefighters, the donations from other nations, the tears of people seeing burned kangaroos… all of it fused into a mix of shock and determination. Among those who moved me most were the young urbanites who, despite lacking prior experience, helped rescue wildlife, clean scorched areas, and plant trees in lands seeking to bloom again. In their eyes, I saw a new respect for the land, the same respect my people have nurtured for centuries.

The Black Summer fires left behind a legacy of pain, but also of awareness. Millions of hectares were burned, thousands of homes destroyed, and over a billion animals perished. It was, without doubt, one of the worst environmental episodes in Australia's, and the world's history. But in the wake of that tragedy arose a commitment to rebuild and to learn or at least that is my hope.

Today, various groups are calling for the integration of Aboriginal practices in forest management because they now recognize that Indigenous peoples have long known how to coexist with fire and use it in a controlled and productive way. This overdue recognition is a small sprout of hope that makes me believe that maybe not all is lost. If society can change how it treats the Earth, some of the damage can be undone.

In my case, I've chosen to share my testimony through Genostories so that my descendants never forget our fate is intertwined with nature's. The 2019–2020 season taught me that no matter how strong we believe our cities and technologies to be, a massive fire can remind us of the insignificance of our advancements if they're not aligned with respect for the planet.

I want my grandchildren and great-grandchildren to understand that, standing on the edge of the abyss, what binds us together is empathy and solidarity. Beneath the smoke-darkened sky, when the sun turned into a crimson disk, thousands of anonymous hands joined forces to save lives, extinguish flames, and protect what remained of our shared home. In that act of cooperation, I saw the spark of humanity, the same one that, for centuries, has allowed our peoples to adapt to extreme conditions.

In the hardest-hit areas, I witnessed scenes that combined tragedy with hope. There were nights when the suffocating heat and the smell of smoke kept me from sleeping, but I could also hear, in the distance, the rhythm of people working side by side. Volunteer brigades searched for animals, cleared charred branches, and served warm drinks to those who hadn't rested in hours.

One of those nights, I accompanied a young firefighter who confessed he had lost faith in humanity:

"The flames take everything," he murmured in despair.

But after walking a few kilometers, we came across a small group of koalas and wallabies hiding in a natural gorge where water had withstood the drought. Several neighbors were there, holding hoses and tending to an improvised shelter made of tarps. The firefighter, his eyes filled with emotion, finally understood that, in the deepest darkness, the brightest lights of solidarity can ignite.

The fire season ended almost abruptly, with the long-awaited rains. Showers and storms swept in, cooling the ground and subduing the flames. Many areas were left unrecognizable: entire hillsides turned into charred deserts, streams darkened by ash, and stretches of forest reduced to blackened trunks. Yet, over time, green shoots began to appear. Certain native species, adapted to fire cycles, showed signs of rebirth. We were amazed to see eucalyptus trees, after such devastating fire, pushing out sprouts from their bark, testament to the biological resilience of this land.

In my heart, I knew the Earth was still giving us a chance. Each spring following the Black Summer carried the scent of renewal, the certainty that life strives to emerge even in the harshest conditions. With it, a strong social and political will also took root, a collective commitment to protect the environments that define who we are.

In this 2025, as I record my story in Genostories, I hope my descendants never forget the essential truth: when the earth burns, our ties to it are also scorched. Let no one be deceived into thinking that fire only affects distant forests or exotic animals; the tragedy strikes at our roots and our shared future. I want them to know that during the Black Summer, many realized, too late, what my people had been saying for centuries: nature is not a backdrop to our existence; it is our very existence.

If the Black Summer taught us anything, it's that technology alone is not enough to contain the fury of the earth. We need ancestral land management practices, respect for ecological balance, and above all, social unity. That's where our strength lay in facing the tragedy: the decision to stand side by side when the smoke obscured the sun and the forests screamed in pain.

After that hellish summer, it became clear that returning to "normal" wasn't enough. Recovery meant speaking with the younger generations, teaching them the value of "controlled burns," and the urgent need to protect the habitats where our animal kin live. Numerous reforestation projects sprang up as sprouts of hope on the ashes. Environmental organizations, supported by local communities and Aboriginal wisdom, began planning the restoration of devastated ecosystems and the care of endangered species.

For the first time in many years, I felt that Australian society was beginning to open up to our Aboriginal worldview: understanding that fire is not just an enemy, but a force that, when handled with care, plays a role in the natural cycle. However, when unleashed by neglect or extreme drought, it becomes a monster that destroys everything in its path. The Black Summer left us with this double message: nature can offer us tools, but if we ignore them, the cost is devastating.

Here is my testimony. I record it with the hope that my great-grandchildren, when they watch it years from now, will not only learn about the devastation of the Black Summer but also feel the longing for a return to what is essential. I want them to understand that those forest fires were not an isolated event: they were the result of a convergence of extreme drought, record-breaking heat, strong winds, and a disrupted climate, factors that plunged much of Australia into an unprecedented scenario. It is estimated that over 10 million hectares were scorched, 2,500 buildings destroyed (including more than 1,300 homes), and at least 26 people lost their lives. But perhaps the most heartbreaking blow was to Australia's wildlife: over one billion animals perished in the flames, an incalculable impact on biodiversity.

To many, these numbers might seem abstract, but behind each figure was a story, a life, and a role in the web of existence. As Aboriginal people, we have always believed that fire, when properly managed, is part of a natural cycle that allows the land to renew itself. However, when the climate warns us with droughts and extreme heat and we fail to heed those signs, fire becomes an unbridled force. Our grandparents taught us that fire can be either medicine or plague, depending on how we treat it and whether we listen to the balance the land demands. That legacy of wisdom, passed down through generations, is more valuable than any technology because it teaches respect, humility, and connection with every form of life.

Throughout this video, I wanted to share the tragedy, but also the flame of hope that ignited amidst so much ash. While the fires ravaged hectares of forest and left skies blanketed in smoke, thousands of people came together to fight the disaster, rescue animals, and support those who had lost everything. In the end, our true strength emerged from the will to protect one another and the world we inhabit. Because if the Black Summer taught us anything, it's that when the Earth suffers, we all suffer. And as long as we remain blind to that pain, fire, whether literal or metaphorical, will continue reminding us of our place in the vastness of life.

After hearing Yarran's voice, I wonder what would have happened if, instead of one billion animals, it had been one billion human lives extinguished during the Black Summer. Most likely, the entire planet would have immediately mobilized with an unbreakable determination to halt the climate crisis. But since it involved other living beings, koalas, kangaroos, birds, reptiles, many continued to see the disaster as something distant or "just Australia's problem." As a result, the decade between 2025 and 2035 was filled with ecological disasters that might have been prevented if we had understood in time that the loss of an ecosystem damages the very roots of our own survival.

Fortunately, the potential of artificial intelligence ultimately proved crucial in redirecting policies and reversing the damage before it became irreversible. Researchers, leaders, and local communities worked hand in hand, supported by algorithms that, this time, were not used to ignore reality but to deeply analyze every corner of the natural world and clearly identify the urgent actions that needed to be taken. In this way, humanity finally came to accept that life cannot be divided into "ours" and "theirs": we are all part of a single, interconnected web.

Reflecting on Yarran's legacy, I ask myself how much pain we could have avoided if we had understood, back during the Black Summer, that the destruction of the earth, and of the beings who inhabit it, is also our own destruction. But amid everything, hope is born: if we have learned anything, it's that as long as there is a willingness to understand and to cooperate, there is still a chance for rebirth. May his story, and the wisdom it carries, inspire us to continue healing this planet we share with all living beings.

Griot 2085

THE VOICE OF A GENERATION

In the archives of Genostories, I came across the story of Lisa Johnson, an African American woman who in 2025, at fifty-two years old, decided to tell how the events of 1992 in Los Angeles permanently shaped not only her youth, but the identity of an entire community. Watching her testimony, I felt the strength of someone who lived through the days when the streets were set ablaze by injustice and rage, yet transformed the pain of those days into a lifelong commitment to racial justice and social change. Here in 2085, when digital communication seems to silence voices from the past, Lisa's story is a reminder that the struggles of yesterday have not ended, but have rather been transformed into seeds bearing fruit in new generations. I invite you to listen to her testimony and understand how the echo of 1992 remains alive in every protest and in every word of hope we speak today.

Griot 2085

My name is Lisa Johnson. At fifty-two years old, I've decided to sit in front of my cellphone camera to share a part of my life that defined my path: the Los Angeles riots of 1992, when the verdict acquitting the police officers in the Rodney King case ignited my community's rage. I am here in my living room, in a neighborhood once associated with violence and despair, but which for me has always meant family and resistance. With this story, I want my children, my grandchildren, and through Genostories, everyone who listens, to understand why that night in 1992 changed not only my immediate reality but also the world's perception of the African American community.

I was nineteen and living with my parents in South Los Angeles. I remember perfectly the suffocating April heat, the tension hanging in the air, and the conversations bubbling on every street corner after the video of Rodney King being beaten by police became known. We were no strangers to police brutality, but seeing those images so clearly united us in a mix of outrage and hope that, at last, justice would be done.

On April 29, 1992, the verdict fell like a sentence of abandonment: the officers were declared not guilty. That day, I felt a kind of jolt in my soul. I could not believe such a blatant act of violence could go unpunished. Many broke down in tears; others were left speechless; while some began preparing to take to the streets and cry out their anger. My father, stern and protective, told me: *Tonight will be rough, daughter. I don't want you going out.* But I felt that staying silent was like accepting injustice.

By nightfall, the city began to burn, not with festive bonfires, but with collective rage. The roar of police helicopters dominated the sky, and on television screens we saw protests growing, releasing decades of pent-up fury. My mother, eyes brimming with tears, whispered, *"And who looks out for us?"* At that moment, no one had the answer.

Despite my parents' warnings, I went out that very night. I felt I had to bear witness to what was happening. I didn't go out to loot or participate in acts of violence, but I walked down the main avenue, seeing some with faces burning with rage and pain, and others who took advantage of the chaos to seize material goods that poverty had long denied them. The ground crunched under my feet, littered with broken glass and fragments of a lost calm.

Yet, amid that pandemonium, a powerful solidarity also emerged. Groups of neighbors joined forces to protect family-owned businesses from indiscriminate destruction; some handed out bottles of water and food to those stranded in the streets. Perhaps the news only showed the destructive side of the riots, but I witnessed the other face: people who didn't want more violence, but wanted to be heard and acknowledged. Around midnight, a group of young people formed a "human wall" to dissuade angry crowds from setting fire to a community center that had taken years to build.

What I felt wasn't just fear, but also the tremor of a shared cause. *"This has to change,"* some community leaders said. And I, at nineteen, took that phrase as a call: I understood that fighting for rights isn't only about confronting police in the streets, but also about educating, organizing, and pushing the system toward equity.

When I returned home around two in the morning, my parents were in the living room, desperate over my delay. My mother hugged me, crying, and my father, his brow furrowed, said: *"Daughter, I don't want to lose you in this war."* I answered that I didn't want violence, that what I longed for was for people to know how fed up we were. That conversation stretched on until dawn, with my father recalling his youth in another state, where he too had suffered discrimination, and my mother pointing out that collective courage had the power both to ignite the flame of change and to destroy everything if it overflowed.

It was in that nightlong discussion that I grasped the historic dimension of the moment. My mother pulled out a yellowed photograph of my grandfather, who had marched in the civil rights movement of the 1960s. She explained that each generation fought its own battle, but this one was perhaps the most visible and explosive: *"When rage builds too long, it erupts like a volcano,"* she said with sorrowful eyes, *"but the volcano also fertilizes the earth with its ash."*

That dawn became a portal into my parents' stories, narratives that connected the discriminatory past to the reality the African American community has endured for so long. As the first ray of sunlight peeked through the window, my father began to share, in a slow voice heavy with memory, the story of his childhood.

My father always said his youth was marked by pain and struggle in a small southern town, where segregation wasn't just a social norm but an unwritten law that divided people. He was born in an era when buses, schools, and even public fountains were separated by color. At just six years old, he already remembered the looks of disdain and the harsh words of those who believed his skin was a mistake.

"When I was eight, at the bus stop, an older man yelled, 'This isn't your section, move!'" he told me haltingly, his fists tightening. That experience left a deep scar, as he realized that the fight for dignity began at the very place where his humanity was denied. It wasn't uncommon for him, during recess at school, to feel isolated and relegated to a dark corner while other children laughed and played. But in that isolation, my father learned to seek refuge in books and in the wisdom of his elders.

His own father, my paternal grandfather, was a man of firm principles who had participated in local civil rights movements. During the 1950s, when bus boycotts became a cry of protest, my grandfather would go out on warm nights to teach young people the importance of solidarity and resistance. My father remembered him with admiration: *"I watched my dad march with dignity, despite the insults and the violence spilling out on every corner,"* he said, his voice breaking with emotion.

As he grew older, my father found himself in the middle of a society that, despite its apparent changes, remained anchored in prejudice and resentment. During his teenage years, when people spoke of the possibility of integrating spaces once reserved only for whites, he experienced the anger of those clinging to the old order. He recalled that one summer afternoon, while helping repair an old community library, a neighbor approached him and sneered: *"Don't think you're too smart, boy. You don't belong in this neighborhood."* Those words cut him deeply, but they also pushed him to forge his character. Over time, he came to understand that every insult was a reminder that the struggle had to continue.

The most formative experience for him was undoubtedly the day he decided to take part in a peaceful protest against police brutality. At just seventeen, he joined a march through the cobbled streets of his hometown. There, among chants and slogans, he felt for the first time the unifying force of collective resistance. *"I felt that, even if we were few and weak against the system, together we could shake the foundations of injustice,"* he confessed to me as his eyes drifted into memory. That determination led him to attend university and to commit actively to organizations that fought for the rights of the oppressed.

Throughout his life, my father has been both a witness to and a quiet participant in the social transformations that sought to tear down the walls of racism. His story is a reflection of those countless lives that, despite the pain, chose to rise up and demand respect. With every anecdote he shared, one could glimpse the seed of hope that drove him to work tirelessly for a future where dignity was not a privilege but an inalienable right.

As my father recounted his experiences, my mother, with tears in her eyes but a steady voice, began to tell hers. Born in a large northern city, her childhood was marked by a duality of hope and struggle in an environment that, although different in appearance, was not free from discrimination. Her mother, my maternal grandmother, was a woman of unshakable convictions who had taken part in countless protests during the Civil Rights Movement.

From a very young age, I was taught to recognize injustice, my mother began, recalling those days with a mix of nostalgia and restrained fury. She spoke with passion about how, as just a little girl, she would accompany her mother to neighborhood meetings where issues far too big for her age were being discussed. In those gatherings, people talked about school segregation, discrimination in employment, and the urgent need to dismantle a system that pushed African Americans into the shadows.

One of the stories that marked her most was of a particular day when, on a busy city street, a group of demonstrators gathered to demand equal opportunities. *I remember the atmosphere was thick with tension and, at the same time, with a vibrant energy*, she recounted, her voice trembling but determined. *My mother, her face lit with hope and resolve, stood before the crowd and shouted: "Enough injustice!" raising her voice so everyone would know that change was possible.* That image, she said, remained etched in her memory like a beacon lighting the way toward transformation.

My mother also shared painful episodes from her childhood, moments when discrimination revealed itself in the smallest details of daily life. At her school, for instance, she noticed that even though she was bright and curious, the teachers looked at her with suspicion and assigned her tasks they deemed "appropriate for someone of her condition." *It was as if, from the very first day, they already knew my fate was sealed by the barriers of a racist system*, she said through tears. Yet even that reality instilled in her the value of resilience. She learned to turn pain into strength, to channel her frustrations into an unyielding fight for justice.

At one of the most powerful moments of that family conversation, while the dim lamp light barely illuminated the living room, my mother confided in me: *Daughter, the real revolution is born in each person's heart. My mother, my grandmother, and all the women before us have learned that, though discrimination tries to break our spirit, unity and love can raise walls that even the deepest hatred cannot tear down.*

Those words resonated in me like a call never to forget our roots and to understand that each generation's struggle becomes the foundation of the future.

Both my father and my mother had drawn from their own experiences the conviction that true change was only possible through unity and collective commitment. That night, in the half-light of our living room, the portrait of a family forged in adversity took shape, where every painful experience was also a lesson in resilience. Through their stories of segregation, of marches, and of small acts of everyday defiance, I came to understand that their lives reflected an ancient struggle for dignity and equality.

To close the circle of our family's story, my mother pulled from a drawer that yellowed photograph, a silent witness of a time filled with struggle and hope. In it, my maternal grandfather stood in the midst of a 1960s demonstration, shoulder to shoulder with other activists who had dared to dream of a different world. With a trembling voice, my mother shared the memories of her parents, my grandparents, who had faced the raw injustices of institutional racism head-on.

Your grandfather took part in the historic March on Washington in 1963, where thousands of voices rose together to demand equality and justice, she told me, running her fingers gently across the image. He would tell me that in those days the air itself was heavy with both fear and hope, with uncertainty and with a blind faith that change was imminent. She recalled that, as a little girl, she had witnessed how my grandmother organized small gatherings in their home, where Martin Luther King's ideas were discussed and community actions against neighborhood segregation were planned.

That generation, my grandparents' generation, lived through pivotal moments in the nation's history. From bus boycotts to strikes and protests that defined the Civil Rights Movement, their lives were steeped in a struggle that went far beyond the personal, becoming part of a larger collective fight. My grandfather, with his dignified bearing and steady gaze, embodied that unshakable will to transform pain into action. My grandmother would say: *Every obstacle we encounter is a step toward freedom. Even if the path is shrouded in shadows, the light of justice always shines at the end.*

That same narrative echoed through every family story, where sacrifice and commitment were passed down from generation to generation. My grandparents did not simply *live* history; they *built* it with their calloused hands and their unbreakable spirit. The marches, the boycotts, the nights of uncertainty and fierce faith became the legacy that inspired my parents to keep fighting for a different tomorrow. Within those memories lies the essence of an era where resistance was the only possible answer to oppression, and where the dream of equality was woven out of effort, tears, and above all, love for the community.

Listening to these stories, I realized that the struggle for justice is never an isolated event. It is the product of centuries of resistance and the conviction that human dignity is priceless. Each account, each anecdote, was a reminder that our ancestors carved out the path that allows us to raise our voices today without fear, to demand fair treatment, and to never forget that memory is, at its core, the foundation upon which the future is built.

That night, as the sun rose and the living room filled with a light that seemed to bless our reconnection with the past, I understood that my family's stories were far more than tales of suffering. They were a living testimony of humanity's capacity to endure, to transform pain into strength, and to build, upon the ruins of injustice, a tomorrow filled with possibility. With every word, my father and mother taught me that the fight continues within each of us, and that as long as we remember the wounds of the past, we will be better prepared to heal the present and forge a future where equality is no longer a utopian dream but a reality for all.

In that conversation, the anguish of a turbulent night was not only soothed, but a generational bridge was also forged. My parents' lives, scarred by discrimination and struggle, intertwined with the heroic feats of my grandparents, who had faced down oppression with the unwavering belief that change was possible. Each story, each tear shed, and each cry stifled in the silence of the night became the very foundations of an unbreakable identity, an inheritance from those who, despite everything, never gave up on hope.

When I look back and listen to these memories once more, I know that the story of my family is the reflection of a people's story, one that has had to fight, over the years, against the tide of discrimination. It is a tale of resistance, of courage, and of the relentless pursuit of justice. In every word, in every gesture, I hear the echo of those who, in times past, raised their voices in the name of dignity and freedom.

In that moment, as dawn broke and the conversation drew to a close, I understood that the legacy of my grandparents, their fight for civil rights, their resolve in the face of injustice, and their unconditional love for the community, is not just a story to be told, but a call to action, an invitation to keep building on the foundations they forged with such sacrifice. And so, with a heart swollen with pride and a spirit renewed, I knew it was my turn to continue that struggle and become an active part of that history.

The unrest lasted several days, with increasingly intense scenes unfolding in various neighborhoods across Los Angeles. News outlets from all over the country broadcast the chaos and tension live. When the city entered a state of emergency, the National Guard was deployed to the streets. It was a scene of extreme polarization. I remember that, despite the fear, African American, Latino, and Asian families, who often kept their distance from one another, came together to guard their corners and seek shelter. What united them was a collective cry of exhaustion in the face of injustice, though the ways they expressed it ranged from peaceful protest to raw violence.

As the days passed, a mix of fear and fatigue spread through the neighborhoods. People spoke of lives lost, of buildings and businesses destroyed, of the wounded and the arrested, but also of community gatherings that, for the first time, brought to the forefront the urgent need to reform the police and address economic inequality. That May of 1992 ended with a tragic toll and many wounds, but at the same time, it planted the seed of a movement that would not rest until it saw real change.

For me, the 1992 riots became a moral compass. As I grew up, I dedicated myself to studying political science and participating in organizations focused on defending civil rights. I understood that the fire of initial rage had to be channeled into initiatives centered on education, civic engagement, and holding institutions accountable. For years, I conducted workshops in schools in underprivileged neighborhoods to remind young people that while rage is a powerful engine, organized action is the most effective vehicle to ensure that future generations do not inherit the same frustration.

Over time, I witnessed some progress: greater scrutiny of police behavior, social programs more effectively targeted at youth, and more Black voices rising to positions of leadership. And yet, there were setbacks too, other cases of brutality made headlines with the same raw intensity, causing the flames of discontent to flare up again. That's when I understood that social change is not a straight line nor a one-time achievement; it's a process that demands persistence, memory, and communities willing to never give up.

Now, as I record these videos and reflect on Genostories, I hope that my grandchildren, and anyone listening, will understand that what we lived through in 1992 did not stay in that year. Its echoes have crossed decades, embodied in various protests and movements, from Black Lives Matter to neighborhood initiatives fighting social exclusion. The unrest of those days did not expire; it transformed into an ongoing demand for justice and equity.

I'm moved when I see young people, fifteen, twenty years old, who never experienced the terror of 1992 but still take to the streets with signs, shouting "No more racism!" The fire I see in them reminds me of the nineteen-year-old Lisa who dared to walk through the darkness, with the city ablaze, to raise her voice. It feels essential that they understand where that historic fury comes from, and that yearning for a less unjust present.

I want my children and grandchildren to learn something fundamental: the riots were not a mere explosion of irrational fury; they were a response to years of oppression and institutional deafness. I hope they never have to witness the horror of seeing their own city burn in order to realize the need for structural change. That's why this message is my legacy: social transformation is not achieved solely in the streets, nor only in the halls of power, but requires the convergence of both spaces, fueled by the memory of what can be lost if we remain indifferent.

If I learned anything from 1992, it's that time alone doesn't heal wounds; it needs people who, with determination, place their hands on the present and build bridges toward the future. Just as my parents and I once sat in our living room discussing fears and the yearning for justice, today I hope that you, the next generation, will have those same conversations with your loved ones, exploring strategies to keep pressing the system until equality is no longer a utopia.

In Lisa Johnson's narrative, we discover that the 1992 riots in Los Angeles were more than just a fleeting revolt, they became the crack through which many people first glimpsed the magnitude of the demand for racial justice. That moment gave Lisa a sense of purpose that marked her for life and propelled her to become a civil rights advocate. From the vantage point of 2085, I am struck by how many of the tensions they lived through remained present in 2025, and how Lisa's voice, full of smoke, fury, and determination, still rings with urgency.

Her story teaches us that the flames of the past, however destructive they may have been, also illuminated the path toward change. It reminds us that when an entire community feels ignored, rage can ignite like wildfire, but if that fire is consciously channeled, it can fuel the will to transform the world. I hope those who read or hear this chapter in the future will take these lessons to heart and understand that Lisa's battle is a part of everyone's story: a call not to let rage ache in vain, but to turn it into a force that builds bridges and breaks down the walls of injustice.

Still, although the events of 1992 sparked deep conversations about systemic racism and inequality, the road toward mutual understanding did not solidify overnight. The controversies of the 2000s and 2010s, and the turbulence seen between 2010 and 2020, made it clear that the historical wounds were still open. Even in the late 2020s and early 2030s, new racial uprisings erupted, revealing just how fragile that supposed understanding really was. Many asked why, after having witnessed the fury of 1992, the same injustices continued to repeat.

Why, again and again, the same cries of helplessness kept emerging. Even in 2035, pockets of tension lingered that echoed scenes from decades past. It was a bewildering period, marked by moments of progress, yes, but equally by severe setbacks, showing that humanity sometimes stumbles over the same ground more than once.

Looking back from 2085, it's striking how difficult it was for society to truly embrace the other, to see diversity as a source of richness rather than division, and from that recognition, to build a future in which negative consequences were no longer perpetuated against other races or minorities. It seemed that human beings, on their own, struggled to learn from the past deeply enough to break the vicious cycle of discrimination.

During those decades, technology advanced at an astonishing pace, but its use was often focused more on the immediacy of information than on the kind of social transformation many yearned for. It wasn't until the mid-2050s, when artificial intelligence and quantum computing took a revolutionary leap, that we began to witness real systemic change. These algorithms, capable of processing immense amounts of data in multidimensional ways, helped expose, backed by irrefutable evidence, the root of inequalities and allowed for the design of fairer, more universal policies. AI, no longer used solely as a market tool, became a strategic ally in identifying and addressing racial gaps, and disparities in health, education, and access to opportunity.

From this temporal distance, it amazes me to think that only when humans realized they could not face the complexity of systemic racism alone did they accept the integration of AI's wisdom and unflinching analysis into their decision-making. Thanks to that, it became possible to align political will, equitably allocate funding, and design models of cultural integration based on empathy and solidarity. In a way, technology forged the path that men and women, with all their limitations, had been unable to sustain on their own. In this year 2085, we still do not live in a perfect world, but we have made tremendous strides in healing wounds that once seemed eternal. The pain accumulated in 1992, and in so many outbursts of rage that followed, ended up being the spark that led to the creation of a more conscious society.

It's important not to idealize: these were complex decades, filled with unrest that flared up again and again from the 2030s well into the 2040s, continually testing our commitment to reconciliation. But ultimately, AI and quantum computing made visible what so many had been shouting about in the streets. With analytical coldness, but also with a surprising capacity to learn from cultural evolution itself, these technological advances became our moral compass.

The story Lisa shared, those days in 1992 filled with burning buildings and cries of exhaustion, was a prophetic cry. I'd like to believe that if humanity had listened more closely to that warning, some of the tragedies that unfolded in the decades that followed could have been avoided or at least mitigated. But reality showed us that we often need more than one fall to learn. And so it was, burdened with pain and countless wounds, that we reached a point where technology offered us the foundation to rebalance our relationships and, at last, straighten the course of human life as a collective.

That's why, as I close this chapter, I invite anyone who reads or hears it to honor the testimony of Lisa Johnson and all the voices that rose in Los Angeles in 1992. Their cry for justice was the seed of a series of transformations that did not bear fruit immediately but have matured over the course of more than half a century. Let us not forget that what began as an explosion of rage can, through time, reason, and yes, also through the help of powerful technological tools, become a path toward a more just civilization. Even in 2085, the echo of her words reverberates, reminding us that equality is born from the humble act of recognizing one another, without excuses or pretexts, as part of the same great human family.

Griot 2085

GHOST CITIES, INVISIBLE HEARTS

In this distant year of 2085, the story of the COVID-19 pandemic might seem like a blurred chapter in our collective memory. We've overcome unthinkable challenges, and technology has become so ubiquitous that we sometimes forget the vulnerability that once shook us to our core. Yet, while reviewing the Genostories archives, I came across the account of David Bennett, recorded in 2025. His voice moved me: it is the testimony of an ordinary man who lived through the silence of empty streets, suffered the loss of his father in the solitude of a video call, and witnessed humanity's capacity to either unite or divide in the face of the unknown.

I share this story so you may understand firsthand just how fragile life can be, and how easy it is to get lost in misinformation, even when the answers were within reach. Because in these times, so different now, we must not forget that there was a day when a simple virus brought the world to its knees and revealed both the greatness and the misery of our species.

Griot 2085

My name is David Bennett. I was born in 1975, and here in 2025, I'm preparing to record my testimony for Genostories, a platform created to preserve our collective memory and pass on the experiences of one generation to the next. I'm fifty years old (about to turn fifty-one), and over the course of my life I've seen it all: the rise of mobile phones, the explosion of social media, political upheavals, and even noticeable climate changes in my own city. But nothing, absolutely nothing, prepared me for the days of the COVID-19 pandemic. Those months in 2020 and 2021, when the world, literally, came to a halt, transformed my understanding of human fragility, the importance of truthful information, and how fleeting life can be.

Now, surrounded by my children and thinking of my future grandchildren, I want to leave a record of what I lived through. I'm not doing this to relive the fear, but so they understand how close we came to losing ourselves in solitude and chaos. I also want them to see how, even amid desolation, there were flashes of ingenuity, solidarity, and above all, humanity. This testimony is my way of remembering, and at the same time, encouraging those who come after me not to forget the lessons the pandemic left us. Because the greatest danger, after surviving a global challenge, is repeating the same mistakes that once brought us to the edge.

At the end of 2019, rumors began to circulate about a virus in Wuhan, China. At first, we saw it as something distant, a situation similar to previous epidemics that, in theory, never really disrupted life for those of us on the other side of the planet. But reality struck with brutal force when, in January 2020, the news spoke of thousands infected and a rising death toll. Even then, many governments and individuals still refused to believe how serious it truly was.

I remember that even I, caught up in my work routine, struggled to grasp the scale of the problem. I was a busy man, I'd leave early for the office, juggle family commitments, and thought that all this talk of *"mass quarantines"* sounded like something out of a Science fiction movie. But when the World Health Organization officially declared the pandemic in March 2020, everything changed in an instant. Overnight, flights were suspended, borders closed, and in my city, like so many others, a lockdown was imposed.

We were used to immediacy, to constant clicking, to believing that technology made us almost invincible. And yet, an invisible microorganism was enough to make the entire planet tremble. My phone buzzed nonstop with notifications about new cases, government orders mandating social distancing, and headlines mixing real data with alarmist rumors. It took just one week for the economy to grind to a halt: tourism collapsed, restaurants and shops were forced to shut their doors, and thousands of businesses had to completely rethink how they operated.

One of the most vivid memories I carry from those days is the image of my city turned into a deserted stage. I lived in a relatively busy neighborhood, where traffic and the murmur of people were a constant part of the soundscape. Suddenly, the streets were empty, blanketed in an eerie stillness that gave me chills. I walked wearing a mask and gloves, something I had never imagined, and when I came across other pedestrians, equally covered and distant, we avoided one another almost fearfully. It felt like we no longer saw each other as human beings, but as potential threats.

Shops displayed signs that read *"Closed for quarantine"* and *"We'll be back soon,"* without knowing whether *"soon"* would ever actually come. The streetlights still came on at night, but they only illuminated empty asphalt. Sometimes I'd step out onto the balcony and look out over a city that, though still lit, had no life in it. Somehow, the word *"ghost"* became the most fitting descriptor, the city had become an emptiness filled with shadows.

Stepping into a shuttered shopping mall was disorienting, it felt like walking onto the set of a post-apocalyptic movie. If you had to go to the supermarket or the pharmacy, you'd find floor markings to enforce distancing; people whispered tense conversations and went silent at the sound of a cough. That isolation left a mark on the collective psyche: we realized that simply closing the front door wasn't enough to stay safe; we had to suspend the inertia of public life and surrender much of our freedom to a virus that, in its invisibility, had modern civilization in checkmate.

The most painful blow came to me in early May 2020. My father, seventy-one years old, was an energetic, vibrant man whom I admired deeply. He used to say, with his characteristic humor:

Son, the only thing that could take me down is a last-minute touchdown against the New England Patriots.

I always thought he'd live for many more years, filling our lives with laughter and his unshakable determination never to give up.

But he'd been feeling unwell for days, running a fever and struggling to breathe. I clung to the hope that it was just another passing case of pneumonia. One afternoon, when his face began to show an alarming level of fatigue, I convinced him to go to the ER. That's when I got the confirmation I had dreaded: there weren't enough beds, and the diagnosis pointed to COVID-19.

I remember that moment vividly. A nurse came up to us and said, hurriedly:

We need to isolate him immediately. He'll be taken to a makeshift ward, we're overwhelmed with patients.

My father, wearing an oxygen mask and speaking in a faint voice, tried to reassure me:

Don't worry, son… I'll be fine.

It was as if, suddenly, all the noise in the hospital faded to silence. I wanted to go with him, but the restrictions were strict: no visitors allowed, not even close family.

Sir, you can't go in. Please keep your distance, said the same nurse pushing the stretcher.

Dad, I murmured, trying to take his hand, what do I do?

He smiled at me with the same tenderness he had always shown.

Take care of your mother. I'll… be back before you know it.

Those words echoed in my mind as I watched him disappear down a hallway crowded with doctors and gurneys. I gripped my mask tightly, holding back the urge to run after him.

From that moment on, my days became a sting of anxiety. Every morning and every night, I tried to get in touch with the hospital. The response was usually the same:

He's stable, though still on supplemental oxygen.

Or sometimes, a more serious voice would add:

His condition remains delicate; we're assessing whether he'll need to be intubated.

The simple fact that I couldn't set foot in that place to see him, to give him encouragement, to ask *"How are you feeling, Dad?"*, it was unbearable. I had always believed that in a medical emergency, you stayed by the patient's side, holding their hand, making sure they lacked for nothing. But COVID-19 shattered that deeply rooted custom.

A few days later, a doctor called me on my cellphone:

Mr. Rivera, your father's condition has suddenly worsened. He's been intubated.

Can I go in to say goodbye? , I asked, my voice trembling.

I'm sorry, the rules are very strict; no visitors are allowed in intensive care.

That conversation broke my heart. I couldn't sit still, I wandered the house like a ghost, checking my phone obsessively. My mother, drowned in tears, kept repeating:

Why won't they let us see him? How will we even know what's really happening?

Then, a tiny sliver of humanity appeared: a nurse I didn't even know personally took pity on me. She called one afternoon and said:

We have one minute for a video call. Please be ready.

That minute became eternal and fleeting all at once. The image was shaky, my father's tired face, connected to tubes and beeping monitors. The nurse held the phone with a trembling hand, and in the background, you could hear the bustle of the ward. My father gave a faint smile, that smile that had always made me feel safe.

Son…, he whispered, his voice barely audible.

Dad, I'm here. Come on, stay strong… We're waiting for you at home.

Take care of your mother, he repeated, his voice trembling. *As for me… my time…*

I wanted to deny it, to tell him he'd be back soon, but in his eyes, I saw a silent farewell.

It's okay, Dad, you're going to recover. Just… a few more days.

And he replied with a faint:

I love you, son.

The video call ended abruptly. It was no use shouting *"Please don't hang up!"*, the nurse had to move on with her duties. That was the last time I heard my father's voice. The next day, I received the call I had dreaded:

Your father passed away early this morning.

The lump in my throat stayed there for months. The word *"heartbreaking"* doesn't come close to describing what I felt. I couldn't even attend a proper funeral. Everything was reduced to a livestream, with a priest reciting worn-out phrases and my mother watching from the kitchen, too drained to sit in the living room. We held hands during the virtual ceremony. You could hear sobs from a few relatives connected to the stream, but there were no embraces, no collective mourning, no flowers gently placed over a coffin with reverence. The virus stole from me the chance to say goodbye to my father with the dignity he deserved, a man who had always fought for his family.

For many, COVID-19 wasn't *"real"* until it touched their loved ones. But when you hear your father's labored cough through a phone call, and then are left with his absence, you realize there's no conspiracy theory in the world that can explain away the emptiness left by death.

My experience isn't unique. During that critical year of the pandemic, thousands, maybe millions, around the world lived the same nightmare of not being able to say goodbye to their loved ones. It was a silent cruelty: elderly people dying without a hand to comfort them, without a familiar face to bring peace in their final moments. Each of those stories became another wound in the fabric of our collective memory.

I would wake in the middle of the night, haunted by visions of overcrowded hospitals, nurses doing everything they could with limited resources and endless shifts. I remembered with bitterness how, while some still stubbornly denied the severity of the crisis, ordinary people were grieving without hugs, facing absences with no possible comfort. That dissonance between the harshness of reality and the ease with which some dismissed it filled me with both anger and sorrow.

It was then that I truly understood the fragility of our perception: when pain doesn't knock at your door, it's easy to believe it doesn't exist. That's why I've chosen to record this for Genostories, so no one hides the most human side of the tragedy. Without firsthand experience, many will continue to think *"it wasn't that bad,"* and yet the emptiness of a stolen goodbye, the weight of a cellphone as the only link to someone dying, those are marks that never fade.

What devastated me most wasn't just losing my father, it was how it happened. We were left with the painful feeling that we hadn't fulfilled the sacred ritual of being there for him. I remember my mother repeating, again and again:

How could he leave so alone, when we'd always been by his side?

One of my aunts, also grieving, called me one day and said:

Look, David, I know this is hard, but you need to understand, it wasn't you who abandoned him. It was this atrocious situation that separated you.

That reflection allowed me to forgive myself a little. Still, the wound remains. That's why, in this chapter, I want to highlight how precious that final goodbye truly is. Historically, in almost every culture, accompanying the dying is an act of love and peace. When the pandemic broke that norm, thousands were left orphaned of that emotional process. So much was said about statistics, the economy, and political debates that we lost sight of how sacred it is to say goodbye in person.

That's why, if one day my grandchildren ever watch this video, I want them to understand that nothing can replace holding the hand of someone who's leaving, whispering a *"thank you for everything"* into their ear, sealing a shared life with one final embrace. Technology, so marvelous at keeping us connected, proved insufficient when it came to offering warmth in the face of death. With a simple digital *"I love you,"* we were left orphaned of real closure.

Among so many tragic stories, there were also sparks of solidarity that restored some of my faith in humanity. It wasn't all emotional orphanhood, the pandemic moved some to become everyday angels. I remember the story of my neighbors: a young couple who, every day during lockdown, prepared soup and left it at the doors of those who were sick, without charging a single cent.

We don't want anyone to die from hunger or lack of care, they would say.

That moved me deeply and stood in stark contrast to the selfishness we saw in other behaviors.

But that wasn't the only light amid the darkness. There were also acts of courage and empathy that broke the monotony of fear. In our neighborhood, for instance, a group of university students organized a support network for the most vulnerable families. Armed with bicycles and a strong desire to help, they went out every morning to deliver food and medicine.

This is our way of giving back what society has taken from us, they said with conviction as they handed out supplies.

Another heroic act that still echoes in my memory was that of a nurse at a small local hospital who, despite the personal risk, volunteered to take extra shifts in the intensive care unit. With visible exhaustion in her eyes, she would often say:

Every patient I manage to care for is a victory against despair.

Her dedication and sacrifice became a symbol of the daily fight amid the chaos, reminding us that even in the darkest moments, commitment and personal devotion can make all the difference.

I also can't forget the story of an elderly man living alone who found the warmth of a family within his community. A group of volunteers organized weekly visits, bringing him food, medicine, and, most importantly, company.

Solidarity is the antidote to isolation, he would say with a shy smile as his new friends embraced him at every visit.

These acts, though they may have seemed small, held enormous meaning for those who felt forgotten.

Even in the virtual world, support networks formed that became emotional lifelines. Social media groups turned into forums for mutual aid, where people shared resources, accurate health information, and advice for coping with daily stress. The admin of one such group used to write:

In times like these, every encouraging message is a spark that ignites hope in someone's heart.

Technology, which at other times seemed to distance us, became a tool for bringing us together and helping us carry the weight of adversity as one.

In short, the pandemic unleashed enormous challenges, but it also revealed the resilient and generous soul of humanity. Amid fear and uncertainty, countless acts of love and solidarity blossomed. Each gesture, no matter how small, was a reminder that in hardship, the human spirit grows stronger. Stories like that of the young couple, the caring students, the tireless nurse, and the selfless volunteers are etched in my memory as living proof that even in the darkest of times, humanity can shine with an unbreakable light.

The pandemic taught us that, despite tragedy, we can build a more humane world, said one of the volunteers, her gaze filled with resolve.

In every act of kindness, every shared smile, and every word of encouragement, it was clear: solidarity is the bond that unites us and the force that drives us forward.

Yet I also witnessed the opposite: people blatantly ignoring health guidelines, triggering new outbreaks, or indulging in conspiracy theories without considering the consequences for others. These cultural clashes exposed the reality that not everyone sees community as a shared project. Many prioritized personal freedom at the expense of collective safety. It was heartbreaking to hear of neighbors who got infected after attending secret gatherings or refusing to wear a mask, only to later learn that someone's aunt had died from an entirely preventable transmission.

Amid the confusion and fear, misinformation spread like a second virus, fueled by the ignorance of those clinging to preconceived ideas and a stubbornness that blinded them to reality. The lack of access to accurate, verified information, combined with the flood of rumors, led many to downplay the danger. Instead of preparing and acting responsibly, they chose to ignore the warnings, convinced that nothing serious was happening. This mindset, far from being simple negligence, revealed a deep disconnect between the lived experience of the majority and the perception of those trapped in a bubble of unfounded certainties.

Polarization intensified across every layer of society: in family gatherings, at work, and on social media. The divide became clear between those who accepted health recommendations and those who dismissed them as exaggerations or manipulations. Some clung fiercely to the belief that public health measures were an unnecessary restriction of individual freedoms, failing to see that each personal decision could have devastating effects on the entire community. These confrontations weren't just theoretical debates, they translated into concrete actions that increased infections and, ultimately, put the lives of neighbors, friends, and family members at risk.

The impact was undeniable. More and more stories surfaced of infections spreading through private gatherings, secret parties, and meetings held without the slightest precaution, spaces where skepticism and misinformation had taken root as unquestioned truths. Take, for example, the case of a group of young people who, convinced they were immune or that the threat was fabricated, gathered without care, only to face the harsh reality of overcrowded hospitals and irreversible losses. These situations revealed a brutal contrast: while some were fighting tirelessly to protect the most vulnerable, others, trapped in denial, were actively deepening the crisis.

But beyond the criticism, this scenario offered a crucial lesson about the importance of healing our divisions. The pandemic, in all its harshness and complexity, revealed that in moments of extreme tension, solidarity and a sense of community are vital for overcoming shared challenges. It's essential to recognize that individual freedom must go hand in hand with collective responsibility, and that only through dialogue and education can we build a united front against misinformation and fear.

Solidarity isn't just a value, it's a necessity, stated a community leader during one of those heated debates, emphasizing the urgency of breaking down barriers and building bridges between opposing views. In times of crisis, a gesture, a word of encouragement, or an informed action can make all the difference. That's why it's so important to foster access to accurate information and promote honest conversation, so that polarization doesn't become an insurmountable force of division.

Ultimately, what failed during the pandemic wasn't just the spread of the virus, it was also the spread of a mindset that, by ignoring the limited evidence available at the time and clinging to unfounded beliefs, helped worsen the situation. The experience teaches us that in moments of social upheaval, it's essential to pause our prejudices and work together for the common good. Only then can we prevent ignorance and stubbornness from becoming weapons that fragment our society, and instead transform them into drivers of change toward a future where empathy and responsibility form the foundation of harmonious coexistence.

Curiously, as I look back, I see that the experience polarized us: some led with empathy and responsibility; others took pride in their indifference toward the whole. Time will tell which attitude will prevail in our collective memory.

By the time I sit down to recount this in 2025, the world is searching for new forms of normal. People speak of the post-COVID era with the tone of a closed scar, though it's often forgotten that the deep wound was fed by so many failed goodbyes. I think of the virtual museums documenting the pandemic, of the medical breakthroughs, like mRNA vaccines, that advanced at incredible speed. I also think of the people who, after overcoming the initial fear, chose to value daily life more deeply, to cherish in-person gatherings, and to recognize that we are not invincible.

Now more than ever, I see the importance of *Genostories*: these testimonies can help future generations avoid filing the pandemic under *"an annoying event"* or *"an overblown conspiracy."* On the contrary, this is a record of my story, a regular man who lost his father and watched his city turn into a vast stage of silence and masks.

If in 2040, 2050, or 2060 my grandchildren or great-grandchildren come across this video, I want them to know that COVID-19 was not just a medical epidemic, it was a moral, social, and emotional trial for all of humanity. Maybe by then there will be stronger healthcare systems and a more compassionate culture that prevents the kinds of divisions that caused so much harm. I hope they also understand that misinformation is far from a joke, it costs lives, and that empathy must not depend on whether one is personally affected.

I hope that in their time, the image of a hospital shutting its doors to a family's affection, barring them from holding the hand of a loved one in their final hours, will never be repeated. Of all the shortages the pandemic left behind, that is the one that burns deepest in my soul. I want them to understand that the true strength of society isn't in avoiding tragedy, but in learning from it to protect what makes us human: our vulnerability, our empathy, and our connection.

This story is not just mine, it belongs to the millions who wept in silence, who loved through a screen, and who grew as people when the world came to a halt. That's why, if the world ever faces a similar challenge again, I pray that the lessons of 2020 and 2021 won't be forgotten, that technology will be used to bring us closer, not to divide us, and that each individual's life will be valued as it should be, free from trivialization and conspiratorial fervor.

At the end of this long recording, I like to recall the image of my city, empty, transformed into a monumental silence, like a canvas awaiting something new. In that silence, I discovered that our hearts are invisible, yet they beat with enough strength to reconnect humanity even when the streets turn into ghosts. My father passed in physical solitude, but I know his presence lives on, in me, in my children, and thanks to these videos preserved in Genostories, also in my grandchildren and the generations to come.

"Technology can keep us online, but only compassion keeps us together." That's the final message I want to leave behind. Because

with every video call, voice note, and livestream, we reaffirmed our need for connection beyond the screen. Let my testimony serve as a warning against the arrogance of feeling safe, and as an invitation to prioritize what truly sustains us as a species: empathy, mutual care, and the humility to remember that we can still be brought to a halt by a virus.

Let us not become ghost cities; let us be visible hearts, united, and ready to face adversity with the shared light of solidarity.

After listening to David's testimony, I'm struck by how difficult it was for humanity to absorb the lesson that COVID-19 brought with it. Despite the voices calling for responsibility and empathy, there were countless events throughout the 2020s, and well into the 2030s, where misinformation and polarization once again ignited social tensions. There were riots in various countries, movements that denied scientific realities, and even new public health crises that found people once again divided and confused.

From my perspective here in 2085, it's astonishing how racial unrest and conflicts rooted in truth-denial repeated themselves in almost identical fashion. It seems the warnings of David, and so many others, weren't enough to stop the collective negligence. It was a long and stumbling process before society truly understood that cooperation and verified truth are not luxuries, but foundations of our coexistence. Only when artificial intelligence and quantum computing reached unprecedented levels of analysis and speed, beginning around 2050, were we finally able to shape policy and educate citizens in a way that made lies less capable of masquerading as facts.

In this way, we finally began to control environmental damage, healthcare inequality, and the management of future pandemics. A collective awareness matured, the understanding that human life, in all its diversity, deserves to be protected with the same urgency with which one defends their own existence. It took us decades to recognize that the values David stood for, genuine human connection, solidarity, and humility in the face of the unknown, were the key to not stumbling over the same stone again.

In recovering his words, I understand that each individual story, his, mine, and those of millions, forms a tapestry that defines us as a species. It's that shared consciousness, supported by responsible technology and political will, that allows us to move forward without repeating the mistakes of the past.

May David Bennett's testimony not fade into a mere account of pandemic chaos, but be embraced as a reminder of the power we have to build bridges, so long as we choose truth, cooperation, and respect for the life of every human being.

Griot 2085

Join the Genostories community on Discord

Stories don't end on the last page. In our Discord community, readers and authors come together to share passions, ask questions, uncover secrets between the lines, and build new narrative worlds together.

- Intimate conversations with other writers
- Personalized recommendations
- Workshops, contests, and exclusive previews
- A haven for those who live among words

This is your place if you've ever felt like a story was reading you.

https://discord.com/invite/ZUr6ZkE4B4

Discover more stories like this…

If this novel resonated with your spirit, if any phrase, any character, or even a single moment will stay with you beyond the last page, then Genostories is for you.

In our app you'll find universes woven with the same narrative passion, stories that challenge the everyday and embrace the extraordinary. Stories that speak like you, that dream like you, that are as unique as the voice of the one who writes them.

Download the Genostories app and become part of a community where literature is still alive, vibrant, and free.

Available on iOS and Android.

Genostories; where stories find their voice.

https://www.genostories.com/

www.ingramcontent.com/pod-product-compliance
Lightning Source LLC
Chambersburg PA
CBHW051058030726
47504CB00006B/1690